... ... gained an edge. "It is my inten... ... Worlds League. This is no secret."

Thaddeus nodded. One thing the leaders of the three most powerful nations in the region shared was the dream of a unified Free Worlds League. Their differences sprang from mutually exclusive convictions about who should rule.

"Mine is the greater claim to the captain-generalcy," Jessica said, echoing his thoughts. "My father fought to save the Free Worlds League when Thomas Marik abandoned it to pursue his own ambitions."

Interesting that you feel comfortable saying that to a Marik. Is that the honesty you mentioned or arrogance?

"Many independent worlds support reunification of the League under my leadership." Jessica's eyes held his levelly. "As do the Rim Commonality and the Duchy of Tamarind-Abbey."

Thaddeus blinked.

"However, much of this pledged support is conditional," Jessica said. "For all my family's moral claim to the throne, there is a physical requirement we do not possess. One that is meaningless in the context of right or ability to rule, but that weighs heavily on the hearts of many loyal to the Free Worlds League."

"You're not a real Marik." Thaddeus stated the obvious.

Jessica did not blink at the adjective.

"To sit on what is, in the minds of most, the throne of House Marik, I must have a blood connection to the Marik family," she said.

Lady Jessica was obviously talking marriage. But just as obviously, she was not envisioning the Free Worlds League unifying under her children or her grandchildren. She meant to hold the throne herself. Impossible, given the conditions stipulated.

Unless . . .

"I see you've grasped it," Philip said.

Thaddeus looked at the man, not sure he grasped anything at all.

"Thaddeus Marik," he said, his formal tone pulling Thaddeus upright in his chair, "will you marry my wife?"

MECH WARRIOR
DARK AGE

TO RIDE
THE CHIMERA

A BATTLETECH™ NOVEL

Kevin Killiany

A ROC BOOK

ROC
Published by New American Library, a division of
Penguin Group (USA) Inc., 375 Hudson Street,
New York, New York 10014, USA
Penguin Group (Canada), 90 Eglinton Avenue East, Suite 700, Toronto,
Ontario M4P 2Y3, Canada (a division of Pearson Penguin Canada Inc.)
Penguin Books Ltd., 80 Strand, London WC2R 0RL, England
Penguin Ireland, 25 St. Stephen's Green, Dublin 2,
Ireland (a division of Penguin Books Ltd.)
Penguin Group (Australia), 250 Camberwell Road, Camberwell, Victoria 3124,
Australia (a division of Pearson Australia Group Pty. Ltd.)
Penguin Books India Pvt. Ltd., 11 Community Centre, Panchsheel Park,
New Delhi - 110 017, India
Penguin Group (NZ), 67 Apollo Drive, Rosedale, North Shore 0632,
New Zealand (a division of Pearson New Zealand Ltd.)
Penguin Books (South Africa) (Pty.) Ltd., 24 Sturdee Avenue,
Rosebank, Johannesburg 2196, South Africa

Penguin Books Ltd., Registered Offices:
80 Strand, London WC2R 0RL, England

First published by Roc, an imprint of New American Library,
a division of Penguin Group (USA) Inc.

First Printing, February 2008
10 9 8 7 6 5 4 3 2 1

Copyright © WizKids, Inc., 2008
All rights reserved

ROC REGISTERED TRADEMARK—MARCA REGISTRADA

Printed in the United States of America

This book is for Valerie,
who is my wife, my other half,
and my personal gyroscope.
Your love keeps me moving forward.

ACKNOWLEDGMENTS

Dean Wesley Smith was the first editor to ever personally respond to one of my manuscripts. He rejected it. But he became my mentor and revealed the secret of success in writing: write, mail, repeat. It's a formula that has not failed me yet. His wife, Kristine Kathryn Rusch, whose uncompromising standards as a writer make her the most formidable of instructors, taught me to be unblinkingly honest in my craftsmanship (and thus work a lot harder than I'd ever imagined I would as a writer). I must also thank Loren Coleman, who first introduced me and a few other innocents to the wondrous world of giant walking tanks and human adventure that is BattleTech. That long-ago conversation led to my joining BattleCorps and getting the experience and understanding I needed to become a novelist in the MechWarrior universe. Of course, that knowledge would have done me no good if editor of editors Sharon Turner Mulvihill had not been willing to take a chance on an old man who liked to tell stories. She has always been there, a constant support to me and—I have it on good authority—every one of her writers, as she labors to bring the stories of MechWarrior to life. In fact, the entire MechWarrior/BattleTech community continues to work together. This novel would not have been possible if folks like Herbert Beas, Randall Bills, Jason Hardy, Blaine Pardoe, David Stansel-Garner, Andrew Timson, Øystein Tvedten and others foolish enough to let me know their

AIM hadn't been willing to drop whatever they were doing and answer random questions and offer advice.

I also would not be here without the members of Soul Saving Station. Once again, they've suffered through months of weekly homilies about BattleMechs and been unstinting in their encouragement and support.

Finally, and most important, my family. The road to this book began over a decade ago when I confessed to my wife that I'd always wanted to be a writer. Valerie said, "It's your dream; make it work." Since that time she and our three children—Alethea, Anson and Daya—have been there for me: Understanding that dad staring into space is working, celebrating every sale, plotting vengeance on editors who reject my stories and looking folks square in the eye and telling them I'm a writer with a straight face means more to me than I can ever explain.

Prologue

Place, unknown
Time, unknown

Where were they?

They were somewhere; somewhere close. She could sense them.

Why had they done this?

And who were they?

She shouted again. Or thought she did. She could not feel her jaw open, felt no constriction of her lungs filling with air, no wind rushing through her throat. No sound. But she shouted. She was sure she shouted.

She had long ago given up on polite inquiry.

How long ago?

She floated in darkness. Or perhaps she was sinking? Or lying on a mattress so soft it could not be felt?

No.

Floating. The lack of up and down, of forward and back reminded her of the weightlessness of space travel—but without the nausea.

Floating, then. But not in space.

She had heard of sensory deprivation tanks—fluid-filled tubes, the occupants of which neither felt nor heard nor saw. But surely she would feel air in her lungs? Hear her own voice as she shouted? Hear her heart beating.

And her heart *was* beating. She knew it. She knew it was beating because she was alive to worry about it beating.

Or was she alive? Her mind was here, was aware, but what of her flesh? She could feel no evidence of anything beyond her thoughts. What of the body that carried her, the face she saw each day in the mirror? Were they still with her? Or had they sloughed away in decay?

She fought down that thought, tried to stop the tide of images, but they returned. Surging to fill her mind, to drive her cowering spirit down into itself. Was this death? All of life, all of faith, all of ambition, all of striving, all of everything, leading to this? To an eternity without sensation? To nothing?

No. Worse than nothing.

Floating forever in darkness was not nothing.

It was hell.

And she was *not* in hell. She was *not* dead.

Her spirit, collapsed down into itself under the weight of fear—of terror—shifted. Adjusted. Her soul—shaped through a lifetime of hopes deferred, compressed through decades of suppression, distilled by countless minute acts of discipline, refined through the loveless fire of her mother's will—confronted cold death in the expanse of a shapeless void.

And snarled.

"I am Julietta Marik!" she declared, silent in the soundless dark. "And I still live!"

1

Court of Parliament
Tesla City, Miaplacidus
Covenant Worlds (Former Prefecture VII)
23 August 3137

Warden Thaddeus Marik sat, sipping tea and contemplating his options.

Thaddeus was aware of Green seated in the comfortable armchair facing Thaddeus' desk, working on his noteputer even as he studied the hooded monitor of the desk unit, and was glad of his agent's silent company.

The Spartan office was soundproofed and the lower two-thirds of the windows turned opaque to restrict his view of the cloudless blue sky—an environment engineered to encourage focused contemplation of the five worlds in his charge, with no distractions.

The Covenant Worlds.

Thaddeus liked the layered meanings of the name. Covenant Worlds had a gravitas devoid of threat that evoked a commitment to promises made. Integrity was a scarce commodity in these troubled times.

Last week's addition of Connaught and Acubens had doubled the Covenant's population and industrial capabilities, and its government was still adjusting to its new size. The raised dais of the Counselors' Chamber, which had been a lecture hall when the Court of Parliament building had been the humanities department of Miaplacidus Christian Liberal College, was still tacky with wet paint.

That the nascent nation needed a parliament amused Thaddeus. Five short months ago, when the Covenant Worlds had been Miaplacidus, Alphard and Nathan, decisions had been made by three men sitting in a conference room in an anonymous office building a dozen blocks from the college.

Court of Parliament, he corrected himself.

"My Marik name does not guarantee nobility of character," he had warned them then, the four of them seated in remarkably comfortable chairs. His personal theory was that the artisans of Miaplacidus were incapable of making uncomfortable furniture. "Nor that I will always act wisely."

"If we were offering you this position—this burden—on the basis of your family name, that argument would carry weight," Governor Tiago Paragon had chuckled. He'd been governor of Miaplacidus under the Republic of the Sphere, and—always minimalists in their social institutions—the Miaplacidians had seen no reason to change that simply because The Republic that appointed him had collapsed. "But we're basing our assessment on what we have seen of you the *man*."

Sir Kiasok Prusak of Nathan had nodded his agreement with an affected deliberateness, which struck Thaddeus as being at odds with his appearance. No doubt the forest of finger-long braids radiating from the young noble's scalp reflected the traditions of Nathan, but Thaddeus guessed the moplike effect made dignity difficult.

Odester Morgan-King had been planetary legate of Alphard before The Republic became Fortress Republic. Now he was vice chancellor of his adopted homeworld and its appointed representative to Miaplacidus. He had couched his approval in ornate language, but in the end communicated no more than Prusak's nod.

In that deceptively informal meeting, Thaddeus Marik had become warden of the Covenant Worlds. Commander in chief, under the Council of Parliament, of all military and constabulary forces in a nation of three—now five—worlds.

Though he had not intended to move into the public eye so soon, once he had assumed the mantle of warden, Thaddeus had felt a sense of inevitability. The very title—harkening back to "warden of the Perimeter Defenses," the ancient title of the Free Worlds League's captain-general during peacetime—seemed confirmation that the course he had chosen was the right one.

And God knew he needed confirmation.

If Thaddeus' assumption had been correct—if the Republic of the Sphere had dissolved as a result of civil war—he would have held thirty worlds at this point. Not openly, but a half dozen independent nation-states would have been beholden to him. Unifying those communities—a step still years away—would have formed an arc of worlds stretching from Phecda to New Canton with his native Augustine at its heart. Commercially and strategically vital, his Marik Crescent would have been the perfect foundation from which to rebuild the Free Worlds League.

But there had been no civil war. Instead, Exarch Jonah Levin had done the unthinkable: simply abandoned ninety percent of The Republic. The resulting chaos thwarted Thaddeus' careful plans.

Of the six pearls he'd planned to string, the six communities he had meant to carve out of the corpse of The Republic, only three remained viable. And only two were within his grasp.

Riktofven had seized *Thaddeus'* homeworld as the capital of the damned Senatorial Alliance. Until he and the remains of his cabal were removed from Augustine, their ill-conceived nation-state separated Thaddeus from the worlds of his Tall Trees Union. Reunification with them was decades away.

The Protectorate Coalition of Rochelle, Alkes, Kalidasa and New Hope was a different matter—and a testimony to Green's skills at forging political rivalries into unions. In recent months the Coalition had fended off a grab by the Marik-Stewart Commonwealth and a Lyran probe-in-force.

Though Thaddeus felt an almost parental pride in their independent successes, there was a downside. The Protectorate Coalition would not now meekly accept the leadership of the Covenant Worlds. Nor would they seek to form a larger union unless and until his Covenant Worlds developed into a nation that commanded their respect.

A process that was taking damnably longer than he had thought possible.

Nathan and Acubens, both agricultural worlds regarded as the larders of the region, and Miaplacidus, a world of artisans and traders, had been only lightly touched by the devastating Jihad of the Word of Blake against the Inner Sphere. Not so, Connaught and Alphard. The retreating Blakists had killed thousands on Connaught in order to cripple the Kong orbital shipyards and the BattleMech facilities on the surface. They'd been less thorough on Alphard, obviously regarding tanks and communication equipment as less of a prize for their opponents. Seven decades later, both worlds were viable but years from full recovery.

Now the Parliament, grown from the original three savvy horse traders to three dozen politicians trying to earn their constituents the greatest advantage, was locked in an endless cycle of debate on how to best consolidate the disparate worlds into a unified whole.

"We need more than just consolidation to make the Covenant Worlds a power in the region," Thaddeus said, breaking the silence. "We need a vital industrial base to support our military and civilian infrastructure."

"Irian is ideal but out of the question." Green stated the obvious, categorizing their options. "They have made themselves a vital trade partner to a half dozen worlds and communities. Joining the Covenant would actually make them *less* secure."

"And if the enlightened self-interest of their neighbors should fail, the generation-long connection of the Hughes family and Oriente through the marriage of Jessica and Philip should signify," Thaddeus added. "Captain-General Jessica and her Protectorate make a formidable argument for leaving Irian in peace."

"The Oriente Protectorate has established a permanent presence on both Ibstock and Park Place," Green said.

"By which you mean to imply they decapitated the Senatorial Alliance for trying to conquer Irian," Thaddeus grunted. "I think they would have taken those worlds no matter who held them. Just as the Marik-Stewart Commonwealth gobbled up Avellaneda and Holt."

"And Stewart."

"Clan Sea Fox traded Stewart to the Marik-Stewart Commonwealth. And even if they hadn't, repatriation sentiments ran high in the populace. Given the chance, they might have sued to join the Commonwealth voluntarily." Thaddeus shook his head. "Hardly a conquest."

"True, sir," Green admitted.

Left unsaid was that the remaining worlds of the Senatorial Alliance—Wasat, Hamilton, Branson, Bernardo and the new capital world Augustine—were stable and entrenched. Not a rock Thaddeus was going to shift any time soon. But shift it he would.

He just needed to forge a large enough lever.

"The Covenant Worlds' alliance with the Protectorate Coalition is proceeding apace," Green reported. "Deoliveira of Kalidasa and Yoe of New Hope are both solidly onboard for mutual defense and duty-free trade treaties. Alkes can be counted on to stay in step with the other former Silver Hawk Coalition worlds. Rochelle's less than enthusiastic, but not actually opposed.

"More pragmatically, the Kali Yama and Kong shipyards have exchanged representatives to discuss helping each other rebuild. There are some interesting matchups between needs and assets." He smiled slightly. Green did not share Thaddeus' fundamental suspicion of serendipity. "Quickcell and Marian Arms are also talking, but there it's sales reps, not engineers."

"Military and economic alliances," Thaddeus said. "How far are we from unity?"

"Three years."

Thaddeus questioned neither Green's answer nor its prompt delivery. Engineering the union had been his agent's primary focus for half a year.

"What can speed that up?"

"Savannah and Remulac." Green had been prepared for that question as well.

Not that the answer required clairvoyance. The two systems sit directly astride the Covenant/Coalition corridor.

"Though their various Technicron industries are not as robust as Irian's, the Barrons of Savannah are emulating the Hughes family," Green was saying. "Multiple contracts in several competitive markets. Their one advantage over Irian is Savannah's close relationship with Remulac. They do not have to depend on outside sources for food."

"That they managed to pull that off implies Technicron is producing more than the IndustrialMech parts they claim."

"There is substantial evidence of heavy IndustrialMech assembly and some impressive military modifications," Green agreed. "If they've resumed *Awesome* and *Quick-draw* manufacture, they're hiding it well. Their big-money exports continue to be high-tech military components."

"Any important marriages we should know about?"

"No, sir." Green smiled slightly. "They rely on a mutual defense treaty with the Marik-Stewart Commonwealth."

"Cousin Anson was not the most stable of allies even before the Lyrans attacked," Thaddeus said. "His forced annexation of Adhafera and Tania Borealis right on Savannah's doorstep must have given them pause."

"Indeed."

"An opportunity to present the Covenant Worlds as a safe haven?"

Green nodded slowly.

"Green, when you have doubts, don't make me ask for them."

"Yes, sir." Green straightened slightly in his chair. "Do we have the military capability to *be* a safe haven, sir? I realize our forces outsize any other nation of our scale, but to stand against the Marik-Stewart Commonwealth and perhaps even the Lyrans . . ."

"You think we need a big brother?"

"Yes, sir."

"So do I." Thaddeus smiled. "Which is why, while you're setting in motion our adoption of Savannah/Remulac, I will be convincing our Parliament to send me to the Oriente Protectorate."

"Sir?"

"It's not so close a bond as marriage, but my grand-mother and Jessica's father put aside their differences to fight shoulder to shoulder against the Blakists," Thaddeus said. "It's a history of alliance I intend to parlay into a mutual defense treaty—which would simplify our strategic position enormously.

"If I can pull it off without making the Covenant a vassal of Oriente."

2

Amur, Oriente
Oriente Protectorate
24 August 3137

"You don't understand!"

Elis watched Christopher's face with interest. She'd never seen him so passionate about anything beyond his next adventure. She would never have expected the Lyran invasion of a realm that had never been more than indifferent toward Oriente to so galvanize him.

Tonight, lit by the half dozen centuries-old incandescent lamps ranged about the family's informal sitting room, Christopher reminded her of . . .

It took her a moment to place the image, and she smiled when the memory clicked: a vidseries that had been popular a decade ago, and one of her guilty pleasures for escaping the pressures of her mother's court. It followed the adventures of a melodramatic defense lawyer who solved impossible crimes pro bono. She couldn't recall the name of the show. The actor's hair had been black instead of blond, but just as curly as her brother's. The crime-solving lawyer had always brought the same focused passion—and the same lack of logic—to his closing arguments that Christopher was now displaying in the face of their mother's implacability.

The difference, of course, was that the lawyer was fictional and always faced opponents who could never quite match him. He always won his cases. Christopher, poor dear, was real and facing Jessica Marik, who outmatched him in every dimension that mattered. He hadn't a prayer of winning his case.

But he persevered. He hadn't stalked off and he hadn't meekly acquiesced. He was pursuing his goal with greater maturity than Elis had ever seen from him.

Of course their mother's announcement of her plan to bring certified Marik blood into their family line had aged them all. Had sobered even flamboyant Christopher.

And Nikol, clever Nikol, favorite daughter and first to tumble to their mother's scheme, had been more stunned by their father's agreeing to the strategy than the plan itself. Now Nikol was watching Christopher confront their mother—her body angled toward the open window and the night and freedom outside, her head turned to watch the turmoil and struggle inside—and she seemed somehow older than Jessica.

"I do understand," Jessica answered, her voice level and steel-hard. "We do not have the resources to dash off to rescue Duke Fontaine. It takes more than your fondness for the old man to conjure up an army where there is none."

"You've said yourself we have more forces than people believe—"

"But not as many as you seem to imagine," Jessica cut him off. "We are strong enough to defend ourselves, strong enough for a few judiciously prosecuted campaigns, but not strong enough to take on the entire Lyran Commonwealth—even if our own borders were secure. And that's exactly what would happen if we tried to interfere with their acquisition of the Tamarind-Abbey worlds."

"But he stood ready to support you!"

"*If* I met the conditions he imposed, conditions you yourself have declared unacceptable."

Typically unfair, Mother. Elis sipped her tea while her brother blustered. *Christopher's the only one still impulsive enough to be thrown by such transparent misdirection. He's perfectly happy to bring Marik blood into the Halas line. He's just disgusted by your decision to do it yourself.*

She stirred, breaking her self-imposed invisibility by leaning forward to set her cup and saucer on the low table in front of the davenport. Nikol's eyes tracked the motion, though Christopher and their mother remained focused on each other.

"It doesn't need to be military aid," Elis said quietly, overriding Christopher's strident tone by pitching her voice to travel beneath it.

Jessica looked at her. Nikol turned her back to the open window to consider her full on. Christopher's overconfident assessment of what the Eagle's Talons could do to Lyran forces rambled for another sentence and a half before his sister's words registered.

"What do you mean?" he asked.

"We have other resources," Elis said. I *have other resources. Three DropShips' worth parked innocently at our nadir jump point and much, much more where they came from.* "We can offer humanitarian aid, or materiel suitable for rebuilding ravaged infrastructure."

Jessica dismissed the notion. "I doubt the Lyrans would be so naïve as to let such cargo pass. Our aid and effort would go to bolster the Lyran cause.

"Nor do we have the material resources to significantly affect the fate of Tamarind-Abbey," she added, coolly consolidating her arguments. "There is a significant difference between having a robust economy and having an economy able to sustain a second, unrelated nation-state in time of war."

Interesting choice of words, Mother.

"The significance of the aid would be its existence, not its amount," Elis said aloud. "We will not be feeding worlds or equipping legions of BattleMechs. Pharmaceuticals, which we do have in abundance, plus other medical supplies appropriate to a war zone. Sheet armor, another surplus, which could legitimately be used for civilian shelters. And salted in among the rest, items of use to liberation units."

"Liberation units?" echoed Jessica.

"Old border world tactic for regaining systems taken from the League," Nikol explained. "Advance scouts would find elements in the local population sympathetic to returning to the Free Worlds and train them in covert ops. Sabotage, information gathering, communications disruption, that sort of thing. Units would act independently, destabilizing the world prior to—"

"I know what a liberation unit is." Jessica's voice was testy. "I had simply not considered how they might be of use to us in our current situation."

Elis smiled inwardly. Settling back against the cushions, she resumed her role of invisible watcher while their mother built on the foundation she'd provided.

"Not every world, of course, but key planets," Jessica said, her eyes focused on something in the middle distance. "In both the Duchy and the Commonwealth."

"Establishing our own resistance cells so deep in their space would require a lot of local intel we don't have," Nikol pointed out.

Always tactical, little sister.

"No doubt resistance groups already exist," their mother countered. "On worlds where they don't, we'll withdraw—inspiring the will to fight where none exists is beyond our practical reach."

Elis admired her mother's ability to make sound routine the task of locating those existing resistance groups on worlds once—perhaps still—hostile to the Oriente Protectorate and occupied by invading forces. On the other hand, it might be. Jessica kept her SAFE operations closely to herself; her daughters had no idea what they were capable of.

"So you're not going to demand they declare loyalty to Oriente as a precondition of aid?"

Nikol's sardonic humor surprised Elis.

"Of course not, dear," Jessica answered. "But they will know who risked the worst the Lyrans could do in order to aid them in their hour of need.

"Something they will remember when our time comes."

3

DropShip **Porthos**
Nadir Recharge Station
Milnerton, Oriente Protectorate
26 August 3137

*D*on't make me kill you.

She smiled at the customs inspector standing in the corridor outside her second-class cabin.

Young, maybe her age in body but decades her junior in spirit, the agent blushed slightly at her direct look, her slightly parted lips. He was cute, she decided, in a *dim-dim* way. Curly red-brown hair that waved in the faint breezes of zero-gravity, nose too thin and jaw too sharp, but his eyes were a delightful blend of green and brown with flecks of gold. Natural? Tilting her head slightly, she caught no telltale trace of contact lenses.

Mistaking her appraisal—as he was meant to—the boy flushed a darker red.

Do you know the contrast makes your eyes glow? she did not ask aloud. She wondered, not for the first time, that Obatala would give individuals of the lesser peoples such beauty. Was it evidence of a spiritual blessing? Or compensation for their limitations? Either way, it could certainly affect her flesh.

Or that could just be my body's joy that the healing creams—thank Babalz-Ayi—have finally eradicated the infection.

She smiled at the thought. The boy smiled back.

Ten days ago she had been swimming naked through the sewers of Amur, escaping from thugs of the demon-woman bent on her destruction. She had felt every bacteria and fungus that attached itself to her body as she moved through the filth; even knowing the effect was imaginary hadn't diminished the sensation of being violated. Once free of the sewers, she had needed two days of stealthy movement—one more than planned—to make contact with the extraction team. Then she had spent four days wracked by fever and crushed by two gravities of acceleration/deceleration pressure as the long-range shuttle provided by the Temple raced to reach the *Porthos* before it left the Oriente system.

Now, three jumps from home, her only concern should be invisibility—acting the part of an anonymous academic en route to a teaching position. And interacting with no one who might remember her. What her plan failed to anticipate—a foolish mistake on her part, in retrospect— was the level of scrutiny that would be given each passenger outward-bound from Oriente.

Which is how she found herself in share-the-breath range of an attractive young customs inspector who—even though he was having difficulty focusing on her immaculate documentation—would definitely remember her face. Nor did her bulky clothes, designed to create the impression her athletic frame carried an additional twenty kilos, seem to diminish his interest.

Either the *caplatas* Jessica had not discerned her identity or had for purposes of her own chosen not to share the assassin's description with her minions. The customs inspectors questioning every passenger and every crew member of the *Porthos* were not specifically looking for a woman of midnight complexion. Otherwise she would be in a holding cell at this very moment.

And within the hour, dead—surrounded by as many of the demon woman's soldiers as she could take with her.

Now her problem was the charming young customs agent, who was stammering a bit as he tried to think of plausible topics for prolonging their conversation after vetting her meticulously counterfeited identity and travel papers.

Which posed the greater danger? His memory of her when a complete description of the fugitive assassin finally reached Milnerton? Or his unexplained disappearance?

The latter would trigger an investigation that would dangerously delay the DropShip's departure. An accident? Aboard the *Porthos* even a clearly accidental fatality would necessitate an inquiry, something the timetable of her escape would not survive. And, as the young agent had arrived and would depart aboard a Milnerton Customs Authority launch, she had no way to arrange his death anywhere else.

So the boy lived. And with him his memory of her.

No doubt when a more detailed description of the assassin who had struck down two of the Marik children reached Milnerton, the boy would match his memory to her false documentation detailing her itinerary. Her side assumed that the strained relations between the Oriente Protectorate and the Duchy of Andurien would make it difficult for local authorities to establish that the cultural anthropology instructor bound for the Mosiro University of Al-Ilb never actually arrived. By then she would be safely home and no evidence would link the deaths on Oriente to the Temple.

As long as he's going to remember me—she let the light of the thought shine through her eyes—*why not make his memory truly memorable?*

The boy's eyes lit up, his breath catching in a ragged exhale. He'd clearly caught the message she was sending.

Shaking her head sadly, she closed her cabin door in his face.

No way she was going to risk triggering a flare-up of that damned infection.

4

"**W**ell," Frederick Marik pronounced, evidently satisfied. Nikol could not tell whether it was the view of the late afternoon garden beyond the open French doors that so pleased him, or the cut-crystal goblet with its triple thimbleful of dessert liquor that he idly swirled or the company of the three Marik women that he found so satisfying. He tended to look at each element of his surroundings with the same possessive assurance.

The early Sunday supper had been artfully arranged. A half dozen minor nobles with their respective spouses invited for their ability to disseminate—and expand upon—gossip, Frederick Marik and Jessica with what the media insisted on calling her "three surviving children."

The media had never been fond of Julietta—Nikol had come to wonder if this didn't reflect some influence of their mother's—and seemed to have written her off. The neurospecialists said there was some indeterminate activity in her frontal lobe, but could not guarantee it was thought. Media reports had described her state as "vegetative" from the beginning. Nikol hated it—they all did—but by the end of the first week, all media listed only Elis, Christopher and Nikol as Jessica's "surviving" children.

Adding to Nikol's jaundiced view of the world was the charade of her parents' separation, which was already under way. Philip Hughes had been absent the last few times her mother appeared in public, which was not unheard of, but unusual enough to cause comment. There had also been reports of Philip being "bitter" and perhaps "reclusive" as he coped with the death of his oldest son.

Nikol knew that for all the haste in its execution, a lot of very careful planning and media manipulation was going into the tale of her father leaving her mother. And Philip had to leave his wife: Jessica must not be seen as setting aside her husband for political gain. Nor could the leaving be bitter or angry. Philip's love and support of his wife was well documented. . . .

Nikol's eyes suddenly stung. She fought the desire to cry by minutely widening and narrowing her eyes. She would not wipe her eyes; she would not let a tear fall.

Elis made some comment to Frederick while Jessica looked on, her head tilted ever so slightly to indicate sincere attention. Nikol imitated the posture without a clue of what was being said.

Their father's unfailing love was the stuff of legends.

If Jessica's media manipulators had tried to propagate the tale he'd left in rage or engaged in some marriage-destroying dalliance, no one would have believed it. Yet Philip had to leave, and leave in a way that made Jessica a sympathetic character, and plausibly available. The sympathy and plausibility were vital.

Not listening, Nikol smiled for no other reason than her mother did.

So—to keep from being screamingly obvious the fact that her mother was about to marry an irritating drone to gain the credibility of his name, her father was going through a breakdown. Nothing terrible. No public frothing at the mouth or fits of rage: quite the opposite, in fact. Tomorrow he was going to ask the court chamberlain to remove his chair from the dais. In coming weeks he would be seen standing around the edges of things, choosing not to take part; he would leave early or not be present at all. Philip would be gradually less and less apparent until . . .

A few months from now—the precise timetable would be determined by the public relations specialists on Torrian Dolcat's team—news would leak from the palace that Philip had decided he could no longer live the public life of consort to a ruler and had gone into seclusion, leaving behind a divorce decree.

Philip Hughes would be vilified and pitied—the story would be spun both ways to different media—and Jessica would bravely carry on alone. By then Frederick Marik would have been coached in his role as loyal adviser and companion. Few in the upper levels of real political power would be fooled by this performance, particularly when Frederick Marik became her new husband. But with a little judicious staging and a few scripted events, the story would play well to the mass media. And be just plausible enough to the general public that it might win Jessica a new level of popular support.

The poached trout from dinner roiled dangerously in Nikol's stomach, and she carefully sipped the sweet wine. She wanted to bolt from the room, as Christopher had done when the other guests had taken their leave. Instead she perched dutifully at the end of the brocade divan, looking interested in their guest. With an effort she focused on what he was saying.

"The Marik clan has always been endogamic." Frederick Marik smiled smugly. "I suppose it's a case of no one else ever being quite up to our standards for tying the knot."

Jessica Marik managed a tiny smile, but Nikol could see how much even that cost her mother.

Either I'm getting better at reading her or she's letting me see how she feels.

Nikol was almost certain it was the latter. What she could not decide was whether her mother was being so transparent because she needed her daughters' support or was trying to manipulate them into pitying her. As though either daughter was likely to forget that the purgatory before their mother was entirely of her own making.

Nikol looked at Elis and was not surprised to meet her sister's basilisk glance.

Finally found something we agree on.

That thought almost brought a smile.

"Of course, my parents were an extreme example." Frederick cocked a conspiratorial eyebrow. "Probably the result of being isolated in the wasteland of The Republic. No way to get back to our roots."

"There are many reasons for marriage," Jessica agreed.

"Perhaps they loved each other," Nikol suggested.

Jessica's eyelid flickered but she did not look toward her daughter.

"Perhaps." Frederick seemed genuinely surprised the notion had been suggested. "But the Marik-to-Marik affinity as well as close proximity is probably what tipped the balance. After all, Calvin Bernstein-Marik was raised like a son by his aunt Kristen Rousset-Marik, younger sister of his mother, Ana. To marry Agatha Hampton-Marik, Kristen's daughter, after being raised in the same household?"

He let his voice trail off, inviting comment—or perhaps agreement. When none of the women responded, he evidently concluded the point needed to be driven home.

"They were first cousins, you see, which violates the incest taboos on half a hundred worlds—"

"And affirms the familial traditions on as many more," Elis pointed out.

Good shot, Nikol thought.

"Perhaps." Frederick's tone was dismissive. "But if the trend among Mariks of The Republic had continued—and if Thaddeus had been born a woman—I'm certain I'd have been expected to marry my sister. No doubt our offspring would have been hermaphrodites."

Frederick chuckled into the goblet as he drank deeply of his liquor. The bowled glass resonated the sound unnaturally.

Good God, he thinks he's just been witty, Nikol boggled. *Maybe even titillating.*

Frederick Marik had presented himself as a self-obsessed bore in every conversation with Nikol since she'd first met the man on Terra; he had proposed marriage twenty minutes into their initial conversation. But he had never revealed himself to be a boor until now. Noting his now-empty goblet, she wondered how much could be blamed on drink.

Two and a half years ago, Nikol had been rescued from Frederick Marik's unwanted attentions at a reception following Victor Steiner-Davion's funeral by Danai Liao. It had been necessary for the Capellan chancellor's sister to physically attack Frederick—disguised as a drunken stumble, of course—to break the man's concentration on his own charm.

Was this same man subtle enough now to be testing their

mettle under the guise of inebriation? Or was he actually such a fool as to allow himself to become incapacitated in their presence?

Either way, Jessica Marik's body language made it clear the after-supper portion of the evening was at an end.

Clear to everyone except Frederick Marik. It took another ten minutes, during which he focused what he no doubt considered to be his considerable charm on each of them in turn, before he was safely in the hands of the servants and headed for the gate.

"That went well," Elis observed drily when they were again alone.

"He does tend to make Anson appear a more suitable candidate," Jessica agreed, with a complete deadpan that surprised a bark of laughter from Elis.

"Was he really that drunk?" Nikol asked.

"Or is he really that foolish?" Jessica asked back.

"He did seem to flirt with all three of us," Elis agreed, her tone thoughtful. "Until today he has been fixated on Nikol."

"So was the change due to his figuring out something is afoot?" Nikol picked up the thread. "Or is omnidirectional flirtation his natural response when in the company of more than one woman?"

"The latter," Elis said flatly. Then amended: "I think. Though I confess I find the idea that there's more to this man than a caricature basically unbelievable."

"Which could in itself suggest there is more to this man," Nikol countered. "Frederick Marik may be an answer, but he brings a lot of questions with him.

"Questions we shall need to resolve in coming weeks," Jessica agreed.

So.

Frederick Marik leaned back, allowing the ground car's acceleration to push him into the neoleather upholstery.

That was informative.

Her Grace the Lady pseudo-Marik was certainly desperate to marry off her spinster daughters; that much was plain. What was not plain was why. Securing heirs, of course, but why now and why in this manner? Perhaps the loss of her first two options had driven home the point that contingencies must be planned.

She certainly didn't seem to pin much hope on young Christopher. Not surprising; he was an abrasive chap with no sense of manners. Usually a lad with the impunity of position and power Christopher obviously enjoyed would have to be restrained from dropping inconvenient offspring all over the landscape.

Of course, Christopher was—or had been—the younger son, he reminded himself. The willing young breeding stock with the greed-glittering eyes would have been ignoring him to throw themselves at his older brother. Frederick could certainly empathize with that situation.

Now, however, the boy's political and sexual star was on the rise. The loss of Janos was tragic, of course, but Christopher was no doubt already considering the horizons from the vantage of his new position.

Frederick wondered what sort of deals with new cronies the boy was striking. He'd certainly escaped from the soirée as though he had something urgent on his agenda. Though truth to tell, there was nothing to hold him at what was obviously his mother's effort to parade the available daughters to the new stud.

Frederick smiled and adjusted his cuff.

And she was desperate enough to put up with behavior that should have earned him the boot by dessert. Even kept him on for a private chat afterward.

The old girl's gotten a serious insight into her own mortality.

He would have to make some effort to discover the particulars of the covey of minor notables who'd been called in as witnesses. There had certainly been nothing about any of them to indicate any need for his consideration, but Lady Jessica pseudo-Marik—

Careful, he warned himself. *Keep admiring your own cleverness and you'll slip and say "pseudo" out loud to the wrong person.*

Lady Marik, Lady Marik, Lady Marik.

He sighed, already missing the clever turn of phrase he'd never use again.

Lady Marik had evidently considered the guests to be of

some importance. Common sense dictated he discover how and where they fit into the suitable-spouse selection process.

And why no maidens for Christopher? One would think binding him to a monogamous relationship of political advantage would be a priority. Unrestrained, a boy of his good looks would be providing heirs abundant.

Unless the lad was a flower, despite all his robust adventurism.

The one does not preclude the other, old boy. Frederick smiled again as he admonished himself. *Wouldn't do to let stereotypes limit one's thinking.*

Even if Christopher was uninterested in women, a marriage of convenience and routine medical procedures would guarantee suitable inheritors of the pseu—of the Marik line.

The Marik line.

That was it. There were no eligible females of the Marik line available—the *real* Marik line, that is. Her Grace was after legitimacy.

He'd known the Oriente Protectorate needed an infusion of genuine Marik blood if it was ever going to gain acceptance among the Houses of the Inner Sphere. That had motivated his decision to relocate to Amur. However, with Lady Jessica so certain of her own legitimacy, he'd anticipated having to educate his rustic nonrelatives of its necessity. Either he was underestimating Jessica's subtlety, or the seeds he'd planted in young Nikol's ear at Victor Steiner-Davion's interminable round of funereal fetes two years ago had borne fruit.

Poor Thaddeus, Frederick thought as the limousine pulled into the gates of his guest estate. *All that hard work being a good soldier of The Republic came to nothing. Where are all your lectures on duty and calling now, Thaddy-boy? Your precious Republic is dust.*

Aware of the importance of the common touch, Frederick inclined his head in appreciation when the footman opened the door of the ground car. Feeling particularly pleased with the events of the day, he went so far as to smile at the maid at the door. His smile grew slightly at her obvious confusion.

Birth order is no match for intelligence, big brother of mine, or for a game shrewdly played. Your lifetime of cutting me off from everything I deserve has come to naught, and the little brother you denounced as a wastrel is poised to inherit the most powerful realm in Free Worlds space.

Glancing at the marbled entry hall of the manor loaned to him on the strength of his name alone, Frederick Marik suppressed the urge to laugh out loud.

Karma, brother dearest, can be a bitch.

5

Augusta, Savannah
Former Prefecture VII
3 September 3137

"He wants what?"

"Targeting systems and replacement components for"—Voline shrugged, turning her noteputer so its screen faced the minister—"a whole shopping list of weapons systems."

Minister of Industry Jim Doonah—until a year ago The Republic's planetary legate on Savannah—sighed. Extending his hand across the cluttered desk, he accepted the noteputer.

"I take it the captain-general never got word of the Jihad," he said, paging through the screens.

"The tone of his letter suggests he doesn't believe the Blakist destruction was as thorough as generally believed," his secretary answered. "Either that or he has a lot of respect for our ability to rise from the ashes."

Doonah grunted. "The tone of his letter is the same tone he uses for everything from death threats to inquiring after your health. Assuming he cared enough about anyone besides himself to ask. He's just an arrogant bastard."

"In that case, I'd say he's simply requesting everything he needs in the hope we actually have it."

"Agreed." Doonah keyed a thumb control, highlighting items on the list. "And in some cases he's right."

"Sir?" Voline made no effort to hide her surprise.

"*BattleMechs?* Ha!" The minister shook his head; deleting one item, he typed in others. "But we can probably spare those G-chassis Industrials. Dieudonne can wait until next production run. We've got some mod kits too. He's got the people to put them together.

"Armor, myomer, fusion drives—all of these are off-the-rack." He handed the noteputer with the highlighted list back to his secretary. "Send them payment-deferred until his convenience. And ask Petrie in Defense over my signature what weapons systems she can spare."

"Sir?" Voline asked again.

Doonah grinned crookedly at her expression. "Confused?"

"Yes, sir," his secretary admitted. "Payment deferred?"

"I think even the bean counters in Budgetary will agree that free support of the Marik-Stewart Commonwealth's survival is a prudent use of our resources," Doonah said. "Anson Marik may be an arrogant bastard, but right now he's the arrogant bastard standing between us and the Lyrans.

"If he falls, we're next."

6

"**M**ilord?"

The voice barely rose above the burble of the fountain at the corner of the broad patio. It was an abstract affair that managed to be both impressive and ugly while rising no higher than his chin. Frederick hated the thing and was glad the architect had chosen to place it to one side; possibly to better facilitate being able to ignore it while admiring the view of the sculpted gardens.

Not that Frederick Marik had been paying the garden the least attention.

He'd spent the last day and a half completely absorbed by a noteputer that had been presented to him by one Dimitri Oshaka, member of Parliament, during a personal visit. It was a beautiful machine: a top-of-the-line Blue Heron, the outer case of which had been expertly embellished with a tasteful rendering of the Marik crest inlaid in what looked to be a sort of mother-of-pearl. Blue Heron was a prestige name brand from . . . he couldn't think of the world. Somewhere in Prefecture II, if he recalled correctly; on the far side of the former Republic.

Won't be seeing any more of these for a while.

The contents of the beautiful noteputer were both fascinating and tiresome: a detailed breakdown of the political situation in the Oriente Protectorate. Captain-General Jessica was not quite the undisputed monolith of power she presented herself to be. There were factions within Parliament, including a significant power bloc that opposed her military expansion.

Of course Frederick was not fool enough to believe this new information was entirely unbiased. Though there was no overt propaganda—or even direct criticism of the captain-general—the word choices and general spin made it obvious the digest had been prepared by members of the loyal opposition.

Frederick looked up, concealing his gratitude for the interruption behind a thoughtful frown, to find the domestic administrator of the house Jessica Marik had loaned him standing at a respectful distance.

"Yes"—Frederick fished for the majordomo's name—"Ballard?"

"This was just delivered, milord."

Ballard presented a buff envelope precisely centered on a silver tray.

Frederick turned over the missive in his hands as Ballard beat a stately retreat. His name was nicely hand-calligraphed, he noted, and there was no sign the seal had been broken. Of course he was sure whatever the envelope contained had been thoroughly examined and recorded. Living in a house provided by Jessica *Marik*—he emphasized use of her chosen name, willing himself to make it habit—and surrounded by servants in her employ, he had no doubt the first was thoroughly bugged and the latter trained informants. Always best to assume every gesture was observed and every nuance evaluated.

Keeping his expression thoughtful, Frederick broke the seal and unfolded the heavy parchment. The needlessly expensive paper was in keeping with the calligraphy, no doubt reflecting a rural concept of elegance.

Frederick stopped himself midgesture.

Rural, rustic—he needed to eliminate all these disparaging adjectives from his vocabulary. He was not now, nor would he ever again be, in the courts of Terra. Oriente was now his home, his arena, and if he was going to be successful here he needed to understand and respect the prevailing conventions. He looked at the envelope with new eyes, noting the quality and weight of the paper. The elegant penmanship implied a scribe, as he doubted anyone casually used a fountain pen with such grace.

Satisfied with his assessment of the medium, he turned his attention to the message.

Member of Parliament Frances Claireborne was requesting the pleasure of his company at an evening soirée the evening of Thursday the ninth. Two days struck him as unusually short notice, but perhaps such last-minute social announcements were common on Oriente. He made a mental note to verify that supposition.

The political analysis on the noteputer Oshaka had given him spoke highly of MP Claireborne. Though she was not presented as actively involved in any of the groups wrestling with the captain-general over points of domestic policy or military adventurism, it took no leap of genius to guess that she was an architect of the loyal opposition.

And the loyal opposition has sussed my potential role in the political future of Oriente. Frederick smiled grimly. *First an expensive gift filled with "unbiased" information to influence my thinking and now warmly welcoming social events to influence my sentiment. Obvious ploys, which means there's probably much more going on below the surface.*

He considered simply typing his acceptance of the invitation into the noteputer. There was no doubt in his mind the machine was as bugged as the house. Anything he typed or accessed would be transmitted to Oshaka's agents.

If he was going to be a player in the game of Oriente politics, he was going to need to develop a secure base and secure information-gathering assets of his own. Establishing an independent household was going to require all of his skills and most of his resources, but it was an essential that he should already have addressed.

Letting his eyes rest on the artfully manicured garden, Frederick Marik considered his options.

7

Talar saw ovKhan Petr Kalasa's expression falter as his eyes met Rikkard Nova Cat's. Nothing overt—a flicker Talar would have missed had he not been watching for it.

Then the Sea Fox leader was across the threshold of the Spirit Cats' command center, hand extended to grasp Rikkard's. An unusual courtesy—or perhaps a display of alliance.

Reading levels of meaning—being aware there were levels of meaning to be read—was new to Talar. A skill he was working to master.

Talar stepped back as the leaders exchanged greetings, his report on restructuring the Touman less important than whatever had brought the ovKhan to speak directly with the Star colonel.

As the leaders talked he took the measure of the Sea Foxes who'd followed Petr Kalasa into the room. A woman of uncommon beauty with surprising violet eyes that met his gaze with equal appraisal, and a powerfully built man half his age who seemed more interested in the room itself than its occupants.

The room deserved attention. When the mountain of rubble above them had been a luxury hotel rising thirty stories into the sky, this had been the nexus of the physical plant: everything from security cameras to thermostats had been controlled from here. Converting it to a military command center, and later the heart of the Spirit Cat enclave, had been a simple matter of connecting new datalines to existing terminals.

Beyond the door through which the Sea Foxes had entered was an underground ballroom of exquisite beauty, while at Talar's back was the office Star Colonel Rikkard used as his personal study. The room where Star Commander Janis had died; where everything had changed.

The beautiful Sea Fox with the compelling eyes and the young Sea Fox of heroic proportions were clearly his opposite numbers; junior lieutenants there to perform whatever errands their ovKhan required. Warriors, but neither dressed nor poised for combat, they projected courtesy, interest and no more than the usual tension of being in the presence of powerful leaders. There was no threat in this visit.

Talar was self-aware enough to be amused at his own diligence in emulating Rikkard in weighing the elements around him. Mere months ago he would have scoffed at the notion of wanting to be anything like the Star colonel.

Before the conquest of Marik, Rikkard's hesitation had always seemed an integral part of the man. When not in combat. In unaugmented combat Rikkard had always been a flawless master who made the most demanding techniques seem effortless. The disconnect between that disciplined prowess and the apparent trepidation with which he approached everything outside the Circle of Equals had been . . . troubling.

Star Commander Janis had seen Rikkard's hesitation as doubt, as weakness. Talar, in the days when he had followed Janis, had believed Rikkard to be haunted by doubts in even the simplest decisions. The confidence of his Star commander, her certainty, had stood in sharp contrast to the Star colonel's questioning of all he saw. He had followed Janis, believing her surety a sign of the truer heart; the clearer vision.

What he had not understood—what Janis had died not understanding—was that her boldness had not been courage, but the reckless bravado of ignorance.

Talar had not grasped this truth in any flash of insight. Indeed, when his Star commander had died by Rikkard's

hand in the Circle of Equals, he had believed all hope of
Spirit Cat survival on Marik had died with her.

It was only through the forging of the new alliance, and
the weeks following the victory made possible by that alliance, that he had come to appreciate that Rikkard had
always seen more clearly than any who followed him imagined. Their leader's hesitation had not been the doubt of
a coward, but the caution of one finding a path through
dangerous ground.

"Indeed?" Rikkard asked.

His Star colonel's sharp tone snapped Talar back into
the moment. He was peripherally aware of the Sea Fox
woman's appraising gaze as he looked to Rikkard.

The fugues we mocked so often, he thought. *Journeys into
understanding*.

"She is not dead, though her older brother is," Petr was
saying. "Murdered in his sleep."

The ovKhan's disgust at such cowardice dripped from
his words.

"She's in a coma. The Oriente doctors believe her spine
and brain stem are irreparable."

She? Oriente?

Talar glanced reflexively to the wall at his left. Against
the far side of that wall, at the juncture where it met the
floor, Lady Julietta had lain. Had landed. Though the spheroid woman was already down when Talar entered the Star
colonel's office on Janis' heels, it was clear Rikkard had
hit her.

He'd never spoken to the ambassador of Oriente, the
daughter of Oriente's leader. But what he had seen of her
had appeared by turns to be both hopelessly bovine and
pompously brittle—a woman of no consequence terrified of
every shadow. He had stood with his back to her in the
Circle of Equals. He had not been in a position to see her
face; to see what was in her eyes when Rikkard paused
above Janis' crippled body and looked to her.

Even if he had been able, Talar would not have looked
at the spheroid. His eyes were fixed only on his Star commander, struggling to regain her feet as Rikkard ignored
her to consider the foreign woman.

Rikkard's stance had shifted—a transfer of tension that

pulled Talar's eyes to his face. There had been—something he still did not fully understand in the Star colonel's gaze as he reached down to catch Janis' flailing arm; to steady her one last time. The final blow had been swift and merciful, ending the Star commander's life between one heartbeat and the next.

For a long moment after, there had been silence, no one moving as Rikkard had swayed, his eyes shut.

In retrospect, Talar realized the beginnings of the change in Rikkard had been apparent at Irian. Though in truth, the signs of any beginning are clear only when one has seen the ending. But even with no knowledge of the ending, the tipping point—the moment of fundamental change—had been clear in Rikkard's eyes as he stood holding the wrist of his lieutenant, dead by his hand.

Now the Sea Foxes brought word that Lady Julietta, the catalyst of Rikkard's epiphany, was in a coma. Worse, the backward spheroid physicians were helpless in the face of her injuries.

It took no spirit vision to anticipate Star Colonel Rikkard's next commands.

Talar glanced to the communications tech. She leaned forward at her station, head turned to keep her eyes on Rikkard even as her finger rested on the TRANSMIT key. Reading the screen in front of her, Talar saw she had already dialed the medical center.

OvKhan Petr Kalasa considered as he strode toward his ground car. Around him the rubble was, if not cleared, at least orderly. Scaffolding and cranes rose from the street. Mandoria was being rebuilt, though no effort was being made to restore the ornate architecture visible on some of the older buildings. Dormuth was being made simpler, stronger—changing to reflect the new order.

Just as the man he had just left had been changed. Though Petr doubted anyone would claim Rikkard Nova Cat had become in any way *simpler*.

Petr had heard the gaze of a Nova Cat mystic described as the "far look." Until now the phrase had meant little. But in Rikkard . . . Throughout their brief conversation, Petr could not shake the sensation that Rikkard's eyes had been simultaneously focused on Petr's eyes and on some horizon point infinitely beyond him. The effect was unnerving.

And yet the Star colonel had none of the otherworldly affect Petr had always associated with mystics. To the contrary, he now radiated a health and vitality he had not possessed when traveling aboard *Voidswimmer* en route to Marik. Rikkard's handclasp had been firm, his conversation succinct and on topic. Nothing to indicate anything other than an ordinary man, alert and on task.

Except his damn eyes.

The nod ovKhan Petr gave his driver as he entered the passenger compartment of the ground car was distracted.

The vehicle was a luxury model of local manufacture, but it reflected none of the unnecessary ornamentation that marred Marik architecture. The vehicle's lines were clean, its construction uncompromisingly solid. The luxury was in the quality of the materials from which it was constructed and the craftsmanship with which those components had been assembled.

The car came to life, its ICE a satisfying rumble barely perceptible within the cabin. There was room enough for his long legs and those of Etgar and Sonja in their rear-facing jump seats. He could think of a half dozen markets where a car of this quality would be appreciated.

"Is it drugs, then?" he asked.

Warriors both, Etgar and Sonja had shown a mental facility that indicated bright futures. *If* their practical judgment and personal instincts attained the potential their test scores indicated. He had no doubt both whelps appreciated the honor and opportunity inherent in his personal interest in their education.

"If the Spirit Cats are using drugs, it is nothing anyone has ever hinted at." Sonja repeated common knowledge.

"More like a trance," opined Etgar.

"They do not appear as sleepwalkers," Sonja countered.

"They?" Petr asked.

"The MechWarrior who was giving the report when we arrived," Sonja said. "He seemed to drop in, then out of the same state."

"I meant trance like an aerospace jockey or a ProtoMech

pilot," Etgar said. "When the information from augmented sensors is flowing through them. As I understand it, some develop an affect like Rikkard Nova Cat's even when disconnected from their augmentations."

"You are describing hyperfocus, multiplex thinking." Petr glanced between the two. "And that requires genetic predisposition, years of training and drugs."

"I do not believe we were witnessing a drug effect." Sonja's tone was thoughtful. "Could this be related to the training and genetics of the Nova Cat mystic caste?"

"I had that thought as well," Petr admitted. "But there have been no recorded exchanges between Rikkard's Spirit Cats and the Nova Cat Clan. To have mystics spontaneously appear seems unlikely."

"Drugs, then," Etgar decided.

"Not drugs." Sonja returned to her original assessment. Then added: "It would take a blood screening to be sure."

"Then acquire a blood sample," Petr said. "Knowing what makes a Spirit Cat a Spirit Cat can be useful information."

"How will I acquire a sample of Rikkard's blood?"

Asking for necessary information instead of pretending knowledge or expressing doubt, Peter noted.

"Not in combat," Etgar said before the ovKhan spoke. "He'd kill you."

"If half the tales are true, in unaugmented combat Star Colonel Rikkard could kill all of us," Petr said before Sonja could respond to the barb. "The young man, however—the MechWarrior with the similar aspect—he will be more approachable."

"Approachable?"

"We will be transporting Rikkard and members of his senior medical caste to Oriente," Petr pointed out. "No doubt his aide will also make the journey. Make friends with the young man."

Petr smiled slightly. "I'm sure an opportunity to collect bodily fluids will present itself."

8

Temple of the Heart of Spirit
Siendou, Unaffiliated Worlds
14 October 3137

"Lucumi," she identified herself. *Friend.*

The ceremonial guard—a man she'd known since they were childhood initiates—nodded his recognition and stood aside, inviting her into the *hounfour* temple with a graceful sweep of his arm.

The broad corridor wound like path through a great forest. The polished pebbles of the floor, like tiny cobblestones, none bigger than her heel and many smaller than her thumb, were cool and solid and comforting against her bare feet. The ceiling glowed softly green, recalling sunlight filtering down through dense branches stretching a hundred meters above her while the walls, dark and irregular, called to mind ancient forests. The path was dim, but it was the dimness and warmth of sanctuary that embraced her.

A pair of rough-hewn torches marked the entrance to the temple itself. Beyond them the corridor broadened into a great circular room, with torches spaced evenly around the walls. She knew the torch fires were fed by gas jets, their flammable mixture balanced to create yellow flames that danced in the gentle breezes, but the effect exactly emulated burning rushes. She recognized them not as counterfeits, but as reverent images.

Breezes that flickered the flames and wafted her ceremonial gown first against her, then away were also elements of the natural world created by artfully hidden fans and vents. The walls were the thatch and adobe they appeared to be, but the jungle did not lie beyond them. The temple was encased within a greater structure of block and concrete. A strange deceit, to hide a temple within a fortress built to mimic a mundane warehouse. Particularly on Siendou, heartland of *Sevi Lwa*, their sister faith. Here in the center of civilization, *hounfour* dedicated to Olorun and Obatala were found in every town. But the secret *Coeur du Vodun*—Heart of the Spirit—had to be shielded from the uncomprehending eyes of unbelievers.

Beneath her feet the stones of a hundred worlds, tumbled smooth enough to prevent injury but uncut, unshaped, were fit together in intricate mosaic. Streams in the true colors of nature seemed to spread away, leading the eye in all directions yet always back to the great pillar in the center. If one did not see the pattern, the floor seemed a random wash of color. But if one looked with understanding, one saw the *veve*, the sacred patterns of uncounted spirits woven together, interlocking into a unified whole.

The *poteau-mitan*, the massive pillar holding up the central vault of the temple, the point from which everything flowed, was the trunk of an ebony tree brought whole from the sacred forests of Terra. Of such size four men with arms outstretched could not have encompassed it, the great tree was surrounded by concentric altars hand-carved from a dozen woods, illuminated by handmade candles.

Father Pauli stood to the left of the pillar, facing the altar of—she could not be sure from the entrance. *If he seeks guidance in struggle, Oggzn. If influence, Oshzn.* Both seemed likely and neither her concern. She pushed the thought from her mind, focusing on her own spirit's path as she approached the great pillar.

After completing his devotion, Father Pauli moved with unhurried grace to join her before the altar of Obatala, mother of creation. He stood in respectful silence as she lit the taper she had made at a candle already on the altar and placed it, with her prayer, in its proper place. When she had completed her respect, she turned to find him smiling at her.

Though Father Pauli was four times her age, his parchment-pale skin was unlined save for the crow's-feet radiating from the corners of his upturned eyes. His hair, still as dark as her own, was gathered at the nape of his

neck in a thin ponytail that hung between his shoulder
blades—testimony to a Draconis thread woven through the
tapestry of his heritage.

Without speaking, the priest extended his hands, palms
like pale leather turned up, catching the torchlight.

In equal silence she laid her naming blade across his
hands. Seven heavy silver crescents, linked to form a necklace but which could, with a twist and push, lock together
into a single blade. Without closing his fingers over the
shining metal, Father Pauli examined the sacrificial weapon,
tilting and angling his hands; blossoms of light ran along
its every edge like liquid fire.

She knew the blade would find favor. Ogun had been
with her as she'd created it, guiding her; possessing her as
her *ti bon ange*, little guardian angel, had danced free in
the rippling heat rising from the hand-heated forge.

Father Pauli smiled again. Approval, and pride in his
pupil, was plain in his eyes. Pressing the ball of his thumb
to the cutting edge, he christened her naming blade with
his own blood.

She felt the sting of welling tears, but neither blinked
nor brushed at her eyes. For her priest and mentor to take
the cut meant for her . . . He elevated her, raised her more
than she deserved.

"There is a task I must fulfill," she said, breaking the
silence in her need to make plain her path.

"What task?"

"I must complete the mission I failed," she answered. "I
must kill all of the *bokor*-woman's brood."

Father Pauli regarded her for a long moment. At the
edge of her vision she was aware of his thumb slowly tracing the planes of her naming blade, coating the knife with
his blood.

"Why must you do this thing?"

"It is an *ebo*."

For the first time Father Pauli frowned.

"An *ebo* is a burden placed upon you by an Orisha Loa,"
he reminded her sternly. "Are you certain this is not a
burden your own pride places across your shoulders? Do
not sin through arrogance."

Her gown rustled and pulled as she drew herself to her full height.

"The demon woman's guards will be ready for you this time," Father Pauli said before she could speak. "They lack *sight* but they are not fools. Do not leave your path on a mission of petty vengeance destined to fail."

"This *ebo* is laid upon me by Ayza: Oggzb has quickened me," she said, knowing the truth shone from her eyes. "It is a burden I delight in, a task for which I thirst."

Father Pauli regarded her for a long moment, the eyes of his spirit searching her soul for any flaw. At last he sighed and extended his hands, presenting her with her blessed blade.

"Fast," he said.

Prepared to accept his benediction, she paused, startled by the unexpected instruction.

"Fast, as I will," Father Pauli said. "If this calling is truly an *ebo* and not some geas laid upon you through sorcery or some trick of your own heart, we will know it together.

"And together we will know how to proceed."

She opened her mouth, then closed it again. She was certain. But if Father Pauli was not, did that not indicate she could be mistaken? Or perhaps the true purpose of the fasting was in his last sentence. *Know how to proceed.* She had her purpose, of that she was sure, but she had only the vaguest notion of how to fulfill that purpose.

Bowing her acceptance of his instruction, she turned her back on the priest and retraced her steps to the temple path.

Behind her Father Pauli watched her retreating figure until she was out of sight.

Then he returned to the altar of Oshzn, where his candle still burned before her threefold image. Bowing his respect to the goddess of sensuality, money and influence, he reached behind the finely crafted triptych and turned off the recorder.

=== 9 ===

Atlanta, Savannah
Former Prefecture VII
21 October 3137

Governor Linette Ferguson of Bordon toyed idly with her gold-plated stylus as she watched Mr. Green watching the presentation on economic diversity. The stylus had come with the gold-plated noteputer case her former staff at the Ministry of Infrastructure had given her as a going-away present when she'd accepted her appointment to Bordon.

Governorship of a planet—even a planet with fewer inhabitants than many Terran cities she could name—was a very big deal in those days. For a history student from the rural backwaters of Tall Trees with an interest in social service, it was far above what she'd imagined would be the apex of her career in service to The Republic.

Who knew a decade later The Republic would be gone?

At the head of the table Bertrand Petersen of the Covenant Worlds made a joke Linette didn't catch. At least she hoped the general chuckles were in response to a deliberate attempt at humor. Glancing at the wall screen behind the speaker, she saw another graphic from the report that had been forwarded to her office the week before. If Petersen was adding anything new to the information, she'd catch it in the transcript.

Being essentially a prospectus presentation to people who understood business, Petersen's presentation had a lot more substance than a political or diplomatic speech, but it was still deadly dull. At least for those who had taken the time to read the material in advance. She saw a couple of investors nodding and taking notes as though all of this was new to them.

She caught Petersen trying not to look like he was looking to Green for a cue and resumed her study of the nondescript man seated near the door. Nothing about him indicated he was anything other than a minor aide, which meant he must be someone worth watching. Not that he actually did anything except sit.

Linette was still planetary governor, still had her gold-plated stylus and noteputer case, but she was no longer a Republic appointee. The people of Bordon had elected her to the position after The Republic pulled back; not because of her charisma or political skills, but because she had never had any agenda beyond getting Bordon back on its feet.

Compared to the devastation suffered by worlds like Galatea or Shiloh, Bordon suffered very little from the Jihad. Its few industrial centers had been bombed almost as an afterthought and it boasted no military assets other than the planetary militia. The planet's real problems had started with Devlin Stone's plan to form a unified Republic through redistributing displaced populations. A significant percentage of Bordon's citizens were first-generation residents relocated from highly industrialized planets in Prefecture II. *Former Prefecture II.*

In theory, the integration made sense. Linette had pored over the documentation for weeks in preparation for assuming office. In the abstract, Bordon's repopulation fit the adding-strength-to-strength model for forward pushing a world's economy. She had naïvely expected to be overseeing a steady upward industrial and economic climb.

The reality on Bordon had not matched the model. The newcomers, steeped in Draconis culture and trained in the use of advanced technology, had little to offer agrarian Bordon beyond the population numbers they represented, and Bordon had little they needed beyond air, food, water and enough gravity to hold them in their beds. The cultural and religious differences alone had been a Gordian knot.

But Linette had persevered, building bridges and getting

people to actually talk to each other. Finding common ground was apparently her gift: to her, it seemed the obvious thing to do; to everyone else, it was amazing. *I suppose if I had to work at it, it wouldn't be a gift.*

The graphic behind Petersen changed to one she hadn't seen before. Linette focused on the economist's words as he ventured into new territory.

The Covenant Worlds wanted Savannah to join them—which made sense given their high level of technology. With Savannah came Remulac, breadbasket of its notoriously undernourished neighbor.

Same with Irian. Why are high-tech worlds the least hospitable? You'd think working to overcome an environment would take too much time for a tech base to develop.

What the people shaping the Covenant Worlds' political strategy didn't realize was that Bordon—with its surplus of technologically savvy citizens—was also wooing Savannah. More as a market than an ally, but there was no reason that couldn't work too. To be part of a larger nation—as an equal member, not as a vassal—would not only give Bordon a wide-open employment market; it would create a way for the world to import the manufacturing technology it needed for economic stability.

Someone on the Covenant Worlds' team had to be apprised of just how valuable an asset alliance with Bordon could be. And from what Linette could see of the power flow within the delegation, that someone was Mr. Green.

Amur, Oriente
Oriente Protectorate

So this is Thaddeus Marik.
Jessica tried to remember him from Victor Steiner-Davion's funeral on Terra, but couldn't. Of course she had seen him; she'd seen all of the paladins, but nothing about him had struck a chord.

Of course, she had not seen him as she was seeing him now, as an envoy of state approaching her throne. His dress uniform, which she'd at first taken for white, was a rich cream, almost a butter yellow, with a Marik-purple cape flowing from his broad shoulders.

And broad was an adjective that suited Thaddeus Marik. Though more weathered, more etched by care, he was clearly Frederick's brother—the same nose, perhaps a millimeter too wide to be handsome, between hazel eyes hard as polished agates. His mouth, his jawline, his hair—once started she couldn't stop herself from continuing the inventory—even his ears reminded her of Frederick. But of a Frederick who had somehow been stretched sideways. For on Thaddeus' face the remarkably similar features were spread farther apart.

For a silly second Jessica considered ordering Frederick to stand beside his older brother. Their heights, as nearly as she could judge, were identical. But Thaddeus' shoulders were wider and his body—clearly well muscled beneath the formal uniform—massed nearly half again as much as his brother's.

The five members of his entourage, each dressed in similar cream uniforms but with half capes of different colors hanging to midback, stopped at the end of the aisle proper. Thaddeus strode the final steps to the focal point in front of her throne alone, and dropped his chin to his chest without breaking eye contact. A military bow.

And those uniforms behind you aren't an honor guard, they're representatives. Your little nation has five member worlds. Jessica resisted the urge to look toward the empty space where Philip had so often sat beside her to receive delegations. *Diplomatic envoys in uniform. Do the Covenant Worlds have their own Chamber of Paladins?*

Ignoring the potentially bad omen, she returned Thaddeus' nod with a smaller one of her own.

"Welcome, Thaddeus Marik. We have heard much about the Covenant Worlds and are interested to learn what brings you to us."

"To pay our respects, Your Grace, and, we hope, to forge bonds of mutual interest. Trade, such as we share with Irian"—Well, of course he knew from whom she'd learned of the Covenant Worlds—"but there are many areas in which we may discover we share common ground."

"There may, perhaps, be areas to explore." Jessica allowed for further discussion without commitment. "I confess I am intrigued by the title with which you signed your communiqué. Warden?"

"The title is an homage to the history of the Free Worlds League." Thaddeus smiled, as though at a fond memory. "As warden I am appointed to command our nation's military, oversee our constabulary and—in this singular case—to represent our interests abroad."

Placing civilian law enforcement under military control is never wise. And to assume diplomatic duties as well? You may call yourself warden to honor the Free Worlds League, but there is far too much of Devlin Stone's Republic in your role, Paladin.

Jessica nodded, accepting the explanation. She followed through the rest of the introductions and assurances of future discussions during the delegation's visit on conditioned reflex, her mind focused on the implications and potentials of small nation states arising in the vacuum left by the collapsed Republic.

Midthought, she let her eyes rest on Frederick Marik, positioned as he now was among her counselors. He was watching his brother's overture with a total lack of attitude that itself spoke volumes. Here was a younger brother, she realized, who had—according to Torrian Dolcat's exhaustive research—lived his life among the halls of power in Geneve and achieved nothing of note beyond a reputation for being a behind-the-scenes deal broker.

When The Republic had begun to collapse, Frederick had run to Oriente. Another court, new halls of power, where—despite revealing himself to personally be something of a boor—he was once again establishing himself as a politically astute adviser.

Thaddeus, faced with that same collapsing Republic, had forged a new nation out of unaligned worlds, establishing his own halls of power ruled by a parliament that was under the impression it had appointed him to their leadership.

Looking from the younger Marik brother to the older, Jessica began to reassess her options.

10

Regulus City
Chebbin, Regulus
Regulan Fiefs
22 October 3137

Lester Cameron-Jones noted the slight stiffening of Gustav
Salazar's spine as he caught sight of Emlia sitting comfortably on the settee angled toward the fireplace. The intelligence director did not believe politics or security was a
proper arena for the captain-general's wife. He reported to
her and consulted with her in Lester's absence, of course—
Lester gave him no choice—but when the captain-general
was in residence, Salazar believed Emlia should be safely
cloistered far from the concerns of state.

To find her ensconced in the formal sitting area of Lester's office during his report to the captain-general offended
his sense of propriety.

Emlia, fully aware of Salazar's opinions, smiled sweetly
as she acknowledged his stiffly minimal bow.

"Anson's response?" Lester asked without preamble.

"Paring away the obscenities," Salazar said, raising his
eyebrows to telegraph the fact he had just made what he
considered a witticism, "Captain-General Anson Marik
suggests you wait until his corpse is cold before you start
trying to plunder his worlds."

"Plunder his worlds?" Lester echoed, his voice rising.
"Does the arrogant imbecile have no understanding at all?"

He shooed away Emlia's caution about his anger with a
wave of his hand before she uttered a word.

Shoving his chair back from the desk, he rose to pace
before the picture windows. His office, quite deliberately,

faced away from the river and the sweeping view of the city. This side of the ducal residence was hedged close by a security wall and a narrow path down which a guard passed every twenty minutes. The noonday sun, reflecting off the yellow stone of the wall and the dense greenery that grew along its base, filled the room with a golden glow. The effect was beautiful—and did nothing to lighten Lester's mood.

"It's not about *worlds*, it's about the Free Worlds League," he said, not caring that he was lecturing two people who understood the political situation as well as he did. "If there is not a seamless transition of authority, the Marik-Stewart Commonwealth will dissolve into chaos. The Lyrans will snap up each orphaned system at their leisure."

"It is possible his eventual failure is not as self-evident to Anson as it is to us," Emlia suggested.

Lester flashed her a quick grin.

"Even if he does not ultimately fall, he's bound to lose control over some of the Commonweath," he said. "If he would just provide us with authority protocols, at least put the mechanism in place for us to step in as the centralized command if he should be cut off . . ."

"The Lyran thrust continues to cut along the coreward third of the Marik-Stewart Commonwealth," Salazar responded heavily. "It is likely they intend to annex that portion of the Commonwealth.

"However, Marik itself has fallen to Clan forces—"

"Clan?" Lester stopped in his tracks. "The Jade Falcons? Or that Wolf faction that's so cozy with the archon?"

Salazar blinked.

"One would be a new and independent adversary," Emlia explained. "The other would be an arm of a Lyran pincer attack."

"I understood, milady," Salazar answered with another minimalist bow before addressing her husband. "Neither. Marik was seized by Clan Spirit Cat supported by Clan Sea Fox."

"I didn't know the Clans worked together like that."

"I often suspect that most of what we think we know of the Clans is disinformation, my dear," Lester said. "No doubt they're quite straightforward and businesslike when not posing for the Inner Sphere's media."

"Indeed," Salazar agreed. "Perhaps more significant is the fact that the Oriente Protectorate has occupied Oceana and Angel II."

"Have they, now?" Lester clasped his hands behind his back and resumed pacing, eyes on the pattern of the hand-woven carpet. "So the witch has graduated from taking Republic worlds Anson annexed to seizing worlds within his sovereign borders."

"It would appear Oriente military operations were coordinated with those of Clans Spirit Cat and Sea Fox," Salazar said in his unchanging tone.

Lester paused again in his pacing, looking to Salazar for confirmation.

"That witch will lie down with any partner who shows the least chance of getting her what she wants," he said.

"Lester!"

Lester grinned at his beautiful wife's expression of alarm, but he neither apologized nor retracted his words.

"The Halas woman claims to hold all the Free Worlds League dear to her heart, yet spits on all the League stands for at every opportunity," he said. "Treason comes as easily to her hand as terrorism when it comes to feeding her avaricious hunger for power."

He slammed his fist against the frame of the tall windows, using the energy to turn him back for his next circuit of pacing.

Clipperton.

Not a day went by that he didn't think of that harmless world—a world without strategic or tactical value that might justify even legitimate military action. Yet it was on Clipperton that the Halas witch had ordered ten thousand innocent people killed. A bomb, planted by a cell of suicide agents who had gone to great pains to impersonate Word of Blake terrorists, had brought a ski lodge and half a mountain down on an unsuspecting resort town. In the blink of an eye, ten thousand six hundred and forty-two blameless men, women and children had been snuffed out of existence—all for the sole purpose of distracting him when Anson Marik and the Marik-Stewart Commonwealth needed him most.

Now Anson was fighting for his life and refused to reach out to Lester as an ally. Instead he issued orders as though the Regulan Fiefs were his to command. And when Lester tried to establish commonsense safeguards, reasonable precautions in the face of Anson's failing military efforts, he accused him—accused Lester Cameron-Jones—of trying to steal away his worlds.

What little trust there was between us perished when I allowed that witch to manipulate me, Lester acknowledged, not for the first time. *But any man would have done the same. And what's past is damn well past. We need to work together if we are going to survive the future.*

Only Anson wasn't going to survive. The man's arrogance led him to smugly mistake clever ploys for strategic planning. A lack of planning that—as opportunity after lost opportunity slipped away—would leave him with no options.

Now, as the Lyran juggernaut ground down the Marik-Stewart Commonwealth, Lester realized he was the last man who could stand against the monster of Oriente and the havoc she would wreak across the Free Worlds League. Perhaps the only man who fully realized how terrible the woman really was.

And now his only ally against her was going into the dark night without passing his authority and resources on to Lester.

He jabbed out a fist again, breaking the skin of his knuckle on the edge of the window frame. Neither Salazar nor Emlia commented.

Much as he wanted to lay the blame at her feet, Lester knew arranging the Lyran invasion of the Marik-Stewart Commonwealth and Duchy of Tamarind-Abbey was beyond the scope of Jessica's ability. Though not beneath her character. Her hiring of Clans to do her dirty work on Marik illustrated well enough her willingness to use treachery against the worlds and the people she claimed to care about so deeply. It was her jackal-like pounce on the wounded nations—rending them even as they reeled under the attack of what should have been the common enemy of all nations of the Free Worlds League—that twisted his stomach into a knot of rage.

He had had no one in position to intervene on Angel II or Oceana or Marik. And his assets on Oriente had been severely compromised, through no effort of Jessica's watchdog thugs. He was an impotent witness to her rape of all for which the Free Worlds League stood.

He—and through him the people of the Free Worlds League—did have resources. But none that were in place to stop what was happening *now*.

Lester stopped pacing and stood looking at the yellow stone of the security wall, clenched fists at his waist.

Stop wallowing in what you can't do and focus on what you can do.

"What were you able to discover about the Rim Commonality?" he asked without turning his head.

"Nothing beyond the fact that Elis Halas evidently negotiated a major concession from the rebel government," Salazar reported flatly. "The behavior of the prime minister indicates he is laying the groundwork, both in parliament and with the people, for a closer relationship with the Oriente Protectorate."

Emlia had once speculated that the director of intelligence would say "I love you" and "My shirt's on fire" with the same deadpan delivery. Lester smiled now at the thought.

"Do we have anything in place that can interfere with this potential alliance?"

"Not directly, sir. But I have accelerated the timetable on Operation Picket Fence."

Lester nodded. It wasn't much, but if Picket Fence did what the strategy wonks said it could, it would hamstring diplomatic efforts of the Rim Commonality's illegitimate government for years. Not actually a direct blow against Jessica, but it would at least complicate her life—if only a little.

Speaking of diplomatic efforts . . .

"Any word on Pembroke?"

"No update, sir," Salazar admitted. "The trade delegation to Tharkad was entering the Coventry system when hostilities developed between the Lyran Commonwealth and the Duchy of Tamarind-Abbey and the Marik-Stewart Commonwealth. There has been no communication with Marquis Pembroke nor any official acknowledgment of our inquiries from the Lyran government since."

Lester nodded at the expected news. The irony of his miscalculation—sending a trade delegation to steal the march on any effort by Fontaine or Anson to form economic ties with the Lyrans on the eve of their invasion—was not lost on him. But the step had been one among many. Not all had been so wrong. And all of them had been—or rather, the purpose behind all of them—was still valid.

He was the last bastion of civilization, battling the poisonous hydra of darkness that threatened to reduce human civilization into a pointless quagmire of bitter, pointless territorial skirmishes.

Lester, that's melodramatic, even for you.

Lester shook his head at the imaginary chiding of his wife even as dear Emlia sat not a half dozen meters behind him.

He turned, startling her with a smile. The answering warmth in her eyes filled his limbs with energy.

"We need our assets within the Halas household active as soon as possible," he said to Salazar. "What's the status on Operation Vole?"

11

Amur, Oriente
Oriente Protectorate
27 October 3137

Damn him!

Frederick's relationship with Jessica Marik and her daughters had changed—for the worse. He thought he

could salvage some of what he had already built. He wasn't
sure how much. But he knew he could legitimately blame
his brother Thaddeus for this.

Things had been going well: routine dinners with the
captain-general and her daughters, a public position among
her advisers, even sitting respectfully behind her during the
occasional public appearance in the hinterlands. A few of
the popular tabloids described him as "cousin and friend
of the ducal family."

Then Thaddeus had shown up, calling himself "Warden,"
of all things. The Republic was dead, but he'd managed to
make himself the big frog in some small pond, and now
came visiting like a head of state.

His own position in the throne room among the gallery
of counselors represented the very real power of influence.
But having a front-row seat whenever Thaddy-boy was invited to negotiate with Jessica *on the dais* had lost its charm
the first day.

And he plans on staying weeks!

Frederick resisted the urge to throw the cut-crystal de-
canter. *Paid for this one.* Hand steady, no trace of his rage
on his face, he poured a judicious two fingers of the local
single malt into the heavy tumbler cut to complement the de-
canter. Replacing the glass stopper, he strolled onto the patio.

The grounds of his new estate were more modest than
those attached to the house Jessica had provided, and it
was twenty minutes farther from the palace, but the high
wall provided privacy and the garden itself was every bit
as delightful. *And devoid of ugly fountains.*

He had followed the advice of Claireborne, and others
more obviously loyal to Jessica, in selecting both his residence and his staff. No doubt everything he did was reported to someone, but he was used to functioning alone
in a fishbowl.

Lacking his brother's firstborn title and status, Frederick
had never been able to cultivate the network of loyal syco-
phants necessary to ensure privacy. And thanks to their
parents' much-touted honesty, he didn't have the coin to
pay for top-notch security either. So he made do, swimming
alone among the sharks, managing to keep his head above
water and looking for a solid place to stand.

Damn him, damn him, damn him!

Smiling as though at an amusing thought, Frederick leaned casually on the railing of the patio and sipped his scotch.

He'd almost made it out of the shark pool and onto dry land before his brother showed up. All he'd had to offer the Halas upstarts was the Marik name. Thaddeus not only had the name; he came with the family title and a gaggle of awestruck peasants calling him warden—and thoroughly trumped the best his little brother could do.

He wondered which of her daughters Jessica would sell for the right to legitimately call her family Marik. Elis as eldest made sense, but she had a cold cunning streak that overmatched even her mother's. Frederick wouldn't have minded being her drone—let her have all the headaches of running a government—but Thaddeus was much more the alpha male. He'd probably opt for Nikol: feisty, straightforward, more at home in her BattleMech than the back rooms of power. Much more Thaddeus' tumble.

Of course, if he marries Nikol, Elis will still be free.

As quickly as it formed, he dismissed the thought. Once the Marik name was secured, Elis was too valuable an asset to be traded away redundantly. She'd be used to secure borders with one of the other rural provinces—Andurien, perhaps, or Regulus. Maybe even Liao, though Frederick couldn't imagine anyone willingly entering into an alliance with that mad House.

Pulling his mind away from idle speculation, Frederick focused on his own predicament.

Marriage into the ruling family was no longer an option, and there was no place beyond Oriente that was both stable and welcoming to Mariks. So. He was stuck here and it was entirely up to him to make his stay as secure and profitable as possible.

Of course he would capitalize on his "friend of the family" role. While Thaddeus bedded Nikol, he'd be by Jessica's side—visibly advising her, publicly being the strong arm she leaned on. If he played his hand well, he'd finish out his years as the beloved uncle of Oriente's next generation of rulers. Not, perhaps, the apogee he'd imagined for himself, but pleasant enough all things considered.

Unless her husband came to his senses and stopped wandering around like a lost soul.

Frederick couldn't understand why the man didn't pull himself together. True, he'd lost a son and a daughter, but so had his wife, and she still had her wits about her. Of course, her power depended on her running her little nation-state efficiently; when one had money on the Hughes' scale, one could afford to indulge oneself.

By the same token, as long as there was a chance Hughes would get his priorities in order and reemerge as Jessica's consort and counsel, it wouldn't do to depend entirely on the captain-general needing Frederick around.

Frederick sipped his scotch, taking the time to appreciate its fire.

So.

Swimming among sharks again. Smaller sharks, swimming in a smaller ocean, but sharks nonetheless.

He needed to learn more about local politics. And local power, since the two were not synonymous.

Time to renew his acquaintance with members of Parliament Claireborne and Oshaka, for one thing. Where he went from there depended on what he learned.

Swimming with sharks was not so difficult. Frederick smiled. All one had to do was *be* a shark.

12

Atlanta, Savannah
Former Prefecture VII
28 October 3137

"**Y**ou're a difficult man to see."

Green looked up from his noteputer, feigning surprise. He'd been holding station in the lobby of the hotel the

Covenant Worlds' trade commission had adopted as its base of operations. One of a dozen low-level functionaries catching up on work away from the conference. Positioned to observe others while escaping notice, he didn't have a plausible escape strategy available when he'd seen Linette Ferguson approaching him with evident purpose.

Governor Ferguson of Bordon was a tall, long-boned woman, the sort some described as "horsey," with close-cropped orange-red hair. Today her nose and cheekbones, highlighted by pale curves that clearly marked the outline of goggles, were sunburned a painful-looking red. In the morning sunlight pouring through the lobby's broad windows, her forest green business suit gave the pale expanse of her unburned complexion an unfortunately bilious hue.

Bordon had been a problem child of The Republic for a generation. The attempt to diversify the population and the industrial economy of the underresourced world had already been pronounced a failure when Ferguson—an inexperienced midlevel manager with neither the wit nor the connections to avoid the assignment—had been saddled with the job of trying to salvage the situation.

Unaware she was captain of a sinking ship, Ferguson had stabilized the economy in less than a decade. Months before Fortress, Bordon had posted its first positive trade balance since the Jihad.

Though the marginal world had never been on his list of potential converts, Green paid enough attention to local politics to know the woman towering over him was credited with holding Bordon together when many more-affluent worlds were sinking into chaos.

"I'm sorry," he said aloud. "Did you wish to make an appointment with Dr. Petersen?"

"No, I understood his economic prospectus the first time he sent it around." Ferguson dropped unceremoniously into an adjacent chair. "Even if he didn't send a copy to me. I want to talk military."

"Excuse me?"

"Reading between the lines," the governor said as she surveyed the lobby. "This *is* a good vantage point. You can see halfway down the corridor."

Green said nothing.

"Reading between the lines," Ferguson repeated. "The Covenant Worlds have more guns than they need. Buried in among all those trade incentives is an assurance of military protection. That's not an assurance people make—or take—lightly. The fact that it's even hinted at says two things.

"This is the part where you ask, 'What two things?' "

Green regarded the governor without speaking. Now that she was shaded from direct sunlight by a pillar, her suit no longer cast a sickly glow over her features. It occurred to him that her face was sunburned because she'd been somewhere other than attending the rounds of talks at the hotel over the last few days. He'd not been consciously tracking her and was now hard-pressed to think of when he'd seen her last.

"Balancing your checkbook?"

"What?"

"Old negotiating trick. To avoid reacting to a question or offer, focus on something else," Ferguson said. "Like thinking about chess during sex to slow things down. The tell is your eyes get a bit glazed no matter how hard you try to look like you're paying attention. In and out of bed."

Green blinked. "I was wondering where you've been."

"If you mean all your life—Tall Trees, Terra, Bordon. If you mean the last two days—fisheries along the Gulf coast. We've been breeding Bordon carp to survive Savannah's alkaline oceans, and it looks like we got one right. If it doesn't eat everything else in the ecosystem, we might have a new agricultural export."

She paused, waiting.

"What two things?" Green asked obediently.

"First, that the Covenant Worlds has an active and mobile military able to encompass a few more systems. In the case of your offer, Savannah and Remulac. Second, that this offer of duty-free trade is a precursor to expanding your borders."

"Excuse me?"

"You are offering to boost the economy and provide security," Ferguson said. "Two things that will endear you—and the administration that makes this security and affluence available—to the people. Do it right, give it a few years and you can get a grassroots "join the Covenant Worlds" movement going with no trouble.

"Based on what I see, I figure five years at the outside." The governor shrugged. "Since it's a cinch I'm only seeing the tip of the iceberg, call it one or two."

How the hell *did I overlook this?*

Green rejected the idea of continuing to sound like an uniformed lackey. Linette Ferguson had obviously parsed a great deal from limited data; events had progressed well past any chance of diverting her with protests of innocence.

"What do you propose?"

"See? It's much nicer when you stop thinking about chess."

Ferguson leaned slightly forward.

"Bordon is secure only because no one wants it," she said. "And no one wants it mostly because no one knows what it has to offer."

Green raised an eyebrow. It occurred to him that he and the governor were clearly visible to anyone who looked their way: his position was unobtrusive, not concealed. However, he could think of no reasonable way to move to a more private location without alerting anyone who had already observed them that something was up.

"Focus," Ferguson reprimanded him. "Way too many of Bordon's people were imported from high-tech worlds. They couldn't bring all their technology with them, of course, but they weren't refugees with only the clothes on their backs. Among other things, they brought their education database—which includes simulator programs far more advanced than anything I saw on Tall Trees or Terra. We've got a generation of techs trained on equipment no one has seen in seventy years.

"Of course, for anyone else it's like learning Greek or Latin, but we are positioned to be an asset to any technologically advanced world."

"You were angling for the Savannah market," Green surmised.

"Bordonians make up about twelve percent of their skilled-labor force," Ferguson agreed. "And we're a lot closer to Connaught.

"In addition, we've been doing a lot of low-tech, easily

sustainable bioengineering. More like your basic cross-breeding. We're moving beyond exporting food to exporting plants and animals tailored to survive on marginal worlds, like that new breed of carp. More important, we've got the people who have been doing this tailoring willing and able to go to other worlds to work on-site."

"In other words, you're a source of specialized skilled labor."

"Short term," Ferguson agreed. "Long term, we're prepared to offer incentives for corporations to build plants on Bordon. Nothing major, of course. Secondary or tertiary assembly points that require little initial capital outlay."

Green considered. "What are you offering?"

"I like that," Ferguson said. "No dancing around, no pretending you're not the agent for the decision makers. Ugly girls appreciate being treated with respect."

Green couldn't help answering her smile.

"Bordon joining the Covenant Worlds would go a long way toward convincing Savannah—and to a lesser extent Remulac—that signing on is a good idea," Ferguson continued. "Of course, I will have to convince my parliament that becoming a Covenant World is the best way to go, but given the current political and economic landscape, I don't expect that to be a hard sell.

"You might have a harder sell convincing your bosses that Bordon is a good ally. Give me a day or two and I can put together a topflight sales kit."

"Governor Ferguson," Green countered. "I think the sales presentation would be much more effective if you came to Miaplacidus and made the pitch yourself."

Not what I came looking for, but treasures often turn up when you're not looking.

13

There were others in the room. Rikkard's battle reflexes counted a dozen to either side, ranking them roughly by threat potential without conscious thought.

Rikkard ignored them, steadily regarding the woman on the throne as he approached. Looking for signs of the daughter in the mother. The relationship of flesh and blood—not merely genetic material—carried with it potential levels of interaction he knew he did not fully understand. Did the spirit gestate with the flesh?

The intelligence he had seen in Lady Julietta's eyes was there, though of a cooler temperature. There was her courage, but not the spirit. Not the same spirit, he amended; for there was a spirit. A hunger, a drive—an assurance the Lady Julietta had not possessed.

"This is an unexpected pleasure, Star Colonel," Lady Jessica said, her words announcing he had approached as far as he was welcome.

A step closer, Rikkard stopped. Two strides and a leap from the woman on the throne.

"Unexpected," he echoed. "Yes. But I would doubt it is a pleasure."

A half smile touched Lady Jessica's lips, but she did not concede the point.

"May I ask what brings you to Oriente?" she asked.

He considered. Not prolonging the moment, but letting his eye measure the others assembled.

A man, broad of shoulder and face, stood beside and

behind the woman on the throne. A man of war, Rikkard saw as he narrowed his focus; but also a man of calculation. One who saw patterns and meanings, but who weighed his decisions on the scale of hard facts.

Rikkard suspected there was a social significance to his placement, but did not know enough of the mores of Oriente to parse it precisely. A champion? Or an ally? That he stood, that there was no place prepared for him on the dais, indicated he was only recently added to the assembly. Was his positioning for Rikkard's benefit?

To Lady Jessica's other side were two very similar women, but younger. One was the veritable image of the ruler of Oriente, regal in her discipline. The other had something more to her bearing, something of the warrior. And eyes that cared as much as they calculated. Daughters? Yes, he was certain these were Elis and Nikol.

With that recognition Rikkard became aware of a thread, a connection, that bound the two to each other and to the woman on the throne. An energy; physical for all it was insubstantial. And the thread, anchored to their mother, wrapped around them and stretched . . .

Rikkard followed the thread with his eyes, turning his head left until he found his gaze met by a man of simple bearing standing just beyond the edge of the dais. Older than himself, the man wore clothes of somber cut without sign of rank or office, as though he were meant to fade into the surroundings of the chamber.

There was the spirit, the placid strength he had first encountered on Marik. Rikkard inclined his head slightly, acknowledging the father of Lady Julietta before turning back to the ruler of the Oriente.

"I do not pretend to understand the relationship between a mother and her daughters," Rikkard said.

If that non sequitur admission, delivered seven heartbeats after her question, surprised Jessica Marik, she gave no sign.

"From what I have observed, trust is a key element."

Tension. Rikkard felt it. With no change in physical position or expression, an electric communication burst into life between the women on the dais.

"Is it considered a betrayal of that trust," Rikkard asked, "for a mother to send a daughter to her death?"

The warrior shifted his stance, the daughters straightened. Others in the room rustled; from behind he heard a shoe squeak and an intake of breath. He did not turn his head, his eyes firm on the unblinking regard of Lady Jessica.

"I have sent no daughter of mine to her death," she stated flatly.

"You sent Lady Julietta, unarmed, to bargain with me," Rikkard said. "You sent her to convince me to waste my forces, destroy my people, fighting your enemies. You sent her with a promise of help so deceptively worded that you could honor its letter in safety while my people died to attain your ends."

The woman on the throne did not move. But steel entered her posture, a fire flared behind the calculation in her eyes.

"If you believe some restitution is owed," Lady Jessica said coldly, "you cannot expect us to honor promises we did not make. We cannot be held responsible for your failure to understand."

"Restitution," Rikkard repeated, tasted the word and nodded his approval. "Yes. A restitution must be made."

"If you are expecting a handout"—Lady Jessica's tone was pitched to provoke—"you will be sadly disappointed."

Rikkard smiled, letting her see he was immune to her insult.

"You knew that I would eventually recognize your deception." He explained the obvious. "That I would, when my people were near the end, understand what you had intended from the beginning—that we die as pawns in your game of conquest.

"And you knew that your *daughter*—Julietta—would be there, in my grasp, when the scope of your treachery became clear."

"Your accusations are unfounded," Jessica said. "And given your circumstance, unwise. If opening negotiations with false accusations is tradition among Clan Spirit Cat, I suggest you become acquainted with the customs of your hosts."

Rikkard smiled again. Not to show he was untouched, but because he found her words—her tactics—genuinely funny. Why were spheroids so relentlessly incapable of honest speech?

"I was looking into her eyes." For a moment he felt those eyes, filled with a fatalistic resolution, regarding him as he stood before the Lady Jessica, just as they had regarded him over Janis' bent but unbowed form. "She expected to die. She was ready to die.

"She knew she had lied in manner, betrayed by implication," he said. "She accepted her shame and her responsibility and stood ready to embrace the consequences."

Rikkard paused, anticipating Lady Jessica's interruption. But her eyes, fixed on his own, did not flicker.

"To give one's life for duty, that is understood," he said. "But to fail and in failing serve the greater good? To forfeit one's honor?"

He shook his head. Part of his mind was aware that no one in the throne room moved.

"She showed me a new thing. Not a new vision, the key to understanding a familiar vision. And through that understanding I was able to save my people."

Again he paused, but Lady Jessica remained still, her face a mask. Even her eyes were without expression. Rikkard realized his words were carrying her into territory she had not anticipated. She was waiting to see where the journey led before responding. She showed wisdom.

Choosing to forgo further explanation, he made a flat declaration of purpose.

"I have come to make restitution."

One of the other women—the youngest, Rikkard thought, though he did not look directly—shifted her weight.

Lady Jessica remained still. She had not followed his final leap. Through no fault of her own, Rikkard admitted to himself, given the length and direction of the jump.

"We have heard your daughter is injured," he said. "Wounded in the spine and brain by an assassin's knife?"

"Yes," Lady Jessica answered in a flat, bitter tone. "She is in a coma."

"The nerves of her spinal column must be reconnected?" Rikkard asked. "Perhaps torn brain tissue mended?"

"Her spine is almost certainly severed," Jessica said, her voice edged with an anger fueled by grief. It was the most genuine emotion Rikkard had seen her display. "The damage to her brain cannot be assessed. The repair you suggest is beyond the capabilities of our finest physicians."

"Beyond the capabilities of your finest physicians." Rikkard echoed Lady Jessica's words a third time.

Hands laid flat on the arms of her heavy chair, as though she gathered strength from the ancient wood, Lady Jessica became a statue of palest alabaster. Rikkard saw—alarm? hope?—*something* in her eyes she did not entrust to her voice.

"You're saying your doctors can heal Julietta?" asked one of the daughters.

Turning, Rikkard saw he had been right. It had been the younger one, Nikol the warrior, who had understood him first.

"My healers have not yet examined your—sister," he answered, aware of the feel of the unfamiliar word. "But with the injuries we have heard described . . ."

Turning his shoulder to the women on the dais, Rikkard sought out the eyes filled with Julietta's spirit. "It is possible that we will be able to make restitution."

This time Lady Julietta's father nodded in return.

14

Zanzibar, Tamarind
Duchy of Tamarind-Abbey
5 November 3137

The wind whipped through the wire fence along the edge of the landing field and through the open frames of the loading gantries, whistling and moaning by turns. Microscopic bits of black sand stung Christopher's cheeks as he squinted against the white glare of morning sunlight on ferrocrete.

Sixteen months ago, seeing the Zanzibar Desert through the tinted windows of a rented limousine, he'd thought the boundless stretch of black sand dramatic, full of what the travel-vid writers called stark beauty. The ever-blowing sand had been a soothing susurration as it slid across the sealed skylight.

Black and gray beneath a crystal blue sky, the desert was still dramatic. Christopher noted the thinnest crescent of one of Tamarind's moons just above the horizon. The bigger one, he guessed. Teteli? Scattered patches of yellow-green vegetation saved the rolling expanse from being completely barren. The plants grew close to the ground, stunted and twisted by the constant wind.

And without the protection of the limo, the constant, sand-filled wind was anything but soothing. It stung his exposed cheeks above the dust mask and threatened to blind him. He should have worn goggles.

It was easy to imagine his flesh being scoured away by the desert.

Just beyond the fence the sluggish Zanzibe River, made nearly as black as the desert by sediment, pushed its sullen way toward whatever sea it fed. Christopher searched his limited knowledge of Tamarind's geography and could not come up with a name.

No place cheerful, of that he was certain.

Christopher had not appreciated the gritty reality of Zanzibar on his first visit to Tamarind, though the DropShip that had brought him had berthed less than a kilometer from the spot where he now stood. The limo had carried him the few dozen meters to the VIP travelers' club, an opulent lounge and restaurant with a sweeping view of the black and brooding desert. Through the polarized windows of that penthouse, the river had seemed like a ribbon of silver across black velvet. The VIP club had sleeping quarters available for those who needed them, but he hadn't. A half hour after his arrival, a civilian VTOL had carried him to the lodge at the base of Otho Mountain on the continent of Padaron. He hadn't seen the desert again until his departure and then also through glass.

No mystery why the historical home of the Marik clan on Tamarind was in the icy heights of the southern continent.

Nobility would want to be as far as possible from this grimy and utilitarian urban sprawl in the middle of a black-sand desert.

And I'm a noble. I know what I'm talking about.

Only he wasn't a noble now, he reminded himself. And he wasn't all that sure he knew what he was doing.

Christopher took pride in the fact that every risk he took was carefully calculated. He knew going in the limits of his skills, his body and his equipment. He studied the waterfall or the mountain or the hurricane from every angle before approaching. When he committed to the challenge, he was ready: the only question in the balance was whether his drive to win was greater than the forces arrayed to defeat him.

No, that wasn't true. The forces he faced generally didn't know he existed. The meteor he jumped would follow its course with or without him; the gravity he battled was an oblivious constant aloof to his displays of defiance. This . . .

He squinted against the glare and grit, measuring the distance between himself and the heavily armed guards at the crew gate.

This was different.

Technically, there was no conflict between Tamarind-Abbey and Oriente. In fact, they had a common enemy in the Lyrans—though that animosity was primarily intellectual in his mother's court.

But he was infiltrating the capital of a sovereign nation. A spy. The fact that he intended to reveal himself to Fontaine Marik meant nothing if he was caught before reaching the duke. His protests of his pure intent would sound like lies.

He could have approached openly—in fact, that had been his original intent. But the ubiquitous Charles had schooled him on the potential consequences. Particularly during their passage through the Lyran-controlled wedge between Tamarind-Abbey and the Marik-Stewart Commonwealth. *Christopher Hughes Marik was too important a target,* he said, *details of his movements a valuable commodity to informants—particularly if that information included mention that his JumpShip was carrying Mules laden with materiel support for Tamarind-Abbey. One* Tramp-*class JumpShip would not have been able to defend itself against Lyran attack; Christopher the scion traveling openly could all too easily become Christopher the hostage.* He doubted the Lyrans would be able to leverage many concessions out of his mother, but why give them the chance to find out?

Christopher shifted the strap of the kit bag on his shoulder. Too late he recognized the gesture as a tell, revealing his own nervousness. As nearly as he could determine by surveying his surroundings through his eyelashes, no one had noticed. A dozen steps ahead the guards at the gate were focused on crewman Jemi Hendricks as she demonstrated that her lyre was indeed hollow and empty.

He had intended to end the charade on arrival in the Tamarind system, but a Lyran JumpShip with a *Corvette* escort parked at the zenith jump point had prevented him from announcing his presence. Who knew how thoroughly the Lyrans had penetrated the Tamarind communications net? One hint he was aboard and not even the *Captiva*'s registration with the adamantly neutral Rim Commonality could have prevented the Lyrans from boarding and confiscating the JumpShip.

One guard was watching Jemi's hips roll as she walked away. The other watched with flat eyes as Christopher extended his identity chit toward the customs officer.

Until the instant he released that coded bit of plastic, Christopher had options. The brown-dyed hair could be a fashion choice; traveling as a merchant able spaceman could be one more jaunt for a bored prince infamous for being determined to experience it all; the clandestine arrival at Tamarind—well, that would have been tougher to explain, but he could have hammered out some story just plausible enough to keep him out of trouble.

But the moment the falsified documents left his fingers, he was committed.

Christopher pulled down his dust mask and let it hang around his neck to allow the guard to compare his face with the ident chit. He tried to keep his face impassive, willing none of his internal turmoil to show. *Hope this guy doesn't watch extreme sports.*

Handing over the forged chit transformed him from sports hero to criminal; he was a spy. Whether or not he was an *enemy* spy depended on how tightly the Lyrans held Tamarind. If they held Tamarind.

The guards—both now watching him as the customs officer fed the ident chit into the reader—wore Tamarind uniforms, not Lyran. A good sign if Tamarind was still independent. Tamarind shipping control had made no mention of the glaringly present Lyrans while clearing his DropShip for landing and assigning its descent route. There were so many layers of possible meaning to that circumstance that Christopher had given up trying to compute them all.

It was completely possible the armed guards were allies, but asking the question could get him killed—or worse, captured to be used against his mother—if the answer was the wrong one.

The first customs officer took a long look at Christopher's face while a second went through his kit. He met the man's gaze levelly, not watching the thorough search. He hoped he'd been right to reject Charles' suggestion of contacts: his jade green eyes were unusual, but were not unique to the Oriente Mariks, and colored lenses were easily detectable.

"Your first time on Tamarind?" the officer asked.

"Aye," Christopher answered. He had no idea if Rim Commonality natives had a regional accent; monosyllables seemed the wisest course.

"Military areas are marked in purple," the man said. "Stay away from purple signage. Also stay out of uptown and residential areas unless accompanied by a resident. There are signs. You're expected to know the law and obey it."

The silent customs agent probing the lining of Christopher's bag paused just long enough to take a plastic card from a dispenser and hand it across the table. Taking it, Christopher saw it was covered in fine print.

"All street markets and taverns near the DropPort are duty-free," the first agent droned, evidently planning to save him the trouble of reading the card. "Gambling is legal only in licensed casinos. Use of narcotics and prostitution is illegal."

Despite the dull delivery, the agent's eyes were sharp, looking for a flicker of reaction as he itemized potential vices. Christopher almost blinked when he added, "This is Friday. Temple services are open to believers only. Sunday Christian services are open for all but have formal dress requirements."

Christopher nodded and accepted his three-day crewman's visa without a word.

Buy what you want, get drunk, bet where we say, but don't screw or get stoned, and be sure to dress nicely for church, he thought. *Rules we can all live by.*

He imagined the guards watching him as he made his way along the narrow walk that led to the public transportation terminal.

Don't be silly. You don't have Jemi's million-Eagle ass.

Christopher grinned. Recognizing the adrenaline rush of survival, he picked up his pace. If he hurried, he'd catch the short tail of the line boarding the dust-covered bus.

15

Amur, Oriente
Oriente Protectorate
6 November 3137

Talar Nova Cat acknowledged Sonja Sea Fox falling in step beside him with a slight dip of his chin, not taking his eyes off the corridor ahead.

The Clan Nova Cat delegation, which included Sonja as a representative of the Sea Fox ovKhan, had been given a limited run of the Marik palace for the duration of their medical mission. Talar had chosen to take advantage of the hospitality by wandering wherever he was allowed, studying the art and architecture. Things that had never interested him until the ornate buildings of Marik had been used as weapons against him.

Two armed escorts in the dark green and purple livery followed a dozen paces behind him as he strolled. A reasonable precaution given who he was and the assassination attempt that had brought Star Colonel Rikkard to Amur. With Sonja now beside him, he did not need to turn his head to confirm that four guards now drifted in their wake.

The residence of the Oriente rulers was dense with history. The hand-carved woodwork represented generations of artisans, each adding to foundations prepared by others. The woods of the floor, visible on either side of the central carpet, appeared at first glance to be a parquet of stained pieces, but closer examination revealed they were parallel planks of natural wood with distinctive grain patterns precisely matched to create a harmonious whole.

It seemed almost sacrilege that the carpet protecting the wood was of machine manufacture.

None of the incidental furniture spaced along the walls touched the carpet. He was certain that for affairs of state, when symbolism was more important than utility, the carpet was rolled away to allow the full beauty of the wood to show.

A detail of a carving that framed an anonymous door caught his eye. Repaired. By the planes of the cuts and flats, he knew the artisan had been left-handed while the original craftsman used his right. He wondered what had damaged the door frame.

"Trade for your thought," Sonja said. Talar caught the tension beneath the banter. It matched the wariness that seemed to haunt her most welcoming smile, her most intimate glance.

What is it you were ordered to discover? Talar thought in her direction. *Ask and we can move beyond this charade.*

Aloud he said: "I was wondering how often violence came to these halls."

"I doubt they have the stomach for much," Sonja answered.

This time Talar did look at her. The same beautiful smile,

the same watcher crouching in the chestnut eyes. He realized she thought he meant physical conflict.

"The battles that rage here are deadly," he said without enlightening her. "And continuous."

"What are they doing?" Jessica asked.

The physician beside her did not answer at first. Jessica realized the woman was studying the scene the same as she was and trying to formulate a meaningful answer. She bit back the urge to demand an immediate reply.

There were seats behind her but she ignored them. In front of her and below, on the other side of sealed glass, her eldest daughter lay under the surgeon's knife. Though there was little to indicate the figure facedown on the table was Julietta: only the nape of her neck and the shaved back of her head were visible, the rest covered by sterile barriers. Blue papercloth shields speckled with drops of her daughter's blood.

She became aware of the hand she was squeezing tightly and looked to her left. Philip met her gaze, a rock of reassurance.

Our *daughter's blood*, Jessica amended.

"Your Grace?" the physician interrupted Jessica's thought.

The rounded accent of Davr Khuna was supposedly legendary in its ability to calm the hearer's nerves, but the soft sound made Jessica want to scream. Not trusting herself not to, she kept her mouth firmly shut and invited the neurosurgeon to continue with a raised eyebrow.

"Your Grace," she repeated, obviously unsure how her words would be received. "Beyond a general grasp of the procedure, I do not know what they are doing."

"Could you explain what you do understand?" Philip asked mildly. "And speculate about what you don't? All I see is our child under the knife, and any information would be a help."

"Of course." The imported expert glanced at Jessica before answering Philip.

"What was thwarting our efforts to help your daughter is that nerves are nerves," she said. "There is no external way to tell a sensory nerve from a motor nerve. And no way to tell a touch nerve, for example, from a heat nerve."

Philip nodded his understanding. The gentle squeeze of his hand reminded Jessica that shouting at the woman for reciting familiar knowledge would do them little good.

"More to the point, while we can reconnect nerve tissue on a gross level, we cannot stimulate its growth," the doctor went on. "What's damaged is damaged. Nerves do not regenerate.

"Except . . ."

Her voice trailed off as she turned to regard the scene in the operating theater below them.

"The person under the microscope hood seems to be testing each nerve fiber," she pointed. "That blue box is connected to microfilament probes. Their surgeon is using them like an electrician's circuit tester."

"Remarkable," said Philip.

"Impossible," the doctor countered. Then remembered: "Your Grace.

"Even more impossible, he seems able to identify halves of severed nerves." She pointed again. Beyond the fact the damned woman was indicating something on the screen above the blue box, Jessica could make nothing of the gesture. "Once he's tagged the matching ends, *he* is connecting them."

Jessica realized the emphasis indicated the second Clan Spirit Cat physician who leaned forward as the first stepped back. His hands disappeared inside a large metal box resting directly on Julietta's exposed neck. His head was bent as he apparently studied a screen built into the top of the box.

"Would it be too much to activate the teaching screen?" the doctor muttered.

Jessica realized the words were not directed at her.

The two-meter-wide repeater screens, positioned to allow medical students in the operating theater gallery to see enlarged images of the procedures, remained dark. She wondered if she really wanted to see the damage to her daughter's spine in such intimate detail.

"So the Clan physicians have the technology and the technique for identifying and repairing nerves but they won't share them," Philip said quietly. "That must be terribly frustrating."

God, Philip, how do you do that?

The doctor nodded, not taking her eyes from the procedure.

"I don't suppose you can tell how it's going?" Philip asked.

"Good, I think.

"Your Grace," she added a moment later, remembering to whom she spoke. "The surgeons have the focused but relaxed body language of pulling off a tough one. . . ."

Again a damnable pause as the woman surveyed the scene below them.

"I do not think this is a fast procedure," she said at length. "We're looking at either the first of several operations, or the first team on a long operation."

"How long?" Jessica surprised herself by not shouting the words.

"Based on what they've done so far," the doctor considered, looking from the mysterious metal box to the wall chronometer and back. "Seventy, maybe eighty hours. I don't really know enough to be sure."

Jessica nodded, forcing herself to be content with the imprecise answer.

"We certainly cannot watch from here for eighty hours," Philip said. "You should get some rest, my dear. I'm sure Dr. M'Bai here will keep us informed."

Jessica nodded again, but did not move.

The Clanner was wrong. I never sent you to die. Your failure I expected, an object lesson to strengthen Nikol, give Christopher some focus. But not your death, never your death. Don't die on me now. Jessica began to turn, then stopped. Pressing against the guiding pressure of Philip's hand, she looked down at her daughter one last time. *Please.*

16

"**Y**ou're lying, boy."

Duke Fontaine Marik had let his hair grow since Christopher had seen him last, and his face had become more drawn and gaunt. But the sapphire blue eyes glaring at him from beneath lowered brows had lost none of their fire.

Christopher imagined he could feel his skin blistering.

"No, sire," he answered solemnly, meeting Fontaine's level gaze with his own.

Getting in to see the duke had been easier than he'd expected, if a bit more painful. The Lyrans did not control Tamarind. Yet. Their diplomatic envoy was cooling her heels at the Lyran embassy while Fontaine organized the Duchy's defenses. No mean feat without hyperpulse generators enabling instantaneous communication.

Christopher had, after a day and a half of wandering the streets, worked his way to the ducal castle by systematically doing the opposite of what every warning sign commanded. His plan had been simple: wait until cover of darkness to get inside the compound, then—safe from the Lyrans by virtue of the security blanket of the Ducal Guard—identify himself.

He hadn't counted on the nightlife of the noble district: ground cars and foot traffic had flowed steadily on every street long after most houses in Amur would have been dark. It was well after midnight when he'd scaled the walls.

Once on the grounds he'd enjoyed nearly twenty seconds

of freedom before security invited him to spend the night in lockup. At least he assumed they'd invited him: he had no memory of events immediately prior to waking up on the floor of a bare cell. From the bruises he could see, he suspected the festivities had included falling down several flights of stone stairs.

While he'd been unconscious, Tamarind-Abbey SAFE had evidently deduced his identity. At least the anonymous men in civilian business suits watching over him when he awoke were SAFE; Christopher recognized the stereotype. They had delivered him here—an anonymous, windowless conference room off an unmarked hall three floors above the holding cell—and left him alone, shutting the door behind.

Christopher had used his time alone to stretch. He'd never been thoroughly beaten before, but he'd been pummeled by enough rocks, waves and trees in his life to know keeping limber was the best defense against the long-term effects of the bruises covering his body.

He'd had to scramble to his feet when the door swung inward, admitting another anonymous civilian, this one two meters tall and twice the age of the men who'd escorted him through the empty halls.

SAFE director, Christopher guessed.

Behind the stranger had been Fontaine Marik.

The duke was dressed in formal, perhaps even ceremonial, robes and did not sit. Christopher decided his arrival hadn't been important enough to wake Fontaine, but the ruler was curious enough to pause on his way to some affair of state to question Christopher directly.

It had taken Christopher two minutes to deliver the bare bones of his mother's assurance of Oriente's support. And her confidence that Tamarind-Abbey would fully support her once she had met the precondition the duke had set.

From Fontaine's glower it was clear the duke wasn't happy with Christopher or the news.

"Don't split semantic hairs with me, whelp," Fontaine said. "You are not telling the complete truth."

"You're right, sire," Christopher admitted.

"Why?"

"Because I cannot tell you everything my mother has in mind." Christopher kept his voice formal. "Negotiations are still pending."

Fontaine glanced to the other man.

Christopher didn't turn his head to follow the look, but from the duke's expression whatever the man communicated was reassuring.

"But her objective is to bring Marik blood into the line?" Fontaine demanded with less heat than a moment before. "A Marik captain-general?"

"Yes, sire."

Fontaine's eyes lost focus in speculation.

"Unless she's selling your sister to Anson . . ."

Christopher did not rise to the bait.

"The only Mariks available are the Rousset-Mariks," the duke said at last. "And they supported the Blakists and turned against the Free Worlds in favor of Stone's Republic."

"They were *used* by the Blakists—as so many were, sire," Christopher countered. "When they realized the cult's true nature, they turned on the Master and pursued him with as much determination as everyone else."

"Not *everyone* else." Fontaine surprised him by chuckling. "It will cause old Lester no end of torment to have a Rousset-Marik presuming to be captain-general.

"The bastard will count him twice a traitor," he added. "First for being descended from Alys Rousset-Marik and second for becoming a paladin of the damned Republic of the Sphere."

"Sire, I didn't say it was Thaddeus Marik."

"You don't have to, boy." Fontaine shook his head. "You as much as admitted it when you defended the Rousset-Marik line."

Christopher said nothing, tacitly conceding the point.

"Thaddeus is the only offspring of theirs that's amounted to anything," Fontaine said. "And paladin of The Republic is about as high as anyone can get—or could get before the damn thing collapsed."

The old duke pursed his lips, frowning into the middle distance. Christopher could almost see the wheels turning as he poked at the idea from every angle.

"If Thaddeus Marik's wandering around loose outside that damn Fortress of theirs, getting back to his roots makes sense," Fontaine said at last. "And him as captain-general would sit well with the League worlds that got traded away and ended up orphans—even if it was his misguided grandmother who did the trading."

Christopher's understanding of the Rousset-Marik betrayal, as his mother called it, ran a little differently but varied only in the details. Only her daughter Agatha's marriage to Calvin Marik redeemed Thaddeus and Frederick in Jessica's eyes. But he said none of this, letting Fontaine spin his own web of meaning.

"Nor does Tamarind forget he's the great-grandson of Kristin Marik. Theresa and Jeremy Brett practically adopted her. That makes Thaddeus the next thing to family in the Duchy." Fontaine glanced to the tall man at the edge of Christopher's vision. "Your mother continues to play the long game well. Elis could do a lot worse."

He cocked an eyebrow, pinning Christopher with a sharp eye.

"Or will it be Nikol?" he asked. "I'll bet a paladin'd appreciate a good MechWarrior for a bride."

"Sire, you're asking me to betray a trust," Christopher said. "I cannot go against my oath or my position."

The old duke's gaze held his for a moment longer. "You're right, boy."

Christopher thought he read approval in the man's nod.

"But you did not need a *Mule* to carry family gossip," Fontaine changed the subject briskly. "What else have you brought for Tamarind-Abbey?"

"Two *Mules*, sire," Christopher corrected, pulling the manifest crystals from his belt pouch. "The *Hudson* remains docked to the *Captiva*, a *Tramp*-class JumpShip of Rim Commonality registry."

The duke regarded him in surprise for a moment, then nodded toward the other man and said, "Billings, my security chief." Christopher handed over the crystals and Billings fed them into his noteputer.

"How did you come by a Rim Commonality JumpShip?" Fontaine asked.

Christopher hesitated.

"The *Captiva* happened to be at Oriente on unrelated business when we received word of the Lyran assault on Tamarind-Abbey," he said carefully. "We were able to inveigle the captain into providing transport."

"Skated close to another one of those family secrets you're not allowed to tell me, didn't you, boy?"

"Yes, sire."

"I'm tempted to ask you how the ship happened to have two suckling *Mules*—which I assume from context are loaded with war materiel—at the exact moment you needed them just to see how you avoid that answer," Fontaine said. "But I'm old and time is short.

"A *Tramp* has three DropShip rings. Is there a third ship you haven't mentioned?"

"Only two were available, sire."

Fontaine nodded.

"I have church in forty minutes," he said, indicating his formal robes. "And when in residence at the Marik Palace, I do not dare miss Mass at the Marik Cathedral. Half the congregation attends only when I'm in town."

Christopher hesitated, but the duke forestalled him with an upraised palm.

"It's best you stay under wraps, boy."

Neither Fontaine nor Billings made a signal Christopher could detect, but the door to the hallway opened instantly. Instead of the muscular men who'd escorted him, a slender young woman in palace-staff livery entered.

"Please take our friend to guest quarters," the duke said. "And find him appropriate clothes."

Christopher opened his mouth, but the duke waved him toward the door.

"What did Oriente send us, Roland?" Fontaine asked his head of security as soon as the door closed behind young Hughes.

"A mixed bag of construction material and ordnance," the SAFE director answered, reading his noteputer's screen. "Looks as though they grabbed everything that might be remotely useful off the shelf."

"Or the shipments were bound somewhere else?"

"Not these precise shipments," Roland said. "The mix is too eclectic. However—

"Delete the ammunition and generic 'Mech parts and the rest of this materiel would be just what you'd need if you were rebuilding an assembly plant," he said. "In fact, add the 'Mech parts back in—call them templates—and you could make a case for someone rebuilding a BattleMech plant."

"And why would the Rim Commonality be doing that, I wonder?"

"The boy's not going to tell us."

"That's a given," Fontaine chuckled. "Not really our concern, anyway. More significant is the empty docking ring and the *Mule* still attached to the JumpShip."

"They're expecting Tamarind to fall."

"And providing us with means of escape," Fontaine said. "I wonder if that was young Christopher's idea or his mother's."

"The difference being?"

"One might be a genuine offer of help." Fontaine adjusted his robes. "The other would definitely be a ploy to put us in debt."

17

Place, unknown
Time, unknown

There was light.

There had never been light before, and now there was. Red. Yes, that was the name; that was the color. The name gave the color meaning. Red light, tinged with orange. And darker lines of red, almost shadows, wandering across the areas of lightest orange. Lines branching like trees, like rivulets of a stream flowing.

Flowing was the clue she needed.

Those are blood vessels. I'm looking at my eyelids.

She thought about that for a while. Looking at red eyelids meant there was light beyond them. For her to see the veins in her eyelids meant either the light was very bright, or her pupils were fully dilated. Opening her eyes was going to hurt.

Was whatever she might see worth that pain? Or were red eyelids enough for now?

She considered the question.

Amur, Oriente
Oriente Protectorate
9 November 3137

Rikkard knew Lady Julietta was awake.

There were changes on the monitor screens; numbers rising, waves becoming more frequent and more pronounced. Nothing that triggered the alarms. Yet. But soon the medical technicians in the room would notice the increasing activity and would respond in whatever way their protocols required.

He felt the eyes of one of the Oriente doctors on him. Turning his head, he was not surprised to meet the gaze of the short woman, the leader of the surgical team that had done all it could before the Spirit Cat healers had arrived. The Oriente physician had a dark complexion, much darker than any in the Nova Cat genotypes the Spirit Cats had brought to Marik, and spoke with a lilting accent Rikkard found pleasant. More important, she worked with the dedicated passion of a true healer. Within the limits of spheroid medical technology, Lady Julietta owed her survival to the efforts of this woman.

Rikkard nodded, acknowledging his debt.

The Oriente physician returned the nod. Then, not yet noticing the changes in the numbers—as the Spirit Cat medicos also had not—she resumed her study of the portable sensor array.

For his part, Rikkard sat on the wheeled stool he had appropriated with his back against one of the few unoccupied spaces along the wall. Hands flat on his knees, he watched the energy gather around Lady Julietta as she pulled herself toward full consciousness.

Dr. Salina M'Bai traced the lines of the medical array with her eyes. There was no way she could ever replicate the device, but if she figured out *how* it was looking for whatever it saw, it could save years of research in developing scanners of this caliber.

Not that technology was her long suit. She was a neurosurgeon by primary training, but over the years she had become a specialist in reconstruction of torn and damaged bodies. Organs, bones, muscles—she could do it all. There was no mystery why she had been the one called when Julietta Marik had been cut down by an assassin's knife.

Salina—and her team, specialists assembled from a dozen sources—had stabilized Lady Julietta; had kept her alive. *Thank God that first security guard on the scene had thought to immobilize her neck.* But for all their expertise . . .

Salina had also been the one to tell Duchess Jessica that nothing else could be done. Lady Julietta could be kept alive indefinitely but, Salina had truthfully said, her recovery was in the hands of a higher power. At the time she had not imagined that the higher power would be the Clans. *Do not be blasphemous. The Clans are the tool of the higher power.*

Salina had advocated keeping Lady Julietta alive. True, there was plenty of evidence that the neural activity they could detect was only the random firings of a network damaged beyond all hope of repair, but Salina had thought she discerned patterns. Intellectually she knew there were no patterns to conscious thought—every brain was wired uniquely—but to her mind those patterns indicated Julietta was still there; still an identity worth saving.

But until the Clan physicians and their unimagined machines had arrived, Salina had no idea how Julietta could be saved.

n't. But if I can figure out just one of these

⸱l she was looking at suddenly flashed green and a rhythmic beeping filled the recovery room. It took Salina a startled half second to realize what was happening. She beat the Clan medics to Julietta's bedside by two strides.

Julietta coughed and spat, a dry rasping sound, as she tried to dislodge the drain tube taped to her mouth.

"Whoa, whoa, whoa, Lady Julietta," Salina said, beating the nurse at pulling an irrigation line and vacuum hose from their pulleys. "Let me get some water in there, wash your mouth out a bit. Relax, relax, you're not choking. That tube's supposed to be there. We'll get it out in a moment. Let me help."

Murmuring comforts, Salina directed a gentle stream of water around the interior of Julietta's mouth, the suction hose pulling the liquid back out again before it trickled down her throat. One didn't risk the esophagus remembering what to do when the patient hadn't swallowed of her own volition for more than twelve weeks.

Lady Julietta had stopped struggling with Salina's first words. She watched wide-eyed as the doctor worked, evidently trying to make sense of what she was seeing.

Most trauma victims did not remember the event, Salina knew. The insult to their system short-circuited the brain before the memory could be filed. It was most likely that from Julietta's perspective she had fallen asleep normally on the night of August fifteenth, then suddenly jerked awake in a strange place with people she had never seen before shoving tubes in her mouth.

Keeping her voice gentle, Salina recounted the missing events. Ninety percent of what she said would be forgotten, or at least stored without processing. The important part was that someone was there, talking to Julietta, comforting her and caring for her. That would register. That would do the most good.

Salina glanced around at the others in the room. The nurse, pan in hand for catching vomit and looking resentful that a mere surgeon had usurped her position; the Clan medics, two reading screens and one standing by with a handheld scanner of some sort; the Clan big shot, the warrior-type with the spooky eyes who had been camping in the recovery room for the last three days, sitting and doing nothing.

"You," she ordered the idle warrior. "Go tell Duchess Jessica that her daughter is awake."

Without a word the man rose and left.

"They can't take her."

"Your Grace, I understand your feelings—"

"How could you possibly?"

"I'm a mother."

Jessica's first instinct was to snap off the surgeon's head. How did being a mother compare to the responsibility of ruling the Protectorate? But before she opened her mouth she realized the other woman was right. She might protest that the possibility of Julietta being held hostage was her gravest concern, but what truly made her blood run cold was the thought of her daughter helpless among the Clan.

"You're right, of course," she said with effort. "Forgive me."

"Think nothing of it, Your Grace."

The physician's accent rounded the words, turning "your" to "yore" and broadening the other vowels. Jessica always felt the urge to tell the woman to hurry up and reach the end of her sentence.

"The Clan doctors have skills and technology we do not," the doctor was saying. "And Lady Julietta is far from being completely healed. She requires weeks, if not months, of observation and therapy. There is a possibility another round of operations may be necessary."

"Surely you can do the observation," Jessica said. "I know you must have skilled physical therapists. If she needs further surgery, we can call them back."

"Your Grace, without their advanced technology we cannot observe accurately. And without accurate and informed observation, we cannot provide the most effective therapy. We may even do harm." The doctor spread her hands. "The best hope for Lady Julietta's recovery lies in her continuing care by the Clan physicians."

"You mean letting them take her to Marik."

The doctor didn't answer, giving Jessica time to work her

way through the necessity herself. Her daughter was alive, she was conscious—wasn't that enough? But Julietta condemned to a life on her back, diapered and connected to tubes, would never thank her for keeping her safe from the Spirit Cats. For not giving her a chance to be whole again.

For a moment Jessica was back in the recovery room, looking down at the shriveled form of her daughter. Her daughter with the oddly luminous eyes—eyes she had never seen before—looking back at her across a great gulf.

What happened to you when you were trapped alone inside your mind? she asked. *What—*

She did not say "madness."

A small part of Jessica—a part of her that was small—tried to think how she could turn this situation to her advantage. She crushed the mercenary instinct. This was her *daughter*. She deserved to be healed.

Besides, said the calculating voice, *she's no use to you in this condition.*

Jessica slashed the air with a short chop, batting the cold voice away. This was her daughter. Nothing else mattered.

"Thank you, Doctor," she said aloud, hoping the formal tone masked the fact that she still could not remember the woman's blasted name from one moment to the next. "You are right, of course. Please see to whatever preparations are necessary for my daughter's journey."

═══ 18 ═══

Marik Palace
Zanzibar, Tamarind
Duchy of Tamarind-Abbey
10 November 3137

Christopher took up position behind the first rank of counselors. He wasn't exactly in disguise, but his conservative cap, following the fashion favored by the upper class, was tilted to shade his eyes. His frock coat and leggings were equally universal upper-class civilian conservative. He looked every inch a local scion who had legitimate, if peripheral, business in the central chambers of the Tamarind-Abbey court.

Which in a sense I am.

The room, ornate by any standards, was draped in purple with just enough touches of contrasting and complementary colors to keep the effect from being overwhelming. Make that manageably overwhelming. Designed by Ortho the Cold at the height of his grandiose excess, the room had nothing scaled to the proportions of a mere mortal.

The arched ceiling seemed high enough for local weather; windows three stories high seemed proportional. There were nearly a hundred people in earshot of the ornate throne, and half again that many in alcoves along the wall opposite the windows: communication consoles that linked the throne room to every ministry of the Duchy. For all its ostentation, the audience chamber was a working hub of government.

Duke Fontaine had left the Lyran archon's ambassador to cool her heels for hours before granting her audience. An old-school ploy to remind the visitor who was in power.

Judging from the duke's attitude, Christopher suspected the forced wait had worn him as much as Trillian Steiner.

Fontaine made no effort to appear at ease on his throne. Christopher knew it was the man's energy rather than the chair's reputed lack of comfort that twisted his body almost sideways in the seat. The duke's hands gripped the arms as though he were about to rip them from their mounts as he glared at the main door, waiting to see Trillian Steiner and hear whatever she'd come to say.

Grand Vizier Sha Renkin stood by the throne. But while his duke focused on the approach of the Lyran envoy, he scanned the room, making sure all was in order for the coming confrontation. Christopher winked when the ice-gray eyes met his, going for some personal contact, but the basilisk gaze passed over Christopher without a flicker.

At last the tall double doors to the audience chamber swung inward on silent hinges. An imposing man entered, wearing the weapons-concealing dress-uniform robes of Duke Fontaine's personal guard, then stood aside. The guard's bald head and apparent age registered before Christopher made the identification: Roland Billings, Fontaine's chief of SAFE. But even knowing, he found it hard to connect this obvious warrior with the nondescript man who had hovered at the duke's elbow.

Clothes really do make the man.

Framed in the doorway was a sleek greyhound of a woman.

Or perhaps Doberman pinscher, Christopher amended as he noted her combat-ready stance. *That would make the big blond guy behind her a rottweiler?*

Trillian Steiner stood, evidently appraising the room before entering. Christopher recognized the ploy to ensure all eyes were on her. He was careful to keep his own features completely blank as her eyes swept over him.

Finally focusing on Duke Fontaine, she stepped across the threshold and approached the throne with measured strides. Her watchdog kept in close step. Surely he realized his position was symbolic. There was nothing a lone soldier—and the graceful precision of his movements identified him as warrior-trained—could hope to do to defend his mistress when outnumbered an entire planet to one.

Still, his stride showed no doubt in either his mission or his ability to carry it out.

Respect, Lyran, Christopher thought in the bodyguard's direction.

Evidently recognizing the obvious cues worked into the mosaic, Trillian Steiner stopped in the center of the audience area and bowed her head with apparent respect.

"A member of House Steiner here?" Duke Fontaine demanded in apparent surprise. "I would ask why I deserve this *honor* but after your nation has savaged my Duchy . . .

"I assume you've come to finish your blood-work."

Surprise almost pulled a laugh from Christopher. His mother would never have started with a preemptive barrage of that caliber; of any caliber. Subtle, Duke Fontaine was not. Or perhaps more subtle than was apparent—going for the shock to see what it knocked loose.

Trillian Steiner was made of stern stuff, he gave her that. Far from flinching at the duke's booming voice, or snapping back a retort to the accusation, she raised her head as though nothing had interrupted her hollow courtesy.

She fixed her eyes on a point just in front of the duke's feet, like a lowly supplicant in the days of Ortho the Cold.

"Duke Marik, I have come here at the behest of the archon of the Lyran Commonwealth," she said in a tone that was both respectful and pitched to reach the farthest corner of the audience chamber. Then she slowly raised her eyes to meet Fontaine's. "It is my hope that you and I may be able to bring an end to these hostilities."

Be sure all witness your innocent intent, Christopher recognized. *Admit no fault and take the high ground. Solid, basic tactics.*

Fontaine regarded her for a long moment. Trillian did not waver.

"You people create false pretenses to start a war," he said, rage in every hard-bitten word. "You invade my nation—a peaceful people—and ensnare us in a bloody conflict entirely of your making. And you now come here and talk of ending these *hostilities*?"

Christopher changed his mind. Fontaine wasn't about to yank the arms of his throne from their sockets. He was about to hurl the half-ton chair at Trillian Steiner. A breath, two, and the oldest living Marik brought his rage under control. The tension did not leave his body, but it became controlled; contained.

"Very well, Lady Steiner." Fontaine's voice was a sheet of ice over a racing torrent. "Tell your cousin to remove her troops. She started this war, she can stop it right now by withdrawing from my Duchy."

Good shot, Christopher cheered internally. He glanced around, but everyone was too focused on the confrontation to spare him a nod of shared appreciation. Except Roland and Trillian Steiner's guard dog. Moving his head in an otherwise still room had earned him a double hit from paired lasers. He smiled his most charming apology and the blank visages returned their attention to the envoy and the duke.

"You were increasing your military presence along the border, Duke Marik," Trillian said, not conceding a point. Then she spoiled her clean tactics by going historical: "And let us not forget that it is the Free Worlds League that has the reputation for crossing that same border and invading our worlds."

Christopher saw her body English shift as she recognized her misstep. Lunging back to the high ground, Trillian added: "Our actions were aimed at ensuring the sovereignty and protection of our people."

Fontaine released his death grip on one arm of his throne to wave away her words.

"Trumped-up intelligence," he snapped. "Outright lies."

Christopher missed the next few words as he became aware of the Lyran watchdog again. The man was slowly turning his head, no doubt looking out of the corner of his eyes as well. He was scanning the room, evidently taking inventory of who was present. Of course her bodyguard would be her intelligence man. Memorizing faces, making note of which worlds were represented and which were not.

Could the Loki agent—for that is what he was suddenly sure the man was—recognize Christopher? The Oriente Protectorate was too far from the Lyran Commonwealth to be a direct threat or reasonable target. But even if the man did not recognize him now, he would no doubt review an image database—compare his memory with records of known Mariks—and spot Christopher. Lord knew the face of Hellion Hughes had been splashed across enough news feeds.

Realizing it was probably futile—after all, the man had looked directly at him a moment before—Christopher shifted his weight slightly. Not quickly, and not much, but enough to eclipse the Lyran with a heavyset judge's crested hat of office. Flexing his knees while keeping his back straight, he reduced his height by a hand span. Legs conditioned to hours on a snowboard could hold that position for days without a quiver. Christopher doubted the usefulness of his impromptu disguise, but had no choice. He did not want the Lyrans considering the Oriente Protectorate a player—a potential threat worthy of attention—in their current conflict.

Fontaine Marik's voice snapped his attention back to the throne.

"Each Free Worlds League nation stands alone until a true captain-general assumes control of the whole," the duke declared. "You cannot easily paint me with the same brush you paint him with, Lady Steiner."

Him? Christopher fished in his memory. *Anson, of course. But distancing yourself from him emphasizes your lack of allies.*

He shook his head, moving a millimeter and a half before he remembered he was staying still to avoid notice. It was too easy to second-guess another's tactics when you were not the one on the spot, but he couldn't help but think Fontaine had made a tactical error with that declaration.

Unless . . . Christopher almost straightened as the thought struck. *He's planting seeds, telling his own people a unified Free Worlds League has his blessing so people will remember even if he's not around to see it through.*

"The Duchy of Tamarind-Abbey has suffered a great deal under your onslaught only because we were unprepared to wage war," Fontaine was saying, his voice still frosty with controlled rage. "But that does not mean we are weak. You will find the worlds that remain are fortified. We will not be caught off guard as we were when you first struck. We will not be intimidated."

"I have not come to intimidate you, Duke Marik," Trillian Steiner said. "I have come to try and find some grounds where further loss of life can be averted."

Christopher admired the cool with which she delivered the bald lie. Did anyone in the room doubt she had come to test Fontaine's resolve? Maybe distract him from the defense of Tamarind-Abbey? Trillian after all was not military; her presence here had no effect on the Lyran campaign. But the duke was the heart and mind of his Duchy's defense. If she kept him busy she slowed his ability to respond, to lead.

Only fear of attracting the Loki agent's attention prevented Christopher's bolting from the room. They had to anticipate Lyran tactics—head them off. Things had to be in motion to diminish the effect of Trillian Steiner's delaying tactics.

How?

Realization of the difference between knowing something must be done and knowing what to do ran a cold, stabilizing shock through Christopher's rising panic. No point in jumping on his horse and riding off in all directions, as his father used to say. Action without a plan was *not* better than no action at all.

He listened with half an ear as arrangements were made for the next audience—his mind filled with what little he knew of Tamarind and plans for the world's defense.

19

". . . a task for which I thirst."

Lester touched a stud, freezing the image of the dark-skinned woman. There was a beauty to her, no denying it; something that sprang from more than mere physical attributes.

Though those were plainly visible. Her ceremonial robe, bleached brilliant white, no doubt to indicate purity, covered her from throat to wrists to ankles. Yet the fabric was sheer to the point of weightlessness and for reasons of static electricity or errant breezes or simple lust, it formed itself to her lithe body—clearly naked beneath the cascading folds—and revealed far more than it concealed.

Lester shuddered.

No, her beauty came from her eyes—or perhaps her whole face, darkly luminous in the light of a dozen torches. Her expression of conviction, of faith. Lester suspected this was what ancient writers had tried to describe when they spoke of transfiguration. But those long-ago scribes had attributed the radiance of inner beauty to a God this woman rejected.

It's the human act of faith—not the object of that faith—that has the power to elevate.

"It seems a shame." Emlia's quiet voice broke in on his thoughts.

Lester glanced at her seated beside him, then twisted his body in the chair, leaning back a bit to look at her properly.

They were in the sitting room of his apartments—all somber woods and muted shades of russet and green; the colors of house Cameron. The wide glass-paned doors that opened out onto his private veranda were shut now against the fury of an autumn thunderstorm. They rattled every few moments as the weather seemed to take notice of the ancient building and buffet it with a hail-laden gust.

The stormy view—which faded to gray mist beyond the railing—formed the backdrop for the flat vidscreen positioned at the far edge of the simple table that served as Lester's desk when he was in quarters. On the table between him and Emlia were the remains of a light brunch—clutter he detested, but he did not want to break their companionable mood by calling in servants to carry away the trays.

The gray storm light from the floor-to-ceiling doors and the golden glow of the incandescent lamps ranged about the room suffused Emlia with a soft clarity.

Emlia's was a different beauty—light where the woman on the screen was dark, and streaks of gray providing silver counterpoint to the golden waves that fell to her shoulders. A smile curved her lips, acknowledging his regard and bringing light—more light—to her eyes. His wife was beautiful in the classical sense, the beauty of Rome or Athens. One of the mysteries of his life was how this magnificent creature had come to love a pale and jagged scarecrow such as himself. And that love, illuminating and informing her every word and gesture, was the source of her own inner beauty.

Faith in things imagined or love for ones who love you? Yours is the greater beauty, my dearest.

"What is a shame, my dear?"

"That girl's religion—*Coeur du Vodun*," Emlia said. "Heart of the Spirit. After you told me about Pauli, I did a bit of research. It's a—I guess you'd call it a radical fundamentalist group—within Sevi Lwa, a religion from ancient Dahomey, on Terra. Quite beautiful, in its way."

"I'm going to regret this," Lester muttered, loud enough for her to hear. Then in a conversational voice: "In what way, dearest?"

Emlia cut her eyes to let him know she was aware of his teasing, but pressed on regardless.

"They believe everything has a soul," she said. "Not just living things, but objects too. How alive they are depends on how much of this life force they have."

"Is it a life source or a soul?"

"Both." Emlia turned a hand palm up. "It's called *Ashe*. It connects everything so everything is one. Whatever you do to someone else, you do to yourself because you're one."

Lester snorted. "That's worse than Hinduism."

Emlia laid a cautionary hand on his sleeve.

"No one can hear us, my dear," Lester reassured her. "I know better than to speak my mind on cherished traditions of Regulus where my words might be noted."

Emlia shook her head, but whether at her own caution or his daring Lester could not be sure.

"I think you'll find *Coeur du Vodun* has more to do with your own Catholic tradition," she said. "That girl is trying to become a saint."

"A saint?"

"They call them O-something. Oshira? Orisha, that's it. *Orisha Loa*. Source of mysteries."

Lester cocked an incredulous eyebrow. His wife was not a fool, and not given to foolish word games. This prattle was leading somewhere, but she wanted him to recognize that somewhere on his own. He nodded slightly, inviting her to continue.

"The pantheon of *Coeur du Vodun* is infinite, always growing." Emlia spread her hands slowly to illustrate. "Everyone who dies becomes a venerated ancestor, with a place at the hearth shrine, and is consulted on matters of family importance . . ."

"An eternity of refereeing in-law disputes." Lester shuddered with comic horror.

Emlia smiled slightly without pausing. "—but the *aborishaloa*—faithful worshipers—who lead exceptional lives, lives devoted to one of the Rada, one of the original Orisha Loa, earn the right to become Petro Orisha Loa— minor gods."

Lester studied the image on the screen with new eyes. Not just faith, but faith alloyed with ambitions of godhood. Interesting combination. "What sort of god is she trying to be, I wonder?"

"I don't know their pantheon," Emlia said, looking at the same image. "But at a guess, one devoted to protecting her people."

A fresh gust of wind rattled the French doors.

Lester cast a weather eye at the storm beyond the veranda and noted the rain was slacking off. He could now see as far as the Brahma River, its broad expanse whipped to whitecaps by the savage winds.

Satisfied the natural world was proceeding normally, he returned his attention to the young woman on the screen. A religious fanatic who believed perfection in murder would lead to her own deification—who aspired to be a god protecting her people. There could be no more relentless a hunter.

And if she was caught? She knew nothing about Cameron-Jones or the Regulan Fiefs. She was a simple native of an unaligned world she imagined Jessica intended to conquer. His people could fill the media with the tragic tale of a young martyr doing her best to defend her home against imperialist invaders.

"You're advising we use her," he said at last. "Send her back in."

"She attains her goal of immortality, we ensure the safety of the Fiefs," Emlia said. "A perfect balance of Ashe."

"Ashe?"

"You weren't listening. Ashe is the life force that binds everything together." Emlia indicated the screen. "Sevi Lwa teaches that the more you understand Ashe, the more you understand the world."

"I understand the world well enough," Lester said, not bothering to hide the bitterness. He didn't take his eyes from the frozen image of the woman.

An untraceable weapon that gives advantage whether she succeeds or fails. He shook his head. *That madman Pauli was a genius for finding these people. Or did he create them by twisting their religion? Either way, genius.*

Five deaths—four and a half, if she kept the vegetable

that had been Julietta on life support—were less than nothing when weighed in the balance against the ten thousand the bitch had ordered slaughtered at Clipperton. Ten thousand innocent lives ended horribly for no other reason than to distract him from going to Anson Marik's aid.

Was Jessica in league with the Lyrans? Had her terrorism been linked to, been a part of, their invasion? It was satisfying to believe so, but Lester knew that whatever else she was, Jessica Halas was too smart to lie down with that particular viper.

How do you hurt a woman who so casually butchers thousands for a moment's political advantage? By making certain that all she does is for nothing.

Lester couldn't take the Free Worlds League away from her. Even without Anson and Fontaine Marik fighting for their lives against the Steiners, he could see enough in the pattern of her manipulations to know the imposter's daughter was within a decade of laying hold of enough worlds to claim she had reforged the Free Worlds League. A League she saw as her personal realm, to be held as firmly as the Davions or the Kuritas or the Liaos held theirs. She imagined herself the founder of a great House, the root and heart of a dynasty.

He lacked the resources to stop her. But he could ensure her dynasty was a dead end. With no children to carry on after her, she would rule knowing that nothing she did mattered. She would die knowing her dream died with her.

A small, small price for the carnage of Clipperton.

"I don't think you're taking the idea of Ashe seriously," his wife accused.

Lester glanced at her, startled that she'd so misread his mood. Then he realized she'd read it well enough and was teasing him gently to remind him he did not face his demons alone.

"If you mean the belief a rock has a soul like yours, then you're right," he answered, reaching out with an ungloved hand. "No tree or rock or forest or mountain could have a soul that means as much to me as yours."

Emlia blinked back sudden tears, far more moved by the rare offer of unguarded contact than his clumsily poetic words.

"Lester . . ." She took his hand lightly.

"Jessica Halas, now," Lester said, looking out at the storm, not thinking overmuch about the feel of his wife's bare flesh against his own. "Her soul. Yes. I'd say her soul had much in common with a rock."

Emlia, not letting his jest mar the mood, held his hand and stared out at the storm.

20

Amur, Oriente
Oriente Protectorate
21 November 3137

"My husband tells me not to waste time trying to manipulate you."

Thaddeus Marik met Lady Jessica's eyes, his fingers a centimeter from the proffered teacup. Her gaze was measuring, he decided; appraising, not challenging.

"I appreciate the sentiment," he said, taking the cup.

So much that happened on Oriente seemed to center on the rituals of eating or drinking. Luncheons, teas, dinners—even after-dinner liqueurs—often served as settings for serious discussions on affairs of state or business. It made one wonder whether obesity was a problem among the power elite of the Protectorate.

The thought made Thaddeus smile as he sipped his tea. Then the flavor registered and he nodded appreciatively to his hostess. Some aromatic herb had been added to the green tea, giving it an invigorating tang that seemed to clear his senses.

The Sunday afternoon lunch had been surprisingly pleasant. Along with fourteen members of the Protectorate's parliament and his brother Frederick, he had shared a light meal of what he assumed were seasonal dishes with the captain-general and her two daughters.

Two of her three daughters, Thaddeus corrected himself. It was too easy to forget Julietta.

He had glimpsed the gray, shrunken form of Philip and Jessica's eldest daughter only once—wrapped in some sort of medical cocoon and being pushed through a hallway on a gurney by a short black woman in a lab coat, accompanied by Star Colonel Rikkard Nova Cat. A vaguely surreal image he would not have seen if he'd kept to the public corridors. Rikkard's small entourage and the Clan medicos—each pushing his or her own cart of medical equipment—had followed close behind.

Details were scarce, but rumor had it Julietta had awakened from the coma she'd been in since the assassination attempt that had killed her brother—*Was it only three months ago?*—and that Clan physicians on Marik would be overseeing her recovery.

Thaddeus suspected part of that was either wrong or deliberate disinformation.

His own brother had surprised him yet again this afternoon. Over the years Thaddeus had come to anticipate Frederick's moods and excesses; worse, the smoldering resentment that had marred their relationship since adolescence. Today, however, Frederick was a changed man. Without a single veiled barb or double entendre, he had been a charming conversationalist throughout the meal, his company clearly appreciated by several of the noble-born MPs.

Thaddeus considered the apparent fact that it had taken the collapse of The Republic and exile—or repatriation, depending on one's perspective—to push his brother fully into his own.

Philip Hughes, now accepting a cup from his wife, had been conspicuously absent at lunch. In fact, until discovering him waiting for them by the tea cart, Thaddeus had been under the impression Jessica's husband was off-planet.

However, since neither of his hosts mentioned either Philip's absence or reappearance, Thaddeus chose to treat his avoiding the public luncheon as routine.

Which it might very well be.

The fact that Jessica herself was pouring tea, and that only she and her husband, Philip, were in the room, indicated this midafternoon repast accompanied a discussion of particular importance—but beyond that assumption, Thaddeus was in the dark. Though the statement about manipulation, and choosing an alternative, indicated—

"The Covenant Worlds," Philip said, breaking into Thaddeus' thoughts. "They sprang up quite suddenly when The Republic withdrew."

"Many worlds that found themselves abandoned have formed communities with their neighbors," Thaddeus pointed out; this was familiar ground. "The Senatorial Alliance that borders Irian formed even more quickly."

"The Senatorial Alliance is the product of negotiations that were under way long before The Republic imploded." Philip leaned back in his chair and sipped his tea. "And even given that advantage, it has proven less stable than the Covenant Worlds."

"By focusing on the needs of the people rather than expansion, the Covenant Worlds are able to consolidate and integrate effectively." Thaddeus matched Philip's relaxed posture as he delivered the party line with thoughtful sincerity. He was aware of Jessica's eyes on him, but he did not glance her way. "The Senatorial Alliance has ambitions beyond the survival of its member worlds. They would have annexed your own homeworld if more powerful neighbors had not responded to their overreaching policies."

Which is better than saying "before Oriente decided to take some of their worlds."

"It must be difficult, having such an alliance centered on your own home." Philip's concern seemed genuine. "Though I suppose it was even more difficult as a paladin of The Republic, knowing that your homeworld was represented by a traitor."

"More than difficult." Thaddeus made no effort to mask his feelings. "It was painful. It is still painful, knowing I can't go home again."

"No love lost between you and the Alliance, then?"

"With all due respect, sir, if you have any contact with

your homeworld, you know the differences between the Covenant Worlds and the Senatorial Alliance."

"Indeed I do," Philip confessed. "In fact, it's my family's suspicion that the foundation of the Covenant Worlds was laid much more carefully than that of the Alliance."

Thaddeus sipped his tea.

Philip was clearly fishing, but doing so with a confidence that implied knowledge. The question was how much of that confidence was authentic and how much a pose.

"The Covenant Worlds combined their resources for the betterment of their people," he said. "The name of the union reflects the leadership's commitment to the best interests of the people. I believe this straightforward objective and unity of purpose have allowed the worlds of the Covenant to flourish more quickly than alliances powered by greed or fear."

"That's a prepared speech," Philip said without accusation. "Clearly meant for press conferences and sound bites."

"Which has no bearing on the truth it contains."

"But it does not contain the full truth." Philip leaned forward. His expression was still deferential, one eyebrow lifted and one corner of his mouth curved upward in a half smile. Thaddeus believed it was not in the man's nature to be confrontational. But that did not mean he wasn't dangerous.

"My advice to my wife that we deal honestly with you was predicated on the assumption that you would deal honestly with us."

"I have dealt honestly and I will continue to do so." Thaddeus kept his tone light. "But I will not violate my obligation to the people who've placed their trust in me simply to satisfy your curiosity."

"Then let me set your mind at ease, Warden." Jessica spoke for the first time since filling Thaddeus' teacup. "It is my husband's theory, and one I now share, that you and we have a common goal."

Thaddeus thought he kept his expression blank, but Lady Jessica evidently saw something in his face she liked. Or at least something that made her smile.

"I have been playing politics for decades," she said. "Out here, where there are no rules. Seeing patterns—and recognizing the forces that shape those patterns—is a survival skill.

"There's a pattern to events around you, Warden. A pattern that implies you are the force shaping them."

Having no idea on what observations Lady Jessica was basing her assumptions, Thaddeus remained silent. Denying the wrong thing could give her information she did not have. At the same time, the fact that he did not have a ready reply made it clear he was involved in *something* he was not sharing. Perhaps even that was more information than she'd had.

Realizing he was about to second-guess himself into paralysis, Thaddeus smiled.

"That is flattering," he said. "But it implies I have far more resources and greater abilities than I do."

"If I had to guess—and it appears I must"—Philip's eyes were on his, watching closely for his reaction—"I'd say you had intended to adopt Augustine and its traditional allies as your base and extend your control coreward, probably as far as Rochelle."

"Indeed?" Thaddeus was pleased by the bland interest in his tone.

"Using the Covenant Worlds as a template, one can see your hand in the formation of the Protectorate Coalition," Jessica said, looking blandly at him as he turned to her. "Patterns, Warden. Riktofven and Ptolemeny tore the heart out of your new nation with their ill-conceived Alliance, but you've persevered."

Almost exactly fifty percent correct, Thaddeus thought toward his hosts as he sipped his cooling tea. *Does that reflect limits to your ability to gather information close to the Capellan sphere, or limits to your skill at discerning patterns?*

Aloud he said: "That the Covenant Worlds are seeking economic and defensive treaties with the Protectorate Coalition is included in our proposal to the Oriente Protectorate. There *are* ties, but one should not build too much on so slim a foundation."

"I will not fence with you, Warden." Jessica's tone gained

an edge. "It is my intention to reunite the Free Worlds League. This is no secret."

Thaddeus nodded. One thing the leaders of the three most powerful nations in the region shared was the dream of a unified Free Worlds League. Their differences sprang from mutually exclusive convictions about who should rule.

"Mine is the greater claim to the captain-generalcy," Jessica said, echoing his thoughts. "My father fought to save the Free Worlds League when Thomas Marik abandoned it to pursue his own ambitions."

Interesting that you feel comfortable saying that to a Marik. Is that the honesty you mentioned or arrogance?

"Many independent worlds support reunification of the League under my leadership." Jessica's eyes held his levelly. "As do the Rim Commonality and the Duchy of Tamarind-Abbey."

Thaddeus blinked. This was revelation—and frank discussion—beyond what he'd expected from an informal tea. Philip had not been fishing; he'd been preparing ground.

"However, much of this pledged support is conditional," Jessica was saying. "For all my family's moral claim to the throne, there is a physical requirement we do not possess. One that is meaningless in the context of right or ability to rule, but that weighs heavily on the hearts of many loyal to the Free Worlds League."

She paused, evidently inviting comment.

"You're not a real Marik." Thaddeus stated the obvious.

Jessica did not blink at the adjective.

"To sit on what is, in the minds of most, the throne of House Marik, I must have a blood connection to the Marik family," she said.

The spurious image of a massive transfusion flashed through Thaddeus' mind, but he squelched it before it reached his face. Lady Jessica was obviously talking marriage. But just as obviously, she was not envisioning the Free Worlds League unifying under her children or her grandchildren. She meant to hold the throne herself. Impossible, given the conditions stipulated.

Unless . . .

"I see you've grasped it," Philip said.

Thaddeus looked at the man, not sure he grasped anything at all.

"For forty years I've been my wife's constant companion, always by her side," Philip said. "But in recent months I've been avoiding her, keeping my distance in public—or not being with her at all. It is generally known that I am going through a period of depression. Soon it will be rumored that I am no longer mentally stable."

Thaddeus had heard of these changes in Philip's behavior, and now faced the man's inability to address the publicly accepted cause of the transformation.

Philip extended his hand toward Jessica and she took it. Thaddeus found himself looking at the clasped hands as they rested comfortably on the ancient wood of the table.

"Sometime in the next few months I will disappear altogether," Philip said, drawing Thaddeus' eyes back to his own. "Soon after that it will be announced that I have left Jessica, divorced her."

Thaddeus nodded at the vision of a future completely at odds with the tableau before him. Politics, and the requirements of power, often demanded a separate form of reality. He deliberately did not consider what must be coming next, but Philip did not allow him the luxury of denial.

"Thaddeus Marik," he said, his formal tone pulling Thaddeus upright in his chair, "will you marry my wife?"

21

Tamarind Planetary Defense Command
Zanzibar, Tamarind
Duchy of Tamarind-Abbey
6 December 3137

Duke Fontaine Marik looked over the edge of the note-puter his director of SAFE had handed him. Christopher Hughes was bent over a situation table, conferring with Force Commander Tobit about some aspect of Zanzibar's defense.

"Would have expected him to be a MechWarrior," he said. "Riding high in a *BattleMaster* or something equally destructive laying waste to the enemy right and left."

"A BattleMech is far too removed from the action for him," Roland answered. "Insulated by armor, isolated. He was in his element on the Haverson Flats, going after Lyran BattleMechs in a Savannah Master."

"Any information on how he managed to insinuate himself into our attack on the Steiner beachhead?"

"Evidently his patented charming smile," Roland answered with a half smile of his own. "No bribes, threats or demands. He presented himself, along with a verigraphed copy of his diploma from Princefield, and said he wanted to help."

Fontaine nodded. The field reports and battle ROMs had documented young Christopher leading a six-tank "heavy" platoon of high-speed Savannah Masters in a daring diversionary attack, pulling Lyran BattleMechs away from the precious Pegasus tanks leading the defensive thrust.

More illuminating than the charge had been his response to the carpet of artillery the Lyrans had thrown down to stop them. The three Savannah Masters that had not followed his exit strategy were destroyed while the two that had stayed on him escaped unharmed.

Fontaine had made certain the whelp did not have another chance to get himself killed on the front lines. Letting her only surviving son commit suicide was not likely to endear him to Lady Jessica—and from the way the Lyran invasion was unfolding, Tamarind-Abbey was going to need the goodwill of every potential ally.

Surprisingly, the lad had proven to be a shrewd strategist. Rather than being underfoot, young Hughes had made himself a valued asset to Fontaine's senior staff. *Or perhaps not so surprisingly—the first time we met, he claimed all his apparent derring-do was successfully applied risk analysis.*

Pulling his eyes away from Christopher, Fontaine studied the figures on the noteputer screen. He didn't need to page down to Roland's projections to know what they'd say.

"How long?" he asked.

"More than a week, less than two," Roland answered. "The First Regulars took heavy losses at the Zanzibe River and they've filled the gaps with provisionals. They're doing well with harrying and hit-and-run, but they won't stand to another full-on assault."

Fontaine frowned into the middle distance, considering.

"Caches are established?"

"Yes, sire."

"Empty the Oriente *Mule*, but don't route anything to the secured caches," the duke said. "Build new ones if you'd like. Then shift the DropShip to Dalad."

He looked directly at Roland, making sure he had the taller man's full attention.

"We're not depending on getting that second week," he said. "As of this moment, Plan Ark is in effect."

22

"Port?"

Thaddeus hesitated.

"Never acquired the taste," he admitted.

"So many of our tastes are forced on us by circumstances," Philip agreed. "I don't remember being given a choice about whether I wanted port and a cigar after dinner. It was the tradition in my family. My first indication my parents felt I'd come of age was my mother clipping one of her after-dinner cigars for me."

"The cheroot was Senator Hughes' trademark," Thaddeus said.

"No, that was my uncle Alexander's trademark," Philip corrected with a chuckle. "Justine adopted it in high school when she discovered it drove her mother to distraction."

Thaddeus smiled slightly at the mental image of the formidable Senator Hughes as a rebellious adolescent.

"There's a brandy, if you'd prefer." Philip broke into his thoughts.

"Please."

"One of the best things about this particular distillation," Philip said, pouring generous amounts of amber fluid into a pair of snifters, "is that no one has ever heard of it. I can still pick up a case for what the concierge pays per bottle for that Loeches Reserve he pulls out for state dinners."

Thaddeus rolled a judicious sip of the liquid onto his tongue and was rewarded with an inhalation of fire that seemed to sweep up through his sinuses to illuminate his brain.

"Excellent," he said.

His host proffered the bottle for his examination.

"The Fuentes Distillery is known primarily for mass-producing wine by the hundred-liter keg for restaurants of average ratings," Philip said. "You'd be surprised at the number of supposed connoisseurs who would rather die than be seen drinking one of their vintages."

"I doubt that I would." Thaddeus was careful not to give his words too much weight. "I know how well the wrong label can affect one's fortunes."

"Point taken." Philip chuckled, pausing to appreciate a sip of his own. "Never tasted a drop or they would know better."

"More for the rest of us."

Philip chuckled again. Then sobered.

"Elis will be taking a case of this with my personal compliments to Michael Cendar in the morning." As part of his growing "estrangement" from Jessica, Philip would not be present when she—and the world's media—saw their daughter off on her journey to her new home in the Rim Commonality. "Hopefully he's sufficiently distant to not be offended by the label and appreciate the contents."

Setting his snifter on the sideboard, he shifted one of two wingback chairs facing the empty fireplace until it was directed toward the French doors opening onto the balcony. He indicated a couch already positioned to appreciate the view before reclaiming his drink and making himself comfortable.

Thaddeus took the far end of the couch, angled to face both his host and the window.

"Saw your grandmother once," Philip said conversationally. "Not to speak to. She was sweeping down the hall, en route to demanding some concession from my father. A woman of great presence."

"My mother did not inherit her dynamism," Thaddeus surprised himself by answering. "But she had that sense of presence in spades. No one ever doubted she owned the ground she stood on."

"Agatha Hampton-Marik was a voice of justice in the Senate," Philip agreed. "Always a friend of Irian."

Thaddeus trusted his voice with a simple "Yes."

"Riktofven isn't a patch on her," Philip rolled on, watching the sun dip toward the horizon. "Greedy bastard with delusions of Machiavelli."

Thaddeus said nothing.

Philip looked at him inquiringly, then seemed to come to a realization. Setting the half-empty snifter on the small table beside his chair, he laid his hands together in his lap.

"Do you really think that was some ham-handed ploy to gain your trust?" he asked. "Recite some praise for your mother and criticize the cretin appointed to replace her in order to establish we're both of one accord? You forget my homeworld is—was—part of The Republic too. My cousin served in the Senate with both representatives of Augustine. I know whereof I speak.

"Riktofven is a manipulative opportunist." He dismissed the leader of the Senatorial Alliance with a backhanded wave. "On the other hand, your mother's integrity was such a fundamental given in Republic politics that mentioning it in the course of a political discussion was the conversational equivalent of breathing."

He settled back in his chair and picked up his drink. "Her loss was tragic."

Thaddeus weighed the words.

"Thank you, sir," he said at last.

Philip dismissed the need for apology with another wave of his hand.

The sun seemed to expand as it touched the tree-lined ridge that framed Amur, stretching to more than three times its diameter as though pouring itself along the horizon. Thaddeus had seen the effect on a dozen worlds, knew it was a simple function of optics, but still found the spectacle fascinating.

"Jessica will no doubt have you investigated six ways from zero," Philip said conversationally. "I'm sure Torrian Dolcat—that's her SAFE director, the swarthy fellow with the good manicure. I'm sure Dolcat will provide her with a thick dossier on your story."

"No doubt," Thaddeus agreed.

He would certainly do no less in her position. In fact, though more operative than analyst, Green had gone a long way toward providing him with full records on everyone of consequence in the Marik court in Amur.

"However, I'll never see that file," Philip said. "I deliberately keep out of the mechanics of running Oriente. So if I want to know something about you, I'll have to ask."

Thaddeus swirled the brandy in his snifter and decided it was very likely Philip was speaking the truth.

"Ask," he invited. "I'll answer what I can."

"I'll hold you to that," Philip said. "Qualifier and all."

Thaddeus lifted his glass, acknowledging his commitment.

"Your mother was one of the great champions of The Republic." Philip sipped his brandy. "You were one of its paladins."

He paused, but Thaddeus remained silent.

"How is it, now that this Fortress is up, that you are on the outside with us?"

This was a question for which Thaddeus was well prepared, one that had come up often and would come up again. His career as a paladin was the greatest stumbling block to his credibility in the Free Worlds League. But this time his prepackaged answer seemed inadequate. The man sitting comfortably in the chair by the empty fireplace deserved honesty. A freshly examined truth, not the polished version he presented to the world.

"The Republic—the ideal of The Republic—was my heart," he said at last. "Just as it was my mother's and my father's. Grandma Alys didn't choose The Republic over the Free Worlds League lightly. Stone's dream presented the best hope for mankind's survival."

He curbed the urge to toss off the remains of his brandy in a single gulp. He sipped slowly, appreciating Philip's patience in letting him gather his thoughts.

"What my grandmother never realized—what I believe my parents never discovered—was that while the ideal was noble, the reality was rotten at the core."

Thaddeus paused, but his host did not comment.

"The realization didn't come on me suddenly," he said finally. "It took the better part of a decade, beginning with my election to the Chamber of Paladins. But once the truth was evident, I couldn't ignore it.

"I know I gained the reputation for being the coldest of the paladins, upholding the strictest letter of the law and no more or less. What people did not realize was that the letter of the law was the only pure thing left. Ezekiel Crow is vilified on Terra for betraying The Republic. But the Republic . . ."

He trailed off.

A shift of weight, a creak of leather chair. Thaddeus could sense the older man considering whether to speak, then choosing to remain silent. He wondered briefly if there were recording devices in the sitting room. Probably, he decided. And just as probably Philip Hughes had nothing to do with them.

"I am a Marik. And Mariks live for the Free Worlds League," he said, looking out the open windows. The lengthening shadows were painting the garden in shades of purple and blue and gray. "For two generations my family turned its back on the League because they were deceived into thinking they served a greater good.

"But there is no greater good.

"I am a Marik," he repeated. "And it falls to me to take what was done wrong and make it right."

Philip stirred in his chair, pulling Thaddeus' gaze from the window. The older man had raised his glass. It took Thaddeus a moment to realize his host was toasting him, his eyes fierce.

Thaddeus lifted his own glass, returning the salute.

The two men sat in companionable silence and watched the sun disappear.

23

Young Hughes had aged in the last week.

From the raised supervisor's platform overlooking the warehouse, Fontaine watched Christopher work his way through the staging area, double-checking manifests, questioning a worker, reading labels—there was little left of the reckless youth who'd first begged an audience a year and a half ago. He saw Christopher's now-habitual frown, and the hard edges of his cheekbones and jaw.

Losing a war does tend to burn away baby fat, doesn't it, boy?

Christopher was brought up short by the sight of the Tamarind throne bolted to a pallet.

Fontaine handed the noteputer he'd been reading to the purser and turned away from the warehouse. The one luxury offered the warehouse manager was a window with a panoramic view of the mountains rimming the north edge of the desert. Though they were now simply looming shapes, dusty purple gray against the indigo sky in the dawn light, their permanence was a welcome counterpoint to the upheaval all around them.

Fontaine positioned himself at the right edge of the window and waited.

Soon enough booted feet bounded up the metal steps with energy the old duke only vaguely remembered. He smiled slightly at the boy's murmured apology to someone in passing.

Courtesy is too often a lost art among our breed.

"See that star?" he asked before the boy could speak. "Low, just above the ridge there?"

Christopher moved to stand by his shoulder and look through the window at the same shallow angle. "Yes, sire."

"That's not a star," the duke said. "It's a hulk, the empty remains of an orbital factory in geosynchronous orbit. It's always there. Do you know what it's in geosynchronous orbit above?"

Christopher was silent for a heartbeat, either searching his own memory or waiting for the duke to answer his own question.

"No, sire," he said when he realized a response was required.

"The Mal Kham Wastes." Fontaine did not take his eyes off the light low against the horizon. "Sixty years ago Mal Kham was a city and the empty hulk above it a shipyard."

"Technicron Naval Engineering," Christopher said, enlightened. "The *Impavido* WarShip project."

"The Word of Blake regarded the shipyards as too valuable to leave behind," Fontaine said. "One more example of how little they understood what really matters."

"Sire?"

"A radically new WarShip was developed here. You'd think that would be something people remembered, wouldn't you?" Fontaine asked. "But a few decades later and no one remembers.

"Do you know why?"

"Actual construction was—" Christopher stopped himself midanswer. "No, sire."

"A factory, any infrastructure, is only a tool, a thing," the duke explained. "The heart of Tamarind is not in our ability to assemble widgets, no matter how complex and expensive those widgets might be.

"What makes Tamarind Tamarind is our art."

He could feel Christopher shift beside him, knew the boy was looking over the ordered chaos of odd-shaped crates filling the staging area with new eyes.

"You're taking the art," he said at last.

Fontaine turned to face the boy for the first time.

"By preserving the art, we preserve the heart of Tamarind," he said. "Those who fight on, the resistance, will resist because they know their heart—the culture that makes us who we are and binds us all together—is safe."

Stepping away from the boy, he looked out over the warehouse. The second wave of trucks was pulling away from the loading dock, carrying their precious cargoes out to the waiting *Mule*. The process would have been quicker at the main DropPort of Zanzibar; but escape from Zanzibar was no longer certain.

"So no, we are not taking guns and supplies," he said. "And we wouldn't even if the resistance didn't need them more. We are taking the heart of the people."

Christopher came to stand next to him. "And taking it with us carries a promise." The passion underlying the lad's words startled Fontaine into looking at him. "It tells the people we're going to bring it back."

See? said Karli's quiet voice in his ear.

Fontaine no longer looked to where his beloved wife had sat as she kept him company. He knew she was always with him, and that was enough.

Our boy is growing up, he agreed.

Then he blinked as he realized what he'd said.

24

Amur, Oriente
Oriente Protectorate
7 January 3138

Jessica could not get used to Torrian Dolcat appearing in the family council room. He belonged in his secure chamber, hidden in the walls and immune from detection. He belonged in shadow. Not standing in the watery sunlight spilling through the high windows that stretched along the southern wall. Though he had done so only twice before, it seemed as though he was becoming too much of a fixture.

We may need to get him his own chair at the table.

The humor of the thought evaporated as she remembered there already were vacant chairs at the table. That the assassin had penetrated their defenses. . . .

"What?" she demanded, her voice sharp with grief and anger at the man who had failed her.

The director of SAFE stopped abruptly at her tone, perhaps three paces sooner than he'd intended.

"Your Grace," Torrian said, including Philip in his bow. Then, with a bow only a few degrees shallower: "Lady Nikol."

Jessica read his body language clearly, as she was meant to; she was certain the man gave nothing away he did not want broadcast. He thought whatever he was about to tell her should be private. But if he wanted privacy so much he should have stayed in his hole.

"Speak plainly, Mr. Dolcat," she instructed.

"Your Grace," Torrian acknowledged, then paused as he seemed to consider his words.

Not good news, then.

"We have reports from agents that the Duchy of Andurien is refurbishing a BattleMech assembly plant," he said. "The intended purpose seems to be the assembly and rapid deployment of BattleMechs along our border."

Jessica felt Philip shift slightly and was aware of Nikol gaping at the edge of her vision.

"That makes no sense." Nikol spoke before Jessica had formulated a reply. "Shouldn't the assembly plant be protected far from the border and only the finished BattleMechs brought up?"

Torrian glanced to Jessica for permission before answering.

"They are refurbishing an existing plant, and as such have no control over where it is located," he said. "In addition, it is much easier to transport components without detection than it is to move BattleMechs. An assembly plant near the point of deployment makes good tactical sense."

"But makes it vulnerable to counterattack," Nikol countered.

"If they complete a few production runs before we discover their location, they'll have all the BattleMechs they need to defend the plant while supplying front-line forces," Torrian said. "We've only just discovered an ongoing process. If they imported components before they began bringing the plant online—a distinct possibility—it's quite conceivable they have enough raw materials to survive any embargo we throw up now."

"How could we miss such a massive transfer of BattleMech components?" Jessica asked, making the effort to keep any condemnation out of her voice. Torrian was too valuable to alienate with misplaced censure.

"The world is a known dumping ground for industrial wastes," Torrian answered. "We tracked the number of ships grounding as a measure of economic and industrial factors, but we did not pay particular attention to what they carried."

"Trojan garbage scows," Nikol said.

"Yes, milady."

Torrian's formal tone told Jessica she'd been right not to point out his failure to detect the covert operation. The man was in no danger of forgiving himself for the oversight.

The important thing is he discovered the plan before *Andurien struck.*

"How near possible deployment points is this assembly plant?" Nikol's question cut across her thoughts.

"One jump from a half dozen of our worlds," Torrian answered.

Jessica watched her daughter calculate. Before Nikol spoke she knew she'd grasped the wrong end of the situation, distracted by the obvious and the tactical.

"I can have the Eagle's Talons ready and mobilized in three weeks," she said. "The only question is, do we want the world and the plant captured or do we just want the plant destroyed?"

"Destroyed," Jessica answered promptly. "Despite this provocation, we have neither the time nor the resources for a protracted campaign against Andurien. No doubt a factor in their decision to attack now. Once their ability to cause immediate mischief is neutralized, we need to focus on the situation in Tamarind-Abbey and the Marik-Stewart Commonwealth.

"In fact, your attention should not waver from the Lyran front, dear." Jessica laid a hand flat against the polished surface of the table, not quite touching her daughter's forearm. "Andurien is a distraction best left to your lieutenants."

"Mother?"

"In fact, I think it may be time to sever your direct involvement in the campaigns of the Eagle's Talons." Jessica watched Nikol's eyes, judging her reaction. "Casson is more than capable of full command. You need to broaden your focus."

Nikol's eyes clouded for a moment. She loved military command. Jessica could only imagine she found the clearcut choices and objectives of the battlefield to be a welcome change from the shifting ambiguity of political intrigues.

But the time has come to put away childish things, dear. You need to step up to the greater responsibility, the burden Oriente and the League requires of us.

"Casson is an excellent commander," Nikol finally replied. "What specifically do you have in mind for me, Mother?"

"The liberation units," Jessica said, keeping her pleased surprise at Nikol's quick adjustment from her voice. "The initial wave of supplies is going well, but a more personal touch is needed."

"Christopher . . ."

"Is, as far as we can tell, doing an excellent job supporting Duke Fontaine and the people of Tamarind-Abbey," Jessica agreed. "I was thinking of the worlds of the Commonwealth. The war is not going well for Anson, particularly with Lester's decision to not support him militarily."

She saw Nikol almost point out that Jessica had chosen to not support Anson militarily, then think better of it. *You're learning.*

"A member of the ruling house personally accompanying relief efforts would go a long way toward encouraging the resistance fighters."

"Not to mention binding them to Oriente," Nikol added.

"No reason not to mention it," Jessica said. "The war is not likely to go well for Anson. We need to have an alternative in place should he fall."

"Then why not go yourself?"

"Generations of propaganda aimed at discrediting me," Jessica said. "A virulent campaign that reached fever pitch under Anson's leadership. It can be overcome with truth— eventually. In the short run, my appearance in the midst of the Lyran invasion would carry far too much negative baggage. In some cases, it may work actively against us. You, on the other hand . . ."

"Have been relatively untouched by the propaganda machine aimed at you," Nikol finished. "And am known as a military leader, not a political manipulator."

"Just so."

"Well." Nikol sighed. "Let's just hope they don't see through my disguise."

25

Ministerial Residence
Zletovo, Lesnovo
Rim Commonality
19 January 3138

Prime Minister Michael Cendar tried not to stare at the force commander's hair as she read the report he'd handed to her.

Alethea Chowla was commander of the Defenders, the elite rapid-strike battalion of the Rim Commonality's armed forces. She was an impressive woman of one hundred and eighty centimeters, massing some seventy well-proportioned kilos and looked every inch the professional soldier.

From her eyes down.

What disconcerted people—what caused those who did not know her to question Chowla's abilities, and possibly even her intelligence—was her hair. Her scalp was covered by six centimeters of starched crew cut dyed an improbable shade of terra-cotta. Her eyebrows shared the color. The artist in Michael appreciated how the color, which could easily have clashed with her cinnamon complexion, complemented her skin tone perfectly.

The French doors lining the northern wall of his private study were wide open, much to the consternation of his ever-vigilant security staff, and the pungent scents of a dozen flowers vied for his attention. Pulling his eyes away from his most trusted military adviser's scalp—something he had grown resigned to doing over the years—Michael looked out over his garden. Row upon artfully nonlinear row of nodding blossoms led the eye to the small fountain, then on to a small but impressive bronze sculpture. He was very pleased with that acquisition. One of Marridee De-Juc's few works wholesome enough to be displayed at the ministerial residence, it was part of his personal collection.

Alethea's snort of derision brought his mind back to the issue at hand.

"Force Commander?" he inquired mildly.

"I hate headaches," Alethea answered, the sharp accent of her native Campoleone edging her words. "And this is a migraine."

Michael smiled slightly at her tone. The force commander's infamous informality was a refreshing counterpoint to the poised gentility of his ministers. It harkened back to her mercenary roots.

Roots that, in the form of her grandparents' command, had held firm to the Commonality's soil when the maelstrom of the Jihad swept more prestigious units—

Michael reined in his mental metaphor before it got too far out of hand.

"We need Westover," he said aloud. "Their ability to produce aerospace fighters, not to mention reliable weapons systems, makes them invaluable."

"They've been invaluable trading partners," Alethea said. "Why all of a sudden do we need them as a member world?"

"You've read the analysis."

"Which was clearly written by people who see acquiring a world that's not so keen on being acquired as a simple matter of telling them we own them," Alethea answered. She smiled suddenly, robbing her words of insolence. "What I do not see is why you, sir, who does understand what annexing a world by force *means*, are considering this."

Michael nodded. It was a fair question.

That she could ask such a question said much about how far the Rim Commonality had come in two short generations. From a feudal state in which planetary nobles concerned only for their own need for power had issued orders, to a constitutional commonwealth in which even the head of state was expected to give an account of himself. Sometimes the magnitude of their progress fairly took his breath away.

And now, through the most ancient practice of the nobility, you seek to bind yourself and your nation to a new Free Worlds League through marriage. He shook his head, not caring that Alethea would think he was responding to her question. *I'm binding myself alone to Elis Marik. That our respective nations follow is simply a fact of our reality, not the driving force.* Then, incapable of deceiving himself: *not the* primary *driving force.*

"There are two factors," he said, answering the force commander's question after what he hoped appeared to be no more than a thoughtful pause. "First and foremost, we do not know how much of the Free Worlds League the Steiners intend to grab. A world with functional aerospace manufacturing capability may be a prize they're willing to reach for."

"And a world that's part of a sizable nation-state is a much less tempting target than a world alone." Alethea lifted the report in her hand slightly, indicating where she'd heard that argument. "By the same token, a coalition of worlds—unaligned, Regulan and Rim—forming a united front would not only save Westover, but stop the Lyrans dead in their tracks."

"The problem with such a coalition is that it's impossible," Michael said. "There are too many factions at work that want control of Westover."

"Including us," Alethea replied. "Tematagi already gives us the corner on BattleMech production west of the Pecos. Adding an aerospace monopoly is just good business sense."

Michael did not let himself be distracted by speculation on what the Pecos was; the force commander's meaning was clear from context.

"That sort of greed-driven military adventurism is not part of who we are," he said.

"Who we are, are the folks who kicked out the Humphreys clan and the rest when they tried to consolidate *us*," Alethea agreed. "Which is why I'm not understanding this."

"The second factor, the one not spelled out in the report," Michael said. "And part of why the coalition you suggest won't work."

"I'm listening."

"How would you characterize our relationship with the Regulan Fiefs with the Steiner threat out of the picture?" Michael asked.

"We're plebian riffraff who threw Humphreys and company out in a fit of madness and can only hope to survive through dumb luck until some other noble family takes us under their wing."

Michael laughed.

"Socially unacceptable and politically astute as always, Force Commander," he said. "What if I told you there was evidence house Cameron-Jones may be thinking they're just the right noble family to adopt us?"

Alethea pursed her lips, squinting into some space beyond Michael's left shoulder.

"They've got us on ships," she said. "But we have double their BattleMechs and we're a hell of a lot better at what we do.

"I'd call it a long and bloody fight."

Michael held up his hands.

"I didn't make myself clear," he said. "No military action is in the offing. The Fiefs are seeking to isolate us politically and economically. They are enthusiastically wooing many of our major trading partners, including Westover, with a mix of economic incentives, offers of military aid and disinformation about our intentions."

It took three heartbeats for the light to dawn.

Alethea spat a word Michael imagined was a curse in her native Hindi. "This is a forgery!"

"Every word of it penned by propaganda experts on Regulus," Michael confirmed. "And it took you in completely."

Alethea riffled the pages.

"I'd swear this was a verigraph on our stationery," she said. "They even spelled my name right."

"Not quite our stationery," Michael corrected. "But close enough to fool anyone not part of our own security team."

"Who else?"

"We suspect every world in the Commonality–Fiefs gap has received a custom-tailored version of this report," Michael said. "Though only Rzishchev and Lengkong have admitted they have copies."

"And we only know about this because Westover came forward?" Alethea asked, still examining the physical report.

"No, we learned about it because Niops VII told us about it." Michael pulled a second report from his folio.

"Niops?"

"Believe me, the reasoning in the strategic analysis section of *their* annexation proposal makes perfect sense." The prime minister shook his head in admiration. "But the basic integrity of the Niopians is completely beyond old Lester's comprehension. I'm sure it never occurred to him that they would simply bring the report to us and ask if it was authentic."

"So . . ." Alethea let the word stretch out. "How did we learn about Westover?"

"Alerted that these reports existed, one of our trade attachés on Westover . . . " Michael hesitated. "*Negotiated* her way to a copy."

"Ah." Alethea's tone made it clear she understood the verb.

Michael focused on sorting papers on his desk, keeping

his head down in a show of looking for something. Despite its weathering, his complexion had always revealed the least embarrassment.

"Is there a mission for my people in this?"

"Actually, yes." Michael hoped he didn't overplay the "finding" of the file he'd been looking for. "I want you to take the Guard on a military goodwill tour to Westover."

"A show of military force to counter rumors we plan on using military force?" Chowla didn't try to hide her incredulity. "That's a bit beyond counterintuitive, isn't it, sir?"

"Yes, it is," Michael agreed.

It took Chowla a moment to realize he expected her to figure it out. She resumed squinting at whatever she saw over his left shoulder.

Michael resisted the urge to turn and look.

"If they think they're going to be invaded by us, they'll try to beef up their defenses," she said at last. "Probably mercenaries, and with the Steiner threat driving up prices, they won't be able to afford the best.

"We go in, all spit-and-polish, to show them what a real military looks like, lay out the four reports side by side, explain they're looking the wrong way for danger and offer a nice mutual defense treaty, maybe a lucrative trade package to boot."

"Excellent reasoning, Force Commander," Michael confirmed. "Westover is probably the lynchpin of the Regulan plan. Once you've brought them on board, it should be a simple matter to convince others to enter into similar treaties.

"Lester Cameron-Jones may well have inadvertently given us the tools we need to form that coalition of yours."

"The Chowla Coalition," Alethea said. "I like the sound of that."

Despite himself, Michael laughed.

=== 26 ===

Nikol was through the DropShip's air lock and into the JumpShip's companionway before the all-clear sounded. Cold seemed to radiate from the docking collars, which only moments before had been open to space. The icy air stabbed the back of her throat and she felt her skin break out in goose bumps beneath her zero-g duty uniform.

Some of the startled crew bowed their heads in hasty acknowledgment while others, intent on their jobs, didn't notice royalty had passed within an arm's reach.

She noticed at least two men miss her completely as they focused on the MechWarrior in her wake. Maria Velasquez was no taller than most ten-year-olds, but proportioned like an exotic dancer. Even in duty fatigues, with her dense black hair gathered in a schoolmarm's bun, the captain attracted male attention of the most direct sort.

Nikol had noted that Velasquez did nothing to either encourage or capitalize on this attention. Based on her own observations, she agreed with the evaluations of previous commanders that there was no question of the woman's integrity.

Only her shadow sense told her Captain Velasquez was keeping silent pace as Nikol launched herself from handhold to handhold along the corridor. The diminutive Martigues native was evidently as at home in zero gravity as she was in the cockpit of her BattleMech.

And given her record, that's saying something.

Of course Ivan Casson was already waiting for them in

the wardroom assigned to the Eagle's Talons for officers' briefings. His normally close-cropped hair was longer than usual, Nikol noticed. The fuzzy blond halo gave him an unaccustomed air of innocence.

Nikol brought her focus back to the task at hand.

"This is Captain Maria Velasquez," she introduced without preamble the dark-haired woman climbing through the hatch. "Captain, this is Force Commander Ivan Casson."

"Maria?" Casson's startled tone matched Nikol's surprise at the familiar greeting. "Good to see you again."

"You too, Cass. Sir," Velasquez corrected herself with a glance at Nikol.

"Captain Velasquez and I attended Princefield together," Casson explained.

Nikol wasn't sure if the atmosphere in the cabin actually picked up an electric charge, but from the two officers' body language she was certain Casson and Velasquez had been more than simply fellow cadets.

"Then I'm glad you already know how to work together," she said aloud, hoping after the fact that her phrasing hadn't come across as a double entendre. "Because we're attaching her 'Mech company to your command."

"Exce—" Casson broke off midword. "*My* command, milady? You command the Eagle's Talons."

"Not anymore, Force Commander." Nikol shook her head. "The personal battalion of the captain-general is now your full responsibility."

"Yes, milady." Casson sounded doubtful. "May I ask why?"

"Why you're in command? Because you're the best. Why I'm leaving? I've been made a diplomat. My last official military act will be taking the *Pontiac* and your light infantry assets with me on my return trip to Oriente.

"I'll be jumping out-system for my first perilous round of cocktail parties and smoke-filled rooms before your first mission."

"Yes, milady." Casson made the acknowledgment a question.

"We're giving you an old-school hit-and-run raid, Force Commander," Nikol said. On cue, Velasquez unslung the orders tube from her shoulder and handed it to Casson. "A full battalion of BattleMechs, heavy guns and battlesuit infantry. Go in fast, hit hard, flatten the objective and get out before a counteroffensive can be mounted."

Casson nodded, weighing the neoleather tube in his hands as she spoke.

"What's the target?" he asked.

"A covert Andurien BattleMech assembly plant right at our doorstep," Nikol answered, enjoying the startled look in Casson's eye. "On a world called Kwamashu."

27

DropShip **Baldwin**
Kwamashu System
6 February 3138

"**W**atch yourself out there, half-pint," a voice called from behind.

Casson stopped in the crowded corridor and turned, waiting for Maria Velasquez to catch up.

"No worries," he said when she was close. "I'm not the biggest target out there."

The diminutive MechWarrior tilted her head to look up at him. "You telling me size doesn't matter?"

Casson grinned at the joke they'd shared since their academy days as the two fell in step. On straitlaced Oriente, such double entendres had been daring for the pair of young cadets. Their relationship at the academy had never gotten beyond suggestive banter. (*If only I'd known what to try,* Casson thought, not for the first time. *God, I was young.*) In the years since, when their paths crossed there just hadn't been the time or the opportunity to explore options not taken.

He glanced down at her as they walked shoulder to shoulder. Or more accurately, her shoulder to his elbow. At one hundred fifty centimeters, Maria barely met the physical requirements for piloting a BattleMech.

Her black hair was braided tight to her skull: the neurohelmet contacts, invisible when her thick mane was worn loose, had been freshly shaved. The little squares of olive skin glistened with contact oil.

"That stuff really doesn't make a difference, you know."

"And shaving hasn't been necessary for a century." She supplied the second half of his usual observation. "But—"

"Even a psychological edge is an edge," Casson chorused with her.

It was a little surprising to Casson that this was the first time they would be going into battle together. It was even more surprising, given their relative performances at the academy, that they were going in with him commanding her.

"What's your take on the tac sit?" he asked, following up on that thought.

"You nailed it in one." The two paused by the entrance to the bay where his *Sun Cobra* was berthed with the rest of Command Lance. "If I had a doubt, I would have said so."

"Of course that's understood," he said with mock gravity. "But it's always good to have your assessment, Captain."

"You medium and light 'Mechs end run through the town." Maria matched his tone. "You should have no trouble outflanking the local garrison while we big boys handle the Duchy regulars."

Casson shook his head, matching her grin.

Those who didn't know Maria assumed she piloted a *Jupiter* to compensate for her tiny stature. The truth was she piloted the hundred-ton 'Mech because it was the only machine tough enough to keep up with her on the battlefield.

Something like a tide passed through Casson. He felt his weight change slightly as the DropShip's crew made some minute adjustment in its breaking thrust.

"Planetfall in one hour," he said. "Get to your 'Mech, Maria."

"Good hunting, Cass," she answered before hurrying to her own 'Mech's bay.

Amur, Oriente
Oriente Protectorate

She watched Mr. Carmichael make a show of reading her résumé. A foolish ploy. If he had not been familiar with its contents, she would never have reached this point in the interview process.

The office was designed to intimidate: a wall of books opposite the door implied the wealth to collect such antiques, while the view of Amur's ducal complex indicated proximity to the halls of power. The furnishings, while classically spare, were of real wood and leather and the art on the walls had been painted by human hands.

Carmichael was as calculated as his office. His black hair, as thickly wiry as her own in its natural state, was trimmed to a uniform centimeter. His hands were immaculately manicured, each adorned with one piece of tastefully expensive gold, and his business suit was of the finest cut and fabric.

The one flaw in his appearance, as far as she was concerned, was the color of his contact lenses. Though she could acknowledge that the green was aesthetically pleasing, it wasn't natural. Why one of the higher race would wear contacts to mimic a feature of a lesser was beyond her.

Perhaps he regarded his body as nothing more than a space he occupied. Like his office, a canvas to be decorated and accessorized as he saw fit. Such a separation from self, from who he was, was saddening. But not surprising.

She had scanned a shelf of books as she'd entered the tastefully opulent office; a flickering glance as she'd surveyed the room in obvious, but not overstated, appreciation. Adjacent titles were unrelated, the bindings having been grouped for greatest visual impact with no thought to the content of the volumes. The wall of books was a library of appearance, not utility. No doubt the interior decorator had purchased them by the linear meter.

The room, the clothes, the contacts—Carmichael was a man wedded to the superficial, who judged the world around him by appearances. How very sad. And very useful.

Her own appearance was artfully managed to conform to expectations. The natural extensions woven into her hair were pulled back into a conservative bun. Her business suit, much less expensive than Mr. Carmichael's, was impeccably tailored and her glasses had just enough style to imply personality without conflicting with her air of competent conformity.

Her only flaw—and she was sure Mr. Carmichael would regard it as such—was her decision not to hide her vitiligo. There was no cure for the disorder that robbed the skin of pigment, but there were dozens of cosmetic cover-ups. To not use them implied both honesty and nonconformity.

In her case, the condition was most apparent in an irregular-shaped swath of pink, pale to the point of whiteness against the chocolate brown of her flesh, that stretched from her right temple to the corner of her mouth. A thumb-sized spot of similar color appeared below her left ear, just above the hinge of her jaw, and again above her left eyebrow. A narrow swath of straw-blond hair rising from the nape of her neck to join the bun and a trace of pink above her high collar testified to the spread of the condition.

The pink-white patches of vitiligo were appliqués of thin plastic. Porous enough to sweat through and flexible enough to conform to facial expressions, they were visually indistinguishable from her flesh. A person of sensitive touch tracing his finger lightly across her face would feel the border between the plastic and her skin—but she had no intention of letting anyone get that close.

Carmichael looked up from his pretense of reviewing her résumé. She saw his artificially green eyes flicker across her vitiligo before meeting her own. An interesting change from men glancing first at her chest. She found his distraction amusing.

But beyond distracting, the irregular patches of vitiligo performed the same function as camouflage. The contrasting colors broke up the outlines of her features, confusing both the human eye and face-recognition security systems. Taken in combination with her straight and longer hair, the discoloration made it unlikely anyone who had met her during her previous stay on Oriente would recognize her now.

"Your references are of course excellent," Carmichael was saying. "The Dalton Investment Group could not say enough good things about your financial acumen. I don't mind adding that your trading portfolio is one of the most impressive I've seen."

"You're too kind, Mr. Carmichael," she said, smiling a polite disagreement that stopped well short of a simper. She had no idea how Father Pauli had produced those sterling records for a young woman who had never lived. "I've made several missteps over the years. I still find the Tobler incident particularly galling."

"As do we all, Ms. Aborisha," Carmichael agreed. "But in every trading environment there is the possibility of fraud. You can hardly be expected to have recognized criminal intent."

"Ayza, please," she said. "And the evidence they were ghosting their assets was there from the beginning."

"But the evidence was only apparent in retrospect, Ayza." Carmichael gave what he thought was her first name an odd lilt—a tell proving he was not an Oriente native. "And your other missteps, as you characterize them, are in every case a situation wherein unpredictable fate confounded well-researched analysis."

"Thank you, sir." She accepted the compliment. To protest praise too vigorously could be as annoying as preening.

From that point the interview wound through its predictable course without incident. He asked for her insights on specific corporations to test her market knowledge and posed hypothetical questions to gauge her trading savvy, mixing in a few well-disguised ethical problems along the way. Well coached and skilled in interrogation, she navigated her way through the potential minefield, gaining a new respect for Carmichael's interviewing skills in the process.

In the end, of course, there was no doubt. Two hours

after ushering her into her chair, Mr. Carmichael rose and extended his hand across the desk.

"I think you will do very well here, Ayza," he said, smiling his first real smile of the afternoon. "Welcome to Sir Frederick Marik's household."

Breezewood, Kwamashu
Duchy of Andurien

The *Firestarter* was candy.

Its armor no match for the massed fire of the *Jupiter*'s autocannon, the Ducky BattleMech seemed to crumple under the onslaught of depleted uranium rounds tearing into it at multiple-Mach velocity. Maria's thermal screen flared as the 'Mech's plasma bottles failed. The machine stumbled forward, but it was more pilot reflex than attack. The area—and the infantry—surrounding the *Firestarter* disappeared in raging flames.

A new threat icon flashed for attention. Maria brought her *Jupiter* around to face the new opponent even as her combat computer made the identification. A *Shockwave*: half her mass and twice her speed. Most common variant mounted an Ultra autocannon, a ten-tube missile rack and a large laser, but a dialog box warned that the versatile design had been observed in combat mounting everything up to Thumper artillery. Her computer wouldn't commit itself to a hard ID of the load-out until the enemy 'Mech fired, but eyeballing the Duchy medium, Maria bet she was facing an off-the-shelf plain vanilla.

Carrying a jockey with a death wish, she amended as the smaller machine charged.

The hangers-on who'd been using the *Shockwave* for cover evidently shared her assessment. An armored personnel carrier peeled away from its heels, scuttling to her left on a cushion of air as a chopper rose from low ground cover and swung wide to her right—splitting targets bent on getting around her to link up with the local garrison. Maria's targeting computer didn't ID the APC, but tagged the VTOL as a model mounting a small laser. Ignoring the gnats, she focused on the BattleMech.

"Come to Mama," she coaxed.

The *Shockwave* jockey held on to his missiles. His large laser and autocannon fired in unison, scoring a gouge of molten armor across her *Jupiter*'s chest and peppering its legs with shot. Cosmetic damage.

Maria unleashed her twin PPCs a half heartbeat later. One blue-white beam went wide, grazing the smaller 'Mech's right shoulder. But the second went true, savaging the Ducky's left leg.

The *Shockwave* almost went down, its knee actuator bending nearly backward under the heavy stream of charged particles. But the pilot lunged the machine through a stagger step that kept it upright and moving.

"Good driving," Maria admitted, noting her target's pronounced limp. He wasn't going to be making sudden left turns.

A sudden wave of heat washed through the cockpit as a damage alarm hooted.

"What the hell?"

Sweeping her scanners left, she tracked the exit arc of the chopper she'd ignored a moment before.

"Talon Charlie One to Talon Actual," Maria snapped at the mic as she ran her eyes over the damage schematic. "Be advised the Duckies have some modified ordnance. A chopper that should have a small laser just beaned me with a medium."

"Armor," Cass' voice came back instantly. "They had to trade out armor for the gun. Hit it with a stick and it will come apart."

"Roger that." Maria acknowledged the obvious advice as though it were wisdom. "Just expect anything that looks harmless to pack more punch than it should."

"Shoot everything," Cass replied. "Got it."

Maria slammed against her harness before she could reply, the straps digging into her flesh. Long-range missiles; nine hits.

"You do *not* shoot while I'm cracking wise," she snarled at the *Shockwave*.

She kicked her assault 'Mech forward, closing on the smaller machine at a walk.

Eyes on her targeting screens, she noted a smattering of yellow lights across the wire-frame diagram of the damage display at the edge of her vision. Nothing serious. Yet.

A Kelswa tank that had been using the Ducky 'Mech for cover edged into view and cut loose with its brace of autocannon. The shells spread wide, scattering damage across her *Jupiter*'s lower torso and chest. Again nothing vital, but the yellow lights were starting to spread.

If she wasn't careful the little nips would add up to a big bite. And she hated big bites.

The APC scuttled out of some hidey-hole to her left. No personnel carrier should have been that close to BattleMechs trading fire. And—now that she was looking at it—she saw that the APC *moved* wrong. The lesson of the overgunned VTOL fresh in her mind, Maria triggered all four of her autocannon at the potential Trojan horse.

The hovercraft slewed sideways, shuddering under the solid wall of raging impacts. Its yaw came dangerously close to a flip before it righted itself.

The fact that it hadn't dissolved in a cloud of shrapnel convinced Maria her suspicions were correct. She watched it for a long second as it staggered for cover, the rips in its skirt sending whirlwinds of dust in all directions. Black smoke belching from every opening convinced her the little machine was out for the count.

Her pause cost her more armor as the Ducky *Shockwave* took advantage of her distraction to land another double salvo. Large laser and autocannon—both solid hits dead center on her chest. Close enough to the low-slung cockpit for shrapnel to etch the ferroglass canopy.

With a feral snarl, Maria unleashed her long-range missiles. Thirty away and thirty hits, covering the medium 'Mech in smoke and flame. Pyrotechnics, she realized. The enemy machine was still intact; still a viable threat.

Not for long.

Pushing her sticks forward, Maria accelerated, bringing her 'Mech to a full run as she closed on the enemy. On any given battlefield there were lots of 'Mechs faster than her *Jupiter*; fifty-four kilometers per hour was not an impressive speed. But one hundred tons of hard metal charging at fifty-four kilometers per hour was close enough to an unstoppable force that the difference didn't matter.

A gun nest she hadn't seen opened fire. Maria gave the troopers points for moxie as the small shells pocked and scarred the battered armor along her *Jupiter*'s arm and leg. Not threat enough to be worth a shot.

The *Shockwave* came clear of the smoke looking altogether too whole to have taken the brunt of her missile salvo. Missiles ineffective, heat too high to risk the PPCs . . . Keeping the main throttle to the peg with her left hand, Maria cupped the control of the autocannons in her right. Aiming the quad battery of autocannons at a full run was more art than science. She looked wide, all but ignored the targeting reticule as her hand and eyes worked in unconscious concert. Good tone. She pressed the studs and the medium 'Mech staggered back, dancing under the hail of depleted uranium projectiles.

The infantry gun crew continued to pump rounds into her back as she bore down on the doomed *Shockwave*. Her right missile rack rocked, a warning light announcing its elevation ring was damaged. Their next shot earned a red light as the round split a rear plate and took out a heat sink.

Maria grunted. Those ground pounders were earning their pay.

Ahead of her the *Shockwave* turned its stagger into a retreat, backing away from the onrushing *Jupiter* with surprising agility over the broken ground. But not with enough speed. She was going to close on this Ducky joker and smash it with her 'Mech's bare hands.

The medium 'Mech launched a final salvo of missiles. The staccato explosions across her 'Mech's chest and shoulders threw Maria left and then right; she bit her tongue when her head snapped back. She cursed. Too cocky: she'd thought she was too close for the long-range missiles to be a threat.

In a second they won't be.

A *clang!* of metal on metal rang through her cockpit and Maria was thrown forward against her harness. In the half second it took her to realize what had happened, it was too late: her *Jupiter* was going down.

The APC—the smoking hovercraft she'd thought was dead—had charged from the side in a last-ditch suicide attack.

The transport hit the inside edge of her 'Mech's left ankle actuator, an impact that did little damage in itself. What had tripped her, literally, was her right leg hitting the APC as it swung forward. The sight of the twisted wreckage bouncing in front of her was little consolation.

Designed to smash the armor on enemy BattleMechs, her *Jupiter*'s arms were more than enough to cushion a fall under most circumstances. But charging forward at full speed was not most circumstances. It was all Maria could do to shield her forward-thrust viewscreen as her assault-class machine plowed face-first into the rocky soil.

The black earth turned the curving canopy into a mirror. Maria shook her head at her reflection, more than a little surprised to still be in one piece.

Mostly one piece.

Damage alarms hooted. What wasn't red on the damage display was yellow, except for her left arm from the elbow actuator down. The dead black told her she'd lost both weapons and mobility for the duration.

Her big worry was the reactor core. The wire frame made clear the housing was damaged, leaking heat at levels that threatened the BattleMech's myomer musculature. And with two—no, four—heat sinks gone, her cooling system barely had what it took to keep her machine from shutting down.

Can't use the PPC I've got left with that heat, she inventoried as she levered her right arm to push the BattleMech to its feet. *Two out of four autocannons online and a missile rack. If I don't try to run, I'm good to go.*

Well satisfied with her survival, Maria shoved the *Jupiter*'s right fist into the ground until her viewscreen came clear of the dirt.

Through the mud-smeared ferroglass she saw the feet of the *Shockwave* close enough to touch.

"Oh, sh—"

Dormuth
Mandoria, Marik

Julietta Marik pushed the walker ahead of her, shuffled to catch up, then stood, resting her weight on its cushioned handles, as she gathered herself for the next step. Looking ahead, she estimated she was about forty meters from her destination. Nothing after negotiating the long curving stairs and the sixty meters of polished Mansu-ri marble behind her. Forty meters. She was fewer than three hundred shuffling steps from the memory room.

The memory room.

That's how Julietta Marik always thought of the inner chamber Rikkard had made his own, adjacent to the command center of the Spirit Cats on Marik. Though in reality the room had more to do with turning points than memories.

She had expected to die in that room, gallant young Captain Tilson of her guard notwithstanding.

Star Colonel Rikkard had expected to die too. Though not in that room at that precise moment—was it only nine months ago? So much can happen in nine months. The most basic building block of all human life, nine months: the journey from conception to birth of a baby. Julietta could recall when the thoughts associated with that analogy would have made her blush. *Death and resurrection seem to make one less a prude.*

Julietta pushed the walker ahead another hand span, then shuffled a foot forward to catch up with it.

Star Colonel Rikkard had expected to die—had expected his people to die—as the result of her mother's betrayal. Instead, he had persevered. The Spirit Cat leader of the Nova Cats—Julietta suspected she would never fully grasp the subtleties of the distinction—had formed an intricate alliance with another Clan, and seemed to be forging something unique.

Someone, half in jest and wholly wrong, had called Marik the Nova Cat Occupation Zone. The citizens of Marik might not yet be in agreement, but what had been theirs was being reborn; not into a Clan-occupied world, but a Clan world. Of course, she had an advantage in seeing this future: she was not looking at the world around her, she was looking into Rikkard Nova Cat's eyes. The vision there was plain.

Push, shuffle, rest. She made her way forward.

Marik was only one world, but it was steeped in the spirit of what it meant to be part of the Free Worlds League. It had been one of many hearts that had made the nation strong. Now it was a world shared by three cultures and—though she doubted any of the three fully understood—they were being forged into something new.

Under Rikkard's leadership, the reforged Marik would be a heart of the new Free Worlds League. She was certain of it. Just as she was certain some of those in the current Free Worlds League would never recognize the rhythm of that new heart's beat.

The first time she had seen this outer chamber—the last time as well, before the Star colonel had sent her home to her mother in defeat—she had been impressed by the beautifully grained burnt-sienna marble. Now, as she watched the toes of her soft shoes appear and disappear from beneath the hem of her simple shift—*Something I would not have been caught dead in nine months ago*—she marveled anew at its luster.

Where did they come from? she wondered. The technicians and builders and cooks and polishers of floors who followed the wave of warriors. Not to mention the children. One saw the warriors arrive, their number and strength widely advertised; and then, sometime later, their entire support infrastructure was just there. In place and functional with no great fanfare.

Push, shuffle, rest—Julietta made her way across the wide room. She knew there were more accessible buildings available for the Spirit Cat nerve center; but she understood this underground chamber was the only one that could be the heart of the Spirit Cats on Marik.

Push, shuffle, rest.

Her mother had expected Marik to fall into Oriente's lap—or had that been Nikol's assessment? Clan Sea Fox was supposed to see the economic advantages of dealing with Oriente rather than the Spirit Cats. Jessica had expected Rikkard and his people to be isolated, and to wither in their isolation. She had underestimated Clan solidarity; and had not realized that the Spirit Cats had sought sanctuary because they thrived on isolation. Enclaves of Nova Cats in the Inner Sphere had long been isolated from the larger Clan, and some of those independent groups had undergone a transformation: no longer able to envision their future as traditional members of the Nova Cat Clan, they sought a separate life elsewhere. Their blood remained the blood of the Nova Cats, however; there was not, and might never be, a Clan Spirit Cat.

Now there was no Oriente garrison on Marik. What her mother had intended as a prison had become a hothouse, nurturing the Spirit Cats in their rebirth.

A young warrior hurried past. Intent on his own business, he swerved wide enough to comfortably pass her as he strode toward the command center.

On Oriente, someone overtaking her would have asked after her health or offered to help or to fetch whatever she was looking for. On Marik it was a given that anywhere she was, was where she wanted to be. If she was going somewhere, it was understood she had the ability to get there unassisted or she wouldn't have begun the journey.

Underlying the brusque courtesy of the Clanners was the assumption she was capable. What had always looked, when she had observed from the outside, like a complete lack of consideration for others was in fact a fundamental respect for an individual's ability to take care of herself.

Though she could not yet say she was used to it, Julietta had to admit the lack of hovering well-wishers, each trying to think of some way to be of use, was peaceful.

"Ah," Rikkard welcomed her across the threshold of the command center with a single syllable.

"Ah," Julietta agreed.

With no break in her three-count rhythm, she altered her course until she was headed toward the open door of his inner office.

"There is a purpose to your visit?" Rikkard asked.

"There is a purpose to my journey," Julietta corrected, keeping a watchful eye on her feet. "To prove I can do it."

Rikkard said nothing, but from the corner of her eye

Julietta caught at least one approving nod from a Clansman at his duty station.

There was a single chair in the inner office, Rikkard's, and Julietta ignored it. Pushing her walker until it was braced against the wall, she swung down the shelf hinged to its frame, converting it into a chair. Reversing herself, she was seated comfortably by the time Rikkard finished whatever business held him in the command center.

"There is an elevator," he said, an indication he was concerned she'd overextended herself. An unaccustomed and effusive display of compassion by Clan standards.

"There are also two delightful elemental warriors, Sigrid and Penelope, whom you've assigned to carry me around like a baby should I need their services," Julietta pointed out. "Those options did not suit my purpose."

Rikkard nodded, accepting the argument.

A half hour of small talk dispensed with in a few seconds. Julietta smiled to herself. *No wonder you think Inner Sphere courtesies to be a waste of time.*

"I received a letter from my mother," she said. "Which I suppose you know, since your courier delivered it."

Rikkard didn't answer.

"You no doubt also know it was long—for my mother— and included an inquiry after my health," Julietta said. "And concluded with a question about when I intend to return to Oriente."

"I do not know," Rikkard corrected. "I did not read it."

In any other culture, the use of the singular pronoun would have implied he'd had others read the letter and report to him. But the Star colonel was Clan. Julietta knew that if he'd wanted to know what was in her letter, he would have read it himself and told her he had done so.

"What would not have been obvious, to someone unfamiliar with my mother," she said aloud, "was that she was asking for a report on events on Marik and information as to your intentions."

"Indeed?"

"Indeed."

She waited, content after her long struggle to reach the office to simply sit and listen to herself breathe.

"Your mother, Captain-General Duchess Jessica Marik, believes you are her eyes and ears among the Spirit Cats," Rikkard said at last. Julietta suspected his stringing all of her titles and names together in one sentence indicated how seriously he took Jessica.

"That is what she believes," she agreed.

"Is she correct in this belief?"

Julietta smiled, letting the lids of her eyes half close. She felt very like a cat.

"Oh no," she said. "Quite the opposite, in fact."

Breezewood, Kwamashu
Duchy of Andurien

"Maria!"

Casson stepped up the gain on his radio, straining for any sound on his friend's frequency. The hiss of static filled the speakers. More significantly, the dozen tiny sounds of a working cockpit did not. It wasn't Maria who had gone silent; her radio was no longer transmitting.

Maria's gone. The realization froze him midmotion, his hands suddenly loose on the controls. The soldier within him added: *What have they got that can take down a* Jupiter?

Blue-white light flared through his *Sun Cobra's* cockpit, snapping him back into the moment. Sensors confirmed what the fact he was alive had already told him; the glare had been the secondary radiation wash of a particle projection beam striking the outside face of his 'Mech's elevated left shoulder. Every time he complained about the 'Mech's hunched "shoulder pads" restricting his field of vision, one of them saved his life by blocking a shot.

He answered the glancing shot from the Kwamashu garrison's *Uziel* with a blast from his own PPC.

The smaller machine took the bolt across its center torso just below the cockpit and staggered back. Given the center-mass hit and the minimal kinetic impact of the particle beam, that stumble meant a pilot overreacting to the shot.

Weekend warriors.

Twisting at the torso, Casson unleashed a second bolt. His thermal display flashed for attention, its sensors displaying the Ducky 'Mech in glowing blue white. Only a failing reactor shield would give those numbers. The *Uziel* had to be seconds away from shutdown. Or worse.

Ignoring the stricken machine, Casson threw a PPC bolt after a fleeing J. Edgar. A clean miss.

Having end-run the dug-in defenders by cutting through the edge of Breezewood, Able and Baker companies were having no trouble pushing back the hastily regrouped garrison forces. In fact, the Eagle's Talons would have reached this point sooner if the city hadn't been practically deserted.

For an industrial boomtown, Breezewood was doing a good impression of a ghost town. The empty urban streets had been perfect for ambushes, and Casson had slowed their pace to scan for booby traps that never materialized.

It was hard to imagine these underequipped and inexperienced troops were all the Ducks had to defend a target as vital as a 'Mech factory.

Of course, if they were all amateurs, Maria would still be kicking butt.

Reports came in on all channels. The defenders were falling back in a disorganized scramble-and-stop pattern that made no tactical sense.

At extreme range ahead, Casson could see a mobile gun crew hastily anchoring their piece behind a low wall. Nothing wrong with the position, but twelve meters to their left was what appeared to be the ruin of a pump house. With thick walls and lots of old metal to fog targeting systems, it was a perfect nest for the small gun.

Brave men, Casson decided, doing their best with no clue how to get the job done.

The rest of the defenders peeled away to the north. Logic—and basic tactics—would have dictated they withdraw into the 'Mech assembly plant. The sprawling industrial compound dominated the tumbledown warehouse district, rising like a walled city above the one- and two-story storage buildings.

Casson clicked his all-channel open.

"They're either trying to draw us off, or getting out of

the way so we walk into a trap," he said. "Either way, the objective's the same. Make for the plant. Anyone who gets out of our way, let 'em go.

"Look sharp for mines, booby traps and ambushes," he added, knowing it was unnecessary. "And sing out. Ten false alarms beat getting your head blown off any day."

Casson moved left a block before advancing on the 'Mech plant. He told himself it was to avoid being too predictable in his approach. Bypassing the local amateurs with the popgun—and letting them live awhile longer—was an unavoidable side effect.

He suspected the real fighting was going to begin when Able and Baker hit whatever force had bogged down Charlie Company. Obviously some Ducky regulars sent to shore up the planetary militia, they would be the real defenders his boys and girls would have to walk through. But from the way this was playing out, he didn't think they were going to meet that particular briar patch until they stormed the complex proper.

"Assault pattern four," he ordered. "Let's try knocking on their front door."

Tamarind-Abbey Defense Command
Tripoli, Gibraltar
Duchy of Tamarind-Abbey

"Damn."

Fontaine Marik looked up at the sound of his security chief's voice.

Roland stood, arms akimbo, scowling at a message screen. His sweat-stained tunic was open at the chest, though Fontaine doubted it offered much relief in the oppressive heat.

Summers in Gibraltar's northern hemisphere were legendary—at least on Gibraltar—for their ability to overcome even the most sophisticated air-conditioning systems. And Fontaine had to admit the air conditioners in his command center were not the most sophisticated.

Rather than call out his question, or wait for Roland to come to him, Fontaine made his way across the command center. More warehouse than military nerve center, the room was mostly silent. At this point command consisted primarily of routing reports of disasters and tabulating remaining resources. The half dozen techs present, all of whom must have heard Roland's exclamation, remained bent over their consoles tracking nothing that needed Fontaine's immediate attention.

He noticed young Christopher had risen from his desk, where he was no doubt running another of his campaign simulations, and was just arriving at Roland's side.

"What is it, Roland?"

"Preston and Zortman have sued for peace," his SAFE director responded. "Surrendered."

"But the Steiners haven't landed on Preston or Zortman," Christopher protested.

"Look at the map, Hughes." Roland's tone was sharp with irritation. "They're hard up against the Lyran border and surrounded by Vedet's forces. The only reason they were leapfrogged by the Steiners is they have nothing to fight over and nothing to fight with."

"They never had a choice." Fontaine cut off Christopher's protest. The boy did not yet understand accepting the inevitable.

He looked at the revised star chart above the communications console.

Alorten, Schererville, Saltillo, Millungera, Labouchure, Niihu, Edmondson, Kosciusko, Simpson Desert, Kilarney— half the Duchy of Tamarind-Abbey. He sighed. *Throw in Tamarind, and they have our heart as well.*

"I've been looking at the intel on Kilarney, and I think I've found something." Christopher broke into his thoughts. "They're maintaining communications traffic like there's a full garrison, but there hasn't been enough DropShip traffic to keep them supplied."

"Any reason they didn't just bring in what they needed to begin with and are just living off Kilarney's production now?"

"Yes, sir." Christopher nodded. "Drought. Two years of

crop failures on Kilarney. It's not a famine by any means, but they don't have the resources to feed themselves and the occupation forces."

"The Lyrans could be letting them starve," Roland pointed out.

"These are Lyran regulars, not Vedet's forces." Christopher's distinction spoke volumes. "If the troops were really there, they'd be importing staples at a steady volume. The volume is not there."

Roland nodded thoughtfully. "They do have a lot on their plate, even for a military the size of the archon's."

Fontaine looked around his command center. Half the consoles powered down, the other half routing assets to survivors or coordinating casualty reports.

"Roland, check his numbers, see if his conclusions are solid," Fontaine said. "If he's on to something, I want a plan to retake Kilarney in my hands soonest.

"It's about time we hit back."

Breezewood, Kwamashu
Duchy of Andurien

Casson ignored the yellow-and-red glow of his damage display. Taking a chance, he stopped his limping *Sun Cobra* at the edge of a circular intersection from which six nameless streets radiated into the surrounding brick and block buildings and pulled up a tactical overlay of the city on his main screen. The faint, scratching whine of the failing gyro beneath him was a minor counterpoint to his own thoughts.

Nothing was going as planned.

The local militia they'd sliced through had been replaced by a garrison force at the gates of the factory complex. Same older, second-line materiel, but a whole lot tougher attitude. And a solid grasp on how to get the job done.

Able and Baker companies had been held at the gate. It had only taken a few sallies to convince him the front door was not the way. They'd stumbled on an alternate route almost immediately, but that had proved more curse than blessing. The trapped Duckies—and these, Casson was sure, had been the crack troops brought in to defend the 'Mech plant proper—had savaged Baker Company with true brutality in their break for freedom.

Disconcerting amidst the carnage had been the sight of Breedelove's *Hatchetman* in Eagle's Talons colors attacking his own troops.

Casson had made bringing down the captured BattleMech his personal business. He'd hung in the battle longer than he should have—taken damage he should have avoided—but Casson hadn't broken off the duel until the Ducky in Breedelove's stolen cockpit had punched out.

He would have blasted the escape pod out of the sky, but his systems were too overheated for his PPC to recharge in time.

At the time he'd counted a cracked gyro housing and gimped left hip actuator as fair trade for victory. Now . . .

It wasn't a question of if the Eagle's Talons would overrun the Duckies, but of when. The damage they'd taken because he'd underestimated the last-ditch defenders—and the hurt he'd taken by choosing to get revenge rather than following the mission—had doubled the cost of victory. But given the balance of forces, victory was inevitable.

With two-thirds of Baker Company destroyed and Able on the ropes, Casson had ordered a fighting withdrawal. Out of the fire and back into the frying pan as the Ducky regulars engaged them again.

Taking cover in the buildings of the industrial district, Casson had regrouped his forces and taken the fight back to the locals in a running battle. A building-to-building, dash-and-blast slugfest that showcased the Talon's superior speed and firepower. Keeping his 'Mechs within a dozen blocks of the walled complex, he quartered the area, stringing the defenders along—pushing them out of the way when necessary—as he tried to locate whatever was left of the slower but heavier Charlie Company.

Not to mention figure out how to destroy the 'Mech plant with a badly battered half of his original force.

"They're breaking off," a voice announced over the command channel. It took Casson's tired mind a long second to recognize Overton, Able-three leader. Looking up from his data screen, he was a little surprised to see the scout lance leader's *Spider* standing at evident rest less than twenty meters away.

"Say again?" he asked.

"They're moving away," Overton answered. "Firing a couple of shots for show, but definitely bugging out."

"Confirmed," Paten chimed in, her battered *Enforcer* entering the traffic circle that had evidently become Casson's command center. "Making haste away from us and the plant."

Casson sighed as he wrestled muzzily with the possible reasons for the Duckies' suddenly cooperative behavior. Looking up at the three-sixty above his display, he could see the walled complex half a dozen blocks behind him, picked out brightly in the midday sun.

"Same choice as before," he said, pulling his attention down to the two MechWarriors in front of him. "They're either trying to lead us off or opening the door for us to walk into a trap."

"It was a trap last time," Paten pointed out. "Think they're repeating the same trick?"

"Not like we have a choice," Overton countered. "The objective is still take out the 'Mech plant."

If there is a 'Mech plant, Casson thought but did not say. Nothing but nothing about this entire setup looked like Duckies protecting a 'Mech plant. Or, he added, surveying the abandoned buildings around them, like a town gearing up to open a brand-new 'Mech plant.

"Circle east," he decided. "Bypass the main gate. Get about one-eighty degrees from that hellhole we opened up. We'll breach there and see—"

His *Sun Cobra* lurched as the ground heaved. The gyro beneath him screamed; only his safety harness kept him from being flung into the viewscreen. Fighting against the 'Mech's sluggish controls and his own tired reflexes, Casson kept the BattleMech upright as the solid concrete of the industrial district undulated like a choppy sea.

"What the hell?"

"Sweet mother of God!" Paten answered.

Casson turned his 'Mech to look in the direction she was pointing; back toward the Duchy 'Mech plant.

Where the 'Mech plant had been.

In its place was a towering column of flame, a conflagration of incomprehensible proportions. Red, orange, green and yellow fire, braided together in impossible patterns and shot through with dense coils of oily smoke, rose like a redwood from within the high walls. And rose. And rose. Until it towered at least a kilometer above their heads.

Looking away from the spreading umbrella of smoke and fire, Casson realized the column of destruction was no longer contained within the walls of the plant. The walls were gone. And, as he watched, the first block of storage buildings disappeared, swallowed by the advancing wall of flame.

"It's getting bigger!"

He was aware of Paten beside him, turning her *Enforcer* away from the oncoming firestorm, pushing the damaged machine to its maximum speed. Overton and his *Spider* were already gone. By the time she reached the far side of the traffic circle, two more blocks of buildings had burst into flames and then vaporized, transmuted from solid to gas by the widening column.

Casson's radiation counter beeped for attention. Whatever was burning was radioactive. Which meant the air itself was becoming deadly.

Casson didn't move. His fight with Breedelove's *Hatchetman* had torn too many myomer bundles. His *Sun Cobra* could barely walk, much less run. He would never outdistance the inferno rising from the ground itself.

Another block of buildings disappeared. The wall of garish flame had become so wide he could no longer see the curve of the column.

Die shuffling away or die standing his ground. Those were his choices.

Back straight, grip solid on the controls of his BattleMech, Casson watched the nearest row of buildings explode into flame.

=== 28 ===

Jessica watched, transfixed.

The column of green, orange and red fire rose toward the sky, spreading until it nearly filled the screen. Bolts of yellow lightning shot along the ropes of black smoke braided through the twisted towers of flame. Blue-white arc-lights flickered—like PPC discharges of unimaginable power—suffusing the scene with such energy the recorder was overwhelmed. In those moments the column of destruction stood out in black relief against a field of white.

Sharp, shouting voices near the recorder, their faint sound offering a sense of scale to the waterfall rumble of the growing conflagration.

The image jerked, shifted and vibrated, momentarily losing its view of the devastation. Her impression was that someone had snatched the recorder from its tripod and was now running with it. A metal sill, a wildly swinging view of the interior of a VTOL. Civilians dressed in medical technician uniforms, Jessica noted.

Then the cloud of fire and death was centered in the screen again. The image was shaky: a handheld recorder on a rising helicopter trying to stay focused on a scene of unimaginable destruction.

The top of the conflagration—the camera panned up to show a spreading umbrella above the VTOL's spinning rotors—was more than a kilometer high. The base of the firestorm . . . the camera jerked back down to show the ground just as a block of buildings seemed to come loose from the ground, to rise up and disappear. Vaporizing rather than blowing apart.

At this altitude and scale, Jessica could see nothing of the details, but one of the shouting voices in the VTOL's cabin was saying something about civilians. Thousands of civilians.

And, barely discernible, a voice was damning Andurien—damning Duke Humphreys—for deliberately detonating a toxic waste dump to deny the "Ories" a victory on Kwamashu.

Underneath the shouting voices someone—some man—was sobbing uncontrollably.

Torrian Dolcat reached out and turned off the playback.

Jessica opened her mouth. And realized she had nothing to say. She felt a touch at her elbow, and it took her a blank moment to realize Philip was offering her a drink of water. She took it gratefully, wondering how she would ever make it without the man the public believed was abandoning her.

Clipperton—

She shied away from that thought. But it came back. She gathered herself and faced the accusation square. In a time of peace she had ordered a terrorist attack on Clipperton, an attack that had killed ten thousand civilians. By that measure, she had no right to be shocked, to be horrified, by what Humphreys had done in battle on Kwamashu.

She had no right, but she found herself feeling it anyway.

Hundreds of his own loyal troops, thousands of his own citizens, who counted on their ruler to protect them, slaughtered for a minor strategic advantage?

What sort of mind thinks that way?

She didn't ask the question aloud. She was afraid that Torrian would answer honestly. It was possible Philip still harbored some illusions about the woman he loved, and she didn't want him hurt.

And Thaddeus—

She glanced at the man chosen to be her husband and found him staring at the blank vidscreen in apparent concentration.

"So," she said at last.

No one else spoke.

"Any chance that was the extent of the damage?" she asked.

"No, Your Grace," Torrian answered. "Our most reliable data is two weeks old, but extrapolating from that information tells us that at least one-third of the planet will be uninhabitable within the year."

Greater than Clipperton by an order of magnitude, Jessica thought. *Why isn't that comforting?*

"How did you come by this recording?" Thaddeus asked.

"It is apparently a copy of a crystal struck by a humanitarian organization that was visiting Kwamashu," Torrian answered. "Dozens of copies have been shipped to major news outlets from Mansu-ri to Calloway VI. We expect them to appear on more-distant worlds as transports reach them."

"So this is not restricted intel, then?"

"Quite the opposite," Torrian said. "There are already riots demanding vengeance."

Another moment of pregnant silence.

"This is going to be an all-out war, isn't it?" Jessica asked aloud, annoyed with herself for needing to ask, yet needing confirmation. "Not a border skirmish."

"More than likely," Torrian agreed.

"Then why isn't it?" Thaddeus asked. "Why didn't the Duchy's forces pour across our border the moment our elite force was destroyed?"

Our border, Jessica echoed in her mind. *Our elite forces. Have you accepted your adoption into Oriente, Thaddeus, or are you letting slip your intention to own the Protectorate?*

"There's a possibility they weren't ready," Torrian said. "This may have caught them by surprise as well."

"Caught them by surprise?" Thaddeus echoed. "This must have taken months to prepare. . . . Or are you suggesting the trap was sprung prematurely?"

Watching Torrian consider his answer, Jessica noticed a single white hair, longer than the others, curling away from his sideburn.

Trying times turn even our young men gray.

"My thought is that an explosion of that magnitude could not be completely natural," her intelligence chief said at last. "The expansion along the ground is far too uniform, and there is a definite sequential feel to the initial blasts.

"Yet I think the disaster itself is natural." He tapped a few controls and the screen came alive with the frozen image of building fragments swirling in the updrafts around the pillar of flame. "The conflagration is clearly out of control within seconds, spreading well beyond the initial blast zone."

"You're suggesting there was supposed to be a firebreak," Thaddeus said. "A ring cleared of flammables broad enough to contain the destruction."

"We struck weeks, perhaps months before they were expecting us," Torrian agreed. "Before the safeguards were established."

"And whoever was at the switch when the Eagle's Talons breached the walls decided to spring the trap anyway."

"One hopes," Philip spoke up, "that he had no idea what he was unleashing."

"Amen." Thaddeus nodded once.

"From a tactical standpoint, the premature explosion is a disaster," Torrian said. "But from a public-relations perspective, it plays to their advantage. Taking a few weeks to gear up a crusade of vengeance is more believable than happening to have an invasion force standing by."

"You're suggesting this recording isn't available in the Duchy?" Jessica asked.

"I have no idea," Torrian admitted. "But since the blast laid waste to one of their worlds and killed thousands of their citizens, I'm thinking the images of the destruction will carry more weight than one man cursing in the background of a trivid recording."

Jessica sat, imagining she could feel the patterns of the table's finely grained wood rising as heat against her palms. Feints, ploys, posturing: that was all she had expected from Ari Humphreys. Nothing—*nothing*—like this.

"How long do you estimate we have?" she asked.

"That will depend on what preparations Humphreys was making and how far along they are," Torrian said. "Weeks, maybe. Probably not longer than a month to a month and a half."

Jessica nodded. She had moved Nikol out of the way—shifted her into the more dangerous ground of diplomacy—precisely so that Thaddeus would be able to shine if a military situation presented itself. No great gamble there; in the current uncertainty, military situations were becoming the norm. But she had never imagined he would need to take charge of something of this magnitude.

Leading the Oriente Protectorate in a victorious war would secure Thaddeus a place in the hearts of the people. Horrible as the Kwamashu destruction was, it presented a perfect opportunity to—

"Your Grace, I must return to the Covenant Worlds."

Jessica blinked.

"My nation and our allies face potential dangers, but nothing on this scale," Thaddeus said. "We can spare the resources to form a joint force to support you."

"I had thought," Jessica said, having to swallow once before finding her voice, "that you would lead the Protectorate's forces against Andurien."

"Impossible, Your Grace." Thaddeus did not quite bow, as he was still seated. "I am warden of the Covenant Worlds. If I go into battle, it is at the head of my own nation's forces."

"He's right," Philip said before Jessica could formulate a response. "Raising an army of allies does more to promote unification than one nation standing alone. Not to mention the fact that being part of the Protectorate's salvation will closely bind the Covenant Worlds—and whomever else Thaddeus persuades to join them—to Oriente."

Her husband patted her hand, a propriatary gesture he almost never made in the presence of others.

"Think of the people, my dear." He smiled; a little sadly, she thought. "An independent hero will make a much more romantic consort than a loyal employee."

29

"Systems check," Corporal Haverson's voice crackled over Marvin's headphones.

Marvin turned his head to look at Haverson, seated immediately behind him.

"Again?" he asked, not bothering with the intercom.

Haverson tore his eyes away from the command periscope to meet his gaze and keyed his throat mic. "Affirmative."

"Corp, the headsets are so we can talk while taking fire," Marvin said. "Sitting in a damn dugout with the engine off, you just talk to folks."

"Besides, you're wasting battery power," Joline added from her post at fire control. Which was about a meter from Haverson's right hip. "Even Beth's on organics."

Marvin smiled as he watched Haverson work out what *on organics* meant. His thought process was assisted by the sight of Beth's lower torso, visible behind Joline's position. Boots on her molded plastic jump seat, elbows on the rim of the open hatch, their sensor tech was hanging out the top of their ancient Hetzer to look around. When all internal systems had a battery life measured in minutes, you did what you could to conserve power.

Either that or have the ancient diesel clattering away behind them, wasting fuel and filling the cabin with stinking fumes.

Haverson wasn't a bad kid, but he *was* a kid. He was

here because he was the new guy and the sergeant didn't want some new recruit smart-ass who tested in at corporal level getting the idea he was a hotshot.

Assignment to the rolling coffin—aka the Hetzer wheeled assault gun—was usually earned by screwing up, either consistently or spectacularly or both. Most troopers pulled H-WAG duty for a few weeks or months, until they'd worked off whatever penance they'd earned; the gun had a high turnover rate.

Marvin, Joline and Beth, crew of H-WAG-7 of the Belleville Urban Defense Garrison, a wholly owned subsidiary of the Mansu-ri Planetary Militia, had served together for the better part of a year and a half. They were something of a legend.

Marvin kept his pilot's chair via the consistently-screwing-up-small-things method. He didn't want anything really big on his record, but he didn't want a lot of work screwing up his tour of duty either. A Hetzer jockey enjoyed a relaxingly near-complete lack of responsibility: after all, how hard was it to drive a tank that spent ninety percent of its time dug in to a defensive position? Perfect gig for the military man of leisure.

Joline, on the other hand, was here because she liked to fight. Not with the H-WAG's big cannon, though she routinely smoked the quarterly qualifier with the AC-20, but with her fists. Preferably in an off-limits bar.

Beth . . . Marvin drew a blank. Except for the fact that, like Joline, the sensor tech didn't believe in sexing the driver, Marvin didn't know a thing about Beth. She'd done something somewhere that put her at the dead bottom of the duty heap, which made her aces with him.

The three of them tended to ignore the command chair, the occupant of which changed every month or so. Fact was that whoever was sitting behind Marvin had pissed off Master Sergeant Amoto, and was just serving their time before getting back to one of the real tanks.

Though that wasn't really fair. The Hetzer wheeled assault gun wasn't a tank, real or otherwise. Like the name said, it was a gun with wheels. Quickcell Kalidasa had built their H-WAG around the Crusher Twenty autocannon, which on the face of it was a very good thing. The AC-20 was an impressive weapon; anything it hit usually disappeared. And with four tons of ammo onboard, the Hetzer could hit things for hours. Unfortunately, the gun was all Quickcell had spent money on. The rest of the vehicle was an engine, wheels, four chairs designed to cause major orthopedic damage, and just enough armor to prevent sunburn.

That last was also a little unfair, Marvin had to admit. Quickcell Kalidasa had mounted appropriate armor on the front, but for reasons known only to the MPM quartermaster, the sides and rear armor of all H-WAGs had been replaced with local plate.

But even without the Militia currying favor by giving unnecessary contracts to local producers, the Hetzer was a cheap ride. Quickcell hadn't even sprung for a turret. The autocannon was thrust straight ahead, its muzzle framing the right side of Marvin's field of view through the open port. The gun could traverse fifteen to twenty degrees in any direction, a percentage hardly worth mentioning. If you wanted to shoot something, you had to point the whole Hetzer at it.

With a top speed that enabled it to barely outrun most crustaceans, the Hetzer was designed to hit the enemy while someone else covered its butt. In practice, the wheeled guns were usually dug in as static defense.

Actually sitting inside the parked coffin was something of a novelty. Usually the crew would be spread around the dugout; the shallow trench cut into a fold of rocky earth, open at the end facing the Navassa plain. Belleville was an industrial center, a city built around Mansu-ri Mining and Manufacturing's extensive mining and manufacturing complex at the base of the Leland Range. The Navassa plain had been a real money-saver for M3; the hardpan of the extinct lake bed was stable enough to be a natural landing field, saving them the expense of building a cargo DropPort.

Of course, anyone trying to take what M3 mined and manufactured at Belleville could see how useful the horizon-wide flat was too. So the Hetzers of the BUDG were usually dug in with their crews spread as far away from each other as possible, grabbing some shade or fresh air or privacy or some combination thereof. But the whole MPM, BUDG included, had been on Defcon three since the Eagle's Talons bought it on Kwamashu.

The entire elite battalion of the Oriente Protectorate, the captain-general's personal unit—disappearing in one shot sounded ridiculous on the face of it. But Marvin had seen the vid and there was nothing funny to say about it, even for him. The Duckies had gone completely crazy just one jump away from Mansu-ri. Even an officer could see that was too damn close for comfort.

So they sat in their Hetzer and waited for the sky to fall. They weren't buttoned up, of course; death by heat stroke appealed to no one, but even with every viewport and hatch open, air circulation remained nothing more than an attractive theory.

The alert tone squealed through Marvin's earphones. He almost snatched his headset off before the words following the wake-up registered.

"Defcon four. Repeat, Defcon four. Belleview Urban Defense, this is Militia Command," the unfamiliar voice was brittle with stress. "Unknown bogies have jumped in system, sub-luna pirate point. Repeat, bogies inside lunar orbit. Best guess planetfall twelve to twenty-four hours. All units, Defcon four."

There was a moment of stunned silence in which Marvin spent trying to remember defense-condition four protocols.

"Oh my God," Haverson said, his voice betraying his sincere desire to be in something—anything—that had a snowball's chance of making it through a battle.

"Don't sweat it, kid," Joline said. "The retirement plan sucks sand."

30

Alethea Chowla hated headaches. And seated across the broad desk of genuine Terran teak was a migraine.

She counted the wide desk as her only extravagance. Or at least the extravagance most difficult to make secure in free fall. The desk was a gift from her younger brother, each panel hand-carved from a tree grown in the region of Terra that had been home to their ancestors. This impractical centerpiece to her mobile command center always gave her a steadying sense of context.

And she needed some steadying now.

Duke Wesley of Westover—an exercise in alliteration if ever there was one—had allowed the Rim Commonality defenders to land, but then insisted they wait on board their DropShips until his military attaché had vetted their "bone fides," as the radio dispatcher had pronounced it. Not unexpected, given the forged internal report describing Rim Commonality intentions that had been provided by the Regulans.

Alethea was prepared for the attitude and ready to fight suspicion with transparency—until she'd met the gatekeeper appointed by the duke. Now she wondered if the greater good might demand she kill him.

"General Bernard Nordhoff," she repeated.

The square man seated opposite her neither smiled nor blinked.

How does he manage to look both stolid and oily at the

same time? she asked herself. *Or do I only think he looks oily because I've read the warrants?*

Alethea held up the noteputer containing the file she'd been reading.

"Archon Steiner and Duke Vedet have covered all of near space with your particulars and résumé," she said. "A disgraced former general of the LCAF who deserted his troops under fire on Simpson Desert. You are wanted by the Lyran Commonwealth for desertion and treason."

Nordhoff neither blinked nor spoke.

"I find it interesting that you show up on Westover offering your services as a mercenary," she said, probing. "The only reason any Free Worlds League world would need your company of mercenaries would be to fight off your former comrades."

"Incorrect," Nordhoff said. "Pirates attacked while the JumpShip carrying the *Titanslayer* was recharging. I ordered my DropShip detached and was able to arrive at Ennis in time to prevent the raiders from making off with an entire production run of *Riever* heavy fighters."

Alethea smiled narrowly. "The timing of that so-called pirate raid stretches credibility just a tad."

"As does your coincidental arrival to negotiate a month after my forces drove off the so-called pirates," Nordhoff countered blandly.

Touché.

Alethea toggled through a few screens. "Duke Wesley says some nice things about your ability to beat back a raiding party while armed with only four staff officers and a mixed company of 'Mechs and armor."

Again the blank nonresponse that Alethea was beginning to suspect was the rogue general's default mode.

"On the other hand, given the Lyran Commonwealth's widely broadcast determination to hunt you down and drag you back home, it could be argued you'd make Westover safer by simply going away," she added.

"I find it difficult to believe the Rim Commonality has intelligence assets within the Lyran Commonwealth." Nordhoff's tone was almost neutral.

"This is the Free Worlds League," she countered. "Infor-

mation is the stuff of life here. We have many more resources, both direct and indirect, than you might imagine."

Or a lot fewer, but this is not a topic for transparency.

"Can you be sure the indirect resources, as you call them,
are one hundred percent reliable?"

Touché again, Alethea conceded. *Regulan disinformation
brought us here. Are you the victim of Lyran lies?*

She rested the fingertips of one hand on the edge of her
desk and let the weight of her wrist hang, stretching her
tendons. The familiar warmth of the richly grained wood
seemed to flow up her arm, relaxing her shoulders and the
knot of tension at the base of her neck. She knew the
energy flow was imaginary, but that didn't diminish its
effect.

Something in the wood—or more likely the studiously
bland affect of the man sitting opposite her—told her Nordhoff was lying. Though intuitions imparted by furniture
were not considered empirical evidence in most courts of
law, the feeling was enough for her.

"The Lyran Commonwealth is offering a reward for your
return that would balance the budget of most industrialized
planets," she said, gauging his reaction to the change in
tack. "Is there a good reason for me to not wrap you in
pink ribbon and present you to the archon with a box of
chocolates?"

Nordhoff pursed his lips.

"Duke Wesley is aware of the lies being broadcast to
discredit me. He fully understands the crisis of conscience
that forced me to abandon my homeland and its inexcus-
able invasion of the Free Worlds League," he said. "It is
your integrity, not mine, that he questions."

*Three for three. A lot of practice trading barbs with
someone.*

"I doubt he would allow your attempt to repatriate me,"
Nordhoff added, smiling his first smile.

Alethea could not tell if that was a misstep or if the
Lyran really thought he could goad her so easily.

Like you've been trying to goad him?

Of course it would never come to a test of military might.
Any hint that she was even considering military action

would solidify Duke Wesley's suspicion that the disinformation Lester Cameron-Jones had so artfully provided was accurate. The first rattle of her sword would scuttle the entire mission.

Alethea was certain the Lyran was nothing more than a traitor lying about his motives. His bored attitude did more to convince her than the Lyran warrant: he was clearly a man feeling smug about getting away with something. But given the duke's faith in the man, her hands were tied.

The glint in his pale gray eyes told Alethea that Nordhoff was aware of—and amused by—her predicament.

You're safe now, joker, but only because I'm smart enough to put first things first.

"So," she asked aloud, "from where we are now, how do I arrange an audience with the duke?"

31

Mansu-ri Mining and Manufacturing Complex Four
Belleville, Mansu-ri
Oriente Protectorate
1 March 3138

"**W**hat the hell is it?" Haverson's voice didn't quite crack, but it was a near thing.

"A 'Mech," Beth answered. "That's all the sensors got."

Marvin kept his eyes on the black-and-white monitor above the open viewport. Hell of a thing backing down an alley at full speed, steering by one straight-back camera feeding an eighteen-by-thirty-six-centimeter screen.

Of course, compared to the alternative—going one-on-one with at least one BattleMech in a confined area—it wasn't so bad.

Ten seconds ago Beth had sung out heavy walking metal

where there should have been nothing and Haverson had ordered, "Take cover!" and Marvin had hit reverse full throttle. That had been three blocks back—ahead—but no one was complaining about how fast or how far he was going to find cover.

Through the front viewport—still open because hell if he was going to take his hands off the yokes to unhook it—he could see sparks flying from the fire escape they'd been dragging for the last block. No sign of the BattleMech, and no indication whether or not it had seen them. Of course, subtle clues like no sign of the BattleMech and no withering fire ripping through their armor gave Marvin hope it hadn't.

"What kind of 'Mech?" Haverson asked. Which was not a dumb question. If it was a lightweight, their trusty AC-20 could take it out in one salvo. But if it was a heavy, sporting enough armor to shrug off their first hit, they wouldn't live long enough to get in a second shot.

Unless all it's got are long-range weapons. In these alleys . . .

Marvin got a grip. Not even the Duckies were stupid enough to send a fire-support 'Mech into the warren of a factory district.

"Fifty, maybe fifty-five tons," Beth answered. "Some kind of energy weapons but we won't know what kind until they fire and a whole lot of dark space that's either a missile rack or an autocannon with ammo."

"What does the tactical database say?"

"That it's a BattleMech, fifty tons give or take, with some kind of energy weapon system hot and ready and a big dark space that's gotta be a missile rack or autocannon with ammo," Beth answered. "I'll be able to tell you more when I see the damn thing. This tactical sensor array is strictly point and shoot."

They hit an intersection that looked big enough and Marvin scissored the yokes. Front wheels crabbed left and rear wheels cut hard in the opposite direction and the H-WAG-7 spun like a top. Bangs and curses all around. The fire escape flew free, taking out a light pole, and the Hetzer finished a two-seventy spin pointing down an even narrower alley.

Marvin gunned the diesel and popped the clutch. Everybody's head snapped back as the machine jumped forward.

"What we got working for us is crappy armor and an internal combustion engine," Beth was saying. "We read like a civilian truck. And running like hell fits that profile."

"We're not running," Haverson objected. "We're making best possible speed to our assigned fallback position."

Uh-huh.

"To the Duckies it looks like running, sir." Beth was the only one who said *sir.* "Which is fine. We'll look civilian until we fire."

"And when we do that, what we got working against us is crappy armor and an ICE," Marvin shouted over his shoulder. The H-WAG lurched as it crushed a phalanx of dustbins. "If we don't take out that 'Mech in one shot, it's going to have us for lunch."

"Or if we do smoke it and it's got a buddy," Joline added. "These things travel in packs, you know."

Marvin slowed the machine. Veering left into what looked like a loading area, he eased in beneath a massive petroleum tank and shut off the engine. They still had half their fuel, but he had no idea how much ground they'd have to cover before they'd have a chance to fill up. The irony of having to conserve fuel while parked under a half-million-liter storage tank was not lost on him.

"We're off bearing for the fallback," he said. "And I think the 'Mech we're not running from is between us and everybody else."

"You *think*?"

"Hard to say with all the metal around us, sir," Beth answered for Marvin. "We know about where it was and about where it was going. There's a good chance it's gotten between us and bud-gee command."

"I hate to admit it," Marvin said before the corporal could think of a rebuttal. "But the officer who pulled the H-WAGs from the dugouts probably saved our butts. We'd have been sitting ducks in the open. In this place, we got options."

"What sort of options?" Haverson asked in a tone that suggested he suspected a trick.

"Do what we're doing," Marvin said. "Park our heavy

metal next to a bunch of bigger heavy metal and hope no one sees us.

"Or take the long way around—get past our 'Mech and his buddies—and meet up with the rest of bud-gee." He scratched his jaw. "Both good, commonsense plans. Smart choices.

"Or"—he looked into the fish-eye mirror next to the review monitor and confirmed he had three sets of eyes on him—"we turn our skinny butts around and go after that Ducky 'Mech. We got a big honking autocannon on this thing."

Haverson sat perfectly still for a long four-count.

"Recommendations?" he asked at last.

Way to lead, kid.

Marvin took back that thought a heartbeat later. Haverson had been with them through two weeks of sitting in a trench. He had no idea what H-WAG-7 could do and giving orders without data from folks who did have an idea was stupid.

"Nobody at Company I want to see," Joline said.

"And this neighborhood sucks," Beth added.

"Like Joline said"—Marvin kept his voice bored—"the Militia's retirement plan ain't worth waiting for."

"Good." Haverson sounded relieved. "Button up, people."

Marvin reached through the open viewport and grabbed the outside lens release—real high-tech, the Hetzer—and pulled the rectangle of curved ferroglass into place. Once it was dogged down, he swung the inner lens in—leaning back to avoid whapping his nose—and secured that. Through some trick of optics he didn't understand, the two pieces of reinforced ferroglass turned the straight-ahead view through the open port into a one-twenty-degree panorama. Things were a bit fish-eye straight ahead and a little compressed at the edges—and the barrel of the AC-20 still pretty well covered his right-side view—but it made steering the mobile gun easier.

There was a clang behind him as Beth brought down the observation hatch, which he knew she hated. Marvin had his viewport, Haverson had his command periscope and Joline had her gun sight, but with that hatch shut all Beth

could do was ride backward and look at cheap monitor
screens that—if Marvin understood what she'd said about
the metal in the factory district—weren't showing her much
but snow.

The automatic ventilation fans apologized for the lack of
fresh air with a whirring sound evidently intended to be
soothing. It certainly had nothing to do with cooling breezes.

"Can you find that BattleMech with the passive array,
Sanders?"

"Yes, sir," Beth answered. "The fusion reactor shows up
on thermal."

"DeMarshand, can you do that whirling turn any time
you want?"

"Always."

"Kline, can you hit what you aim at while deMarshand
is pushing this bucket full-tilt?"

"Piece of cake."

"Backward?"

"Even better."

"What's the plan, ki—Corp?" Marvin asked.

"Sidle up as close to that 'Mech's backside as we can,"
Haverson said. "Then pop out into whatever street it's on
and charge. Kline, you will have one block in which to take
your best shot. DeMarshand, at the first intersection, do
your spinning turn and *back* into the side street at full
speed."

"So if the 'Mech comes after us, it'll be facing our gun."
Marvin nodded, approving.

This kid's got skills.

"Can we do it?" Haverson asked.

"With or without blindfolds?" Joline countered.

Marvin fired up the diesel.

Marvin's first hint things weren't going right was the
front of the damn Ducky 'Mech where the back should
have been. Either the 'Mech had been backing up, or the
pilot had spun around to face them just before they'd
charged into the street. Which of course was four lanes
wide and devoid of anything you could hide a forty-ton
truck-with-gun behind.

He got a quick impression of very broad shoulders with

a box on each one and a medium laser on a one-eighty swivel mount where the head should have been. Then he focused on dodging as much as the road allowed as three laser beams lashed out.

One went wide, distracted by a metal building, another tore up the asphalt and the third, the head laser, slashed along the top of the Hetzer. The vehicle surprised Marvin by not melting into a puddle of molten lead.

"Hold straight!" Joline ordered.

Marvin pointed his nose at the 'Mech's right ankle, which should have put Joline's barrel about centerline, and accelerated. Full tilt in a Hetzer wasn't much; he hoped it was enough to confuse the 'Mech's targeting computer.

The yokes jerked in his hands as the H-WAG-7 rocked hard and veered right. He thought they'd been hit, then realized Joline had taken her shot. He fought the yokes, pulling the machine back on center.

Two blocks ahead of them, the Ducky BattleMech started to curtsy, its left knee joint bending sideways.

The box on its right shoulder belched smoke.

Marvin had just enough time to wonder if that was some sort of secondary explosion before the missile hit. Missile, singular, as in one out of six. Five blasted the pavement around them and the single hit blew up against their front armor just above his viewport. One of the few places on the coffin that could handle the explosion.

He had a brief glimpse of the 'Mech turning as it fell, its profile revealing the headless machine's cockpit stuck forward from its belly.

Then he executed a ninety-degree turn into a cross alley at speed. More bangs and curses behind and Marvin thought he felt the inside wheels lift free of the pavement.

"That was a *Night Stalker*!" Haverson said.

"His Beagle," Beth answered. "He saw us coming."

"Hell of a shot," Marvin said to Joline while the other two debated BattleMechs, their voices sharp with the adrenaline of survival.

"Aren't you supposed to be backing up?" Joline asked conversationally.

Marvin shook his head, slowing the Hetzer to a walk in the relative safety of the alley.

"That 'Mech ain't chasing us anywhere," he answered, then raised his voice. "Wasn't that a light?"

"Medium, forty tons," Haverson answered. "Heavy scout, Capellan design."

"So it's not the fifty-tonner we weren't running from?" Three-heartbeat pause.

"No." Haverson's voice was ten years older. "Sanders, see if you can find another fusion drive on infrared."

"Told you these things run in packs," Joline muttered.

32

Valken, Gallatin
Lyran Occupied Zone
Marik-Stewart Commonwealth
6 March 3138

Nikol Marik shuffled through the gate of the Lyran checkpoint, her duffel kit slung over her shoulder. She kept her eyes downcast and tried to keep her back straight and her shoulders hunched at the same time.

Defeated but not complacent, that's me, she imagined, transmitting the image into the guards' minds, willing them to see a beaten figure who hated the occupation forces but lacked the will to do anything about them. Too cocky and they'd do a body search just to take her down a notch. Too compliant among a population known to hate the Lyrans and she'd arouse their suspicions.

"Papers."

She dropped her duffel on the table, undoing the cinch for easy inspection before digging her ID chit and work order out of her shirt pocket. No worries there. The forged ID was some of SAFE's best work, and the work order was authentic: two weeks at double rations for helping clear rubble from the latest bomb blast.

Ten months after Gallatin officially fell to the Lyrans, and they were still dealing with insurgents. The hate emanating from the guard scanning her bag was palpable.

Small talk is not a good idea.

"Keep this on the outside," ordered the man who had checked her paperwork.

Without acknowledging she'd heard the instructions, Nikol clipped the ID to the top buttonhole of her thin jacket before stuffing the work order back in her shirt pocket.

Looking disappointed he hadn't found anything, the guard with the scanner shoved her bag at her. She fumbled to catch the open duffel before its contents spewed over the ground. Without looking up at either guard—or the gun tower overlooking the checkpoint—she hurried on her way.

Nikol stayed on the main thoroughfare, one of hundreds of walkers in a zone where vehicular traffic was banned. Sunday was traditionally a day of rest, but the luxury of observing tradition was one of many things the Lyran occupation had taken from the people of Gallatin.

The boulevard passed from the industrial district—and the destination on her work order—into blocks of modest apartments; housing for the factory workers. She saw two children sitting on the stoop of a tenement building, sharing a large picture book with no words on the cover. At the next alley she turned left.

Two blocks along the narrow street she passed beneath an elderly woman perched on a fire-escape landing to catch the warmth of the afternoon sun as she worked at her needlepoint. Nikol did not look directly at the woman and the woman did not look up from her hoop.

At the next building Nikol stepped suddenly sideways and shouldered aside a rusting metal door with a massive padlock. The door, padlock and all, swung silently open, almost dropping her into a bare room lit only by the sunlight following her in. The moment she was clear of its swing, the massive door shut silently behind her, filling the room with darkness.

Standing still, she waited a two count for the lights to come on.

When they did she was not surprised to find they were all directed at her. In the shadows at the edge of their glow she could make out half a dozen men and women with weapons leveled at her.

"So," said a man's voice, evidently from some point behind the first rank of armed sentinels, "what has Oriente sent us?"

A really terrific hostage if this does not go according to plan.

"We don't have much *to* send," she admitted, squinting in the lights. "Though the Marik-Stewart Commonwealth is taking the brunt of the assault, every nation along the borders of the Free Worlds League is being pressed by one enemy or another."

Her phrasing was tailored for this audience, allowing them to hear that her mother regarded their plight as more dire than that of Tamarind-Abbey. By not spelling out the fact that the only enemies "pressing" Oriente were Andurien and the Senate Alliance, she also created the impression that the Capellans were moving against the Protectorate. Building a sense of common bond without actually lying.

Though if the shadowy figures with leveled weapons felt a sudden upwelling of camaraderie, they were adept at hiding it.

"And what is this not much you are sending?" demanded the same male voice, with no change in inflection.

"This trip—pharmaceuticals, mostly, and other humanitarian supplies," Nikol answered. "Give me a list of supplies you need and I'll bring what I can next time."

"This trip? Plan on making us a regular stop on your trading runs, do you?"

"A regular stop? Yes, for as long as possible. But this is not trade. You're on the front lines fighting for the Free Worlds League. We're just doing what we can to support you."

"Mighty generous." The tone was sarcastic.

Nikol said nothing. Still blinking as her eyes adjusted to

the light, she waited for the person directing the challenging voice to make a decision.

"Who are you?" the voice demanded at last. "Why should we trust you?"

"I am Nikol"—she hesitated half a heartbeat—"Halas-Hughes Marik, daughter of the captain-general of the Oriente Protectorate."

At least one of the weapons trained on her moved; a black barrel elevated into the light as a carbine was raised from hip to shoulder. Nikol did not acknowledge the threat, keeping her eyes focused on the point from which the voice originated.

The silence stretched. Nikol was certain the speaker was conferring with someone, but she could not pick up the faintest whisper.

"So are you just here as the daughter of Lady Halas?" the voice asked. "Or do you have some official capacity?"

"I don't understand the question," Nikol said, ignoring the insult to her mother's name.

"Are you just a rich kid playing dress-up, acting alone, or do you have some official capacity in Oriente's government?" the voice all but sneered. "Do we address you as captain-general junior?"

You said be politic, Mother, but this is a military engagement.

Clenching her jaw, Nikol took a step toward the voice.

"You can call me anything you damn well want as long as we are both fighting for the Free Worlds League," she snapped. "But if you want to waste time on titles, you can call me the minister-general, because right now my job is getting to as many League worlds as I can and doing everything I can to make sure they *stay* League worlds."

Nikol glared around the circle, trying to pierce the shadows above the gun barrels, to find the eyes of the men and women holding the weapons. Not a muzzle moved.

"Now, you can send me on my way or you can do the Lyrans a favor and shoot me—or make them truly happy and turn me over to them," she said, turning her attention back to the voice. "*Or* you can accept the fact that any attack on any Free Worlds League planet is an attack on every member of the Free Worlds League, and take support when it's offered.

"Your choice."

The silence around her stretched.

33

Cendar Estate
Zletovo, Lesnovo
Rim Commonality
3 April 3138

Elderly. Elis watched as Michael Cendar received a verbal report from a force commander with oddly colored hair at the edge of the veranda. *Why did I ever consider him elderly? Have I aged so much in two years?*

Sipping her iced herbal tea, she admitted to herself it was possible. The politics of Oriente tended to accelerate the aging process.

More likely it was a maturing of her perceptions. She had learned from her mother how to observe political adversaries and allies; to weigh their potential threat or utility to the gram. From that perspective, Michael Cendar had been breathtakingly beautiful. But as the young woman Elis looking at the man Michael, she had mistaken the weight of responsibility for the burden of age.

Now, lounging in what Michael called an Adirondack chair—a far more rustic bit of furniture than anything found at cousin Gen's estate—enjoying a purposeless conversation as a long summer Sunday afternoon wound toward evening, she was discovering her future husband was much more vital and entertaining than the prime minister she remembered.

He's of an age with Thaddeus, she thought generously.

And a good bit less stuffy. Practically an untamed spirit by Rim Commonality standards.

Elis intended to do a bit to alter the standards of Rim Commonality society herself. In her role as the daughter of a distant duchess visiting a cousin twenty-one months ago, her refusal to wear corsets and insisting on only half the standard volume of fabric had been a quirk that amused social columnists. Now she was the fiancée of the prime minister, and her uncompromising stand on fashion was being viewed with alarm by the bulk of Commonality society.

If you find what I do to your couture disturbing, Elis thought toward the matrons of distant Zletovo, *wait until you see what I do to your government.*

"Good news, I see," she said as Michael returned. "Always something to be hoped for when mysterious soldiers appear."

"Forgive me." Michael's smile disappeared. "I am so used to keeping my duties separate from . . ."

His voice trailed off.

From the women you bring to your private retreat, Elis finished mentally. *Fortunately for both of us, a successful marriage of state does not require virginity.*

"Prime minister is not a hereditary title," Michael said. "A vote of no-confidence could be called at any time, and I could go back to being merely Lord Cendar."

"With your approval rating perpetually mired somewhere north of eighty percent through twenty years in office, that could happen at any moment," Elis agreed solemnly.

Michael laughed, a remarkably easy sound.

"What I meant was, administration of the Rim Commonality has always been something apart from the family life of the prime minister," he said. "We are about to usher in a new era in Commonality politics."

Elis nodded. The captain-generalcy of the Free Worlds League had once been an elected office, open to anyone. How many generations—and how many missteps—before it had become a Marik monopoly? People believed in blood, trusted heritage. The time was not too distant when only Cendars—or Marik-Cendars—could hold the highest office in the Rim Commonality.

As the first Lady Marik-Cendar, Elis would have no official standing in the government. At first. But that would change, and her husband-to-be was committed to being a part of bringing about that change. After twenty-some years of sole responsibility, he was looking forward to sharing the burden.

"So who was that messenger?" she asked aloud. "And what was her good news?"

"Force Commander Chowla of the First Rim Commonality Guard—"

"She must be over one hundred."

"Granddaughter of *that* Force Commander Chowla." Michael overrode her interjection. "And the good news she delivered is that she has arrived about a day ahead of Duke Wesley of Westover and his diplomatic party."

"Ah."

Michael was very proud of the new alliance he and the duke would be thumbprinting into law at the end of the week. One of Lester's schemes gone one hundred and eighty degrees wrong, it was the first in what Michael was sure would be a series of interlocking treaties with unaligned worlds beyond their borders. Treaties that would secure the Rim Commonality against anything the Regulan Fiefs—or the Duchy of Andurien or the Marian Hegemony—could muster.

"Next time—"

"I will present her to you," Michael agreed. "And you will receive all diplomatic reports firsthand, at my side."

Elis nodded complacently, sipping her tea.

Corsets are only the beginning.

34

"**A**re these figures accurate?"

"To the last decimal." Ignoring the fact that their relative up-down orientations were sixty degrees askew, Green met Thaddeus' gaze levelly. "The entire roster of assets available to form the Covenant Worlds First Expeditionary Force."

Thaddeus glanced left and slightly up. Colonel Timur of the Covenant Worlds Militia confirmed the assessment with a nod that set him bobbing at the end of his tether.

"It's almost an embarrassment of riches." Thaddeus thumbed through the screens again.

"The influx of Bordon's skilled labor gave Connaught greater flexibility in allocating support personnel, allowing them to safely deploy twenty percent more aerospace fighters than anticipated."

Thaddeus half listened to his lieutenants' reports as he reread the data.

Heavy on conventional forces. Savannah responded with only technical support and components, but Marian Arms either had a lot more ordnance in mothballs than anyone suspected or has outstripped expectations on rebuilding. He shook his head. *Disinformation is the stock-in-trade of the post-Jihad, even among our own member worlds.*

"Though not willing to cede command of planetary aerospace assets to other worlds," Timur was saying, "Connaught acknowledges their single *Miraborg* is overloaded and has accepted reallocation of several lances to Nathan and Alphard DropShips."

Still differentiating between planetary militias and the Covenant Worlds as a whole. Inconvenient, but true to their Free Worlds League heritage.

"The Protectorate Coalition contingent," Thaddeus said aloud. "These numbers exceed projections by almost sixty percent."

"Yes, sir," Green acknowledged. "I'll be reassessing our intelligence resources on Kalidasa."

"Normally I'd agree with you. But while I'm leading the Expeditionary Force against Andurien, you are going to be my eyes and ears on Oriente."

"Understood."

Tapping a few keys, Thaddeus tied the noteputer into the wardroom's projector. The data he'd been squinting at now occupied a three-square-meter screen against the far bulkhead. He spent a few minutes adjusting the information into an organizational chart. He was aware that he was micromanaging, taking on tasks that rightly belonged to Timur's staff. Had probably already been executed in much greater detail by Timur's staff, in fact. But he needed to manipulate the facts directly to set the variables in his own mind.

As he shifted and regrouped numbers, he was aware the digits represented thousands of men and women floating weightless, even as he did, within a hundred-kilometer radius of his position. Part of his mind wondered if they felt his machinations, like ghostly threads binding, then loosening as he tapped the keypad.

"The new assets are a bit lopsided, and as Connaught's aerospace illustrates, not all are willing to be fully integrated." Thaddeus frowned as he thought aloud. "Structuring this force is going to be as political as it is strategic. Without more 'Mechs, we'll need to find a way to leave behind some of these conventional forces and support personnel without hurting anyone's feelings."

"Perhaps they could be loaned to the Oriente military for the duration?" Green suggested. "That would not only help cement relations, it would form a physical connection between the militaries—a potential building block for future alliance."

"Support units tend to be subsumed," Thaddeus explained. "If we try to integrate them into Oriente's military, they'll be absorbed—disappear with no gain to the Covenant Worlds."

For another half minute he adjusted the organizational chart in silence, adding and subtracting connections, rearranging groupings. At last he felt he had a firm enough grasp of the situation to plan.

"Colonel Timur," he said, shutting down the screen. "I want a working organization plan in place by Monday. Is three days enough?"

"Yes, sir."

"We'll not have the luxury of shakedown exercises before we engage the Anduriens, so keep units that share some history together as much as possible," Thaddeus advised, aware his words were redundant for his commander. "Once the structure is right on-screen, it will take, what, a week to get the units reorganized and distributed among the DropShips?"

"If that, sir."

Thaddeus considered a moment. Had he forgotten anything? Aware of two sets of eyes on him, he nodded once, decisively. "The Covenant Worlds Expeditionary Force will jump out-system on May second."

Dormuth, Marik
Oriente Protectorate
26 April 3138

Dayton Withers refrained from adjusting his collar as he watched the ovKhan of the Sea Foxes and the Star colonel of the Spirit Cats read the analyses he'd prepared. Actually, only the ovKhan was reading the noteputer screen, evidently absorbing every detail; the Spirit Cat had tabbed through a few pages, then set the machine on the table.

It was a perfectly ordinary round table, cheap wood meant to be covered with a tablecloth. Something out of a midpriced restaurant, Dayton guessed. Meant to seat either six or eight depending on how formal the arrangement was. What made the table unusual—besides his sharing it with two Clan warlords—was the BattleMech-sized chandelier directly overhead and the magnificent ballroom stretching away in all directions.

Dayton was never comfortable negotiating with Clanners. It wasn't just their touchy egos, though those were legendary; it was the fact that their cultural assumptions proceeded from a fundamentally different worldview. Honor, for example, meant something akin to appearing above reproach while doing everything necessary to win, because only those who won were able to pass on their genetic material.

Pass on their genetic material. Not having kids—families—that was the core of the difference.

But prickly egos and the brittle definition of honor meant he'd had to word the captain-general's proposal carefully. Her bald statement of what she wanted the Clans to do for Oriente had lacked her usual subtlety.

Read like a direct order, in fact.

"Thank you, Penelope."

Dayton followed the sound to discover a giantess had emerged from the row of columns to his left. It took him a moment to realize he was looking over the head of the speaker. Between him and the elemental, a woman was propelling her wheelchair forward with rhythmic thrusts.

Captain-General Jessica's daughter, Dayton realized. The lady Julietta.

Evidently satisfied her charge had been delivered safely, the giant woman turned without comment and disappeared into the shadows.

"Please do not get up," Julietta said as Dayton gathered himself.

"Milady," he acknowledged, turning his near-rising into a seated bow from the waist as she wheeled the last few meters to the table.

The Spirit Cat leader looked toward Lady Julietta, and Dayton thought he smiled. At least the corners of his mouth twitched and his eyes seemed to lighten. The Sea Fox ovKhan did not raise his scarred head.

Dayton noted Lady Julietta's face was flushed with exertion, but not alarmingly so.

"It is good to see you well, milady."

"Thank you, Sir Dayton. Pardon my lateness, but when nerves are healing they sometimes need to rest. The motor nerves to my legs do not seem to be in the mood to work this morning."

"I can only imagine how frustrating that must be." Dayton did not mention that he could easily imagine how terrifying it must be to fear every setback might be permanent.

"Thank you, Sir Dayton."

Lady Julietta's genuinely appreciative tone made him wonder if she'd read his thoughts as well. Or perhaps living among the laconic Clanners these weeks left her starved for common courtesies.

"Fourteen pages to explain a proposition that required two sentences," the Sea Fox ovKhan announced.

"Only fourteen?" Julietta asked before Dayton could frame his apology. "Then Sir Dayton has already made an effort on your behalf. Though he'd never admit it in our presence, it is a credo that diplomats are paid by the word."

The ovKhan's grin was distorted by scar tissue, but genuine. Dayton could not remember ever seeing a Clanner smile with anything but malice.

"That would explain many spheroid contracts."

"What are the two sentences?" the Spirit Cat leader asked.

"Oriente would like us to garrison Abadan and Avellaneda, two worlds they've carved from the corpse of The Republic, while they send their troops to fight Andurien."

"They are ceding worlds they cannot hold?"

"You did not wait for the second sentence," the Sea Fox pointed out. "Following their victory over Andurien, Oriente will reinstate their garrisons and express their gratitude to us in any form we desire up to a mutually agreeable value."

"Mercenaries." The Spirit Cat spat the word.

"Essentially."

"Not quite," Julietta put in before Dayton could speak. "Oriente is the Oriente *Protectorate*—a form of governance in which a stronger world protects others. True, they control the protected world's dealings with other planets, but the world itself is autonomous. Marik is part of the Protectorate, though Oriente does not presume to interfere with Sea Fox trading practices. All spheroid powers in this region know that if they attack Marik, they will have to deal with Oriente."

"We do not need their help."

"No. But the fact that you have it without asking means other nations give careful thought to how they approach you," Julietta countered. "By asking us to assume a part of their role as protector, Oriente could be acknowledging a rise in Marik's international stature."

Could be, but isn't, Dayton thought. Then: *"Us"?*

He looked sharply at Lady Julietta, but her eyes were focused on the Spirit Cat leader and unreadable.

At least to him. The Clanner clearly saw something, for he nodded slowly, visibly considering Lady Julietta's words.

"This world is our haven, whether Oriente presumes to take any credit for that or not," the Spirit Cat said. "To extend the security we enjoy to protect other worlds can only be honorable."

Dayton kept his sigh of relief from escaping.

Definitely her mother's daughter. As smooth a save as I've ever seen.

The only false note in Dayton's mind was Lady Julietta's smile when he nodded his thanks to her. A small thing, really, considering the coup she had just pulled off for Oriente, but one he would always remember.

Lady Julietta looked very much like a cat that had swallowed a canary.

Starlord-*class JumpShip* Soledad
Zenith Jump Point, Savannah System
Former Prefecture VII
3 May 3138

"Sir!" The sharp syllable cut through the darkness of Captain Morristein's cabin.

A moment later someone on the bridge remembered emergency protocols and overrode his environmental controls, flooding his sleeping chamber with light.

By then Morristein had recognized the voice of his gamma-shift watch officer, now distorted by alarm.

"Go, Vincent," he said, slipping the tethers on his sleep net. Anything worth waking him up for was something he was going to have to make the bridge to handle.

"Unidentified jump signatures!" his third officer all but shouted.

"Multiple?"

"Yes, sir," Vincent confirmed. "Tally two—now three—*Merchant*-class JumpShips total. Close formation."

The disruption wave of three K-F jumps in close proximity . . .

"Are we clear?" he demanded, then cursed himself for a fool. The fact that he was alive to ask the question meant the *Soledad* was outside the primary event radius.

"Affirmative." Vincent's voice was calmer with each answer. Passing on the responsibility had a way of steadying the nerves. "Range thirty-seven thousand kilometers."

"Transponders?" Morristein asked, pulling on his soft neoleather duty boots. Their high-traction soles gave him an extra set of grippers for maneuvering in zero-g.

"None yet."

Morristein palmed open his door and launched himself down the short corridor to the bridge.

One JumpShip had run when the *Soledad* had jumped in-system four days ago, its K-F wave-front damaging one of its orphaned DropShips. A quick check of local star charts had revealed a half dozen agricultural worlds, a few industrial centers ravaged by the Blakists and a combination artists colony and tourist trap. With no one in the wilderness of the ex-Republic it could summon to relieve Savannah, that ship had run and kept running.

Whoever these raiders were—and only raiders would jump into a system in combat formation—they had no idea a Lyran battalion had seized Savannah. Some wayward pirates were about to get the shock of their lives.

At this range, it was possible that signals from the newcomers' automated identify friend or foe transponders hadn't reached them yet. Or it could be the mystery ships had jumped in "dark," a standard pirate and raider tactic since the dawn of the K-F drive.

"Make signal, all general channels," he ordered as he crossed the threshold into the command center. "Inform the newcomers they are now in Lyran space. Order them to stand down and prepare to be boarded."

He noted Vincent wasn't occupying the captain's chair in the center of the bridge, evidently preferring to float near the duty stations. He supposed the position gave him a better vantage of the screens, but the captain's repeater screens served the same purpose.

"They're deploying DropShips," the ensign on scanners reported. "Tally six."

That was not good. If there had been enough time for the

sensors to report DropShips detaching from the JumpShips, there had been enough time for the ships' transponder signals to reach the *Soledad*. The intruders were coming without identifying themselves.

"Is the *San Jeronimo* up to speed?" he asked, securing himself to his chair.

"Yes, sir." Vincent pressed a hand to the earpiece of his headphones. "Captain McCethan reports *San Jeronimo* at battle stations, intercept course laid in."

Morristein nodded. The fast and heavily armed *Kuan Ti*–class assault DropShip ordered to blockade the jump point was a match for any mix of fighters or DropShips a band of raiders was likely to cobble together. Or would have been under most circumstances.

Three JumpShips is more than anyone anticipated, Morristein admitted to himself. *And that bowstring-tight formation . . .*

Best keep this fight as far from the Soledad *as possible.*

"My compliments to Captain McCethan and tell him to proceed with intercept."

"Transponder signal," announced the communications officer.

Vincent bounced to the woman's station, gripping the back of her chair to steady himself. Morristein tapped a contact, pulling her display up on his own screen.

Covenant Worlds? He read the unfamiliar IFF signature. *Local strong-arm with delusions of grandeur?*

"Signal in clear on general channel seven," the comm tech added.

"Multiple bogies!" the ensign on scanners called out. "They've launched fighters."

"How many?"

"A wing, sir," the boy answered. "Maybe two. One of those DropShips must be a carrier."

"Amend that," Vincent said. He'd bounced across the bridge to hang over the young ensign's shoulder.

International law required combatants to identify their affiliation, not broadcast details of their force composition. Determining that required sensors, and officers who understood what those sensors told them.

"With that mass and energy . . . ." Vincent turned to face

Morristein. "It's a *Miraborg*. Current tally twenty-four fighters inbound, varying masses. No solid IDs yet."

A Clan DropShip? "Covenant" with whom?

"Get me Captain Henry," he ordered.

"*Apopka* here," Janet Henry's voice responded instantly from the overhead speaker. "Go ahead, *Soledad*."

Morristein hesitated. He was captain of the JumpShip, not commander of the military forces he was transporting. Colonel Daily had left his fighter carrier behind rather than risk it against a world with no appreciable air defense, but had not ceded command of the craft to the *Soledad*. Technically he could not directly order the deployment of the aerospace fighters aboard the *Okinawa*-class DropShip, but the situation demanded centralized response with no time for all of the formalities of offering compliments and making suggestions. He didn't know Henry well, but he decided to count on her pragmatism outweighing her adherence to protocol.

"Launch fighters," he ordered. Then, just in case, added, "Please."

"Already scrambled, sir," the carrier's captain answered, her word choice making clear her acceptance of his command.

"Keep the *Apopka* to close-defense position," Morristein ordered. "Deploy fighters to support the *Jeronimo*."

"Suggest holding six back to form defensive screen, sir," Henry answered. "In case any of the bogies get through."

"Agreed." Morristein bowed to her better knowledge of her fighters' capabilities. "We'll deploy our *Mark-VII* to your command."

Duke Vedet had replaced one of the *Soledad*'s deep-space shuttles with a military landing craft. It was of limited use in space, but Vedet had believed its six pulse lasers made it a viable close-defense option for the unarmed *Star Lord*.

Six aerospace fighters, a landing craft and the *Okinawa*-class fighter carrier in close defense formation: enough to handle anything that fought its way past McCethan's *Kuan Ti* and the rest of the *Apopka*'s wing? Morristein hoped he wouldn't have to find out.

He reminded himself that in a solo facedown of this sort,

who they were was more important than *what* they were. His small task force represented the might of the Lyran Commonwealth Armed Forces. The LCAF outmassed and outgunned anything a minor Free Worlds League state or Republic castoff could muster.

"Put the incoming signal on bridge speakers," he ordered.

"—your choice," a baritone voice said.

"Missed that, Covenant Worlds." Morristein kept his voice clear and level. No need to bluster. "Be advised that you are interfering with a lawful police action of the Lyran Commonwealth. Stand down and order your fighters to return to their berths or face the consequences."

"This is Warden Thaddeus Marik of the Covenant Worlds," the baritone voice responded with an equal lack of bluster. "And no invasion of our sovereign nation is lawful."

Morristein blinked at the name. He considered the various implications of a widely known former member of the Republic of the Sphere's failed oligarchy now calling himself "warden" of a new nation-state for all of four seconds before discarding it as irrelevant.

"We will debate whether an ad hoc association of worlds constitutes a sovereign nation some other time, Paladin," he answered. "The fact remains that no Covenant Worlds are recognized as such by the Lyran Commonwealth. More to the point, Savannah has been supplying arms and materiel to our enemies.

"Therefore, I order that you withdraw immediately or face the full force of the Lyran Commonwealth Armed Forces."

He watched the chronometer, mentally marking the point at which his words reached the rogue paladin commanding the upstarts and predicting when Marik's reply would reach him.

"DropShip formation splitting up," the sensor officer reported before the second hand reached the halfway point. "Tally four boosting toward planet."

"Again no hard ID," Vincent said before Morristein demanded *useful* information. "But from mass and burn it's probable there are two *Union*s, one *Fortress*, and one

Seeker planet-bound at one-point-five g's. The *Miraborg* is staying with the *Merchant*s, with the last six fighters deployed as a screen, and a DropShip is positioning itself between them and the *Jeronimo*'s approach vector. Not enough burn to be sure of mass, but best guess is an *Intruder*."

Doing the math, Morristein deduced a heavy battalion was going after Daily's battalion on the surface. An even fight for the Sixth, if they weren't already neck-deep in a firefight with Savannah's planetary militia.

"Send all data to Colonel Daily," he ordered. He glanced at the chronometer, confirming that Marik's reply was overdue.

"Obviously your forces deployed before you received my transmission," he said into the overhead mic. "I'll repeat my order that you withdraw from the system or face the full force of the Lyran Commonwealth."

"In that case, I'll repeat the choice which you say you missed," Marik said conversationally. "Unless you surrender the *Soledad* unconditionally, we are going to take out your sail. Then we're going to pare away enough hull and structure to make a jump suicidal.

"Your options, Captain Morristein, are surrender now and live, or have our construction crews space your remains later. Your choice."

"You're bluffing, Warden." Morristein sneered the title. "This is a *Star Lord* JumpShip. You wouldn't dare."

"Our Kong shipyards on Connaught build *Star Lord*s," Marik said without heat.

Morristein dismissed the claim that Connaught was building *Star Lord*s. Lyran military intelligence would have known. And if there were Republic JumpShip facilities within reach, Duke Vedet would not have wasted his time on a minor irritant like Savannah.

"A lie, Marik," he pronounced.

The silence stretched as his words crawled through the distance separating the JumpShips.

"Think what you like." Thaddeus Marik's voice remained maddeningly calm. "The fact remains that without your surrender, we will maroon the *Soledad* here and wait until you and your crew starve to death. Then it's only a matter of repairing any sabotage you thought of while dying using parts we have onboard. And slopping around a bit of bleach to remove the stench of your decomposition."

"Sir!" Vincent reported, ignoring the open microphone. "The attackers are flaring wide to bypass the *Jeronimo*. Captain McCethan is ordering fighters to intercept."

"Make no mistake, the *Soledad* is now property of the Covenant Worlds," Thaddeus Marik was saying, his words transmitted before Vincent had spoken. "Your only choice is whether or not you and your crew live to be repatriated.

"You have until the first shot is fired to decide."

Morristein chopped the air with his hand. Vincent correctly interpreted the gesture, relaying to the communications officer the order to kill the radio.

Whatever assets the Covenant Worlds possessed couldn't match what the Lyran Commonwealth could bring to bear. In theory. However, they weren't facing the might of the Lyran Commonwealth. Just a single JumpShip that had ferried a battalion of expendable troops to a backwater world. This thrust at Savannah was a minor, punitive sortie while Duke Vedet focused on his campaign against Stewart.

Depending on how the war against the Commonwealth worlds went, it could be weeks before Duke Vedet realized he hadn't heard from the Savannah mission. And likely more weeks before he became curious enough about their fate to dispatch anyone to find out what had happened.

If he had the resources to spare.

If anything, he'd send a scout ordered to quickly assess the tactical situation and return. Whether fire was exchanged with the Covenant forces holding the jump point or not, the *Soledad* would almost certainly be presumed lost. The most they could hope for from Vedet was the minuscule chance he'd order a punitive strike to avenge them.

Despite Morristein's invocation of Lyran might, this was not a confrontation between the Lyran Commonwealth and the Covenant Worlds. This was between him and Thaddeus Marik: whatever resources he had against whatever forces the self-styled warden could bring to bear.

"Attackers have revectored," the scanner officer reported. "Wing has split. Twenty are bearing on *Soledad*. Four are on course through the sail."

"Through?" Morristein echoed. "Not to?"

"The fighters have passed skew flip point," the officer replied. "They cannot stop in time."

"Time to weapons contact?"

"One minute twelve seconds."

Morristein studied the situation tank. He could feel the seconds slipping away from him, but he forced his mind to slow down; to think.

Our fighters are outnumbered almost two to one. And with a Miraborg *and an* Intruder *to contend with, the* San Jeronimo *is no threat to their JumpShips. If they abandon us, the* San Jeronimo *and* Apopka *might make Savannah, but unless Daily wins, that's just delaying the inevitable.*

If the Covenant force really was willing to damage the *Soledad* . . .

"Tactical channel," Morristein said.

The communications officer flipped a toggle on her console and a green light glowed on the arm of the command chair.

Morristein cleared his throat. Glancing at the chronometer, he made a note of the day and time his career ended.

"Captain McCethan, Captain Henry." He cleared his throat again. Just as he didn't technically have the authority to order them into combat, he did not have the authority to enforce his next order. He could only hope their common sense would prevail.

"The *San Jeronimo* and *Apopka* are to stand down from battle stations," he ordered. "All fighters return to berths."

"General channel," Morristein said. A second telltale came alive.

"This is Captain Bernard Morristein of the Lyran Commonwealth *Star Lord* JumpShip *Soledad*," Morristein said clearly. "We surrender."

Eyes on the situation tank, he watched for some sign anyone cared what he said.

37

Picasso, Ariel
Marik-Stewart Commonwealth
16 May 3138

"We did not expect the captain-general to respond so quickly."

The round viscount reminded Nikol of someone, but she couldn't quite place the memory. Perhaps there were generic similarities shared by civil servants who had comfortably secured their place at the pinnacle of their career and intended to hold position until retirement. Something that enhanced the sense of smugness.

Though Minister—Fallow?—didn't appear smug. He seemed understandably perplexed that a member of Oriente's ruling house had appeared on his doorstep without warning. He was still standing, too startled to offer her a seat or to resume his own, behind a broad desk adorned with a neat stack of papers and three datascreens.

If nothing else, the man can multitask.

"The captain-general will not receive your request for another week," she answered aloud. "Your courier discovered I was on Oceana and wisely chose to deliver the message to me while her JumpShip was recharging. It was her good fortune that I have been appointed to speak for the captain-general in all matters pertaining to the current Wolf-Lyran crisis. However, at the request of your courier, I sent her on to Oriente so that she might complete the letter of her original mission."

"Ah."

"I apologize for not announcing my presence when I arrived in-system. With the situation being what it is, I thought it best I travel incognito."

"Oh no, think nothing of *that*, Minister-General. A purely reasonable precaution." Her host nodded vigorously. "Please do not mistake my surprise for any form of censure."

Nikol blinked at his use of her "title."

Just how complete is the grapevine out here?

Evidently coming to himself, the viscount got her settled into a chair and established that she desired nothing to eat, drink or smoke before finally sitting down behind his desk. With three taps the datascreens went dark and an economical sweep of his arm dropped the stack of papers into a shallow drawer. Clasping his hands on the bare desktop, he made it clear that Nikol had his undivided attention.

As he busied himself clearing the desk, Nikol took the opportunity to glance around the planetary administrator's spacious but clearly functional office. A modest flat-image picture, displayed where a visitor's eye would naturally fall, depicted a younger and decidedly more slender viscount standing beside an excavation of some sort, one hand resting on a sign that read FARROW.

Glad I saw that before I misspoke his name.

"Two aspects of your request to the captain-general struck me, Viscount Farrow." Nikol played her opening salvo. "First, that you felt it likely Ariel would be both attacked and left undefended. Second, that you addressed your appeal to Captain-General Jessica Marik, not to the government of the Marik-Stewart Commonwealth. I wanted to hear your reasoning directly from you."

Farrow nodded.

"What do you know of Ariel?"

"No major manufacturing, no known military presence," Nikol recited from the dossier she had read coming in-system. "A center for the arts, particularly trading in fine and decorative visual and kinetic pieces."

"Are you familiar with our sand sculptures?"

"I have heard of them." Nikol began to wonder where the viscount was leading her. "Though I have never seen one."

"You never will, unless you are present when one is

being created. They are deliberately transitory, and tradition forbids that any be permanently recorded." He indicated the picture of his younger self beside the sign. "The most you will ever see is an image of the artist beside his work, framed to document only that the sculpture existed, not what it looked like."

"I see," Nikol lied.

"Lady Marik, can you imagine trying to base the economy of an entire planet on the sale of paintings and the creation of sculptures that never last more than a fortnight?"

"You're saying Ariel has other assets."

"Civil servants and data management," Farrow confirmed. "There are Ariel citizens involved with the nuts-and-bolts day-to-day running of planetary administration on a dozen worlds in this region. Keystone is perhaps the most dramatic example. The McMahon family is rightly focused on rebuilding the industrial infrastructure lost to the Blakists. All other aspects of planetary operations, from schools to sewers, are handled by our people."

Nikol nodded, accepting the information on face value but making a note to have her own people confirm it independently.

"Ariel's central location makes us a natural data and communications hub, as well," Farrow was saying. "Every major banking institution and information distribution network has a presence here—administered by their people, of course, but staffed by ours."

"Are you implying you have access to all of that data?" Nikol asked. "Or that you have information on the inner workings of neighboring worlds?"

"Oh, good heavens, no." Farrow's genuine shock was nearly comic. "I meant that if the Lyrans or the Wolves discover how central Ariel is to the administration of the Marik-Stewart Commonwealth, they will loot us, expecting to find a trove of vital information."

Nikol did not bother to disabuse the viscount of his misconception. The Wolves and the Lyrans were bent on acquiring real estate—worlds they could shape in their own image. Data of the sort Farrow described would be of tertiary interest to them at best.

Now, if Ariel were a clearinghouse for military *information . . .*

It was easy to see what had happened. Viscount Farrow had appealed to Anson's administration for defense that he thought was glaringly vital, and had been ignored. As the man responsible for the safety of a world with no military assets, he'd then turned to the only other ruler he thought could possibly help.

Taken out of context, there was nothing about the planet Ariel that would inspire the Oriente Protectorate to come to the world's aid. But Ariel as a symbol—the first world of the Marik-Stewart Commonwealth to reach out to Captain-General *Jessica* Marik . . .

"My instinct is to help," Nikol said aloud. "But your position—as you said, central to the trade of the Marik-Stewart Commonwealth—presents certain political and logistical problems."

"The politics I will leave to you, Minister-General," Farrow assured her. "But logistics are our lifeblood. In fact—"

The viscount stopped, as though surprised at what he had been about to say. Nikol watched the internal struggle play itself out on his mobile features. Farrow, she decided, was a man ill-suited to politics or poker.

"Our position on so many worlds does give us certain insights," Farrow said at last. "Nothing that would violate our employers' trust in our discretion, but a firm sense of where the winds are blowing."

"I understand," Nikol prompted.

"Even without the Lyran-Wolf invasion—" the viscount stopped himself. Visibly adjusting what he'd been about to say, he added: "Given the current situation, it is likely that Captain-General Jessica Marik may soon find she has a need for Ariel's services in coordinating the administrations of several worlds in this region."

38

Thaddeus Marik slammed sideways, the harness digging into his flesh as *Kriegaxt* rocked under multiple missile impacts.

Seven hits, the tactical computer informed him, and the wire-frame schematic of his *Warhammer IIc 4* mapped minor armor losses along the right torso. Collapsing plumes of dirt testified to eight misses. From their pattern, the missiles had been descending when they struck.

More important, his tactical scanner showed no enemy 'Mechs. Turning to face the direction from which the missiles had come, he saw only rolling grassland stretching to the horizon.

That's not grass, Thaddeus corrected himself, then smiled at his own literal-mindedness.

The purple fronds of what the locals called heather—some rising as high as his 'Mech's knees—bore no resemblance to grass. But the rippling waves of resilient plants yielding beneath the breeze would have been familiar to prairie dwellers on a hundred worlds. Grassland was as good a name as any.

The rolling terrain was more significant than the vegetation covering it. The composition of the soil did not block sensors, but the topography confused the tactical computers. The folded earth created false horizons below which the computers did not scan; since the angles varied with every fall and rise, the computer's automatic algorithms did not compensate effectively. Valleys and ravines were often invisible until they were too close to ignore.

Replaying the sensor log, Thaddeus was not surprised to see fifteen long-range missiles rising out of solid ground. Something in a narrow arroyo had launched an indirect barrage. No doubt the sniper had already vacated the position, moving to another vantage point, but Thaddeus pointed *Kriegaxt* at the missiles' point of origin and shoved the throttle forward.

"Ex-one-alpha to Ex-one-company," he broadcast on the tac channel.

"Copy, one-alpha," a crisp alto voice responded immediately.

Sergeant Alma Peterson, commanding Boxer lance, Ex-Force First Company, Thaddeus identified.

He didn't know who had first called the Coventry Expeditionary Force "Ex-Force"—a name that sounded too much like a B-vid action serial for his tastes. But it was obvious that his people enjoyed the name, maybe precisely *because* it was so cheesy, so he adopted it without comment.

It's the little things that bind a unit together.

"Snakes in the valley," he reported. "Repeat, indirect enemy contact, apparent ravine in grid tango-seven. Moving to investigate."

"First Boxer lance moving to support," Peterson said. "ETA one forty."

Thaddeus double-clicked a standard affirmative.

Boxer-one was four mediums, all jumpers and all faster than *Kriegaxt*. He couldn't have asked for a better support mix in this situation. Still . . .

Eyes scanning the deceptively rolling ground ahead of him, Thaddeus advanced on the missile launch-point. Fully aware that going into single combat made as much sense as the warden taking a personal role in the ground search, he intended to settle this skirmish before the other BattleMechs arrived. That gave him—he glanced at the chronometer—one minute and thirty-two seconds.

Though he couldn't see it, he knew the ravine the sniper had fired from was now in range of his own brace of ATM-6s. A status check confirmed that the variable-ordnance short-range missile launchers were feeding from the high-explosive magazine. Perfect for laying down a devastating carpet of fire. But he wasn't going to risk an indirect salvo.

The tactical situation on El Giza was complicated by hundreds of civilian settlements scattered about the prairie. The First Expeditionary had already stumbled across one community of several hundred civilians hidden from sensors by a fold of earth. Thaddeus could not imagine how they sustained themselves—he saw nothing that looked like organized agriculture, much less industry—but entire villages seemed to dot the landscape. Or would, if they weren't universally located at the bottom of invisible valleys.

Worse, the lack of trees meant the buildings were constructed of local adobe over frames of metal scavenged from who knew where. This gave a distinctly military spin to initial readings whenever the sensors first detected a village.

He didn't think a MechWarrior would use civilians as cover, but Thaddeus had seen too many things that shook his fundamental beliefs in the last decade. He would not fire without visual confirmation of his target and risk blasting a village simply to avoid weathering another flight of long-range missiles.

In the days of the First Star League, El Giza had been a major trade nexus and Defense Force base on the border between Capellan space and the Free Worlds League. The regional center of communication and entertainment industries, it had boasted a thriving academic culture, with scholars from all over the rimward half of the Star League attending its many universities.

With the collapse of the Star League, the military, intellectual, industrial and economic resources that had made the world a cultural mecca became its greatest liability. A rich prize, the world had changed hands violently a dozen times before the Free Worlds League wrested control away from the Capellan Confederation. By then the planet had been effectively destroyed; what had not been plundered had been razed to deny rivals any advantage.

As a valueless backwater, El Giza had passed through the Jihad unscathed—or, more accurately, without suffering further destruction. As far as he knew, even Daoshen Liao's obsession to "reclaim" all worlds formerly Capellan did not extend to this barren planet.

The Duchy of Andurien considered the world strategically valuable if not intrinsically. Near the major trade hub of Mosiro, this was the base of operations for the Fourth Andurien Cavalry—a grandiose name for what was essentially a heavy mixed company tasked with pirate control. A gutted world and tiny military presence would be bypassed in most campaigns, left for the occupation forces to deal with. However, their proximity meant the Fourth Cavalry was in a position to support the Second Andurien Guards on Mosiro.

And Mosiro was the Ex-Force's objective. A vital industrial and transportation center, the world was the economic lynchpin of the coreward third of the Duchy of Andurien. Taking Mosiro was key to cutting off the Duchy's ability to make war against the Protectorate.

While Thaddeus was confident the First Expeditionary could defeat the Second Guard, sound strategy dictated they neutralize the Fourth Cavalry on El Giza before engaging Mosiro's defenders.

The Fourth Cavalry comprised light, fast machines, well suited to fighting raiders but no match for the heavier assets of the First Expeditionary in a stand-up fight. Which is why the Anduriens had used their speed and mobility to disappear when the Covenant Worlds' forces arrived.

What surprised Thaddeus was that they did not withdraw completely from the planet. Making a stand alone against the superior Covenant force made no sense strategically or tactically. The Cavalry should have joined the Second Guard at its first opportunity—and Thaddeus had made sure they had the opportunity. Instead, they had dug in, harassing the Marik troops from concealed bases.

The tactic had slowed the Oriente advance for a few days while they dug out the Cavalry, but the Duchy force was being destroyed piecemeal. The cost was far too high to buy Mosiro a few extra days. But Thaddeus dared not leave the Cavalry at his back, so the Second Guard was getting nearly a week to prepare for his assault while he rooted out their cousins on El Giza.

The staple scene of holovid war stories since time immemorial, in which a DropShip pinpoints all enemy assets from orbit, was a fiction of the entertainment industry. Even with the most sophisticated sensors available, a

DropShip could miss a major base unless it knew where to look. The problems increased exponentially when hunting for scattered units determined to elude scans. Planets were *big.* An effective search required coordinating orbital scans from DropShips with aerospace flyovers and straightforward walking the ground and looking. And Thaddeus, warden of the Covenant Worlds, required some time in the cockpit of his BattleMech to work out the frustrations of command.

The ground dropped away before him. Lost in thought, Thaddeus was a half second late in responding and yanked back on the stick, throwing the machine's center of gravity past its heels. He brought a leg back in time to prevent a fall, but the lip of the bank crumbled under the weight of one heel. The MechWarrior shuffled quickly, working to keep his eighty-ton BattleMech from tumbling into the ravine.

Anywhere else an erosion gully like this would be a raw scar. How fast does this heather grow?

Alarms hooted as heavy metal boiled out of the ground to his left.

Stepping back from the precipice, Thaddeus swung his left particle projection cannon to bear without turning the BattleMech's torso. The blue torrent of hyperaccelerated particles crossed paths with four flickering ruby firestorms. Heat filled his cockpit as the combat computer reported four solid hits, medium pulse lasers melting armor from his arm and side.

The computer identified the birdlike shape racing to cross behind him as a *Men Shen.*

A fifty-five-ton machine with twice the speed of the *Warhammer,* armed with four pulse lasers and a long-range missile rack and guided by a sophisticated Beagle Active Probe sensor system, the Hellespont-built machine was a perfect pirate fighter. Or raider. What it was not good for was going toe-to-toe with an eighty-ton bruiser like Thaddeus' *Kriegaxt.* The Fourth Cavalry pilot would use his superior speed and maneuverability to bring down the larger 'Mech.

Or try to.

Not bothering to follow the faster machine's flight, Thaddeus snap-pivoted the *Warhammer*'s torso right. Dead-reckoning the course and speed, he triggered both ATMs, laying down an oblique pattern of twelve high-explosive missiles across the Andurien's path.

None of them hit, of course, but the *Men Shen* squatted back on its odd double-kneed legs as the pilot threw his machine back and sideways to avoid them. In the heartbeat it took the BattleMech's myomer muscles to overcome inertia and change direction, the machine was standing still.

That moment was all his targeting computer needed to get a lock.

The twin lightning bolts of his *Warhammer*'s paired PPCs flashed garishly against the purple of the heather. They converged on the *Men Shen*'s left hip assembly, just ahead of the laser mounts; two solid hits only meters apart. Armor exploded away as the 'Mech staggered.

Wreathed in the oily black smoke of burning myomer, the Andurien planted his good leg and pivoted to face Thaddeus. Fifteen long-range missiles launched the same instant as twelve short-range missiles left the *Warhammer*'s tubes, but their longer acceleration curve meant the LRMs were still in the air when the *Men Shen*'s forward-thrust cockpit disappeared beneath a firestorm of high-explosive impacts.

TEN HITS, Thaddeus read from the tac screen just as the Andurien's posthumous retaliation hit.

Twelve explosions walked across *Kriegaxt*'s chest and shoulder, destroying the right-side missile launcher and staggering the machine backward. Fighting the tillers, Thaddeus kept his machine upright.

"Ex-one-alpha, this is Boxer lance," the young voice sounded in his ear. "We have you on visual. What is your status."

Thaddeus eyed the Andurien BattleMech in front of him. The forward third of the machine had simply come apart, structural members peeled back as though his salvo had triggered some sort of internal explosion. He'd never heard of that effect and wondered at its significance.

Half your missiles entered through the cockpit, he reminded himself. *Don't overthink this.*

"Ex-one-alpha?"

"Affirmative," Thaddeus answered. "Tally one *Men Shen*

down. No sign of any others. Not that that means much out here."

"Concur, one-alpha," Peterson answered. "First Cat lance reports what appears to be the remains of a city bordering grid zebra fourteen. Looks like it hasn't been lived in since the Star League."

Thaddeus rotated his BattleMech until he was facing north-northwest, toward zebra fourteen. From the vantage of his low rise at the edge of the ravine, he could see a smudge as broad as his thumb along the horizon. It looked to him like nothing so much as a ridge of dirt.

"Meaning Sergeant Morris thinks there's something inside."

"That's affirmative, sir."

"The ravine this Andurien was using to sneak up on me looks like it leads back toward his location," Thaddeus said. "Let's follow it and see what he's found."

39

Amur, Oriente
Oriente Protectorate
30 June 3138

Jessica Marik fought the urge to rise out of her seat and twirl.

She'd almost danced when she'd heard the Lyrans had attacked the Marik-Stewart Commonwealth. Now she wanted to declare a day of dancing in the streets.

Anson Marik is dead!

The words were a tuneless song singing through her head as she reread the report.

A gust of wind rattled the windows of the solarium, startling her. She glanced through the insulated glass surrounding her, surprised to see the garden subdued in shades of green and russet and washed in the watery sun of autumn. News of this import should have caused the garden to burst into full spring regalia; her spirit demanded bouquets and birdsong.

As if in answer, a lone mockingbird swooped from cover to pounce on some unsuspecting insect. She watched for a moment as it stalked across the grass. Every few steps it rose to its full height and spread its wings, hoping to startle another potential prey into revealing its presence by fleeing.

There's a metaphor there, but I'm not sure for what.

Jessica's only regret at Anson's passing was that the arrogant pustule would not be alive to see her ascend the throne of the reunited Free Worlds League. If he weren't already dead, that would kill him.

She smiled as the mockingbird pounced on another bug.

"The Lyrans claim he died begging for his life," Philip observed, reading his own copy of the report. "Anson never begged for anything in his life."

Jessica's smile grew warmer as she considered her husband's profile while he read, oblivious of her observation. Technically her ex-husband now, though the only changes to their relationship had been for the better.

Philip often observed with some satisfaction that he was able to spend much more time with his wife since "leaving" Jessica. His seclusion in the family quarters of the palace gave him greater access to her than when he'd been traveling about as her representative. The only regret he expressed about his "missing" status was the loss of his beloved thrice-weekly golf game.

"More to the point," Jessica said. "If he'd been alive enough to beg, the Steiners would have kept him alive enough to be used for propaganda."

"The Marik-Stewart news feeds say he went down fighting, a gun in each hand," Philip read.

"I would think a gun in one hand and a leg of mutton in the other more likely."

"Jessica," Philip reproved mildly. "We need to show some respect for the dead."

"I have no intention of showing respect for a boor who made clear at every turn he despised me when alive," Jessica said. "Privately. Publicly, of course, there will be a poignant yet not maudlin declaration of our grief as we proclaim a day of mourning."

"Do you think you're up to delivering such a declaration without giggling?"

"I have people, Philip," Jessica said primly. "Trained professionals who can stand in my stead as I recover from the emotional shock of this news."

Philip chuckled, a sound she'd heard more often since his "exile" had relieved him of duties.

You never wanted power, did you, dearest? A quiet life with me is all you've ever desired.

"Why Stewart, I wonder?" Philip was reading the report again.

"What?"

"If I'm reading between the lines correctly, a sizable number of his forces got off-planet," Philip said. "Why didn't he go, too? Why make a stand on Stewart?"

"Perhaps he got cut off," Jessica said, but the words did not feel right. "Or perhaps he just got pissed off."

"Dear, neither duchesses nor captains-general should talk like guttersnipes," Philip observed. "But I think you're right. Going out in a blind rage sounds just like him."

"We should get word to Nikol to be on the lookout for the forces that escaped," Jessica said. "Without a Marik-Stewart Commonwealth to fight for, they'll be looking for a home."

"Difficult to imagine," Philip said, "a world without the Marik-Stewart Commonwealth. I had always expected the irritation of Anson Marik to be a constant in our lives. He was always the biggest opponent to your captain-generalcy."

"Physically the largest," Jessica agreed. "And the loudest. But not the most dangerous."

First Regulan Hussar Command
Mohenjo Daro, Regulus
Regulan Fiefs

"Damn that arrogant bastard!" Lester Cameron-Jones crumpled the report in his fist and slammed it down on his desk. "If he weren't dead, I'd kill him."

"Sir?" Salazar asked.

The man blinked when Lester turned on him. It did him good to see a man twice his size daunted by what little threat he represented.

Don't be an ass, Lester corrected himself. *It's your position, not your rage that gives him pause.*

My rage. I'm thinking—I'm not thinking—*like Anson.*

Lester turned away from his SAFE director. He wanted to pace, but this was the military-issue office he used when at Base Mohenjo Daro. A quarter the size of his study at the palace in Chebbin, it simply didn't have the room for serious pacing. He contented himself with four stiff steps to the window and stood there, left hand massaging his right fist. He was getting too old to punch unyielding metal desks.

On the exercise ground the mixed forces of the Steel Hussars, resplendent in full dress colors, were forming up for his annual review. The sight of the military power at his disposal calmed his nerves.

He was self-aware enough to recognize that deriving comfort from so superficial a source indicated just how raw his nerves were. Regulating his breathing, he willed his pulse to slow.

"Anson Marik has died," he said, breaking the obvious down into words of one syllable for his chief of intelligence. "Without leaving me one command protocol, one breakdown of assets, one *comm number* to call."

"That gluttonous bastard always said he wasn't leaving much behind. But *this*—"

Lester realized he was growling through clenched teeth and paused. With an effort he relaxed his jaw. Lowering his shoulders required a bit more effort. He wished Emlia were here. Discussing issues with her was far more satisfying.

"There was supposed to be a contingency plan in place, a way for me to continue the fight for the Marik-Stewart Commonwealth if he fell," Lester said—still angry but sounding, he hoped, a bit more rational. *Anson is the one who throws tantrums. Was.* Turning away from the orderly arrangement of war machines beyond the window, Lester deliberately strolled back to his temporary desk, which was still covered with the readiness reports that a moment ago had been interesting reading. "Instead, Anson Marik chose to believe himself invincible and made no plans for continuing his realm after his death. With no unified defense, the worlds are going to fall piecemeal to the Lyrans and the Wolves.

"And with almost all of his forces massed at the other end of the Commonwealth, I have no way to reach them quickly, no way to coordinate command." Lester noticed he'd raised his fist again and lowered it. "The Commonwealth is going to fall because of one man's arrogance."

"My impression has always been that the Marik-Stewart Commonwealth was very much a nation of personality," Salazar said in his maddening monotone. "Perhaps Anson Marik made no plans for its survival beyond his death because he knew that without him there would be no Marik-Stewart Commonwealth."

Lester looked sharply at his subordinate, but the larger man's face remained as blandly impassive as his voice.

"You're saying that the Commonwealth no longer exists?"

"My assessment is that it ended on June fifth, when Anson Marik fell."

Lester felt his eyebrows climbing toward his hairline.

Every now and then, Gustav. Every now and then you remind me why I keep you around.

His mind racing, Lester turned again to regard the Hussar BattleMechs and armor arrayed in neat rows on the exercise field. Salazar and the urgent communiqué he carried had delayed the scheduled review. The morning sunlight glittered off every polished edge and plane of heavy metal. Weapons hungry for use.

"If the Marik-Stewart Commonwealth no longer exists," he said, "there are worlds that depended on its protection that are now helpless in the face of the Lyran-Wolf onslaught."

"That is my thinking, Your Grace."

"Salazar, prepare me a detailed analysis of the Atreus system. Everything we know about its defenses and assets." Lester's tone was thoughtful. "That's a vital world—a symbolic world—that needs our protection. But we'd best be prepared in case the citizens don't see the Fiefs taking them under our wing in quite the same light."

"Already done, Your Grace," Salazar said, producing a noteputer from his attaché case. "I took the liberty of preparing tactical analyses of the Alterf and Ionus systems as well."

Lester made no effort to hide his pleased surprise as he took the noteputer from his security chief's hand.

"Mr. Salazar," he said as he keyed the machine on, "would you be so kind as to inform Colonel Petrovski that the First Hussars should stand down from review? Then ask that he and his staff officers join me in the situation room posthaste."

Tamarind-Abbey Defense Command
Tripoli, Gibraltar
Duchy of Tamarind-Abbey

"Damn."

Fontaine Marik looked up from the noteputer and met Roland's eye. Outside, a winter storm had turned the noonday to a swirling cauldron of grays and whites—more blow than blizzard, it made travel impossible.

"Damn," he repeated flatly.

"What happened?" Christopher asked.

The question startled Fontaine. He'd half forgotten the boy existed despite the fact he'd been in conversation with him when Roland arrived.

The duke handed the noteputer across the chessboard, letting the young man see for himself.

He was beating me anyway, he thought, looking over the array of the interrupted match. *Checkmate in . . . four. I let myself get distracted by that damn rook feint of his.*

"Anson Marik is dead?"

"On that both the Lyrans and Commonwealth agree," Fontaine said. "Though there is some disconnect on the details."

"The headline says suicide," Christopher read. "Then the article goes on to detail twelve bullet holes in his body and head, only three of which could *not* have been lethal, or at least critical. Who okayed a stupid release like that?"

"Trillian Steiner oversees propaganda and disinformation," Roland said. "But I agree that lacks her usual finesse."

"More important than how he died is the fact that he's dead." Fontaine extended his hand for the noteputer. "Without him there's no core to the Commonwealth."

"Nonsense," Christopher said. Then added at the duke's expression, "Sir."

It wasn't the lack of address that had startled Fontaine, but he let it pass, interested in seeing how the lad analyzed the situation.

"A chain of succession and transitional protocols are fundamental to any government." The lad waved as though able to indicate the precept floating somewhere in the air above the chessboard. "The new leadership won't be as flamboyant as Anson was, but the Commonwealth will survive."

Ah.

"A chain of succession and transitional protocols are fundamentals of government to careful planners like your mother and old men aware of their mortality," Fontaine explained. "Anson believed himself invincible, and governed his nation as though he were immortal. It is widely known that he counted no one his heir. You can take it as a given that there's no orderly shift in command structure planned for any individual or body."

Christopher's expression of surprise was almost comic. Then it transformed into something decidedly more thoughtful. Wordlessly, he turned to the window, staring out at the swirling snow with furious concentration.

Fontaine half smiled. He was willing to acknowledge Christopher was his master at chess and had heard rumors of his skill with dice; but those were games of skill and probability. The boy was going to have to learn to school his expressions—to not visibly announce his every thought and feeling—if he was ever going to win at poker. Or rule a nation.

Roland began to speak, but Fontaine forestalled him with a raised finger. Watching his young protégé, he waited for the lad to quit worrying whatever bone he'd latched on to and give them his thoughts.

"This can work to our advantage," Christopher said at last.

"How so?"

The boy turned from his contemplation of the weather to regard Fontaine levelly.

"If the Commonwealth is coming unraveled without Anson at the center, the worlds are going from a united nation to individual planets," he explained. "Capturing solo worlds is easier than waging war with a nation. But capturing many individual worlds is a time-consuming process."

"Meaning you expect the Lyrans to suspend their campaign against us and focus their resources on the orphaned worlds of the former Commonwealth."

"It makes sense."

"So does abandoning most of the Commonwealth to the Clans and concentrating their forces on crushing Tamarind-Abbey," Roland pointed out.

"Only if their objective was to share equally with the Wolves," Christopher countered. "Or in this case, give them the lion's share for little effort. Generosity is one charge that has never been leveled against a Steiner."

Fontaine smiled at the assessment but did not comment, content to let Roland and Christopher sort it out.

"Which speaks to the point that we do not know the full scope of the Steiner objective," Roland said. "To gain territory, yes. But how much? To destabilize any effort to reunite the Free Worlds League, almost certainly. But how do we know they will be content with the death of Anson? There are other Mariks still alive who could rally the League."

Some more than others, Fontaine thought, watching Christopher's face as he absorbed each of Roland's points. *And some of* them *not blood Mariks.*

"All of that's true," Christopher conceded. "But there are patterns to the Lyran's behavior. Their attack on Merton showed they are as interested in acquiring unaligned worlds as they are in destabilizing nations."

And taught the Steiners that choosing the wrong targets can strengthen a nation. Fontaine allowed the corner of his mouth to quirk at the thought. *One poorly managed sortie and Tamarind-Abbey's rapid response had accomplished what a decade of negotiation had not. Both Merton and Sackville had sued to join the Duchy that now shielded them from Lyran annexation.*

"Even if their eventual goal is the destruction of Tamarind-Abbey and the death of Duke Fontaine," Christopher was saying, baldly stating the issue as though Fontaine were not in the room, "in the short term they're going to have to focus their efforts on assimilating as many of the Marik-Stewart Commonwealth worlds as they can. Otherwise Clan Wolf won't just be a presence on their border, they'll have enough worlds to be a major nation-state of their own."

Roland nodded slowly. "It's going to be a feeding frenzy."

"The Lyrans have a deep bench and deeper pockets." Christopher glanced at Fontaine, including him in the conversation. "So it's too much to expect them to pull all of their forces out of Tamarind-Abbey. But . . ."

"But their attention is going to be elsewhere." Roland picked up the thought. "And with so many combat-ready assets so close to where they need them, siphoning off a few and leaving skeletal garrisons in their stead makes logistic sense. Particularly on worlds that haven't been giving them any trouble."

"Like Tamarind."

"Like Tamarind."

Fontaine nodded as his lieutenants looked to him. Having the liberation units left on Tamarind keep their heads down and focus on intelligence-gathering had been Roland's idea, and it was a good one. The quiet worlds were occupied by fewer—and less experienced—soldiers.

"We can springboard from Loongana," he said. "But I see no way to take Tamarind without tying up Simpson Desert. A heavy feint would do it, but . . . we'll need to plan for a joint campaign."

"And a quick one." Christopher pointed out the obvious. "We can't give them time to redistribute forces and get reinforcements in place before we've kicked them off the planet."

"Doable?" Fontaine asked. He felt Karli nudge him and realized he'd framed his question in one of Christopher's most oft-used terms. *Influence works both ways.*

For his part, Christopher nodded quickly, then caught himself and looked to Roland for the answer.

Good catch, boy, Fontaine thought in his direction as the two waited for the SAFE director to work through all the checks and balances.

"Yes," Roland said at last. "Particularly if we don't move immediately. The Lyrans will expect a cathartic response to Anson's death. Give them several weeks to decide we're doing nothing and a couple more to quietly rotate what forces they will into the Marik-Stewart theater, then make our move."

Fontaine proffered Roland's noteputer.

"Gentlemen, assemble the command staff. Bring them up to speed." He smiled. "I want to see plans and contingencies detailed by next Monday. That gives you eleven days to design a two-planet campaign.

"In the meantime, I want a few annoyance raids— nothing substantial and nothing spinward of Edmondson. The Lyrans are expecting us to react, and we won't disappoint them." His felt his smile grow to a predatory grin. "But we won't alarm them too much either.

"I want them comfortable and complacent right up to the moment we take back our home."

40

The commercial center of Mosiro lay in ruins.

Thaddeus walked the broken streets, feeling the grit under his boots and smelling the smoke of fading fires.

The afternoon sun prismed off a field of broken glass; the façade of a high-rise office complex had become a drift of diamonds at the feet of a gaping metal frame. Squinting against the glare, he looked up at the tower's skeleton, imagining how it had looked before Ex-Force had arrived.

He knew his security people hated his out-front approach to leadership. Intellectually he knew it was not wise: his death could undo every military victory his people had fought so hard to earn. But he could not deny the drive within him, the need to be in the thick of things, to put his bare hands on the work he was doing. Perhaps it was a reaction to his years of manipulating events from behind the scenes, waiting for the opportunity to act. Or perhaps it was a premonition of the decades ahead of him; diplomatic missions and backroom deals as he worked to forge the disparate nations of the Free Worlds League back into a stable union.

Or as stable as it ever was.

Thaddeus paused in the center of an intersection, an open space that made him an easy target. His people had secured the area, but all it took was one sniper. . . . He could feel the battlearmor squad escorting him click into a higher level of readiness as they surveyed the empty boulevards and scarred buildings.

Looking back the way he had come, he could see *Kriegaxt* standing where he'd left it at the edge of the riverside park. The replacement missile rack and the armor patches were still in dull primer, but the overall effect was still resplendent in the white light of Mosiro's sun.

Pride in things, Thaddeus chided himself. *Not a good trait in a leader. The people must come first.*

With that thought and no word to his bodyguards, Thaddeus strode to the relative security of a covered walk. In the final block approaching the government center, the street was a broad mall, closed to vehicular traffic and dotted with decorative fountains and abstract sculptures. A row of restaurants lined the right side of the mall, and metal awnings, molded to look like street-market tents, extended their seating areas into the open air. Thaddeus had no idea whether the lightweight metal offered anything more than symbolic safety, but his guards deserved the gesture of caution.

Reports and the holovid images he'd seen testified that the planetary capital of Al-Ilb was very nearly intact. Carved as it was from the face of a kilometer-high cliff above a forest, the city was practically inaccessible, at least to the volume of traffic a commercial center required. Al-Ilb was devoted to the arts, a city of museums and concert halls, the largest mosque rimward of Terra, and a major university. None of them viable targets. And for once the Anduriens had followed the rules of war and kept their own forces away from the city.

Al-Hassam, on the other hand . . .

Here the fighting had been building to building. Long after sound tactics dictated the defenders withdraw or surrender, the Second Guards and Mosiro Planetary Militia had thrown themselves at the Expeditionary Force. In the case of the Militia, it made a sort of sense; they were defending their home from invaders. But the Second Guard could have withdrawn as a viable force and repositioned themselves to fight again on another world or to retake this one. Instead, they had . . .

Wasted themselves, was the only term that came to mind.

Thaddeus wondered if this pit bull tenacity, this focus on the immediate while ignoring the greater context, reflected

Humphreys' own orders to his military or a character flaw in the Andurien people. For anything so costly and so futile could only be a flaw.

Anduriens had struggled to throw off invaders and occupiers of one stripe or another for generations, if Thaddeus recalled his history, always with very limited success. This war was giving him an insight into those centuries of frustration.

The covered walk ended as the mall opened into a piazza hundreds of meters on a side. Thaddeus knew there were traffic tunnels beneath the town center—his infantry had spent days clearing the MPM out of the twenty-block warren—but here there was nothing to indicate this was not Terra over a thousand years ago. The architecture, like the climate, reminded Thaddeus of northern Africa or the southern coast of Spain.

Mindful that his security detachment would have preferred he travel by APC or stayed in his 'Mech, Thaddeus set a course that carried him close to what little cover was available as he crossed the great square.

To his left was the mosque, imposing in its simplicity and strict adherence to classic design. Directly ahead, resplendent in white local marble and tile, was the planetary government complex. There, Thaddeus knew, were all the prosaic offices that regulated the wide-ranging commerce that flowed through Mosiro's DropPort as well as the world's domestic infrastructure, hidden behind a façade that rivaled the finest palaces on a dozen worlds.

Miaplacidus could learn something from this noble simplicity.

Behind him, flanking the broad mall through which he'd entered the piazza, were the state museum and the concert hall. His briefing digest on Mosiro had included something about the significance of the local opera, but the details eluded him.

Here among the fountains, dry and silent now, and the sculptures and the carefully tended plants and trees, nothing disturbed the illusion of serenity. There was no provision for vehicular traffic, and Thaddeus noted that none of the modern buildings just a few blocks away was visible from the central square.

And try as he might, he could find no evidence of the final desperate battle for the city.

With the notable exception of Sergeant Peterson's Ostroc.

Angling right, he made his way toward the incongruous BattleMech and the Ministry of Information building it was guarding. Rivaling the government offices in size, the Information Complex housed one of the most extensive libraries of physical books in the Free Worlds League, an equally extensive compilation of astrophysical observations collected since the days of the Star League, and the planetary headquarters of SAFE.

It was in this last that the Covenant intelligence officer had found something he thought Thaddeus should see directly.

Watson was waiting for him at the door, evidently anxious to escort him to the SAFE office. His civilian coat, as much a uniform as Thaddeus' MechWarrior gear, was open in the midday heat. Thaddeus surmised the building's central air-conditioning was not working.

Thaddeus missed Green, but appreciated Watson's competence. Where Green had mastered the art of being blankly invisible, Watson cultivated a completely harmless image. Though he was not fat, his wardrobe choices and the way he carried himself created the impression of portliness, and his twinkling powder blue eyes and perennial smile could put even the most suspicious at ease.

The dashingly handsome superspies of holovid adventure fiction were just that—fiction. When it came to covert operations and intelligence gathering, it was the blank and the harmless that got the job done.

"We've analyzed this recording every way we know how," Watson was saying as they stepped into a windowless interior office. Work lights were aimed at the walls and ceiling to fill the room with a shadowless indirect light. Cables snaked from a portable generator to power the lights and several pieces of equipment. "I can state unequivocally that it is pure and untampered with."

"Which is a problem?"

"Sir, I think it may be a very big problem."

Watson clicked a button, starting the playback.

A large monitor came to life, filling with the infamous

view of Breezewood, Kwamashu, moments before the monstrous explosion that had killed—was still killing—nearly a third of the planet's population. Thaddeus watched the scene beyond the talking man. A spokesperson for Humanity Without Borders, a humanitarian agency that specialized in medical and hunger relief, he was explaining they had come to help with civilian health concerns and discovered a battle on the planet.

Even braced for it, Thaddeus still started when the BattleMech complex blasted out of existence. Green and purple and orange and red, shot through with lightning, the column of flame burst free from the pits of hell. Thrusting toward the sky, it hurled buildings and debris and— invisibly tiny at this range—people hundreds of meters into the air. Then it expanded, consuming block after block in an insatiable conflagration. A fire burning so rapidly it was one continuous explosion.

He'd seen the recording a dozen times—hundreds, if one counted the nights its memory had kept him awake—and it never failed to fill him with horror. Still, he forced himself to watch as the team of volunteers broke and ran, tumbling into their VTOL. The cameraman—Thaddeus always marveled at the man's dedication—aimed the recorder back out the open door and tried to keep the image of the growing destruction centered as the pilot fought to keep the aircraft steady in the hurricane winds.

Invisible in the cabin behind the camera, members of the relief team moaned and sobbed. And one voice, faint but clear, damned Oriente for killing thousands of civilians— for destroying a world simply because they couldn't conquer it.

An icy hand gripped Thaddeus' heart.

"This is authentic?"

"We've tested it every way we know how."

"But the recording we saw," Thaddeus said. "Damning the Anduriens—"

"Tested six ways from zero," Watson confirmed. "Equally authentic. No editing, no dubbing, nothing added or deleted to either recording."

"What the hell does that mean?"

"Most immediately it means someone with manipulative

technology that exceeds anything we know about manufactured both recordings," Watson answered. "In the broader sense—*why* it was done and by whom—I have no idea."

Thaddeus stood, staring at the monitor. The last image of the recording was frozen on the screen: the huge column of flame canted at an angle as the VTOL banked into a turn. It occurred to him that was a very apt metaphor for what had just happened to his world.

41

Atreus City, Atreus
Former Marik-Stewart Commonwealth
22 July 3138

Lester glowered at the ruins of Atreus City.

The name of their capital says everything that needs saying about the imagination of these people.

The wind ruffled his hair, funneling between buildings to kick dust and scraps along abandoned streets. The area was secure; without need of armor, Lester rode in an open ground car. He stood, steadying himself with a firm grip on the open frame of the roll cage, the better to survey the fruits of conquest as the vehicle made its way through the late afternoon sunlight.

The city around him had not been ruined by Regulan forces; there had been no fighting here. Nor had it been ravaged by the Blakists. The self-styled "city of dreams" occupied an island continent far from the manufacturing centers of Corin and Lanan that had borne the brunt of the fury of their scorched-earth retreat. No, Atreus City had crumbled under its own greed. Even at the height of the Free Worlds League's glory, the capital had been known for its excesses. On a world that needed to import over a third of its food, obesity had been the number-one health problem before the Jihad.

Now . . .

True, the only refugees on the streets were those too sickly to escape or too fatalistic to consider fleeing. But they were skinny, their short stature bearing witness to a lifetime of malnutrition.

How could Anson have let this happen? Lester ignored the fact that the process had run its course long before Anson had assumed power. *This was once the heart of the Free Worlds League.*

No doubt conditions were better on Paltos, the isolated island continent that thrust out of the sea nine thousand kilometers west of Atreus City, long the stronghold of the aristocracy. There were scores of family-held fortresses and retreats hidden away among its narrow valleys and stony ramparts, and even now was the only part of the planet that Fief forces did not hold uncontested.

Nobles and their private armies. None of them was a match for the Regulan forces in open combat. But they were able to hold a rocky island of little worth. There was no point in wasting resources and good Regulan lives digging the popinjays out of their warrens. With nowhere to go and no way to get there, the aristocracy of Atreus was under virtual house arrest.

The white marble and chromium palaces that had housed the many ministries of the Free Worlds League towered like the mausoleums of gods, covering the hill that rose to the north of the city proper. The slanting sunlight caught the white planes and silver accents, reflecting a brilliance painful to unshaded eyes. Looking away, Lester found his eyes resting on the shuttered façade of a museum that had once been a mecca for artists and historians throughout the League.

"We have to rebuild."

"Sir?" Salazar answered.

Lester had forgotten his stolid SAFE director riding beside him, sitting on his side of the rear seat as though it were a straight-backed wooden chair.

His hair doesn't move in the breeze.

Lester considered remaining silent. He'd been talking to

himself, not intending his words to reach anyone else. But it occurred to him he would be having this conversation with his right-hand man sooner or later. Once begun, it made sense to get it out of the way.

"This place, this city," he said aloud. "We need to rebuild it."

"Sir?" Salazar repeated. "Atreus City has no value, intrinsically or strategically, and the cost of restoring it to its former stature would be prohibitive."

"Agreed," Lester said. "Its former stature was that of a glutton. But the ideal of Atreus City—not the reality—is a powerful symbol. Think of it as restoring the spiritual heart of the Free Worlds League."

Lester rocked right as his driver swerved to avoid a pothole. He imagined he could hear Salazar's cogs turning.

"A powerful public relations coup," the man agreed at length. "Certain to have an impact on both independent worlds and worlds of the former Commonwealth."

Lester nodded.

"But," Salazar added, "public opinion has only limited impact on diplomatic overtures and even less on military objectives. Do the Regulan Fiefs have the resources to both rebuild Atreus and pursue their broader objective?"

Eyes forward, Lester nodded again, not caring whether his seated lieutenant could see him concede the point.

The acquisitions of Alterf and Ionus had been almost bloodless. Given a choice between being brought under the protection of a nation of the Free Worlds League and the heel of the Steiner boot, both worlds had been happy to host Regulan garrisons. But the battle for the hearts and minds of the people of the Free Worlds League would not be won with guns. Nor with public-works projects that did little but refurbish unoccupied buildings—no matter how historically significant.

"Full restoration of only the House of Parliament, then. Symbol of what made—makes—the Free Worlds League unique," he said. "Perhaps a general cleanup of other significant buildings. I'll leave that to your experts on public opinion."

A child, perhaps five—or possibly as old as ten and

stunted by malnutrition—stared at Lester's passing ground
car with hollow eyes.

God.

"The people, Salazar, the children." Lester felt his
voice rough against his throat. "We need to get food here.
Medicine. The people need us more than the damn
buildings."

A pause, maybe a breath, then Salazar's voice with more
heat than Lester could remember ever hearing before.

"Yes. Yes, sir."

42

Talos City
Asellus Australis
27 July 3138

Lord Garith Talos tugged down the carefully starched cuffs
of his formal shirt. Again. He'd been doing that often of
late; the white linen had developed a habit of disappearing
inside the broad sleeves of his frock coat.

He'd experimented exactly once with complaining that
his clothes had somehow gotten smaller. Lady Joslyn had
promptly informed him the problem lay with his expanding
waistline, not his shrinking wardrobe. The generous cut of
his brocade coat concealed the taut stretch of linen across
his midsection, but there was no concealing the fact his
increased volume made his sleeves ride up.

However, ordering new shirts would be admitting to what
his wife called his middle-age spread. Worse, it would be
an admission that he didn't expect to ever get back down
to his former weight, and that was one defeat he would
never acknowledge. All he needed was a bit of discipline

and a regular exercise routine—a resolution he considered
frequently but had yet to act on.

To be vain and lazy is a deadly combination.

Stepping out onto the dais, Garith paused. Conversations
across the audience chamber ceased or faded to murmurs,
and the rustle of heavy fabrics announced that those who'd
been seated had risen to their feet.

He extended his left hand without turning his head and
felt his wife clasp it firmly. Together they strode to the two
wooden armchairs flanking the center of the low platform,
relics of his many-times-great-grandfather's declaration that
the Talos family would rule without pretense or ostentation.

Garith made the traditional show of steadying her chair
as Joslyn sat—as though the two hundred kilos of Australis
oak would shift under her weight. She *hasn't lost her fighting trim.* She smiled appreciatively and he bowed slightly,
smiling in acknowledgment, before taking his own chair.

Australis Hall was not grand as palaces went. In fact,
Garith had seen pictures of hotels on Tharkad that made
it look pedestrian. But he loved its simple geometry and
the clean, spare lines of the audience chamber. This building had been the home of his family—of his world's autonomous rulers—for twenty generations.

Until eighteen months ago, when Nikol Marik had announced from the cockpit of her *BattleMaster* that Asellus
Australis was part of the Oriente Protectorate. Just as So-
phie's World and Sorunda and Lungdo and Asellus Borealis had all come under Oriente's "protection" in a matter
of weeks. Apparently Jessica Marik had decided the formerly independent worlds needed Oriente to defend them
against Anson Marik's imperialist campaigns.

True, the Marik-Stewart Commonwealth had been extending its borders, but into star systems abandoned by the
collapse of the Republic of the Sphere. Oriente was the
only nation absorbing its free neighbors against their wills.

Garith had found it almost impossible to reconcile the
steely-eyed MechWarrior informing him his sovereign
world was now a vassal state with the awkward colt of a
girl lost in her mother's shadow on an informal visit—

God, was that only three years ago? Three and a half.

Pretending he didn't know why a ducal audience had been called midweek, Garith looked to his court steward.

Unrolling the traditional scroll, the steward considered it for a moment as though selecting one item from many on the blank parchment, then announced:

"Marquis Cristobol Forcythe of Oceana, Etgar Sea Fox, Talar Nova Cat, and Lady Julietta of Marik."

Of *Marik? Not just Marik? Or more properly, Halas-Hughes Marik? And what the hell does* the *lady mean?*

Though the newcomers had been announced least to greatest—and young Forcythe being listed as less important than the Clanners was significant—Julietta Marik led the procession making its way down the broad aisle. She walked with two crutch canes, each a metal tube with a band that wrapped around her forearm and a simple peg handhold for her to grip, but there was no uncertainty in her deliberate advance.

Flanking her was a giant who looked like a Greek god from a sword-and-sandal holovid and a man of normal proportions with a disconcerting stare. In their wake came Forcythe. Garith first noted Cristobol was the spitting image of his father, Thom, then realized he was moving with the easy confidence of a man among equals.

By tradition guests of any rank stood when addressing Garith and Joslyn, but only an ass would keep a woman standing who needed canes to walk. Without being told, the steward stepped forward to position a chair for Lady Julietta Marik. *The* Lady Julietta of Marik.

She stopped him with a look that sent him scurrying back to his station.

"Lord Garith, Lady Joslyn." Julietta nodded to each in turn. "Well met."

"Well met," Garith returned the oddly truncated greeting. "It is an unexpected pleasure to see you on Asellus Australis. We have heard little of you since word of your tragic attack many months ago."

Not counting the rumor of you haring off to join the Clans.

"My mother is not one to share family gossip," Julietta agreed. "As it happens, I now live on Marik."

She paused, but Garith did not rise to the bait. He'd be

polite, it was not in his nature not to be, but he would not do Lady Julietta's work for her.

"Many believe I serve as Oriente's envoy to the Clans Spirit Cat and Sea Fox," Julietta said before the silence stretched. "But my role is more that of cultural adviser. Even after so many years of exposure, the ways of we spheroids can be confusing."

She smiled slightly and Garith found himself smiling with her.

"One political concept the Clans find interesting is that of *protectorate*—worlds autonomous to themselves, under the protection of more powerful states, yet not possessions of those states."

"The example of the Oriente Protectorate—"

"Is a bad one," Julietta cut him off. "My mother, Duchess Jessica, knows that solidarity of purpose is vital in the current crisis. Unity of response is vital in war, making the complete autonomy of a protectorate's member worlds impossible."

Garith said nothing. He'd intended a subtle reminder that his own world had been annexed by Oriente against its will. He suspected Lady Julietta of tricking him into replying, then cutting him off before he'd made his point.

"*Your* world, Lord Garith, has been under the hand of the Oriente Protectorate these last seven months, has it not?"

What?

Garith's mind raced. What could be her purpose in first stopping him from mentioning Oriente's occupation of Asellus Australis, then bringing it up herself? Whatever game they were playing, Lady Julietta was at least two moves ahead of him. In any case, he could think of no way to avoid her direct question.

"The hand of Oriente, as you characterize it, has been light, Lady Julietta," Garith said smoothly. "We simply provided food, facilities and such supplies as the garrisoning forces required, in exchange for the protection they offered against Commonwealth aggression."

"The Marik-Stewart Commonwealth no longer exists," Julietta pointed out. "And if you are referring to the Lyran

Commonwealth, you should be aware that Oriente forces have been stripped away from the Wolf-Lyran front to support the taking of Atreus."

"We are aware of the campaign to liberate Atreus from the Regulan Fiefs," Garith answered, trying to judge where Lady Julietta was bound. "And while the Oriente garrisons on Asellus Australis and Asellus Borealis have been redeployed, my understanding is that the bulk of Oriente forces remain between our worlds and the Wolf and Lyran aggressors."

"A blend of Oriente forces, former Marik-Stewart regulars and local militias holding Bedeque, Bainsville and Autumn Wind," Lady Julietta said. "That is the extent of the Oriente Protectorate's bulwark against Clan Wolf and the Lyran Commonwealth."

Garith heard the murmurs sweep through the audience chamber and was hard-pressed not to glance at his wife for reassurance. There was no direct contradiction between the information Lady Julietta presented now and the situation as explained by the commander of the departed garrison, but the *impression* had been . . .

"What of Rasalas?" he asked. "Washburn? Keystone?"

"Fallback positions. Provisioned, but not garrisoned beyond their own planetary militias."

A second wave of murmurs, and this time Garith did look at Joslyn. Her normally rich nutmeg complexion had taken on a sallow tone as she stared at Lady Julietta. Shock had drained all blood from his wife's face. Not for the first time he wished the damned chairs were placed close enough for him to hold her hand.

"I do not mean to imply any duplicity on the part of Oriente in this," Julietta said, as though responding to his thoughts. "Or any immediately pressing threat."

No mind reading there. She must know everyone who hears her words is thinking the same thing.

"The dangers Oriente faces are daunting. Even with the Andurien War winding down, the Protectorate's forces are stretched in every direction," Julietta was saying. "Duchess Jessica has placed every soldier she can spare between Asellus Australis and the Wolf-Lyran occupation zone. Her problem is that there simply are not enough troops available to guarantee the safety of the worlds that have come to depend on her.

"Which is why she came to us."

Us? Garith's ears pricked at the pronoun. *Lady Julietta* of *Marik. Marik the planet. She's declaring herself separate from her mother.*

"I had assumed," he said carefully, "that Marik was a part of the Oriente Protectorate."

"An assumption shared by many." Julietta nodded. "Logical, on the face of it, but false. That assumption may have influenced Oriente's decision to call upon us for help in this time of overextension.

"You are aware Clan Spirit Cat was asked to provide protection for several worlds while the forces that had stood garrison were deployed elsewhere?"

"For the duration of the campaign to liberate Atreus, yes," Garith said. "Am I to infer from what you have shared that you are now proposing something different?"

Lady Julietta smiled.

On other worlds, deals like the one Garith thought he saw lurking in her eyes were struck in private, unacknowledged meetings. But the leaders of Asellus Australis were renowned for the transparency of their rule. There would be no closed doors, no clandestine negotiations here. What needed to be discussed needed to be discussed in the presence of the people it affected most.

He'd seen ambassadors and emissaries and world leaders balk at that requirement. He suspected that it had cost Australis many lucrative deals. But he also knew his people were better and more honestly served because the tradition was in place.

And now, for the first time that he could recall, in Lady Julietta was someone who seemed to genuinely approve of the practice.

"No one outside of Clan Sea Fox knows the extent of their trading empire," she said, opening with an observation that seemed in no way related to what had gone before. "Yet both the size of their mysterious fleet and their ability to deal with anyone for anything is legendary."

No response suggested itself, so Garith remained silent.

"Etgar speaks for Clan Sea Fox, on behalf of his ovKhan Petr Kalasa."

The holovid costume hero stepped forward, his shoulder a hand span higher than the top of Julietta's head.

He's not an elemental, Garith realized. *He's just a big man.*

"We've familiarized ourselves with your world's agricultural exports." His voice was a surprising tenor. "What you call wild grain has almost unlimited market potential. There is nothing with quite the same combination of flavors and nutrition available."

"Our trade treaty with Oriente—"

"Has been grossly unfair," Etgar cut him off, nodding as though agreeing with Garith's point in the process. "Based on an undervaluing of your wild grain's potential and Oriente positioning itself as your primary market."

Garith became aware his mouth was still open with the unfinished sentence and closed it.

"What are you proposing?" he asked.

"A protected trade agreement, with Clan Sea Fox as your sole distributor," Etgar said. "We renegotiate your current contracts and explore new markets for your products. After deducting our commission and fees, you can expect a thirty to forty percent increase in your net."

Garith decided he was missing a connection. There seemed to be nothing to tie Etgar Sea Fox's words to what had gone before.

"All of our imports would pass through you as well?" he asked, grasping at one straw he thought he understood.

"As part of the protected trade agreement, of course." Etgar nodded. "In this case our commissions and fees would about equal the reduction in costs, so in all but a few items there will be no change in price from your perspective."

Garith was aware of the silence in the audience hall. He took some consolation from the fact that no one seemed to understand where this conversation was headed.

Unless . . .

"You say protected trade agreement. Who is protected how and from what?"

"Asellus Australis is protected from all comers by Clans Sea Fox and Spirit Cat."

Garith snapped his gaze to Lady Julietta.

"You expect us to turn our world over for Clan occupation?" he demanded.

Lady Julietta smiled, and Garith was pleased to note the expression lit her eyes.

"Remember I told you I'd been teaching the Clans about protectorates?" she asked. "They like the idea very much. Your complete autonomy in exchange for all trade in and out of Asellus Australis. Profits from the trade pays for your garrison, which means if the Spirit Cat forces guarding your world need something Clan Sea Fox hasn't already provided, they pay you fair market value—a fair market value determined by your vendors. Thus, at no loss to the people of Asellus Australis, your world is under the protection of the fiercest warriors in the region, and your entire system guarded by a navy even the Lyrans fear."

Those last two claims might be hyperbole, Garith recognized, but they were close enough to the truth not to matter. But self-supporting? No net cost to Australis?

"To what end?" he asked.

"Captain-General Jessica Marik is reuniting the Free Worlds League." Julietta made the announcement as though it were a foregone conclusion.

Garith blinked once.

"When the Free Worlds League reforms, Asellus Australis will join her." Julietta raised her voice to reach every corner of the audience chamber. "But not as an individual world with no say in Parliament. Asellus Australis will have a voice in guiding the Free Worlds League as an honored member of the Clan Protectorate."

43

Even prepared for it, Jessica was transfixed by the images on the monitor.

The unimaginable destruction of Breezewood rose like a deadly flower, filling the sky: the mad dash to the VTOL, the final shaky images from the rising aircraft—all of it was horrifying, and increasingly familiar.

As the spreading firestorm destroyed the city below, Jessica heard the spokesman's shouting voice, distorted by the VTOL's cabin, saying thousands of civilians were dying in the blast. Beneath the shouting, a man sobbed at the horror he was witnessing.

And, barely discernible, a voice damning Oriente—damning Jessica—for deliberately detonating a toxic waste dump to deny the Duchy a victory on Kwamashu.

Torrian stopped the playback.

Jessica fought the urge to ask him if the recording was authentic. The SAFE technicians on Oriente had already confirmed Watson's field assessment. *Both* recordings were indisputably unaltered originals. No doubt his people would be devoting several sleepless nights to determining how it had been done.

"So this is why you stopped the war?" she asked.

Thaddeus didn't blink.

"I stopped the advance on Andurien," he corrected. "We hold Kwamashu, Antipolo, El Giza and Mosiro."

"No thought of giving them back?"

"No." Thaddeus ignored her sarcastic tone. "I have ordered humanitarian aid and authorized the quartermaster to negotiate contracts for rebuilding infrastructure damaged in the conflict."

Jessica nodded. Jobs, and letting the people rebuild their own worlds. Far better for solidifying relations and loyalty than letting idle and resentful natives watch the invaders construct replacements for what they'd destroyed.

"So we are keeping the worlds?" It wasn't really a question.

Thaddeus ignored her, turning to look at Torrian.

"We'll need your people on-site. Military intelligence is ill-suited to finding liberation units among the civilian population."

Torrian nodded. Jessica did not miss the fact that her SAFE director accepted the assignment without looking to her for confirmation.

"More to the point, we need to figure out who made these recordings and why." Thaddeus turned back to her. "And you know the situation better than I. What, if anything, do we tell Humphreys?"

Well done, damn you, Jessica thought, regarding the wide-set hazel eyes leveling their sincere question in her direction. *Establish that you're able to evaluate and give orders on your own, then acknowledge you need me. Partnership, not service. You said that in the beginning.*

I'll let you keep the illusion as long as you don't expect the reality.

She glanced at Torrian, but found her SAFE director regarding the monitor screen in a brown study.

"The author of this is not a mystery." As expected, both men focused on her. She let her fingertip lightly trace the grain of the ancient table as she met each one's gaze in turn. "Daoshen Liao."

Thaddeus grunted.

"Even by his standards—" Torrian began.

"The fact that his standards—and only his standards— come anywhere near encompassing something like this pretty well focuses our search parameters," Jessica said. "This trap took months to set up, and involved the slaughter of tens of thousands—hundreds of thousands—of innocents. Neither time nor strangers' lives mean anything to a madman who thinks he's an immortal god."

"Playing devil's advocate," Thaddeus said. "My understanding of the political situation is that Humphreys has always considered war an option. Could the recording we first saw be the original and the one distributed throughout Andurien worlds a doctored copy?"

"Ari has always coveted the worlds he thinks a war might gain him," Jessica corrected. "He's had his eye on everything from Fujidera rimward since he was old enough to read a star chart.

"But actually start a war?" She arched an eyebrow at Torrian. "Until we learned of the Kwamashu BattleMech facility and saw the recording of the explosion, I didn't believe he had the stomach. Or the backbone."

Torrian did not flinch under her gaze.

"We were manipulated," he admitted. "And well. Andurien does not have the technology to produce a forged recording crystal of this quality."

"Another tally on the Daoshen side of the scale," Jessica said. "Only the deep pockets and hidden resources of a major House could have pulled that off."

"The Lyrans—" Thaddeus stopped himself. "Never mind. There's a difference between playing devil's advocate and grasping at straws. Oriente and Andurien are too far from Steiner space for the archon to bother."

And points to you for not mentioning that her campaigns threaten your own Covenant Worlds.

"Daoshen Liao is focused on carving up the corpse of The Republic. But he can't afford to leave what he sees as two potential competitors on his flank," she said. "Setting us against each other is cheap insurance—particularly since Oriente never supported Daoshen's war on The Republic to his satisfaction. It would amuse him to support Humphreys against us." She frowned at the frozen image on the screen.

"Knowing we were duped into conflict, I am not comfortable prosecuting the war any further than we have." Thaddeus' voice broke in on her thoughts. "By the same token, we have gained valuable worlds, worlds I think are worth consolidating."

"So just keep what we have and declare the war over?" Jessica felt the edges of her words.

"Win back Manchu-ri, consolidate the worlds we've acquired and stop our advance," Thaddeus advised. He indicated the monitor screen. "This horror occurred on Duchy soil, costing us nothing but a battalion of soldiers prepared to die for Oriente.

"If we go public with these conflicting recordings while the war is still hot—cry foul while facing the wrath of Andurien avenging its murdered civilians—it's possible even some of our own citizens will believe we're only trying to escape the consequences of our actions.

"Particularly if our trying to stop the fight too soon inspires Liao to throw the Capellan Confederation's weight behind the Andurien cry for justice."

Jessica smiled at the thought despite herself. Such duplicity would be vintage Daoshen.

"Fight the war to a standstill." Thaddeus leaned forward earnestly. "Pour all we can afford into winning the loyalty of the worlds we've acquired, make the people citizens instead of captives, *then* make a public disclosure of our discovery.

"Instead of being a desperate attempt to stop a war, it becomes the final step in solidifying a peace."

"Ari's going to want his worlds back," Jessica pointed out.

"You said yourself he's always dreamed of having everything rimward of Fujidera," Thaddeus said. "We're just giving him something bigger to dream about."

Jessica felt another smile pulling at the corner of her mouth, but successfully fought impulse. Half-closing her eyes, she regarded Thaddeus Marik thoughtfully.

Partnership, she thought. *Might be worth consideration.*

Pirate Point, Autumn Wind
Wolf Occupation Zone
Former Marik-Stewart Commonwealth

Nikol let her body float in zero gravity, marveling that she still felt the weary weight across her shoulders even when there was no up or down.

There was no organized resistance on Autumn Wind. Like Gannett, like Danais, like Concord and oh-so especially like Helm. On Helm she had expected something. If only fueled by the outrage of the massacre, there should have been something.

But the Clans hated resistance fighters. They regarded guerilla warfare as cowardice, murder without honor. To them, anonymous attacks on unwarned targets were symptoms of a sick society. And they responded accordingly.

If an occupation soldier was killed in a neighborhood on a Lyran-held world, the Lyrans would go through the area door to door. They would search every house; examine the identities and backgrounds and relationships of everyone there. Sometimes they would find the killer. Other times they would find nothing. Most often they found some other criminal activity that would have otherwise gone undetected.

If an occupation soldier was killed in a neighborhood on a Wolf-held world, the Wolves would go through the area door to door. And they would kill everyone. Every man, every woman, every child within a five-block radius of the soldier's body. And they would leave the bodies of the people they killed—let them rot where they were and shoot anyone who tried to bury a family member or a loved one.

If being a resistance fighter meant running the risk of seeing your children rot unburied, the price was too high. The Free Worlds League systems held by the Wolves were lost. They would stay lost until the League was strong enough to push the Wolves out of League space. And from what she had seen on Autumn Wind and Gannett and Helm, that was not going to happen any time soon.

Anson Marik had been dead two months now. It had been just over a month since her mother had ordered her to find the Silver Hawk Irregulars. Nikol thought she knew where they had gone: they'd taken themselves off the Lyran-Wolf sensor net. But she hadn't gone after them yet.

She was the minister-general. She'd made up the title herself, at gunpoint, and that made it official. And her official duty was to minister to the people of the Free Worlds League; to make sure the worlds of the League stayed free.

The Silver Hawk Irregulars didn't need ministering to.

At least not as badly as a lot of worlds that were under the heels of the Lyrans and the Wolves.

Nikol had not so much ignored her mother's instructions as she'd weighed them against the needs of whole worlds. Interplanetary triage. She had gone to the worlds she thought needed her most and found too, too many of them to be beyond her power to help.

Her mother wanted the Silver Hawks. She would get her mother the Silver Hawks. Soon. A few more weeks wouldn't matter. And there were two, maybe three worlds between where she was and where she was fairly sure they'd gone to ground. Worlds without Clan Wolf; worlds she could help.

Nikol took a deep breath and expelled it in a long sigh. She bobbed at the end of her tether.

Enough.

Grabbing the safety line, she pulled herself to the bulkhead. Moving swiftly from toehold to grab-ring, she pulled herself toward the captain's ready room. She was the minister-general. There were worlds that needed her.

44

Amur, Oriente
Oriente Protectorate
8 August 3138

*N*ot sure what to make of things, are you, brother?

Frederick sat at his ease, legs stretched out in front of him and fingers laced across his stomach. Thaddeus had not quite adopted the Oriente habit of feeding you something every time he wanted to discuss something; which in this case was a shame, because a drink would make the evening perfect.

Thaddeus had called him into a private conversation for the first time since he'd tried to sound out Frederick on the Carbonis issue. That his little brother was a genuine force in Protectorate politics seemed to put him off his stride—not an advantage Frederick often enjoyed.

For his part, the war hero had done well for himself. The army he'd raised from that cobbled-together alliance of his had proven to be the darlings of the Andurien War. And Thaddeus—as their leader *cum* ambassador *cum* close adviser to the captain-general—enjoyed a popularity usually associated with trivid heartthrobs.

Quite a change from your cold reign in The Republic, eh, Thad?

Of course, he'd come a long way too—which is what so disconcerted his brother. And that spoke volumes about his relationship with his brother.

It was blatantly obvious Thaddeus had never considered Frederick to be anything other than an ornamental drone, buzzing about social events looking for an advantageous union. Or two. To find him situated as a power broker, particularly on such glamourless issues as domestic commerce, was just outside the former paladin's preconceived little world.

Of course Thaddeus thought military campaigns and politics ruled the fate of nations. He hadn't tumbled to the fact that commerce was the true driving force, running deeper than nations or ideologies. The yin-yang of supply and demand was the constant from which all human endeavors sprang.

"There's a situation." Thaddeus broke the surface of Frederick's comfortable thoughts with a handful of wooden words. "Something not yet on the public horizon. It has been determined that you should not only be aware of, but have a role in upcoming events."

"Indeed?" Frederick asked, more intrigued by who was doing the determining than any bit of political intrigue Thaddeus was about to reveal. "It's good to know you're still thinking of me."

A flush spread across his big brother's broad features. More of a darkening from chestnut to russet given the amount of sun the war leader had been getting. It occurred to Frederick that continuing to play the fop was a misstep. Annoying pompous Thaddeus was amusing in the short run, but not wise in the long.

Particularly since something of substance seemed to be in the offing.

"I'm sorry, Thaddeus," he said aloud. "Old habits and all that."

"I have never understood—"

"Nor I," Frederick cut him off. "But I suspect from the setting and your opening remark that now is not the time to revisit our mutually exclusive perceptions of the past twenty years. I apologize for my comment. Please continue explaining the situation."

The stunned surprise on Thaddeus' face was comic. Frederick fought the urge to find a reflection and discover if he'd sprouted a second head.

Just violating expectations.

Frederick could almost hear the creak of unoiled gears as Thaddeus considered him for a long moment.

"I begin to see Philip's point," he said at last.

Frederick knew he didn't actually jerk at the mention of Jessica's estranged husband, but it was a near thing. To his knowledge no one had seen Philip Hughes in weeks and his whereabouts were the topic of frequent speculation. That his brother, who had quite definitely been nowhere other than the Andurien front and the diplomatic residence adjacent to the ducal palace, was evidently in contact with the man threw a new and unexpected light on events.

Now who's being the fool of his preconceptions?

"I was unaware you—or anyone—had spoken to Philip in some time," Frederick admitted. No point in not rising to what was obviously bait. "I take it he is on Oriente?"

"He's in the room," came a voice from behind.

Frederick pushed himself forward, twisting to look over the high back of his chair. Philip Hughes was at the sideboard, pulling the cork from a squat bottle. He would have risen to his feet, but Philip waved him back down.

"You're hoarding the Fuentes brandy again, Thaddeus," Philip said as he poured generous dollops into three snifters.

"A reasonable precaution," Thaddeus answered solemnly, "given the known supply is limited to a single planet."

Frederick didn't bother trying to keep his face impassive as his mind boggled at the easy familiarity the men shared. He was quite certain his brother had not made a joke since age fourteen.

"It seems there's more to this situation of yours than I imagined," he said aloud.

"Oh, quite a bit more," Philip agreed, handing him a snifter. "None of which can leave this room."

"I understand."

The brandy was excellent.

There was an edge of tension to the room, of course. Philip and Thaddeus were midprocess in broaching some proposal. But Frederick perceived that sharp note did not disturb the pair's informal comfort.

Philip never left Oriente. He's been holed up here the whole time and Thaddy-boy has been keeping him company.

Contemplating the layers of significance behind that realization, and the possibilities beyond, threatened to swallow all of Frederick's attention. With an effort he tabled speculation and focused on the situation at hand.

"I think it will take me a while to regain my feet after discovering you alive and well in the palace, Your Grace," he said. "I'd begun to imagine I'd developed some skills in ferreting out the goings-on about Amur."

Philip chuckled.

"I'd noticed," he said. "Not much to do on house arrest other than observe the world around you."

"House arrest?"

"Self-imposed seclusion, then," Philip corrected. "Though to be honest the only thing I've missed these past months has been my golf. Used to play two, sometimes three times a week."

"I've recently taken up golf," Frederick said, keeping to common ground.

"One of the reasons I suggested we bring you onboard," Philip said. "You puzzled-out where and how we locals conduct business behind the scenes, then took steps to become part of the process. You've also been shedding the more flamboyant of the foppish mannerisms that—and here

I'm guessing—used to stand you in good stead in the halls of Terra.

"In other words, you adapt intelligently to changing situations."

And it seems everything is a "situation."

"Thank you, sir."

A glance to Thaddeus assured his older brother was watching the exchange with interest. And perhaps a bit of bemusement.

"Though Jessica must remain on Oriente in the current crisis, I will be journeying to the Rim Commonality for our daughter's wedding," Philip said. "In fact, I'll be giving her away to Michael in the wedding ceremony."

The unusual turn of phrase threw Frederick for a moment. Then he remembered the arcane practice of the father transferring ownership of his daughter to her new husband. He hadn't realized anyone still did that.

The farther one moves from Terra, the farther back in time one goes.

He was about to comment to this effect when he realized the other two were watching him expectantly.

"A test of analysis?" he guessed.

"Essentially," Philip agreed.

"Your presence and adherence to the old forms will give the union legitimacy in the eyes of the traditionalists." He pointed out the obvious. "At the same time, your apparent estrangement from your wife and the Protectorate throne will make you a lightning rod for those who oppose the closer ties between nations that the marriage represents. A quick and easy test for dissenters.

"Of course, the fact that your estrangement is only apparent means a reconciliation of sorts in the future, no doubt brokered by your daughter with the help of her new husband." He sipped his brandy. "This will capture the hearts of the sentimental, making the coming alliance popular as well as practical."

Thaddeus was looking at him with the complete lack of expression Frederick knew indicated his brother was making an internal reassessment.

Are you really so surprised I'm not an idiot? Brother dearest, you do not know the half.

"Accurate," Philip said, nodding his approval, "as far as it goes."

Which leads us to the "situation" part of tonight's presentation.

"Shortly after our departure—at a time determined by our propagandists—it will be announced that the duchess Jessica has decided to remarry," Philip said. "This coming October she will wed her dear friend and trusted adviser Thaddeus Marik."

Frederick was glad he had not been sipping his brandy when the words registered. He had to struggle to keep from gaping as he looked from Thaddeus to Philip and back, half expecting them to burst out laughing at him for falling for their prank. There was no trace of humor in either expression.

"You're serious," he said unnecessarily.

"Very," Philip confirmed.

The room seemed to drop away as Frederick's mind turned inward, wrestling with the new information.

"That brings the Covenant Worlds—which, if I understand the current crop of foreign relations rumors, will soon include everything from Acubens through Rochelle?— solidly into Duchess Jessica's camp. Halas becomes a *Marik* House." He was vaguely aware he was babbling as he brainstormed, but didn't particularly care. "Irian. Irian is alienated—"

"A public relations minefield," Philip admitted. "But those who matter in my family are fully onboard."

Frederick nodded acknowledgment of the information as he rolled on.

"The reconciliation with the Rim Commonalities is bittersweet, creating the illusion of checks and balances. Redux of the dissenters' lightning-rod effect, perhaps alienating Regulus the more, but that's an irrelevant matter of degree, while attracting some of the more independent worlds.

"Thaddeus adopts the Halas-Hughes children, of course. That creates a crop of legitimate Marik heirs without having to—"

Frederick stopped abruptly, shocked that he'd been out of control enough to almost blurt out his next thought.

"Don't be concerned," Philip said, evidently assuming Frederick had embarrassed himself by alluding to Thaddeus begetting children with Jessica. "It will be a marriage in name only."

I thought she was trying to marry off one of her daughters. The game was being played at a level I didn't even recognize.

More disconcerted by that realization than anything the others had revealed, Frederick missed their next few sentences as he resorted past events in light of this new information. When he came to himself, he realized Philip and Thaddeus were looking at him expectantly.

"I'm sorry," he said. "I was lost in thought."

"It is a bit much," Philip agreed.

"We were saying your role in this will be to bridge the private sectors," Thaddeus said. "You can be the conduit through which the financial powers of the Rim Commonality and the Oriente Protectorate communicate.

"Your status as a Marik and what will become known as your complicated relationship with me puts you in a unique position to broker economic bonds that might otherwise take years to develop."

"As often happens among the friends of a couple who divorce." Frederick nodded. "Thaddeus remains loyal to the ex-wife while I—" He broke off. "You're asking me to go to the Rim Commonality."

"Of course."

"Sorry," Philip added. "We'd assumed that was the part where you were lost in thought."

Frederick nodded, his mind racing.

Farther away from Terra, and farther back in time. There's no point in becoming a bigger frog if the ponds become too small to accommodate you. He sipped his brandy, aware of the others watching him. *On the other hand, there's only so far one can go peddling influence within a single nation-state. To be a power broker between nations—to be the nexus through which influence flows—that is a future without limits. The Rim Commonality is too small, but directing commerce within a reunited Free Worlds League from behind the scenes? Just about right.*

"This really could reunite the Free Worlds League,

couldn't it?" he asked aloud. Publicly, particularly when the public of the moment were two of the most influential men in the Protectorate, one must always focus altruistically on the greater good.

Thaddeus nodded, his face in the crumpled expression Frederick recognized as indicating strong emotion. Philip's smile was less emotional, but his eyes were bright.

"We may very well be on the road to putting it all back together," he said.

Frederick nodded in his turn, giving the thought process another few seconds.

"Gentlemen," he said at length, packing his words with sincerity, "I can think of nothing I'd like better than to be a part of this venture."

Smiles and nods all around. Philip poured another round of brandy.

For his part, Frederick listened as the other two discussed the finer points of the reunification plan, his mind on his own future.

When swimming among sharks, don't settle for becoming a shark. Become the biggest damn shark in the ocean.

45

Amur, Oriente
Oriente Protectorate
11 August 3138

She stopped two steps across the threshold.

The *bokor*-woman's consort sat across the hearth carpet from Frederick Marik's armchair, a snifter of brandy cradled in his hands. He knew her. He had seen her on a daily basis years before, as a minor clerk in the Marik Palace administration. The killer of his son.

"Quite a shock, eh, Ayza?" Frederick chuckled. "I thought he was dead too."

"Sorry, sir," she said, resuming her businesslike stride toward her employer.

"Philip, this is Ms. Aborisha. She's become my good right hand when it comes to analyzing what this damnable Protectorate economy is up to. I'm thinking she will be an invaluable asset on our mission."

"Charmed, Ms. Aborisha," Philip Hughes said, rising to his feet with an old-fashioned courtesy the ruling class almost never wasted on their minions. "Sir Frederick has said nothing but good things about you."

"Thank you, sir." She did not extend her hand, fearing contact would break the illusion of her disguise. Instead she bobbed her head, playing the commoner overwhelmed in the presence of noble power.

As expected, the monster's husband smiled condescendingly and waved her toward a third chair. Not the straightbacked wooden one she normally chose—that was against the far wall near Frederick's deceptively useless-looking rolltop desk—but one of the four identical wingback armchairs grouped in front of the fireplace.

Careful not to sneer at the obscene softness of the cushion, she perched on the edge of her assigned seat.

She wished she had worn her hair loose so that she could screen her features. She reminded herself the eyes of the lesser races naturally slid off the features of the people—and the pink patches of her ersatz vitiligo could confuse even a practiced observer. Her body language: she focused on doing nothing like her former self as she looked to her employer with professional attention.

"Nothing said in this room leaves this room," Frederick said, reciting his household's standing policy for Philip's benefit. "Ayza, I have a proposal for you. Technically, I could simply make it an assignment, but this venture will take at least months, quite possibly years, and requires a level of dedication that only one who is truly committed can bring to the table."

"Yes, sir."

"What do you know of the Rim Commonality?"

"Originally a feudal aristocracy of some half dozen

worlds. In the aftermath of the Jihad, the exclusive rule of the nobility was overthrown and a representative commonality established," she recited by rote as she tried to deduce where the unexpected turn was leading. "Now composed of fifteen worlds, the current government of the Rim Commonality is not recognized by the Regulan Fiefs nor the Duchy of Andurien, but enjoys solid trade relations with the Duchy of Tamarind-Abbey and the Marik-Stewart— I'm sorry, former Marik-Stewart Commonwealth and a cordial if less robust trading relationship with the Oriente Protectorate.

"I would need a day to prepare a thorough economic analysis."

A day to contact the half dozen sources that had been prepared in advance to assist her in her mission and restructure the digested analyses they provided into something that sounded original. Father Pauli's thorough attention to detail was an inspiring example of dedication to a cause the men facing her could not begin to understand.

"That won't be necessary." Frederick smiled with a possessive pride.

Good to own proficient servants.

"In three days we—by which I mean Sir Philip Hughes and I—will journey to the Rim Commonality." The smile became predatory. "We will be attending the wedding of Lady Elis to their prime minister, Lord Michael Cendar."

She nodded.

Two of the evil one's daughters had slipped away before she'd arrived on Oriente; and the third gone before she was properly established in Sir Frederick's household. That none she sought were within reach had tested her faith more than any other event since her choice to ascend the Path. Long nights of prayer and days of fasting had strengthened her spirit, but brought her no closer to fulfilling the *ebo* laid upon her by the Rada.

Her eyes turned inward, the voices of the drones becoming a distant buzz.

The spawn she'd wounded now lay in bed-ridden exile among the Clans. That was her only comfort. The too-pretty boy faced, and no doubt cowered before, the Lyran horde in some forsaken corner of space, the wanton warrior daughter skulked through the darkness between worlds, and the middle child—the daughter touched most deeply by her mother's evil—had fled to the fringes of the sphere. All were beyond her grasp.

"Sir Philip will be laying the groundwork for a more formal political relationship between the parliament of the Protectorate and the senate of the Commonality." Frederick Marik's mundane syllables penetrated her thoughts, pulling her out of her self-pity. "While I will be doing what I can to transform that cordial but anemic trading relationship you described into a ferrosteel economic partnership.

"I think you'd be an invaluable asset in that endeavor." Her breath stopped.

"This will mean a substantial elevation in your position. You will be working on behalf of the Protectorate, not as my personal assistant." Frederick smiled, smug in his imagined control of her fate. "But it also involves protracted residence in a foreign nation and learning a new market and unfamiliar economic system from the ground up."

She sat transfixed, all thought of posing forgotten.

The *caplatas* of Oriente was sending her consort to support her spawn in spreading her web of evil across an innocent nation. Worse, once she had bent the unwitting satrapy to her will, could there be any doubt she would solidify her grip by absorbing—conquering, destroying—the worlds between the Commonality and the Protectorate? How many worlds? Twenty? Thirty? All would fall beneath the dead-hearted witch's will. Including beautiful, holy Siendou.

Surely Ayza the protector, whose name she had adopted for this holy mission, had guided her to this place, this moment. She offered up a prayer of repentance that she had ever doubted the Orisha's wisdom.

The seed of the monster, the mate of the beast, the tool of the destroyer: all three would be under her blade in a foreign land. A land whose leader was being drawn under the thrall of evil through his wedding bed. Or who might already be a willing partner in his people's enslavement, trading their souls for the satisfaction of his lusts.

Four deaths—four glorious sacrifices—that would wound the *bokor*-bitch to her cold and lifeless heart, thwart her plans of conquest and save an innocent people from her avaricious evil.

She thanked *Olorun* for this opportunity—this affirmation.

A pop of burning wood in the fireplace brought her back to Sir Frederick's sitting room–office and the two nobles watching her. Waiting for her answer. From the insipid smiles spread across their pasty features, she knew they had seen the exaltation of her epiphany flowing through her. No doubt they attributed her evident excitement to appreciation of their tawdry proposal.

She wondered that they did not burn to ash in the radiance of her spirit.

"Sir Frederick, Sir Philip," she said, aware of a new huskiness in her voice. "I can honestly say that my only prayer is that I be equal to the task that has been set before me."

46

Amur, Oriente
Oriente Protectorate
28 August 3138

"**W**hat has she done?" It took all of Jessica's will not to throw the noteputer and its offending report into the fireplace. "What has she done?"

"It is the Clans Sea Fox and Spirit Cat that—"

"With her as their envoy," Jessica cut off Torrian's explanation. "Don't try to placate me when I'm holding your damned report in my hand."

Unable to contain herself, she rose to her feet and paced the length of the sitting room. Turning on her heel, she caught Torrian in a lost expression before he professionally smoothed his features.

God, Philip. Where are you now?

Halfway to the edge of nowhere helping Elis secure her power base in the Rim Commonality, she answered herself as she paced back toward the fireplace. The time stamp on the message hadn't escaped her notice. One week ago. One year to the day from the night the assassin had plunged a knife into Julietta's throat.

The pop and crackle of the wood burning in the over-sized fireplace seemed to mock her. The evening was really too warm for a fire, but up until a moment ago the dancing flames had given her comfort. Now . . .

"We were the ones who asked them to garrison those worlds—" Torrian's words cut across her thoughts.

"Because Clanners don't take worlds except by conquest. Play to their honor and worlds they were asked to protect would be safe. Wasn't that the argument?" Jessica demanded. "She put them up to this. She taught them how to gain worlds and honor their oath at the same time.

"Clan Protectorate!"

Torrian opened his mouth and shut it again, wisdom stilling his tongue.

The plan had seemed so simple, so straightforward in a world twisted with labyrinthine politics. The Clans were the perfect tool for freeing up Oriente's military to deal with Andurien. Clan Sea Fox wanted safe trading partners and there weren't enough Spirit Cats standing after the conquest of Marik to take a world that didn't want to be taken. But kilo for kilo the Clanners could outfight any army in the region—at least that was their reputation. The mere presence of a Spirit Cat defensive garrison on Abadan and Avellaneda would be—had been—enough to persuade raiders to look elsewhere.

When that vile reptile Lester had seized Atreus, it had seemed only logical to extend a plan that was working. Stretching the Clanner's resources was far more logical than dividing Oriente's. The Lyrans were too intent on wrestling the Wolves for worlds closer to their border to strike so far rimward, and the Senatorial Alliance was in no condition to invade anyone. Garrisons for Angel II, Oceana and the Asellus systems would be more symbolic than necessary—a reassurance to the populace.

It had never occurred to her the Clans would annex the worlds by invitation. It was unheard of; it was unthinkable.

It was brilliant.

Why? Jessica raged silently against her oldest daughter. *Why* now *do you finally apply the lessons I spent a lifetime teaching you?*

"After the liberation of Atreus we will have the resources available to reestablish our control over the region," Torrian ventured again. "Though the Clan Sea Fox fleet is legendary, only a tiny fraction is actually present, and we know the Spirit Cats have enough resources to defend, at most, two systems against simultaneous assaults."

"By the time Atreus is ours, the Clan Protectorate will have established diplomatic ties with a half dozen nations," Jessica countered. "You've read this damn declaration. Clan Sea Fox is requiring all their trading partners to recognize their sovereignty. Anyone who wants to confound Oriente is going to follow suit."

What's next? Elis marshaling the Rim Commonality to strike at Oriente? Nikol resurrecting the Marik-Stewart Commonwealth to snatch Atreus from my grasp?

Philip, damn you, I should never have let you go away. For a wild moment she considered recalling him. *He couldn't yet be more than three jumps away.*

Jessica reined in the rising tide of self-pity with an effort. Looking at her hand, she was a little surprised to see that the noteputer hadn't shattered in her grip.

"Thank you, Torrian," she said. "That will be all."

Alone again, she resumed her chair by the fire, hoping to draw some comfort from its warmth. Taking a careful sip of her still cool Riesling, she considered the noteputer and its contents. The Clan Protectorate's declaration of sovereignty and Torrian's strategic analysis.

Tabbing back to the beginning of the files, Jessica began reading again.

Brilliant.

Liberation Base
Torville, Loongana
Duchy of Tamarind-Abbey

"Julietta's alive!"

Fontaine Marik grinned at the obvious joy on young Christopher's face.

"A new nation has declared itself, the Clans are doing something that has never been done before, your mother—her dream of unifying the Free Worlds League—is now pressed on three sides and yet you, lad, see right to the most important part of the matter," he said. "Your sister is indeed alive. And from the evidence, doing quite well for herself."

The wind was picking up. Fontaine squinted against the blowing dust, trying to gauge the readiness of the DropShips. Foolish, of course. He could get more accurate data sitting in the comfort of the hunting lodge Viscount Damatto had provided, reading updated reports on his noteputer. But nothing quite matched the visceral effect of an eyes-on inspection. It grounded events in reality, not ordered phosphor dots.

And it got him out into the fresh air, which—he reminded himself as another dust-laden gust nearly triggered a fit of coughing—was something he had said he needed.

His plan to retake Tamarind in the wake of Anson's death had been delayed nearly a fortnight. Not only had the damn Steiners been more cautions about relaxing their guard than he'd anticipated, the planetary militias of Merton and Sackville, the Duchy's newest members, had been unwilling to risk assets they felt they needed in retaking a capital world toward which they felt no real loyalty.

Why tell us you have the damn troops if you won't let us use them?

Fontaine took a deep breath—risking inhaling another half kilo of blowing dust—and calmed his nerves, grateful for Karli's steadying hand on his shoulder. Two weeks of rearranging rosters to make up for the lack was all it had cost them. And there was always a chance their apparent inactivity had helped the plan, making the Lyrans more sure the spirit of Tamarind-Abbey had been broken.

Beside him, Christopher navigated across the dusty ferrocrete by instinct, reading the reports on the noteputer screen and trusting his sense of space to keep him from falling down a gopher hole. Roland, Tamarind-Abbey's director of SAFE, kept station on Fontaine's other flank as the three made their way across the DropShip field.

Julietta of *Marik?* Fontaine returned to the declaration the courier had delivered. *She's carved a new nation for herself out of the carcasses of both The Republic and Anson's Commonwealth, snatching the prize right out of Jessica's hand in the process. She may not have the blood, but her moves are pure Marik.* Fontaine chuckled. *Those Clanners will never know what hit them.*

Aloud he said: "How does this affect us strategically?"

"Not at all, Your Grace," Roland answered. Even though they were well out of earshot of any who might have overheard, he spoke in the formal tones of court whenever they were outside the confines of rooms his people had swept for listening devices. "In addition to Oriente, the Clan Protectorate borders the Covenant Worlds, the Senatorial Alliance and a region of the former Commonwealth we believe Clan Wolf intends to annex."

"Meaning if they want to jump one way they have to turn their backs on at least one hungry neighbor with a knife."

"Essentially, Your Grace," Roland agreed. "It is doubtful Oriente will divert any of the resources it has committed to the Atreus campaign to the new front. The Clan Protectorate will be too preoccupied with cementing stability to be a threat. And as an objective, Marik is well below Atreus on Oriente's priority list."

"Meaning everyone else is playing with someone else and out here it's just us and the Lyrans?"

"Essentially," Roland repeated.

"Good." Fontaine nodded, looking up at the nearest DropShip. "I like an even fight."

Regulus City
Chebbin, Regulus
Regulan Fiefs

"How many worlds?"

"According to their declaration, seven, including Marik," Gustav Salazar answered with the passion he usually reserved for commenting on the weather. "Abadan, Angel II, Asellus Australis, Asellus Borealis, Avellanada and Oceana."

Lester was aware he was standing, with no memory of getting up. He was peripherally aware of the last pages of the report he'd been reading drifting to the emerald carpet of Emlia's sitting room.

"And only Marik taken by force?"

Salazar nodded.

"Ha!" Lester scrubbed his hands, unable to contain his glee. "The bitch lay down with vipers and the damn things bit her in the ass."

"Lester!"

"Sorry, my dear." He grinned at his wife, feeling not the least bit contrite. "But that's exactly what happened."

He began pacing, having to plot an oblique course between the overstuffed chairs—how could the woman he loved not notice the saffron-flowered russet upholstery clashed with the carpet?—to reach the window. Turning on his heel, he barked his leg on an incidental table, but the sharp pain did nothing to dampen his mood.

"She brought in the Clans to bring down the Free Worlds League because she thought she could control them. Instead they took a page from her own book and stabbed her in the back when she was most vulnerable. Oh, the delicious irony."

This time Emlia's smile answered his own, her eyes dancing with shared delight.

"There is more," Salazar said.

"News?" Lester asked. "Or irony?"

"Both, I believe, sir."

"Gustav, I believe that is the first bit of humor I've ever heard from your lips."

"Sir?"

"Lester, don't tease the man."

"You're right, of course, my dear." Lester composed his features into a solemn mask. "My apologies, Mr. Salazar. What is this additional information?"

"The spokesperson for the Clan Protectorate, and evidently chief of their foreign affairs, is Lady Julietta Halas-Hughes."

Lester felt a chill wash through his body. "Julietta Hughes?"

"Yes, sir," Salazar confirmed. "Though she now identifies herself as Lady Julietta *of* Marik, evidently indicating the planet."

Emlia made an appreciative sound, earning her a glare from her husband.

"Legitimately linking the Marik name to hers while making it clear she stands separate from her mother *and* conforming to the Clan tradition of no unearned last name," she explained. "Elegant."

Dismissing the trivial point, Lester focused his glare on his chief of intelligence. "What happened to her coma?"

"I reported that she had regained consciousness some months ago. The Spirit Cat physicians—"

"Took her to Marik, I know," Lester snapped. "She was bedridden. What happened?"

"I have no assets within the Clan enclave," Salazar said. "Inferring from available evidence, Clan medical technology exceeds anything we anticipated."

"Damn it!"

"Lester?"

"Is even the smallest victory snatched from us?"

"Dearest, I don't believe you're appreciating the irony Mr. Salazar mentioned," Emlia said. "Or perhaps it's Ashe."

Lester stared at his wife blankly.

"Where is the irony in that—*woman's*—unholy whelp being alive?" he demanded. "She should be dead."

"Leaving Jessica with no heirs is one justice." Emlia smiled. "But isn't this justice of a different sort? Jessica living to see her dream torn to shreds by her own children?"

47

Christopher glanced between his datascreens and the heads-up display, confirming their empty fields matched.

No one appreciates how much double-double-checking goes into being a daredevil. He grinned.

With no targets in range and no sensors sweeping his way, he eased his BattleMech forward, following the curve of the aqueduct leading into the Padaron water desalinization plant. The bulk of Teteli Company was spread out to his left, moving cautiously through the metal-heavy manufacturing district. Only Missy Carter was to his right, the purple icon denoting her *Hercules* hovering at the edge of his heads-up as she paced him along the far side of the aqueduct. He knew she could see him as they passed each arch of the elevated waterway, but the over/under barrels of the twin extended-range medium lasers jutting from the right chest and shoulder of his BattleMech blocked his view in her direction.

Prevailing on Duke Fontaine to let him be part of the liberation of Tamarind had depended on his promise to pilot a BattleMech and not one of the light, fast vehicles he preferred. The duke had expected him to select a *BattleMaster* or something equally indestructible. His choice of a fifty-five-ton *Cronus* 5M had almost ruined the deal; would have landed him in the situation room with the duke and Roland if Force Commander Talbridge hadn't convinced Fontaine the fast, rugged machine offered as sure a guarantee of survival as any 'Mech could in the battlefield.

Acing the live-fire qualification exercise had helped.

Though he'd only had a few weeks to become familiar with this particular *Cronus*, the design had been his favorite at Princefield. However, an owner with more faith in firepower than trust in electronics had swapped out the C3 unit for an extra ton of missiles to feed the four-tube streak missile launcher that rose above his cockpit. Christopher liked the thought process, and knowing he was going into combat with twenty-five additional salvos was a comfort.

Coming to another intersection, Christopher paused again to scan ahead. Intel placed at least a demi-company of Lyran BattleMechs in the industrial district. So far no one in Teteli Company had made hard contact with anything remotely threatening. Given the heavy fighting Tamarind Company was reporting nearer the center of town, this was wrong at a number of levels. Instinct said rush ahead, move to support their comrades already in the thick of it. But common sense, and Lieutenant Whittaker, commanding Teteli, said move slow and look sharp. The tactical situation had ambush written all over it.

Ahead of him the pavement was drenched. Seawater spuming over the side of the aqueduct above made a permanent rainstorm about a dozen meters across. The keepers of the waterway were evidently protesting the Lyran occupation by either deliberately letting the system overflow or not clearing the channel of debris. Probably both. It wasn't much as acts of resistance went, but every little bit helped.

Rainbows danced in the falling water, the morning rays pouring through a cross street washed the pavement and the pillar of the aqueduct in golden light. If the stream had been in the shadows between buildings, Christopher would have missed the charred circle extending beyond the soaked ferrocrete. Something had scorched the ground. Not weapons fire, more like a burning vehicle or . . . *jump jets*?

Turning his *Cronus* to face the open arch beside him, he squirted a narrow microwave signal toward the *Hercules*.

"Can this sluice support BattleMechs?"

Missy's machine stopped midstride.

"I'm not sure. It doesn't look overengineered, but architecture ain't my field." There was a pause. Christopher hoped she had the wit not to focus her sensors on the aqueduct before they were ready to engage whatever enemy might be up there. "I sure wouldn't risk anything big up there. A scout maybe?"

"Hughes to Whittaker," Christopher said on the tac channel.

"Go, Hellion."

"Carter and I think there might be a scout 'Mech on the aqueduct. If we're right, we're standing right under him."

"Keep walking," Whittaker ordered. "Try not to look like you saw him. If they've got a spotter in the trees, you can bet they've got a heavy in the bushes to protect their eyes. Stay sharp."

"Thermal!" Missy shouted before Christopher could answer. "Fusion reactor powering up bearing three-oh degrees relative. Range two-nine-oh."

The lookout's defender Whittaker had expected, on Missy's side of the waterway.

"Multiple start-ups," someone shouted into their microphone. "Tally . . . three in zone baker. Hard contact grid baker-tango."

"Alpha lance, gamma lance, form on me," Whittaker ordered. "Beta lance, form on Carter. Take out the guard dog and blind the bird dog."

Christopher aimed his extended-range particle-projection cannon at the arch of steel and stone thirty meters above. He hesitated. What would a PPC do against the structure? Taking blind potshots might rattle the Lyran spotter, but taking him out was going to require a clear shot. He backpedaled into the street.

"Got a *Falconer*," Missy called out as the Lyran heavy broke cover on her side of the aqueduct.

"ETA twenty seconds." Ngyuen, leader of beta lance. "Pull back through the arch. Lead him to us."

"Blinding the bird dog," Christopher announced.

Stomping his foot controls, he launched the *Cronus* into the air.

A triple stream of laser darts cascaded along the length of his BattleMech as it cleared the lip of the waterway. The wire frame lit up with reports of lost armor—nothing vital.

Christopher feathered his jump jets, cutting his arc short

and twisting to bring his torso weapons to bear on the Lyran 'Mech. Twin contrails marked the passage of short-range missiles through the space where he should have been.

The tac display labeled his opponent a *Battle Hawk* as his finger spasmed on the fire control. All three lasers went wide, boiling the water that rushed past the smaller machine's hips.

Christopher kicked his jump jets hard. Coming down in moving water in a torrent ten meters wide and at least four deep was not something a BattleMech was designed to do.

His respect for the Lyran pilot doubled as his legs were swept from under him. Flexing the knee actuators to their maximum, Christopher just managed to keep his torso upright. He swung the thick arms of the *Cronus* up and out, parallel above the surface, lest the current grab them and drag his machine over backward.

Did not anticipate this.

Fortunately he was still facing his opponent, now a hundred meters upstream. The lower of his over/under-mounted medium lasers was underwater, and waves were breaking over the small laser below his cockpit. He didn't think that would affect them, but to be safe he triggered only the upper laser. Ghostly in the sunlight, the green beam splashed across the *Battle Hawk*'s chest, melting armor in a ragged scar just below the escape pod.

Nothing vital there.

Tapping in a code, he primed the four streak missiles in their tubes above his cockpit. At near-contact range he didn't wait on the targeting computer, firing his salvo the instant the missiles went hot.

The *Battle Hawk*'s right arm bent impossibly back as explosions blossomed across its shoulder and chest. The light 'Mech shuddered, staggering toward the kneeling *Cronus* in the grip of the torrent. Planting its legs wide and reaching out with its good left arm to grip the edge of the aqueduct, the Lyran seemed to get control of his machine. At least it stopped staggering toward Christopher. But it continued to shudder, vibrating faster than the rushing water should have caused.

Gyro?

As if in answer to his question, the head of the *Battle Hawk* seemed to explode upward. The escape pod arched up and out over the rim of the aqueduct.

Without the pilot to keep it upright, the Lyran BattleMech, still vibrating as its massive gyroscope reeled in its mount, tumbled forward. Christopher's hope that the machine was massive enough to resist the drag of the current evaporated as the headless shape scraped ponderously toward him.

If the smaller machine jammed against his, he would never regain his feet. Even if the *Battle Hawk*'s shredding gyro didn't damage his *Cronos*, he'd spend the rest of the liberation trapped in the aqueduct until someone came and rescued him. Or he could punch out and take his chances running around the streets of Padaron in cooling vest and shorts threatening Lyrans with his laser pistol.

Desperately working the joysticks, Christopher tried to get his legs under him. Bent back, they were directly beneath the muzzles of his jump jets. Firing the jets would destroy his legs, and an off-balance and legless BattleMech would not land well. At all.

He was facing upstream, and so the wall of the sluice was close to his right arm. Unfortunately, the only hand the *Cronos* had was on its left arm, which was about six meters too short to reach the other wall.

Swinging his right arm up, he brought the ER PPC down hard on the stone wall, trying to make the heavy cylinder find purchase. On his third try the cooling vanes caught on some imperfection. Pushing down with all the pressure the arm servos could muster, he was able to bring the *Cronos*' right leg forward and up, getting the foot planted firmly on the bottom of the sluice.

The 'Mech rocked.

Looking up, Christopher expected to see that the *Battle Hawk* had finally reached him, but the Lyran machine was still a dozen meters away. He watched it a moment to confirm the current was still pushing it slowly along.

How much water moving how fast can push a thirty-ton BattleMech—

The *Cronos* rocked again.

Christopher realized the rushing water, which had been

level with the muzzle of his small laser moments before, was now flowing around the lower edge of the cockpit canopy. The water was rising.

Except . . .

The far wall looked higher than it had before. And the stonework glistened wetly above the rushing water.

He wasn't cockpit-deep in rushing water. He was cockpit-deep in rushing water in an aqueduct thirty meters above the ground. An aqueduct that had never been designed to support a fifty-five-ton BattleMech. And there were an additional thirty tons of heavy metal creeping closer every second.

His 'Mech wasn't what was rocking.

Christopher stomped his jump jets just as the wall under his right arm collapsed.

48

Zletovo, Lesnovo
Rim Commonality
23 September 3138

Hopelessly homely, Frederick Marik thought, inclining his head as the young woman with the wide blue eyes was introduced. *But with a family name like Bey-Hughes, Lady Genevieve could grow a second head and still have her pick of any young scion antispinward of Regulus.*

As a cousin of Elis Marik, the soon-to-be wife of the Rim Commonality's prime minister, Lady Genevieve's stock was about to go up substantially. Frederick decided he liked her eyes.

As he had expected, fashions and society on Lesnovo harkened back to mores outgrown by Euro-Terran culture twelve hundred years ago. With the exception of hands, there was no bare flesh below the throat on men or women, despite the oppressive humidity. Though he imagined the preponderance of light silks and lace in both men's and women's fashions indicated an oblique attempt to keep cool.

Most startling to him were what he assumed were corsets of some sort worn by women of every age and class. He couldn't see their exact design beneath the dresses, but they evidently constricted the midriff tightly, then flared out at the top. The net effect was an improbably tiny waist and breasts thrust up and forward as though set on a shelf. The breasts themselves were properly covered, of course— usually with silk, though some of the younger women at the reception practiced brinksmanship with yokes of translucent lace—but the effect was just a bit disconcerting.

A quick glance at his personal assistant confirmed that Ayza shared his bemusement at the local fashion.

"Lord Marik." Their hostess snagged his arm with what he suspected was socially daring familiarity.

Lady Gladys was, if he was tracking familial connections properly, both the maternal great-aunt of the blue-eyed Genevieve, whom Elis Marik addressed as "cousin Gen," and Philip Hughes' second cousin. Or third.

Reflecting on the fact that aging dowagers should be spared the hellish corsets, Frederick missed her next words as she steered him toward a sober group of men and women. And standing out as sober at a Lesnovo fete required a bit of doing.

Sharpen up, old boy. Until you know the lay of the land, every encounter is vital.

"I'm sorry, Lady Gladys, but I missed that last," he admitted. Charming honesty was always the best policy. At least when there was a danger that playing off a lapse might lead to a strategic faux pas.

"It *is* a bit convoluted, I shouldn't have thrown it all at you at once." Lady Gladys slowed her pace a bit to allow an extra moment of conversation before reaching the group. "The short form is, these are the prime movers in the Goth Khakar cartel, which controls trade in the coreward third of the Commonality. Economically, they are closely tied with—"

"Independent worlds coreward of your borders and the Duchy of Tamarind-Abbey?" Frederick guessed to cut short her explanation.

"And you said you'd missed it." Lady Gladys patted the arm she still held. "They have some serious concerns about how this impending alliance will affect their trade relations."

Frederick was peripherally aware of Ayza trailing slightly on his flank. With a glance and a nod, he summoned her to come abreast as Lady Gladys introduced him to the group.

Technically, Ayza was not of the same social class as those attending this afternoon's gathering. The contrast between her Oriente-style business suit and the local finery, combined with her unfortunate disfigurement, tended to emphasize this, making it difficult for her to mingle as an equal. But Frederick wanted her out of his shadow and clearly established as a major player from the beginning. Her role in integrating the economies of the two realms would be made easier if she was perceived by all involved as a person of substance.

Particularly on this backwater—

Shoving his elitism where it belonged, Frederick smiled and extended his hand to the evident leader of the cartel. Introducing Ayza Aborisha as an economic analyst, he set to work building the Free Worlds League.

Amur, Oriente
Oriente Protectorate

Jessica settled back in her chair and nodded to Torrian. Her intelligence chief dimmed the lights without a word. There was a moment of twilight before the flat-screen monitor came to life. The resolution was sharp, sharper than most holovids, and Elis' smiling face seemed close enough to touch.

She's been getting too much sun, Jessica thought, then chided herself for being a fool. *That's makeup. Elis recorded this before she left. Before we knew what her sister was up to.*

Her daughter appeared to be sitting in a sunroom of some sort. Visible beyond her was a broad window through which could be seen a garden of vaguely exotic plants. Jessica was certain the image accurately represented the appearance of a garden in Zletovo on Lesnovo a month ago, when this recording was supposedly made.

Torrian's people did good work.

"If you are seeing this, you know that my mother granted my wish," the recorded Elis was saying. "I wanted to be the first to tell everyone on my home of Oriente and all through the Protectorate some wonderful news.

"At first, to some who do not know my mother well and who do not understand all she has been through, this may not seem like good news. But . . ."

And here Elis sighed, visibly gathering herself before pressing on.

"There is some bad news that must precede the good.

"You all know that tragedy touched our family over a year ago. A tragic loss that wounded my father in ways few can understand. I know it is generally assumed that he left my mother, though there has been no formal announcement. He did leave. But not because he no longer loved my mother. He left because he could no longer endure the pressures of public office, no longer bear to live in the house where his eldest son, my brother Janos, died. Though they will always care deeply for one another, he could no longer be a husband—a daily companion and support—to my mother."

Jessica wished she could sip her tea, but she'd set it down before she was fully settled and now it was out of reach. She considered leaning forward and stretching for the cup, but decided the tea had probably grown too cool to enjoy.

"For those of you who have been wondering what became of him, I am now authorized to tell you my father has come to the Rim Commonality and will be living for a time at the estate of cousins here on Lesnovo."

The recorded Elis paused for a long five-count, giving her listeners the chance to absorb the shock.

Jessica liked the strength in her daughter's face. Her delivery struck just the right note: emotionally vulnerable without being maudlin. And clear-eyed—clear-eyed was important. The public expected the Mariks to be clear-eyed in all they did.

"I asked Father to join me in recording this news, so everyone who cares about him will know that he is as genuinely pleased as I am, but he said that he is not ready to face the public yet. Not even in recorded form. He did ask that I tell all of you who have been praying for him that he is doing much better. He hopes to be able to tell all of you—and to show all of you—someday soon."

Again Elis paused. Her eyes seemed to turn inward and a small smile curved her lips. The very image of a young woman reflecting on something good before sharing it.

"As I adjust to my life here on Lesnovo and prepare for my wedding, which should be happening about the time you see this recording, I do miss my mother. But I know that in these trying times her people need her on Oriente. The universe does not stop because a mother wants to go to her daughter's wedding.

"Or because a daughter wants to go to her mother's."

A broad smile lit Elis' features, radiating delight.

"Though no man can take my father's place in my mother's heart, someone I know is admired and respected by all of us has come to be her steady support, her trusted adviser, her daily companion and her very dear friend. Even before we left Oriente, my father and I grew to know and appreciate this man's steady dependability, his solid moral judgment and his unswerving devotion to the ideal of the Free Worlds League. He is a friend to us both. And we were both delighted to learn that he has grown to be something more to my mother."

Jessica didn't think it possible, but Elis became even more radiant—positively luminous with joy as she leaned toward the camera with transparent eagerness to share her news.

"My friends—my family of the Oriente Protectorate—it is my very great pleasure to announce that at sixteen hundred hours Amur time on Sunday, the thirtieth of October, 3138 my mother, Captain-General Jessica Marik, will wed Warden Thaddeus Marik.

"Please join our entire family in celebrating her joy."

The image froze, imprinting Elis' delight on the viewer's

mind; then the screen faded to a restful blue before going dark. A moment later the room's lights were restored.

"Well."

"Indeed," Torrian agreed. "Consensus in my department is the holovid industry missed a golden opportunity. She made that recording in a single take."

Jessica nodded.

Elis always had the gift of making herself invisible. The ability to project any image she wants must be a natural extension of that talent.

"When does this go public?" she asked aloud.

"In about a week." Torrian retrieved the data crystal from the reader and carefully sealed it in its case. "That timetable will give local nobility time to attend without giving any potential opposition time to organize."

"I would think anyone opposed would take to the streets the moment they heard."

"I was speaking of political opposition, Your Grace."

"Of course."

"Public opinion is always mercurial. We have several interventions in place should Lady Elis' announcement prove not to be enough in and of itself."

Jessica nodded, accepting her security chief's assessment. Perversely, she found herself wishing Philip was seated next to her.

Perhaps have him give me away at the ceremony. That would be a scene for the evening news. She smiled at the image of disconcerted wedding guests trying to cope gracefully. But the chair beside her was empty and there was no one to share the moment. *This is not going to be as easy as I'd thought it would be.*

Stretching forward, she picked up the porcelain cup of herbal tea. She'd been right; it was cold.

49

"**D**amn!"

"Roland," Fontaine said wearily. "You really must develop some alternative response to unexpected news."

"Sorry, Your Grace," Roland said, holding up the verigraph he had been reading. "But under the circumstances . . ."

"Simpson Desert?"

"No, Your Grace."

The Lyrans had been more deeply entrenched on Simpson Desert than on Tamarind, obviously expecting Fontaine to take the stepping-stone world before attempting to liberate his capital. After two months of conflict, the world was still in conflict, but it was basic strategic arithmetic that if the Lyrans won Simpson Desert their next step would be an assault on Tamarind.

Without further explanation, Roland rose from his workstation and carried the verigraph to Fontaine's broad wooden desk.

Fontaine took the document, trying to glean some clue to its content from Roland's expression before reading it. Giving up on divination, he angled the page to catch the light from his study window.

He felt the blood rush from his face at the second line. "Damn."

"Indeed."

Young Christopher—not looking so young since his fall at Padaron—turned from his study of the garden. The gesture required he move his whole body, for his neck and right arm were encased in rigid casts, the later braced so it extended out from his shoulder.

Fontaine had seen the battle ROMs—both Christopher's and his lancemates'—and had listened to expert testimony to the effect that the last corkscrew flight of his broken BattleMech represented some of the finest piloting anyone had ever seen. None of that had curbed his anger at Christopher for taking such a risk. Or with himself for letting the lad talk him into giving him the opportunity.

The only good that had come of the event, as far as he could see, was a new sobriety in Christopher's attitude; perhaps even some evidence of the early onset of wisdom.

"What is it?" Christopher asked.

Fontaine raised the verigraph in his hand, then stopped midgesture.

The lad had been by his side for nearly a year. Stuck with him through the loss of Tamarind and been part of retaking it. A small and foolish part, perhaps, but the boy had endeared himself to the people of Tamarind-Abbey at every turn. None doubted his basic decency or his commitment to the Free Worlds League.

And yet . . .

No matter how much Fontaine had come to regard Christopher as a son, there was no forgetting whose child he was; who had raised him. Jessica Halas-Hughes Marik had her hand in every aspect of the boy's life. He was not just her flesh and blood; he was her creature, shaped by her will to carry out her plans.

Eleven months ago, in a room not far from this one, Christopher had refused to reveal those plans. Standing—rightly—on his honor and his duty to the Oriente Protectorate.

But there was another possibility, one Fontaine had not considered at the time. Perhaps the boy had refused to talk because he knew his mother's plans—and knew those plans would turn Fontaine's stomach.

Letting the boy read the verigraph himself would give him time to school his features, to formulate his response. And leave Fontaine forever wondering. The way to find the truth was to look him straight in the eye and hit him with it cold.

"Your mother is marrying Thaddeus Marik."

"Thaddeus—"

Christopher's mouth opened, then closed convulsively.

Fontaine felt the muscles of his back and shoulders relax as he saw the lad's complete surprise writ large across his features.

"Um." Christopher frowned, then seemed to gather himself. "Is my father all right?"

Fontaine blinked. He hadn't even considered that aspect.

"Yes," Roland answered. "Toward the end of the document it says he has relocated to the Rim Commonality with your sister Elis. Both he and she give their blessing to this union."

"I see."

"Sit down before you fall, boy," Fontaine snapped. "Roland, get him some water. Or do you want something stronger?"

"No," Christopher said, lowering himself to the window seat. "No, sir, I'm fine. I'll want to get a message to my father."

"Of course, of course." Fontaine glared at the verigraph in his hand. "This is my damn fault. I told her what she needed to do to unify the Free Worlds League—to get my support—and she did it. The woman is playing this game at a level the rest of us can only imagine."

Regulus City
Chebbin, Regulus
Regulan Fiefs

"I take back everything I have ever said in defense of Jessica Halas."

Lester didn't respond, lost in the sight of Emlia as he'd never seen her. Her chin was up, her eyes so wide their irises were ringed in white and her nostrils were flaring. She looked like nothing so much as an enraged charger; a valiant mare ready to rend enemies beneath her hooves. He'd seen her angry before, seen her outraged, seen her indignant. This was . . . different.

Frightening in a strangely attractive way.

"She has allied herself with the Clans," he said. "Turned on her own people, invaded Andurien, killed thousands of innocents in her thirst for power and this—marrying Thaddeus Marik—is what fills you with rage?"

"Thaddeus Marik?"

"Mind you, he's a Marik, with all the unstable delusions of grandeur that implies," Lester said. "But as far as Mariks go, he's one of their better efforts. Morals of a snake, of course. He started out as Republican scum but he can't help where he was born. And unlike his late and unlamented cousin Anson, he's earned all those medals pinned to his chest. She could have done a lot worse."

"No." Emlia's voice was edged with finality. "She could not have done worse."

"Given her choices—"

"Lester, sometimes you are an ass."

He froze, his shoulders lifted midshrug, and stared blankly at his wife.

"Her husband, Lester." Emlia bore down on the words. "She set aside her husband. She defiled her family. She ended her *marriage*!"

Emlia stopped herself. Fists clenched at her sides, chest heaving, she glared at Lester with a rage that bordered on madness.

"She ended her marriage," she repeated in a calm tone that did not match her eyes. "Traded her husband for the Free Worlds League.

"Jessica Halas is beyond redemption."

50

Speranza Nova DropPort
Speranza Nova, New Hope
Protectorate Coalition
30 October 3138

Lieutenant Zeke Carleston thought about getting out of the Ibex. After a moment his legs agreed with him and swung left.

The medics had told him—everyone had told him—that the hesitation between order to move and move wasn't noticeable. Or barely noticeable. He'd timed it himself, recording himself on a borrowed holocorder. One-half to two seconds and everything in between. That was the delay. With no rhyme or pattern to when it was what.

Getting over the doorsill was a bit of a trick, but he'd had months of practice and there was no visible hitch in his boots' arc from the floorboards to the running board. Holding the door frame with both hands, he levered himself upright and eased one foot from the running board to the extra bar step that had been welded beneath it.

That had pissed him off the first time he'd seen it. The hand controls for the Ibex—those made sense, if only from a safety standpoint. He could accept those were necessary even if he didn't like them. But the baby step? It singled him out; it announced to the world that the driver of this Ibex needed extra help just to do his duty. He'd stormed over to the motor pool—in the methodical, thoughtful way his fried brain required—just in time to see the last set of step rails being welded on the final Ibex. Every damn vehicle in the compound had baby steps. He'd wanted to cry.

Turning on his heel—fast for once—he'd stormed away before anyone caught him at it.

Zeke could see the VIP he was supposed to pick up sauntering in his direction from the service tunnel leading up from beneath the civilian cargo-hauler that had brought her to New Hope. At least he assumed it was her. At one hundred and fifty meters he couldn't make out the identifiers he'd been given: female, red hair, green eyes.

His Ibex was sixth in a line of vehicles standing by at the requisite distance from the pad to carry any passengers or any off-duty ship's crew into the city, and a lot of the taxis were recycled military, so his didn't stand out. The first clue to tell his pickup which was her ride was Zeke standing by the left front fender of the Ibex. Like the taxis, a lot of the drivers were recycled militia from a half dozen worlds, or militia dependents. Mismatched military surplus was pretty much standard dress among them, and standing by the taxi was standard driver behavior. But his was the only khaki sporting service ribbons he'd earned: and Marik-Stewart Commonwealth ribbons pinned to a duty kit with no rank insignia was the confirmation his passenger would be looking for.

Speaking sternly to his legs, Zeke moved deliberately to the front fender, passenger side, of the high-wheeled Ibex to wait for his ride to spot him.

His *Ocelot* had done this to him. Or he'd done it to himself trying to keep his light BattleMech on its feet while taking fire from two Lyran heavies. The last barrage of lasers before the autocannon toppled him had fried the control interface. Fighting for balance with the safety lockouts gone had created a feedback loop in his neurohelmet. His legs were fine—or had been once the bones had set—but his brain always had to take an extra second to figure out how to route commands past the burned-out patch in his motor-control center.

Extra half second to two seconds. Not much, but enough to ensure he'd never pilot a BattleMech again. Nothing the medicos could do about that.

Or about the ghost pains. There was nothing wrong with his body; his injuries had all healed beautifully, but every now and then the pain receptors in his brain fired. No reason, no trigger anyone could find. Just sudden shooting pains tracing nerve paths through his body. He had a prescription for heavy-duty pain meds for when it got bad, but the drunken lack of control they induced scared him worse than the pains. He'd taken two in the three months he'd been out of the hospital.

Before Helm he'd commanded BattleMechs, what amounted to two-thirds of a company in the deliberately skewed command structure of the Silver Hawk Irregulars. Now he commanded the new recruits, overseeing the DIs who did the real work of molding them into soldiers and making sure the neophyte Irregulars had a thorough understanding of the Silver Hawks' unconventional battlefield tactics.

Or running errands for Colonel Cameron-Witherspoon. The CO liked having him around for some reason. Called him a talisman once, which made no sense. He figured he was a screwup who hadn't been put out to pasture because they couldn't spare any MechWarriors to wipe the new kids' noses.

His passenger made her way down the line of taxis, smiling noncommittally at each driver and glancing at their chests for service ribbons. Someone behind her called out about taking first in line and not being so damned choosy, but she ignored the voice.

Red hair, though he would have said more strawberry blond, *check*; and she was a bit younger than he'd expected. Her green eyes swept blankly across his, then dropped to his chest.

She came to attention so fast Zeke thought he heard her spine pop. Fingertips to brow, hand straight as a blade, she snapped and held a formal salute.

Which was stupid, Zeke thought, since she was in mufti. And as he understood it, supposedly under cover. But there was no denying the green eyes shaded by her hand glowed with genuine respect.

With an effort he hoped didn't show, Zeke snapped his heels together and came to full attention, returning the salute.

"I appreciate it, sister," he said, dropping his arm. "But we're both *ex*-military these days. And MSC ribbons don't mean much now that the Commonwealth is gone."

"A lot of good people died fighting to save Helm," she answered, not matching his familiar tone. "And the Order of the Saber is the Order of the Saber no matter where it was issued."

"They were handing 'em out like party favors in the last days."

"I very much doubt that." She ran her eye over his Ibex, not smiling as she spent an extra second on the canvas cargo pack that concealed the twin man-pack gauss rifles on their swivel mount. "You keep a clean machine. Would you give me a lift into the city?"

"Ten eagles," Zeke quoted the standard rate. "And no war stories."

She handed over the fare and Zeke held the rear passenger door open for her, trying not to envy the easy grace with which she swung into the vehicle.

As he made his way around the front of the Ibex, the driver of the taxi ahead of him blocked his way.

"There are rules, bud. Courtesies. First hack in line gets the fare."

Zeke looked up at the bigger man. He looked in shape, but with a weightlifter's build, not a fighter's. Six months ago, before Helm, Zeke could have taken him down, though he'd probably have taken some damage in the process. Now . . .

"The fare chose me," he said.

"Because you put on a show." The driver waved an up-turned palm toward the line of cars and trucks ahead of Zeke's. "You should have directed her to the first taxi. We start competing, we get a price war and everybody loses. You just screw up the system playing dress-up like that. What if we all started buying medals to pull the riders?"

The big man met Zeke's eyes and stopped moving midgesture.

"Oh. Damn. Sorry. That was out of line." Shuffling his feet, the driver looked at the ground, then down the line of trucks and cars, then back at Zeke. "Look, we've all gone through stuff, and we're all going through stuff. Some worse than others. But we gotta stick together. Next time, wave the fare to the first hack in line, okay? Give us all a fair shake."

"Next time," Zeke promised.

The big man sketched a wave that was almost a salute and headed back to his battered van. There was a small crowd of civilians wandering out from the DropShip. Zeke wondered how many of them were support troops for his passenger.

"You're pretty high profile for a guy from an outfit that doesn't exist," his ride said as he punched the diesel to life. "No effort to hide the extra armor?"

"Half the working stiffs in the Protectorate Coalition refugeed out of some defeat," Zeke answered. "Military surplus is the norm on most planets."

He didn't add that he never wore his service ribbons unless given a direct order.

"Protectorate Coalition," his passenger said. "Doesn't have quite the same ring as Silver Hawks Coalition, does it?"

Zeke spared her a glance in the rearview. Jade green eyes met his with nothing but curiosity. Good poker face. His ribbons must have really shocked her to break that façade.

"This isn't the Silver Hawks Coalition anymore, ma'am," he said, eyes on the road. "The Hawks got divided up between the Lyrans and the Milton Combine and whatever the hell it is the knights and paladins of the ex-damn-Republic are doing on Callison and Marcus. The Protectorate Coalition is the closest thing to a Silver Hawks state that's left."

"And that's good enough for you?"

Zeke spun the wheel, the surefooted Ibex turning like it was on rails, and headed up a gravel road that wound into the hills above the main route into the city.

"Is it sergeant, then?" his passenger asked when it became clear he wasn't going to answer her last question.

"Lieutenant."

"Ah. You carry yourself like a top kick."

"Thanks."

She chuckled, the sound more genuine than her give-nothing-away eyes.

"So, how fare the Silver Hawk Irregulars on New Hope?"

"I wouldn't know, ma'am."

"Fair enough."

His passenger sounded like he'd given the right answer. Which was a little reassuring considering the fact that they both knew he was driving her toward the headquarters of an outfit he'd just denied knowing anything about.

"Do you have a name, Lieutenant?"

Zeke toyed with asserting he didn't know for a moment, then answered.

"Ezekiel Carleston," he said. "Generally just Zeke."

"Good enough, Zeke. You can call me Nikol."

"Like hell, ma'am."

"Excuse me?"

"I know brass when I smell it, ma'am."

"Guilty as charged," she admitted. "I *was* brass up until about nine months ago. I was discharged."

"Discharged from where?"

She hesitated. He caught it in the rearview mirror, the flicker of her eyes as she tried to decide what to answer. And he caught the moment she decided to tell him the truth.

A pothole rocked the Ibex hard left and jerked his eyes back to the road.

"The Eagle's Talons," she said behind him. "Oriente Protectorate."

Zeke didn't bother with the curse.

Jade green eyes. Red-blond hair. Oriente Protectorate. MechWarrior. Miss "you-can-call-me-Nikol" was goddamn Lady Nikol Halas-Hughes *Marik*.

"Never heard of 'em," he said.

Amur, Oriente
Oriente Protectorate

The wedding itself was an anticlimax.

Jessica adjusted her gown slightly, hoping the motion wasn't noticed. The dress and cape were heavier after six hours, more restricting than they had seemed during the fittings. Of course, anything would have felt oppressive after the state ceremony and endless reception. The gown was tailored to appear both airy and regal, and whenever she caught a glimpse of her reflection, Jessica had to admit the designers had succeeded brilliantly. Not white, of course—with five children one did not pretend to be a virgin when entering a second marriage—the layers of fabric were a pearlescent off-white, the highlights of which subtly captured and blended the traditional colors of Houses Marik and Halas.

That last was important. While she declared herself Marik, Jessica never denied her Halas blood. Though she had to admit that honoring her father and his role in trying to hold the Free Worlds together in the face of the Master's treachery had often been a difficult tightrope. The greatest Marik in recent decades had not been a Marik at all. And the worst villain in the history of the Free Worlds League— of the Inner Sphere—had.

To revere the Marik name, the Marik ideal—to aspire to Marik greatness when the current generation of Mariks were so unfit to rule, so ignorant of what it *meant* to be Marik—

Jessica brought herself up short. She knew her features were too well schooled to have allowed her inner turmoil to show. By the same token, there would be a tell, a sharpness of tone, an abruptness of gesture, that would be seen and remembered. She wanted nothing to spoil the perfection of this day.

Besides, she thought, glancing to her new husband, *there are a* few *Mariks left worthy of the name.*

Even Frederick, once he was no longer a potential spouse, had proven himself to be an asset. More a politician, more a mover and shaker than a leader, the younger brother had made himself an invaluable asset in managing the private sector so vital to Oriente's economy.

Jessica nodded and smiled at the marquis Danbury of Nova Roma as the elder statesman raised his glass in her direction. His approval of the union had never been in doubt. The opportunist supported her merest whim in the hope of currying favored status.

His support, and the support of dozens of world leaders the Protectorate over, did not diminish the fact that Jessica had expected drama of some sort, if only in the popular press. The public relations manipulators had been—what was that odd verb they used? *spinning*—spinning for weeks. Preparing the public first for the announcement of the wedding and then for the ceremony itself a barely decent month later.

Despite all the artful preparation, all the groundwork and carefully positioned endorsements and inducements, they—Jessica—had braced for a public outcry. Her dear Philip was still beloved by the people. Even his abandonment of her was seen as the natural response of a gentle man who had been crushed to the point of breaking. He was not a Marik; it was acceptable for him to be broken by tragedy—just as it was inevitable that she would persevere. For her to so quickly replace him with another should have generated more . . . *something*.

"You seem to be a popular choice, Thaddeus," Tiago Paragon chuckled, a rumble from deep in his chest.

Thaddeus looked up at the governor of Miaplacidus, now president of the Parliament, de facto ruler of the Covenant Worlds.

"I had not realized popularity was a factor."

"You lie well, Thaddeus, but you and I both know the popular will of the people is essential to Duchess Jessica's plans."

Thaddeus considered continuing to play innocent, but realized there was little to gain. Paragon was not his friend, precisely, but the giant was closer to being one than any other political ally.

"I had some concern that this alliance would not sit well with the Covenant Worlds," he admitted. "But it's not the sort of thing about which one can consult."

"Indeed." Again the deep rumble of humor. "Though I would have liked the opportunity to ask her if her intentions toward our warden were honorable."

Thaddeus smiled at the image.

"I have been on-planet less than a week and have been called on by every mover and shaker in the Oriente Protectorate." Paragon traded his empty champagne flute for a full one from a passing tray. "Your nuptial vows have elevated the Covenant Worlds through several strata of political power."

"You will not be surprised to know that was something I considered."

"Any chance you could make that a law?" Paragon asked. "That the captain-general of the Free Worlds League must always wed the warden of the Covenant Worlds?"

Thaddeus felt his face freeze for half a heartbeat.

"There is no captain-general—at least not of a unified Free Worlds League."

"There will be, Thaddeus." Paragon leaned closer, his eyes laser bright despite the show he was making of tossing off flutes of champagne. "And you had the good sense to marry her."

Thaddeus glanced toward where Jessica was holding court with several nobles, some of whom he recognized. Evidently feeling his gaze, she turned her head to look directly at him. Seeing all was well, and who was with him, she smiled and Thaddeus felt himself smiling back.

"That's what I mean," Paragon said as Jessica turned back to her own conversation.

"What?"

"You two actually like each other." Paragon gestured with his empty glass. "This isn't just politics."

It occurred to Thaddeus that he had not seen Paragon actually drink the champagne. He glanced suspiciously at the topiary at the governor's elbow.

"And that—the genuine respect, if not friendship—isn't something that has passed unnoticed. I told you, politicos have come a-courting. You can tell a lot about the political waters by how the wooers woo."

"Indeed?"

"Indeed."

"And?"

"And what? I told you. You're a popular choice. Nobody believes this is any sort of romance, but no one doubts you are allies—not just political powers formalizing an alliance. That makes a big difference."

"The duchess' people spent a lot of Eagles and effort on making sure the people realized this is a genuine romance," Thaddeus pointed out.

"Well, I can't answer for people, I've been speaking to politicians," Paragon answered. "But I think that if you took the public's pulse you'd find pretty much the same thing. Some buy the romance, I'm sure, but most see two friends uniting in the face of loss and hardship. I wouldn't be a bit surprised if her media wonks weren't spending more time and money on that than the fairy-tale romance angle."

"You could be right."

"The big problem, of course, isn't the Protectorate. She—you both—control most media and influence those you don't. The Protectorate loves you." Paragon gestured again, evidently indicating the wide world beyond the reception hall. "Your greatest challenge is going to be when you take this show on the road. Ex-paladin of the ex-Republic, commander in chief of an eight-world—soon to be twelve-world—nation. You lead a combined force in a war that knocks Andurien and Humphreys back into Canopus, then marry the most powerful duchess in the Free Worlds League, a woman nearly two decades your senior. Trying to sell you, the two of you, as the guiding light of a new *free* Free Worlds League is going to be an uphill battle. Without your media staff spinning the news feeds, you're going to look like an opportunist. One who doesn't mind using 'Mechs to get what he wants.

"No, my friend. The marriage was the easy part."

51

Zeke escorted Nikol into the Silver Hawks headquarters, staying just ahead of her with his oddly deliberate gait. Her military training and sense of courtesy combined to make her want to match his stride, but there was a hitch to his rhythm that kept them constantly out of step.

Around them the upper mountain air was crisp, but not cold. It was summer and even at this altitude the night air did not reach the freezing temperatures Nikol associated with mountain retreats. The Silver Hawks' main base appeared to be an abandoned ski resort—at least, she doubted the Alpine cottage in which she'd spent the night was authentic.

Why she had been required to spend the night before meeting the commander of the Silver Hawk Irregulars had not been explained. From what she knew of the outfit, it had not been a ploy to put her in her place by forcing her to cool her heels unnecessarily. More likely than not the colonel had been somewhere else—a somewhere else Zeke would no doubt die before divulging.

The anteroom to the command center was the lobby of what had clearly been an inn in happier days. Wood beams angling up into a steeply vaulted ceiling, a fireplace too large to be practical and a noncom standing behind a chest-high counter. Nikol deduced that the double doors toward which Zeke was leading her opened into what had once been the dining room.

Colonel Cameron-Witherspoon didn't look like what

Nikol had expected. He looked younger—rawer. More a front-line skirmisher than the thoughtful strategist she always pictured when she thought *colonel*.

Of course, according to her intel he'd been a force commander when Anson ordered him to get the Silver Hawks Irregulars off Stewart. She didn't know who had dubbed him colonel; he may have just taken the rank on himself to save arguing with planetary militia brass. That thought appealed to her.

"Good of you to see me, Colonel." In mufti, she didn't salute. *Should have remembered that at the DropPort.*

"When a stranger comes bearing gifts, the least you can do is see who they are." Cameron-Witherspoon's voice sounded decades older than his face. "Never expected to see a Halas-Hughes Marik this far from Oriente."

Nikol inclined her head in acknowledgment. The Halas-Hughes, unheard of in the Protectorate, was the norm throughout the worlds of the former Marik-Stewart Commonwealth and former Republic, and she tried not to read too much significance into the fact that both nations were now *former*. That Cameron-Witherspoon added Marik was a courtesy.

"We try to go where we're needed, Colonel," she said aloud.

"Not where you're wanted?"

Take this head-on.

"There was bad blood between my mother and Anson Marik. The lack of blood too, come to that." *Spiked* that *cannon.* "But that was the past. This is the present, and we need to be looking to the future. History is important, it should not be forgotten, but the question we need to answer now is, where do we go from here?"

"Canned speech?"

"Canned? No. But one I've repeated on a half dozen worlds in the last six months," Nikol answered. "The truth doesn't change with repetition."

She opened her shoulder bag and pulled out a noteputer. She waited four seconds as the DNA scanner confirmed her identity from her thumbprint and deactivated the security and handed the tablet to Cameron-Witherspoon.

"That's our inventory," she said.

"And you're giving all this to the Silver Hawks?"

"If you need it. But it'll make it damn hard on the next worlds down the line if they have to wait for us to resupply from Oriente before we get to them."

Cameron-Witherspoon grunted and focused his attention on the screen.

She saw his shoulders straighten as the numbers registered. Anyone who saw that inventory had a pretty good idea how big a fleet she was hiding from the Lyrans. And the fact she was showing him that list told the Silver Hawks commander how much she was trusting him. *So much of communication is in the presentation.*

Giving Cameron-Witherspoon time to digest the information, Nikol glanced around the command center, careful not to look as though she were trying to assess the Silver Hawks' assets. It was pretty standard issue. Central table, ring of communications consoles, situation map—any staff officer from any military in the Inner Sphere would have felt right at home. And the map, which could have been blanked for her visit, revealed . . .

"A force that isn't supposed to be here, and you're defending New Hope?" she asked Zeke.

"I wouldn't know, ma'am."

Nikol fought the urge to grin at him. The man was unflappable. He hadn't blinked when his colonel said her name either, which meant he'd known who she was since the DropPort.

So much for our security.

"Our presence here let half the Protectorate Coalition Militia go haring off after Warden Marik when the Covenant Worlds rushed to support your war with Andurien," Cameron-Witherspoon answered her question. "If Coalition security did their job, Covenant is a bit bemused by their unexpected generosity."

"The Protectorate Coalition sees the Covenant Worlds as good allies?" Nikol asked.

"More than allies," Cameron-Witherspoon corrected. "Anyone who can read the signs can see it's shaping up to be a union."

"Do you like that?" Nikol asked; then: "Forgive my asking. But my people are pretty thoroughly cut off out here.

A big part of my job is figuring out where it's safe to surface. Knowing the political situation is a big part of *that*."

"Formation's a bit weak through the middle," Cameron-Witherspoon said. "The state would be too easy to cut in half through the short axis. But it looks like a good fit."

Nikol nodded and said nothing more, waiting as the colonel went through the noteputer screens, tabbing items his people needed.

"There's a second half to your canned speech," he said at last.

"Pardon?"

"Your reputation precedes you," Cameron-Witherspoon said. "This generosity just gets your foot in the door. You're laying groundwork for your mother taking over the Marik-Stewart Commonwealth."

Well, at least he didn't hint at it.

"I am laying groundwork, as you call it," she acknowledged. "But not for my mother or anyone else to take over."

Cameron-Witherspoon grunted, returning his attention to the noteputer.

Nikol judged that her first impression of a front-line scrapper had been right. Cameron-Witherspoon wasn't a man to waste words—or time—on someone else's agenda. If she read the tac-sit right, this was going to be her one and only chance to reach him.

"The Free Worlds need to be reunited," she said, careful not to rush as she jammed days of discussions into a single salvo. "The people deserve a League large enough and powerful enough to defend them against the predatory Houses that think an accident of blood gives them the right to conquer and destroy on a whim. These little nation-states—Covenant Worlds and Regulan Fiefs and, yes, Oriente Protectorate—can't do it. We're being eaten alive from the outside and tearing ourselves apart from the inside."

That brought Cameron-Witherspoon's eyes up from the inventory screen.

"I happen to believe my mother would make the best captain-general, but I know that's just my opinion. The leader of the Free Worlds League must be chosen by the people of the Free Worlds League, through our Parliament, because the captain-general does not rule the people. She— or he—serves them."

Nikol felt Zeke's eyes on her profile. In fact, she was aware that no one in the Silver Hawks command center was even pretending to monitor their consoles. All eyes were on her. And she kept her eyes locked on Cameron-Witherspoon's.

"I'm laying groundwork, but not for a takeover," she repeated. "I'm laying groundwork for the day the people of the Free Worlds regain their vision and remember that who we are is not about whether we live in the Oriente Protectorate or Tamarind-Abbey or the Regulan Fiefs or the Duchy of Andurien or the Rim Commonality or the Silver Hawk Coalition. We are the League. And the people of the League stick together. No matter what our differences. It's what makes us who we are."

Nikol stopped talking. The critical part of her mind, the mother-trained political part, told her she'd gone on too long, sounded too much like a stump speech. She squelched the doubt—and the urge to say more—and waited for Cameron-Witherspoon to respond. She could hear her breathing, she could hear her pulse and she was sure that if anyone dropped one she would hear a pin fall to the dining room carpet.

For a moment—surely not the days it felt like— Cameron-Witherspoon regarded her, his eyes narrowed and his lips pursed. Then he thrust the noteputer toward her.

"I think this will about cover it," he said. "You can work out delivery details with Lieutenant Carleston."

52

"**O**ne minute, Your Grace."

Thaddeus nodded to the young man directing traffic at the wing of the broad stage, aware his expression was grim. He still had the urge to look over his shoulder whenever anyone addressed him as Your Grace. The title, the marriage to Jessica, did not actually trouble him, but he was honest enough to admit he was not fully comfortable with it.

Warden, he liked the title Warden. He'd earned that one. Your Grace, and Count of Oriente; those he had married. He had yet to earn them. He shied at the mental image the idea of earning the right to be called Jessica's husband conjured.

"Is everything all right, Your Grace?"

"Yes." Then, seeing the stage manager flinch at his abrupt tone: "A painful memory, nothing more."

"There are plenty of those to go around," the stage manager agreed.

Thaddeus didn't wonder. The battle of Mansu-ri—the series of battles of Mansu-ri—had earned the heretofore unremarkable world a place in legend shared with few others. Like Coventry and Kathil in wars past, Mansu-ri had earned the right to be called meat grinder. Months ago, this little man beside him directing traffic for this honor ceremony could have been crouched behind a ruined wall, training his carbine on approaching infantry. Now he waited in the wings of an opera house making sure a visiting noble didn't screw up his entrance.

"You're on, sir."

Thaddeus half smiled. The man had been remembering, and in memory had fallen back on military address.

Still smiling grimly, Thaddeus strode into the lights. Returning the salutes of the officers assembled onstage, he moved directly to the podium. Gripping the edges of the empty oak pedestal, he looked out over the assembly.

The dignitaries were off to either side, in uncharacteristic humility yielding the center to those who'd earned it. Though Thaddeus thought the humility looked a trifle smug on some.

In the balcony and beyond were family members, press corps, whoever else thought being here was worth the inconvenience of the lines and the lack of public transportation.

The center of the opera house was occupied by the true stars of this evening's performance; for a performance it was. They stood arrayed before him as though he were the one worthy of respect.

Soldiers for the most part, with the occasional civilian resistance fighter thrown in. The men and women who had defended Mansu-ri. And through their valor, their dogged refusal to give up, had decided the fates of a half dozen other worlds.

Their valor and Humphreys' ego.

Unwilling to let Mansu-ri go once his forces had landed, the duke had committed men and resources from other worlds to retaking the planet. Men and resources he could not afford. His fixation on Mansu-ri had reduced the world to rubble. But more important, the former and underdefended Andurien worlds of Kwamashu, Antipolo, El Giza and Mosiro now flew the flag of Jessica's new Free Worlds League. *The* new Free Worlds League.

And Wallacia wears Liao green.

Realizing the men and women before him were still standing, Thaddeus released his grip on the podium. Stepping around front and center, he brought himself to stiff attention and saluted.

There was a rustle and pop as four hundred soldiers snapped to and returned the salute. Some left-handed, Thaddeus noted. He held his position for a long three-count, then brought his hand down crisp, index finger aligned with the purple piping of his dress trousers. Rustle, slap, the hands came down.

"At ease," Thaddeus ordered. "Sit."

When they had complied, Thaddeus looked back at the podium. There was a recessed screen displaying the text of the speech his staff had prepared, honoring the gallant warriors of Mansu-ri. A speech that seemed completely inadequate in the face of those assembled.

"My name is Thaddeus Marik," he said unnecessarily. "And I have come here to honor those to whom honor is due. Those who have earned it.

"The Oriente Legion of Merit is a medal—a little pin, actually, two swords and a palm leaf. Pretty, in its way, made of platinum, jade and amber. But its value, like the value of any medal, comes not from the materials from which it is made nor its appearance. The value of a medal comes from the fact it is awarded to those who have demonstrated valor and heroism in combat. What the regulations and public declarations do not mention is that this heroism is measured not in the great acts which become the stuff of legends, the pieces of history we all learn. True heroism is in the little acts, the internal ones, the ones no one else sees.

"For it is there on the inside—in our hearts and in our minds—that the battles that matter are fought."

He paused, and heard no sound beyond his own breathing. Turning his head slowly, he tried to meet every eye before him. Every eye was on him. Every eye that could be. In the front row sat a man in tanker dress, his eyeless face scarred by what could only have been laser fire. A woman, her own face lined by healing lacerations, gripped his arm, directing him toward the stage he couldn't see. A one-armed boy who didn't look old enough to shave flanked the sightless soldier.

Something about their tableaux held his attention. He directed his next words directly to them.

"No one but a fool goes into combat unafraid. No one but an idiot never doubts himself, never questions what he does. And none but an egotistical bastard ever thinks he deserves a medal." He lifted his eyes, again sweeping the ranks of seated warriors. "We who survive will always believe we could have done more to save those who fell. The plain truth is, there was nothing we could have done. Whatever choice seems clear now, whatever option, now obvious, not taken then—is an illusion. What we do in the clarity of combat is the only thing that can be done. Our best in the midst of a hell those who have not been there can only imagine.

"And you have all done that," he said. "And your best was better than anyone else could have done."

Again he stopped and again the only sound on the dais was his own breathing. He raised his eyes to the gallery and the balcony beyond the assembled soldiers; to the families and the onlookers.

"Now I have come, chosen because my Marik name and bloodline dictate my authority and my responsibility, to recognize these valiant men and women for their courage, their valor and their tenacity in defense of their world and their nation," he said. "The Oriente Legion of Merit is awarded to—and here I quote the regulations—to warriors who have demonstrated outstanding bravery and wisdom.

"That last clause sets it apart from medals awarded for courage or martial prowess. It recognizes that each of these men and women made a choice. They *decided* to stand and fight for what they believed. And, having made the decision, they fought not only bravely, but intelligently, making their every blow for freedom count.

"Traditionally, the awarding of the Legion of Merit confers membership into a society of warriors known for both their hearts and their minds.

"I submit to you that this tradition is flawed.

"We who were not there at the darkest hour, when all seemed lost and there was no hope except that which burned within them, have no power to either confer or deny anything to those who were. We can only acknowledge that which these valiant men and women have earned by their own strength and blood."

He lowered his gaze to regard the soldiers.

"I come as a representative of the Free Worlds League to present you with the Oriente Legion of Honor," he said.

"But more fundamentally, I come as a man, as a fellow soldier of the Free Worlds League, to tell you that I am proud to call each and every one of you my brother.

"Or sister," he added with a slight smile to the tanker in the front row. "Do not feel honored that you are meeting me. Know, rather, that it is my great honor to meet you."

Pulling himself to attention, Thaddeus saluted.

The brief moment of silence was broken by a single shout followed by thunderous applause from the gallery.

For the next forty minutes, Parkinson, commanding general of the Mansu-ri planetary militia, read off the names of each Legion of Merit recipient, along with a brief description of how they'd earned it, as each soldier marched or was wheeled or led across the stage. Thaddeus handed each a boxed medal and clasped a hand firmly for the cameras before they were ushered over to the row of senior officers who actually pinned the ribbons to their chests.

Thaddeus fought the feeling he was trapped in a combination publicity event and high school graduation.

There's a difference between generating publicity and building morale.

Thaddeus listened with half an ear to the recitations of how each recipient had earned the right to cross the stage under the lights and clasp his hand. Some of the tales were truly inspiring—others harrowing.

He'd been partially right in his pegging the blind man, the boy and the woman as a tank crew. They were the survivors of a Hetzer wheeled assault gun that had taken on a lance of Andurien BattleMechs in the first day of the Duchy's initial invasion, delaying one prong of the attack long enough for the planetary militia to rally and throw them back. In a way, the skirmish was a microcosm of the Andurien campaign; a reflection of the egotistical thinking that had undermined the Humphreys strategy throughout. The lance should have rolled past the armored gun, particularly after it had immobilized one of their number. Instead they'd lost their momentum—and lost their overall objective—by throwing away their tactical advantage to hunt down an ultimately inconsequential target.

When he'd handed out the last Legion of Merit, clasped the last hand and murmured the last "good work," Thaddeus came to attention for the third time and again saluted the men and women who had defended Mansu-ri against the Andurien onslaught. The dignitaries around them rose to their feet, a beat ahead of the families and press and onlookers filling the gallery and balcony. The opera house thundered.

Thaddeus wondered if the politicians' ovation was mere show. Then wondered if they wondered the same thing about his own emotional display. He decided he was over-thinking again. There were times when the honesty of the moment overwhelmed schemes and agendas and machinations.

53

Dormuth
Mandoria, Marik
3 February 3139

"**W**hat have we?"

Talar Nova Cat was not surprised to see Lady Julietta framed in the doorway of the command center.

Star Colonel Rikkard raised the verigraph. "An invitation to join the Atreus campaign."

Lady Julietta stepped forward, the tips of her canes clicking on the polished marble floor.

"Isn't that just a blockade to thwart the expansion of Lester Cameron-Jones' sphere of influence?" she asked.

"It has been," Rikkard agreed. "But your mother is now proposing a retaking of Atreus."

"Inevitable that she would want to with the Andurien War ended." Lady Julietta stopped a few paces from Rikkard. With a glance, she included Talar, making the conversation an open triangle. "But, especially with the war just ended, Oriente does not have the resources to take on the full might of the Regulan Fiefs."

Rikkard nodded. "Which is why we are being invited."

Lady Julietta frowned thoughtfully into the middle distance. Talar tried to reconcile this commanding presence with the bovine creature who had occupied that body before it had been broken—and could not. It was as though a completely different person had somehow taken up residence in her flesh.

No, he corrected himself. *As coal becomes a diamond. The element is the same, but pressure has changed its structure.*

"Who else?" Lady Julietta asked.

"From context, everyone." Rikkard consulted the verigraph again, evidently confirming his impression. "Each nation-state of the Free Worlds League is being asked to send what they can to a united force."

"Under Oriente command?"

"Of course."

"Impossible."

"I had already reached that conclusion."

Lady Julietta smiled. "I was reacting, not advising."

"Ah." Rikkard nodded solemnly.

"This forms a tightrope," Lady Julietta said, frowning again at some point in the air between Rikkard and Talar. "Waters full of shoals."

"And conflicting metaphors," Rikkard agreed.

Lady Julietta blinked, then rolled her eyes ruefully.

Their easy familiarity . . . Talar felt as though he were party to a private moment, not a discussion of strategy.

"If I understand you," Rikkard was saying, "your advice is we not do what we are asked, but that we not remain idle."

"There are always levels to everything my mother does," Lady Julietta agreed.

"What hazards do you see?" Talar asked, overcoming his feeling that he was breaking in on a private conversation.

"My first thought is this invitation is the first step in making us a vassal state." Lady Julietta nodded toward the verigraph. "However, if the Free Worlds League re-forms and the Clan Protectorate did not take part in liberating

Atreus, we will forever be one down in any political negotiation."

"Dishonored?"

"Essentially, yes."

"Then perhaps," Talar suggested—aware that not long ago he would have declared boldly—"a challenge for leadership."

"Pointless," Rikkard answered.

"Even if we won," Lady Julietta explained, "none of the other nations would follow us against Regulus. Mother and Oriente have a legitimacy we lack. A tradition of loyalty."

"Yet we must do something," Talar pressed, aware of a rising frustration. "We cannot remain idle."

"That's a given."

"What?"

Lady Julietta and Star Colonel Rikkard exchanged a long look. She answered Talar without turning her head. "That requires a bit more thought."

Mount Huffnung, New Hope
Protectorate Coalition

"Zeke, we've been invited to a party."

"Sir?"

Cameron-Witherspoon looked up from his noteputer, giving Zeke a lopsided grin.

Zeke didn't bother trying to curse. He'd answered the summons to Cameron-Witherspoon's office expecting orders. Instead it looked like he was in for one of those meetings where his CO talked in riddles, using Zeke as a sounding board as he worked his way through some problem.

At least this time Captain Byers was present. She'd keep Cameron-Witherspoon from getting too out of hand. He flicked his eyes toward her and she nodded fractionally, promising to do just that.

No taller than Zeke's shoulder and crowned with a cloud of gray curls, the captain looked like nothing so much as someone's grandmother—an effect reinforced by a receding chin, apple red cheeks and wide-set eyes of innocent puppy brown. The uninformed, seeing her in duty khakis, usually assumed she was a retired librarian forced by hard times to shop in military surplus stores.

The informed knew Edith Byers had been in her teens when the Blakist occupation forces had dubbed her the Kaladasa Ghost, one of the most successful and vicious resistance fighters of the Jihad. Now well past the age when most career soldiers retired, the former guerilla warrior commanded the Silver Hawk Irregulars infantry, and trained the covert and liberation units that had been giving the Steiners and Wolves hell on a dozen worlds.

The fact that she was here told Zeke this was more than Cameron-Witherspoon considering hypothetical options. Something real was afoot. And his commander, who thought better out loud, needed someone to talk to who would not answer back.

Zeke didn't like being Cameron-Witherspoon's sounding board, but knew the only way to get through the ordeal was to shut up and listen until the colonel ran down. He ordered his legs to brace apart at parade rest and clasped his hands behind his back.

"Sit down, Lieutenant." Cameron-Witherspoon extended the noteputer toward him. "Tell me what you make of this."

"Thank you, sir." Zeke did not sigh at the realization he would not be getting out of the office any time soon. He hated the sessions where he was supposed to answer worse than the ones where he just stood and listened.

Byers smiled a sympathetic grandmotherly smile.

There was a long minute of silence as the two officers watched him tab through the noteputer screens.

"At a guess," he said at last, "this is the Oriente Protectorate's plan to take Atreus away from the Regulan Fiefs with the serial numbers filed off. There's no hard data on who's where, but from the grouping of the star systems and travel times, there's a major force built up on what has to be Tongatapu and a smaller force on Loyalty.

"Here." He thumbed down a page. "They take Ionus and Alterf respectively, then converge on Atreus. While *here* there's an alternative plan where they leapfrog the secondary targets and hit Atreus fast."

Neither officer said anything.

"Or you could take the same arrangement of stars, switch Loyalty out for Zollikofen, trade Alterf for New Earth, and swap Ionus and Tongatapu for Altair and Styx. Then this becomes a plan to invade Terra."

Byers' laugh was a single bark.

"I think we're safe in assuming this is a broad summary of the Atreus campaign," Cameron-Witherspoon said drily. "What can you tell me about the troop numbers?"

"They're deliberately fuzzed," Zeke answered promptly. "But I'm pretty sure Oriente doesn't have the volume of assets that plan indicates."

Cameron-Witherspoon nodded, then glanced over at Byers. If she was supposed to add anything, she missed her cue.

"Did I ever tell you about Captain-General Anson Marik's last words to me, Zeke? Not when he ordered us off Stewart, the last time he briefed me—nearly two weeks before." Cameron-Witherspoon raised a hand, palm toward Zeke. "Before you tell me you don't recall, that was a rhetorical question. I've repeated those words in one form or another every day of my life since Stewart fell, a dozen times a day.

"He called me into his inner sanctum. I was expecting some blustered rhetoric about stopping the Lyrans and Wolves on Stewart. Or, if Daggert had talked some sense into him, some questions on how to do the most damage to them on a fighting withdrawal. Instead he asked me who I served. I said him, of course, the captain-general. He called me an idiot. And he was right."

Zeke knew better than to *yes, sir* that last sentence, but it was tempting. Not that Cameron-Witherspoon was an idiot; quite the opposite. His savvy had kept the Silver Hawk Irregulars a viable fighting force when lesser men would have given up. He'd follow Cameron-Witherspoon through hell. He just hated letting a perfectly good straight line go to waste.

"He said I served the people. That the Silver Hawk Ir-

regulars served the people of the Silver Hawk Coalition.
No captain-general, no politician, no institution. The people
of the Silver Hawk Coalition."

"Yes, sir."

"I asked him if we fought for the Silver Hawk Coalition,
what the hell we were doing on Stewart. He told me that
stopping the threat before it reached the Silver Hawk
worlds was the best way to defend those worlds." Cameron-
Witherspoon shook his head. "At one level I knew that
was bull. We weren't going to stop the combined Lyrans
and Wolves, not by ourselves—and even though we weren't
the last MSC unit standing, we were the only one cohesive
enough to put up any kind of organized fight. I thought he
was blowing smoke.

"What I didn't know, what I didn't understand until he'd
ordered us off-planet just as the Wolves and Steiners were
on the ground and committed—" Cameron-Witherspoon
stopped himself. "No, that's a lie. I didn't understand until
after I heard he was dead."

Zeke glanced over at Byers, who had surely heard this
recitation as many times as he had. She was watching
Cameron-Witherspoon with unwavering attention. Satisfied
he wasn't the only one still moved in his gut by the tale,
he looked back to his commander.

"I didn't understand until later that he was using us as
a lure, as part of something greater. He was doing all he
could to save the people of the Marik-Stewart Commonwealth. Not the Commonwealth, that was lost as soon as
the Wolves and Lyrans decided to carve us up. He gave
his life so the *people* of the Commonwealth had a chance."

The silence stretched for a full minute before Captain
Byers spoke up.

"Ian, what has this got to do with Oriente taking Atreus
away from Regulus?"

"Oriente isn't taking Atreus away from Regulus,"
Cameron-Witherspoon said mildly. "Captain-General Jessica Marik is calling on the unified Free Worlds League to
retake our capital."

"Sir?" Zeke was startled into breaking his own rule of
silence.

"This very broad campaign summary was part of a proposal submitted to the Protectorate Coalition Senate by Captain-General Marik." Zeke noted Cameron-Witherspoon spoke the title without sarcasm and the name with neither Halas nor Hughes. "She posits a Free Worlds League uniting to take back Atreus, then working to build a new nation on the foundation of the old."

"The logistics of such a cobbled-together campaign would be a nightmare," Byers said. "Rebuilding the Free Worlds League government? A thousand times worse."

"The political side I don't pretend to know about," Cameron-Witherspoon said. "The military side? If the member nations buy into the idea of a reunified Free Worlds League military, it can be done. The FWLM did it for generations."

Zeke opened his mouth, then shut it again.

"Spit it out, Lieutenant."

"Sir, I track the part where Captain-General Jessica Marik made this proposal to the Senate and the Senate passed the campaign summary along to you for assessment, but I don't understand what this has to do with the Silver Hawks. You said yourself that Captain-General Anson Marik made you understand that our duty, our loyalty, is to the Silver Hawk Coalition. If we're considering any campaigns, shouldn't they be about retaking Shiloh? Or Callison and Marcus?"

"In the long term, yes. We will not rest until all the Silver Hawk worlds are free," Cameron-Witherspoon said. "But in the shorter term—and as part of the long term—it comes back to serving the people of the Silver Hawk Coalition, not the government.

"And I think a case can be made that the people will be better served as citizens of a unified and potentially powerful League than of individual and isolated enclaves."

"Okay." Zeke drew the word out. It was clear to him his commander, and by extension the Protectorate Coalition Senate, had decided to support the plan. He just wasn't sure they were right.

"I'm counting on your judgment for the details of the campaign, Lieutenant." Cameron-Witherspoon confirmed his worst fears. "I'm sending you on ahead to liaise with the centralized command. If you have any doubts, let us know.

"Otherwise Captain Byers and third battalion will be joining you on Tongatapu."

Third battalion; mostly heavy infantry and light armor. That left two BattleMech battalions and a bit more guarding the Protectorate Coalition. Not as bad as the full commitment Zeke had been dreading. But still . . .

"Sir, it's not the campaign I'm worried about so much as the aftermath." Zeke tried not to rush his words. "Once Atreus is secured, what prevents the captain-general from reneging on her promise? We don't know her, and what we do know is not good. *Duchess* Jessica Marik has been known as the enemy of the Silver Hawks for my whole life. How can we trust her now?"

"That's the beauty of it," Cameron-Witherspoon answered. "We don't have to."

"Sir?"

"Captain-General Jessica Marik is putting together this campaign, though her husband probably has a lot more to do with the nuts and bolts than she does. It's her plan, so going in the Oriente Protectorate has overall command. Simple, commonsense logistics. But—" Cameron-Witherspoon grinned. "Once she pulls it off—*if* she pulls it off—Oriente doesn't have the muscle to face down the rest of the Free Worlds League.

"When the dust settles, who rules the Free Worlds League will be up to the people of the Free Worlds League."

54

Fidelity, Loyalty
Former Marik-Stewart Commonwealth
13 April 3139

Alethea Chowla turned up the collar of her tunic as she strode along the broad walk. The wind was little more than a breeze, and the temperature what nine out of ten people called "comfortably cool," but she was the tenth person in that survey; she was cold and she hated the feel of blowing air tracing across her freshly shaved neck.

The late morning sunlight was watery but clear, bright enough to make the black and leafless branches of the slender trees lining the mall stand out in sharp contrast to the slate blue stone sheathing the public buildings. Autumn, she guessed, though she didn't know enough about the local climate to be sure.

"I like the black," said Nordhoff, keeping easy pace beside her. "Though I suppose it's more a midnight blue. Much more businesslike than the clown orange."

Alethea remained silent, in no mood to discuss her hair. Especially not with the bland weasel who had parlayed a coincidence of timing into command of the Westover Militia.

If she'd had her way the man would never come within ten jumps of Atreus; but she didn't have her way. Westover built aerospace fighters and, despite the generally accepted story of limited production over the last six decades, had committed four wings of *Stingrays* and *Rievers* to Operation Homecoming. Her people were going to be doing the fighting on the ground, but to get to the ground they needed the aerospace under Nordhoff's command to punch through the Regulan orbital umbrella.

Strategically, the oily turncoat clicking along the pavement beside her was as vital to the liberation of Atreus as she was. Alethea squinted against the headache that thought brought on.

"Why aren't your people here?" she demanded.

"They are here," Nordhoff answered easily. "Or more precisely, they are aboard their carriers holding station at the nadir jump point."

"I mean *your* people, the Lyrans. They stopped two jumps short of one of the biggest JumpShip yards in the Free Worlds League."

"I wouldn't say one of the biggest," Nordhoff contradicted.

The fact that he easily ignored her verbal jabs while quibbling on irrelevant points annoyed Alethea more than the verbal barbs he fired in return. Worse, she knew he knew that.

"While a JumpShip production facility, even a damaged one, might look like a prime objective, Loyalty is simply too far into League space to be held. They'd have a long, easily severed neck—much the same reason the WarShip yards at Ionus were left untouched." Nordhoff sounded as though he were schooling a cadet on the obvious. "Lyran forces came as far rimward as they did in this region because Vedet had his own agenda. Competent advisers warned him Laureles presented unnecessary risk for negligible gain."

The mall broadened into a smallish square in front of the Count's Palace, home of Liberty's Senate. Alethea hoped today was the last day the senators' chamber served as temporary headquarters for the antispinward arm of Operation Homecoming. She was ready to get off this rock and into the action.

"Now, that is beautiful."

Despite herself, Alethea followed Nordhoff's gaze to the *Tirana* memorial rising from the center of the piazza. There was no denying the effect of clean, angular lines leading the eye upward, reminding the observer of the heroic battle fought thousands of kilometers above.

"Any monument to men and women who died fighting for freedom is beautiful," she said.

"True," Nordhoff agreed. Then added: "But I've seen some god-awful ugly ones."

Alethea chose not to answer.

Hunching her shoulders against the quickening wind, she mounted the palace steps, hurrying toward what she hoped was their last briefing.

Zenith Recharge Point, Aitutaki
Free Worlds League

OvKhan Petr Kalasa hung at his ease, untethered, but within easy reach of a half dozen handholds.

Around him the bridge of the *Voidswimmer* was nearly silent. All batteries were charged, all systems ready. His command would set the officers around him into furious action, cause the great ship that carried them to wrap space around itself and *jump* through a dimension men only pretended to understand. At his word the JumpShip would leap instantly to a place the sunlight now caressing its hull would not reach for another thirty years.

The thought filled him with a peace no ground dweller could understand.

"Were their academy not destroyed, we could raise an army here." Rikkard's voice came from relative above. Petr tilted his head to look directly at the Spirit Cat securely clipped to the bulkhead. "Lady Julietta tells me this world has sworn undying hostility toward the fiefs of Regulus."

"Oh?"

"A spheroid tangle I did not follow. Apparently there was an unforgivable betrayal on some point of politics." Rikkard smiled slightly. "In my search for tranquility, I find I must learn more and more of the convoluted social machinations of the Inner Sphere."

"It is not really difficult." Petr shrugged, then flexed his left leg to counteract the imparted spin. "Everyone—Clan or spheroid—does what they do because they believe it will gain them that which they want. Discover what they want, and why, and everything else becomes clear."

"I believe you have just revealed a core belief of the Sea Fox."

"We have never claimed it was a secret," Petr acknowledged solemnly. "Just that it is honorable."

"A truth I easily accept," Rikkard answered.

"More easily than you accept the honor of our current position?"

Rikkard did not answer.

"This is a transaction, an investment in the future," Petr said, reminding his friend of ground they had covered. "For the Clan Protectorate to flourish, the Free Worlds League must be strong. Though there is no tangible return in the short run, our Clans and the worlds we protect are best served through this action."

"One can accept truth while still finding it strange," Rikkard answered.

"Comm, I wish to record an announcement of who we are and why we are at Atreus," Petr said, following his own thought. "You will load it for clear transmission on all major channels the moment we arrive. I don't want to take fire from allies who don't know we exist."

55

Ministerial Residence
Zletovo, Lesnovo
Rim Commonality
19 April 3139

There would be no better time.

After today, there would be no time at all. For months she had maintained the illusion of economic analyst by rewording reports prepared by the rest of the staff, adding her own insights into the personalities of the people in-

volved. But yesterday Frederick had asked her to personally assess a proposal from a cartel the very nature of which
was obscure. Without access to the resources Father Pauli
had established on Oriente, she had found the columns of
numbers and screens of graphs opaque. Her cover would
not survive five minutes' conversation with the monster's
accountant.

At first glance, a disaster. But on deeper thought, an
obvious prodding by Ayza. She had delayed too long. And
today was perfect.

She moved briskly down the sunlit corridor; broad windows along the southern wall made the passage a virtual
solarium. Several French doors opened on to the formal
veranda and the garden beyond. After a quick glance to
confirm both were vacant, she ignored the view.

So many things were different. Midafternoon, not night,
and dressed in the informal business attire of a consultant,
not the white ceremonial dress that had passed for so many
months as a nightgown. Cendar and the creature Elis he'd
taken to wife were in their chambers. It was a Wednesday
tradition in the Cendar household, going back generations,
she'd been told: conducting business in their private sitting
room, meeting the functionaries who actually did the work
of running their government without ceremony or servants.

If she believed in luck, she would have called the conflu-
ence of the Cendar family tradition and Frederick Marik
forcing her hand a coincidence. With the wisdom of her
faith she recognized that Obatala had ordained both, setting events in motion generations ago that would lead to
this one fated afternoon.

She turned from the corridor into one equally broad with
sage green walls and a floor of dark polished marble. Here
there were alcoves, each a shrine to a piece of art; paintings
and sculptures, no doubt considered priceless by someone,
individually displayed. A museum without patrons or
guards. This deep within the house, there was no security.
This was Lesnovo, not Oriente, a peaceful world with no
political dangers requiring armed defense.

She longed to duck into one of the alcoves, to scrub the
dye from her hair, to peel the pink appliqués from her face,
to shed the obscenely restrictive clothes. The Orisha's work

should be done purely, sky clad and without masks. But for the work to be done at all, she must do nothing that would draw attention to herself.

The demon daughter Elis and her husband—victim or willing accomplice no longer mattered—would be alone and unguarded and at their ease. A faceless minion, unscheduled but not unexpected, would enter. Subservient, obedient, apologizing for having the gall to breathe, she would wait her turn until others left if need be. If not, she would approach directly.

Cendar first; for though they were both soft consumers used to living off the efforts of others, by his very mass he would be the stronger of the two. Then Elis—no doubt screaming her horror—would fall beneath her blade.

From that point it would be a simple matter to lock the door. If anyone knocked she would tell them through the speaker that the prime minister and his wife did not wish to be disturbed. Until Frederick and Philip—the tool of the *caplatas* and her mate—asked permission to enter.

Then she would open the door. And usher them in to justice.

Perhaps while waiting for them, secure behind the locked door, she would shed her disguise and the ridiculous clothes. The image of the pasty old men spending their last moments unable to choose between staring at the horror of the slain husband and wife or the nakedness of her body amused her.

After their deaths, there was no escape. She knew of no tunnels beneath the estate grounds, had no safe houses planned on this alien world. She would run, of course. Live and kill for as long as she could. How long she lived did not matter. Her *ebo* was complete. Her place among the *petro*—whatever it would be—was set with the deaths of the evil one's pawns.

Great would be the monster's suffering.

She paused, setting her neoleather folio on an incidental table between alcoves. Reaching behind her to release its clasp, she pulled the necklace of her naming blade from beneath her shirt. Worn always next to her skin, but hidden from eyes that might recognize it, her weapon was warm and ready. With a practiced twist she aligned the crescents, locking them into a single lethal blade.

Still smiling at her image of the old men's confusion, she clasped the knife flat against the folio and resumed her path.

Ten paces ahead, the door to the prime minister's private apartment opened.

"Fascinating."

Green watched Michael Cendar and Elis Marik—Elis Marik-Cendar—exchange thoughtful looks.

Such a short time together and they're already beginning to function as a team.

The sitting room of the suite Cendar had set aside as an inner sanctum was modest, or would have been if one did not realize the few distinctive pieces of art decorating the walls were priceless originals. Though there were several armchairs, husband and wife had chosen to share a divan that had been turned so that its back was to the fireplace. The effect was to make the traditional conversation area into an informal work space, allowing them to sit in physical contact as they dealt with visitors.

"You have not laid out all of this for my mother."

"That is correct," Green acknowledged. "It is my understanding that Sir Thaddeus will explain all phases of his program to the captain-general at a later date. If he has not already."

"Well, I for one am grateful to Riktofven."

"Madam?"

"If he hadn't squatted his Senatorial Alliance right in the middle of your patron's plan, the Oriente Protectorate would be facing a much more savvy adversary than Anson Marik ever was." Her smile did not quite take the edge from her words.

"Sir Thaddeus never intended an adversarial relationship with the Protectorate, milady," Green assured her. Then honesty—and her one cocked eyebrow—compelled him to add: "Although he did believe healthy competition enabled a nation to refine its purpose."

Cendar chuckled.

"Each of these communities, as he calls them, was based on mutual advantage and interlocking goals," he said. "No coercion, no significant bribery, no assassinations, and no funding of revolutionaries. Very civilized—very Free Worlds—and very well thought out. And, if I'm reading between the lines the way you and Thaddeus Marik intended, you deserve a good deal of the credit for the hands-on engineering of these communities."

"Thank you, mi—sir."

"Let me spare you the next part of your presentation by guessing that the purpose of this little confessional display is to convince me to adopt your tactics, adopt you, in fact, to cement our unaligned neighbors to the Rim Commonality. And through us to the Free Worlds League as a whole."

"Essentially, yes, sir," Green acceded, faithful to Thaddeus' order of complete transparency. "Though of course it will take several months for me to gain a meaningful understanding of the region, it was thought that I would be of use in that regard."

I think I've sounded more pompous once before, but I can't recall when.

Again the husband and wife exchanged looks.

"Leave these files with us, Mr. Green," Elis spoke for both of them. "We will speak with you again after we've studied them more thoroughly."

"Yes, madam."

Realizing he was dismissed, Green snapped the cover of his noteputer shut. With a final bow that was little more than a nod, per Prime Minister Cendar's stated preferences, he turned to let himself out the door.

A ruling family that holds court wearing casual dress in their private sitting room without a single servant in sight. I am not *on Oriente anymore.*

Bemused, he crossed the simple foyer and opened the door into the main corridor.

Carrying his own golf clubs was a small thing, but Frederick relished it. In the first place, carrying the slender leather case projected an impression of vitality. In the second, not

relying on a servant off the links or a caddy on made clear
that he was a man who did not expect others to do work
he could do himself.

Neither persona would have been recognized by those
who'd known him in the courts of Terra. But the courts of
Terra were in no position to help him now. Adaptation was
the key to survival—the key to winning.

Of course, he felt a bit less clever this afternoon. After
a few hours of chipping around the informal links—
everything about Cendar's estate seemed to be informal—
Philip had sent his caddy and clubs ahead in the car and
chosen to walk back to the main house. Before the car had
gone a dozen meters, Frederick had regretted his casual
declaration he'd be fine carrying his bag, but of course
there was no calling it back.

Thanking God he'd had the wisdom to carry a simple
tube and not the massively compartmentalized contraption
Philip favored, Frederick concentrated on keeping a spring
in his step. The hedge to their left enclosed one of the
gardens, he was sure—a suspicion confirmed when they
passed a low gate and he saw the formal veranda with its
splashing fountains.

"Let's go in the back, here," he called to Philip, who had
continued on toward the front. "I think that's the glass hall
that leads to Michael and Elis' chambers, isn't it?"

Retracing his steps, Philip stood beside him surveying
the garden.

"That'll save us ten minutes," he agreed. The gate latch
opened at his touch.

Have these people never *heard of security?*

Adjusting the strap across his shoulder, he hurried to
catch up with Philip.

Green nodded to the dark young woman with the pied
features in the hall. Frederick's financial wizard, he recognized, the one tasked with fitting the Rim Commonality's
economy into that of the Protectorate. She would be a very
valuable asset when it came to puzzling out how to build
local communities.

He gave her a second glance as they passed, considering

how to approach her with the proposal. The glitter of something silver between her dark fingers and the black neo-leather of her folio caught his eye.

Was that a knife?

"Excuse me—"

She spun, folio flying, her right arm scything to slash the secretary's throat.

Only his throat wasn't there.

The mousy man had rocked back, faster than she would have thought possible, just enough to avoid her strike. His brown eyes were wide with amazement, his expression confused. A fool saved by his reflexes.

Adjusting her stance midmotion, she stepped close, thrusting her blade into his heart.

Into the space where his heart had been.

Not chance this time, not blind reflexes. The pale brown man danced clear of her attack with a fighter's grace, determination replacing the confusion in his eyes. She followed fast, flowing after him, keeping him retreating, preventing him from finding his own stance; setting his defense. *Slash. Feint.* She closed, pushing him into an alcove. *Thrust.*

His noteputer deflected her lunge as he spun past her, out of the alcove. His shoes squeaked on the marble.

A grunt of effort in her ear and pain exploded from her ribs to her elbow.

Switching her naming blade from the numb fingers of her right hand to her ready left, she turned to face his new position. Assessing her damage, she realized the little man had rabbit-punched her in the nerve cluster below her right shoulder blade when he pirouetted out of her way. She rotated her right shoulder, working out the numbness.

Her opponent circled to her right, keeping to her damaged side. But not too far right. He stayed between her and the door to the prime minister's apartment.

She hesitated. Feigning a stumble, she dropped her guard to lure him closer. The secretary—whom she suspected was no more a secretary than she was an accountant—did not take the bait.

But neither did he run. Of course he didn't call for help; no one beyond the prime minister and his whore would have heard him, and the little man evidently knew calling them to face her blade was a bad idea.

She jabbed and the battered noteputer deflected her thrust.

Tremors shot the length of her right arm. There had been a lot of power behind that punch. If he had gone for her neck instead of her pressure point, he'd have snapped her spine.

Why didn't he kill me when he had the chance?

Jab. Slash. Kick.

Each attack deflected. No counterstrike. No grapple. She had him on strength, he had her—barely—on speed. Yet he did not attack. It was as though he meant to wear her down with his defense. A moment later, the penny dropped.

The little man meant to capture her alive.

His last thought would be how foolish that mistake was. Seeing her opening, she moved in for the kill.

Frederick's first impression was of two people dancing in the hall.

Then Philip shouted and began to trot toward the figures.

It took Frederick a second longer to realize the dancers were fighting. The man was Green, Thaddy's agent. And the woman was—Ayza?

Green went down. A knife flashed silver in Ayza's upraised hand.

"My God."

Unlimbering his golf bag, Frederick charged.

"Elis!"

She paused, turning to the sound of the voice. The *bokor*-bitch's husband was tottering toward her, his arms upraised and his mouth working with effort. From the look of him, he'd die of heart failure before he reached her. The fool Frederick was running too, passing the older man with his stupid golf bag in his hands. Frederick she'd have to kill.

The little man writhed on the floor, hand covering the bloody socket where his eye had been, and tried to scissor-kick her legs out from under her.

She laughed, jumping lightly over his futile effort, and

brought her naming blade slashing down. His throat parted like a sausage, the final spray from his carotid arteries misting blood to cover her arm and chest.

To be absorbed by the stupid clothes.

Distracted by her disappointment, she was late in rising to meet her fresh attacker.

Thrusting his golf bag ahead like a battering ram, Frederick slammed into her, carrying her to the floor by sheer mass and momentum. There was a clatter and crash—flying golf clubs and a vase knocked from its pedestal—as he tumbled over her.

She rolled with him, on top of him, and thrust her naming blade deep.

His flesh twisted, pulling the knife aside. She almost released the hilt in shock before she realized she'd driven the blade into his empty golf bag. Yanking her weapon free of the leather, she pulled her legs up, her business skirt riding up over her thighs until she was kneeling astride his writhing form, pinning him to the floor.

Reversing her grip, she drove her naming blade down into his face.

Frederick caught her wrist, stopping the blade a handsbreadth above his eye. His other hand joined the first, straining to push her arm back. But he was old, and weak, and had never been a warrior. She paused, her face as close as a lover's, and let him think he was winning.

The old man staggered closer, wheezing as though he had run a hundred kilometers. The scattered golf clubs rattled across the marble floor as he fell among them and fumbled to rise. She didn't bother to turn her head, focused on the feeble man struggling between her legs. She only hoped the *bokor*'s husband lived long enough for her to kill him.

Something pushed her, nudged her hips. She realized Frederick was trying to kick her, his knees barely reaching her back. Smiling she leaned down, close enough to see her breath stir his eyelashes.

"Try bucking me off," she cooed. "That feels so much better."

He blinked.

She pushed her naming blade a finger's width closer to the sagging flesh of his face, making sure he understood it was *she* and not he who delayed his death. The naked terror rose in his eyes. She laughed, delighting in her power.

The darkness took her.

56

Free Worlds League Military Command Center
Jakarta, Tongatapu
Former Marik-Stewart Commonwealth
20 April 3139

"This is a chimera," the broad man across the situation table cursed.

"Sir?" Zeke asked.

The markers on the map showed units, not individual BattleMechs. How the warden-general could spot a single forty-ton cavalry 'Mech at this scale was beyond him.

Thaddeus Marik looked at Zeke, as though surprised to find him there. Although it was the warden-general who was out of place, haunting operations HQ in the middle of gamma shift. Around them the command center was nearly silent. What orders needed to be given had been given and for now most staffers, including former liaison Zeke, were just double-checking numbers and conserving energy for when they'd need it.

Zeke met his hazel gaze placidly. He had decided he liked Operation Homecoming's overall commander. He overthought problems, like Colonel Cameron-Witherspoon, but he didn't expect lieutenants to stand by and listen while he worked his way through options aloud.

"This," Thaddeus Marik said, indicating the map of

Atreus and the proposed incursion points. "A chimera. I've cobbled together a liberation force out of mismatched parts I know nothing about."

He tapped an ID at random. "The First Rim Guards. Sounds like a ground car accessory. Dossier card says a battalion of heavies and mediums with a handful of scouts. How do I know how best to use them?"

"The First Rim Commonality Guards were a merc unit when they fought the Blakists sixty-some years ago," Zeke said. "Got hired by the government for winning. They like fast, multitarget engagements."

"That's on the data card?" Thaddeus Marik asked, frowning at the strip of plastic in his hand.

"Perhaps, sir. I got it from talk around the junior grade officers' club."

The warden-general cocked an eyebrow.

"They're staging on Loyalty, two jumps from here," he said. "How did they come to be the topic of gossip at the jg club?"

"Never known distance to affect scuttlebutt, sir."

"Point taken, Lieutenant." He indicated the table with a wave. "Don't suppose you have similar rundowns on all these units."

Jake surveyed the table. "A few, sir. Most of these I've never heard of. And most of the ones I have you've already got where they'll do the most good."

"I've the recommendations of each of the commanders, of course. I did what I could to match units with each other and with objectives." The warden-general sounded weary. "But these people have never fought together. No plan survives contact with the enemy. Tomorrow will be . . ."

The warden-general surveyed the table for a long moment.

"Tomorrow at this time, these men and women will be improvising, under fire from a determined enemy, with almost no idea what to expect from their comrades." He shook his head. "It's a chimera."

"Sir?"

"Ancient Greek mythology. Chimera, daughter of the whirlwind," Thaddeus Marik explained. "She had dozens

of forms, but in every case she was the mismatched parts
of animals that had been forced together by the tempest.

"My favorite configuration had the head and forelegs of
a lion, the head and wings of an eagle, the head and chest
of a goat, the haunches of a dragon and a long, venomous
snake for a tail. Another head."

Zeke tried to hold the image in his head and failed.

"That sounds like . . ." He looked down at the situation
map with its projected landing points for dozens of units,
each with its own logo; each with its own history and abilities and tactics, no two quite alike.

"That sounds like this."

Ministerial Residence
Zletovo, Lesnovo
Rim Commonality

"Do you suppose it was the same woman?" her father
asked. Again.

Philip was seated, still looking lost in the high-backed
chair by the fire. But, Elis thought, looking less slumped
than he had hours before. The sitting room windows were
dark with night—or predawn, she corrected herself. None
of them had slept that night. Nor could she recall anyone
eating, though food had come and gone.

The medicos had urged her father and Frederick to the
infirmary, but both had refused to go. They seemed to gain
some energy from the company of Michael and Elis, and
the two were glad to have them.

Conversation had been desultory, wandering in spates
between silences through all manner of trivial topics before
returning to the attack. The beverage of choice was a
mulled wine, kept warm in a frequently replenished de-
canter by the hearth. It lacked the potency to put any of
them to sleep, but Elis felt a distance from her limbs that
warned against sudden movements.

"I don't see how it could have been the same individual."

Elis answered her father's question. Again. "But there are too many similarities for coincidence."

"An organization of some sort?" asked Frederick. He was still ashen, but the focus she had come to associate with him was reasserting itself.

"Probably," she agreed. "Of course you realize that when word of this gets back to Mother, every woman of Afro-Terran descent on Oriente is going to be subjected to a thorough background investigation."

"Oriente?" Her father asked with more animation than she'd seen since the attack. "All of the Free Worlds League. Your mother is not one for half measures."

Michael was turning the weapon in his hand. Twisted one way, it became loose crescents of silver strung together. Twisted the other, the crescents locked to form one curved blade, like a chef's boning knife, longer than his hand. "This is needlessly complex," he said.

"And clearly handmade with considerable craftsmanship. A sliver of silver very like that tip lodged in—" Her father's voice broke off. After a moment he added: "The Clan physicians were able to remove it safely."

"This looks to be a ceremonial weapon of some sort." Michael continued to turn the blade in the light. "Perhaps she was a member of a cult of some sort. Like a Thuggee."

"Thuggees use garrotes." Frederick sipped his wine. "But I take your point."

"Worth looking into."

Elis was watching her father. He had seemed to slump again, staring into the empty fireplace.

"Are you all right, Father?"

"Hmm? Yes." He shook his head. "I've never killed anything larger than a cockroach before. Took me a while to recover that time too."

Elis couldn't think of a response to that. She still hadn't adjusted to the image of her kind old father smashing in an assassin's skull.

"I had no idea a driver could be so deadly," Michael said into the silence.

"Niblick."

"Excuse me?"

"Iron with a steep slope," Philip explained. "A driver

would have bounced off—too broad. The niblick—nose-on, like an axe—is shaped to put what swing I have into the point of a metal wedge."

"Wait." Michael was staring at his father-in-law with new eyes. "You took the time to select your club and decide how to swing?"

"Of course." Philip sounded surprised at the question. "Wouldn't want to duff a shot like that."

57

Operation Homecoming
21-27 April 3139
Scout-*class JumpShip* Olho
Zenith Jump Point
Atreus System
Regulan Fiefs

Captain Doreen Patel relaxed in her command chair.

The cramped bridge was silent but for the occasional beep of equipment announcing some process begun or ended. Both sensor arrays were manned with technicians intent on their external screens. Screens Doreen knew were blank because the row of repeater screens suspended just above her line of sight were blank. The pilot sat at her ease; with the coordinates locked in and the jump drives at warm idle, she need only press one button when the order came. The engineering station was empty, but its boards showed all systems optimal; batteries fully charged.

Doreen had heard of captains who stood their watches in ready rooms—reading, relaxing or catching up on reports— depending on their bridge crews to alert them should they be needed. Doreen had every confidence in her crew, but she was constitutionally incapable of serving her watch anywhere but in the *Olho*'s hot seat.

"Sir!"

Doreen came upright, her eyes fixed on the repeater screens. Points of light were appearing, bracketed by numbers she could not read.

"What have we got?" she asked, not bothering to increase magnification on her repeaters. More points of light sprang into existence.

"Multiple jumps, pirate points . . ." The tech paused, double-checking his readings. "Every one we plotted and then some."

Doreen nodded, aware she'd lost a bet. She'd been among those anticipating a few incursions of large-capacity JumpShips in tight formation; a massed attack to punch through Atreus' defensive umbrella. The Halas raiders had evidently opted for the swarm assault, hoping to flow through the defenders' net by presenting too many targets for them to engage at once.

In the end, of course, it didn't matter.

"Transponder codes," the second tech reported. "Every one broadcasting Free Worlds League Military."

Doreen snorted.

On the repeater screens the light-point count seemed steady.

"All in?"

"Looks like it," the senior tech confirmed.

"Compress all data for fast squirt," Doreen ordered. "Mr. Orton, take us to Hellos Minor."

Hunter-*class* JumpShip Renard
Pirate Point 34,000 kilometers above Zenith Jump Point
Atreus System
Free Worlds League

"Their forward observer has jumped."

"Aitutaki."

Alexander Plateau
Corin, Atreus
Regulan Fiefs

"Eyes to fist two," the voice crackled in Andrika's headset. "There's a third aggressor unit, lance of heavies, bearing oh-four-seven relative, grid fourteen-twenty. Using the ridge for cover."

"Grid fourteen-twenty," she confirmed aloud, letting the forward observer know she'd heard him, and making sure her gunners heard her as well. "Let us know when they enter fourteen-eighteen."

Taking their cue, the two gunners above and behind her elevated their matching turrets for indirect fire. Fourteen-twenty was just out of range, but it was right next door to fourteen-nineteen, within range of the thirty long-range missile tubes her JES III mounted. And next to fourteen-nineteen was fourteen-eighteen—the far kill zone for the mix of ballistics and missiles David Company's Second Platoon could bring to bear. Even though she couldn't see them, Andrika knew the other four fire support tanks of DC2 were targeting fourteen-eighteen right along with her. Dug in and camouflaged, the fifteen long-shooters of David Company were tasked with stopping any Halas raiders trying to take the Imperator Autoweapons plant from the south.

The huge ImpAuto manufacturing facility, crouching among the cliffs and ridges overlooking a few thousand square kilometers of wheat fields, was naturally defended to the north and west by cliffs of razor-edged crags even mountain goats avoided. The natural approach was east, where the plateau dropped steeply down a stony flat routinely used by DropShips. That's where all the 'Mechs were pointed, waiting for someone stupid enough to use the front door.

To the south were ridges of soft limestone and narrow valleys of silt and bog. A few million years ago, she'd learned at her briefing, it had been a coral-filled bay surrounded by rock. Now it was about halfway through eroding down into a bog, which made it practically impassable for heavy ordnance. Which in turn meant somebody was bound to try it.

So far three somebodies had. Or maybe just the three lances of one company. First Platoon and Third Platoon had each turned back raider probes this morning. Two up and two down as fast as the defenders could fire.

Andrika and her crew sat in silence, waiting for DC2 to get its turn.

"Eyes to fist two." She jumped at the sound of the spotter's voice, then grinned at her own nerves. "Tally four hostile heavies, dead center grid fourteen-eighteen."

"Fourteen-eighteen sweet spot," Andrika confirmed. "All together on my mark, ladies and gentlemen. Three, two, one, *shoot!*"

Around her the JES III rocked as the missiles launched.

Without instructions her gunners worked the cycle, loading fresh missiles into the hot tubes while the first flight was still rising. Thirty seconds before safety protocols allowed, but Andrika had always believed the chance of a thermal trigger in the launcher was infinitely better than being caught with no birds ready to fly.

"Hits, hits," the forward observer reported. "They are turning tail. Repeat, hostiles withdrawing at speed."

"That's three," Andrika said.

Alexander Plateau
Corin, Atreus
Free Worlds League

"That's three," Edith Byers said, watching the mixed contrails arch over her head. "We owe the Angel II militia a round of drinks for drawing that kind of fire."

"Tally is fifteen tanks," Lieutenant Evergreen reported, turning a field noteputer so she could see the tac display. "Except for these two outriders here and *here*, their formation is pretty standard. Arcs give lots of mutual cover."

"But it's all long range." Lieutenant Lude frowned at the data tags. "What have they have for close in?"

"Most likely nothing." Evergreen traced arcs on the screen. "They're set up for a fast pullback into the plant. Odds are the heavy defenses are inside the facility perimeter, where they can bottle up aggressor 'Mechs."

"Too bad we left all our 'Mechs on New Hope," Byers said solemnly. "Looks like we'll have to skip the trap demonstration and blow the tanks in place.

"Tell off satchel details."

For a moment she was tempted to assign herself one of the targets, but wisdom prevailed. She still felt like a teenager, but she moved like a middle-aged woman. Which was good for an old girl, especially in the heavier pull of local gravity, but not good enough for sneaking up on an emplaced tank. Either she'd get killed or some kid would get killed covering for her. Either way, the tank crews would know what was up before all the satchels could be placed. The whole company could get away clean if she screwed up early enough.

Speaking of which . . .

"Tell the snipers to go ahead and take out the forward observers," she ordered. "Before one of them observes *us* and decides to tell somebody."

Hampstead Refining and Machining
Imstar Aerospace
Lanan, Atreus

Aletha Chowla stomped her jump jets, launching her seventy-five-ton *Thanatos* over the building. As her BattleMech cleared the roofline, she launched medium-range missiles, widest spread. Twenty missiles blanketed the courtyard, two vehicles dissolving into fireballs before her targeting computer could identify them.

Trucks or APCs, she guessed, basing her assumption more on their total destruction than anything else.

She swung her 'Mech's left arm wide as she landed, sweeping the extended-range large laser and medium pulse laser over as wide an arc as possible. Finger on the trigger, she searched for a target while her missile launcher re-loaded itself.

Nothing moved. Sensors gave back mountains of hard-ened armor in every direction.

The problem with clearing an aerospace fighter plant is everything is heavy metal.

The problem was, some of the heavy metal was the First Regulan Hussars—a tougher unit than the pirate bands the Rim Guards usually faced. She'd lost a lance of good peo-ple learning to respect the Hussars' discipline and tactics.

"Don't shoot, it's me." Marcus Green III's *Raijin* stalked from the mouth of an alley opposite the building Alethea had jumped. The main entrance to the courtyard was to her left, east, opening onto the main thoroughfare.

"Our trap netted two trucks, Marc Three," Alethea warned. "We may be the trapp*ees* instead of the trapp*ers* here."

Sensor readings were jumpy in a factory the size of a medium town packed to bursting with ordnance waiting to be assembled, but at long range they had thought some-thing big had dodged into this parking area. Nothing had jumped. The alley was too narrow for anything bigger than Marc's machine; all of the doors big enough for a 'Mech were shut and none of the buildings had new holes.

So either nothing was here, or one of those big doors had been open seconds ago. She knew what Marc was thinking: the twin turrets above and behind his cockpit ro-tated through their arcs independently—covering as much area as possible with the particle-projection cannon and clustered medium-pulse lasers.

"Out the front," Alethea ordered. "We're too boxed in here."

Marc altered course without a word.

Considering the ranges around her, Alethea primed the missiles in their tubes before moving to follow. An armful of twenty "hot loads" was potentially volatile, but she sus-pected anything that came at her would be inside her medium-range missiles' minimum range before she could shoot.

Jumping would have been the fastest way out; both her *Thanatos* and Marc's *Raijin* could clear the surrounding buildings easily. And be easy targets for anyone set up to shoot them down. The fact that she'd jumped in without incident meant nothing. Nobody ever got hurt falling for a trap—it was when you tried to break out that things got bad.

When they were between the buildings, halfway to the street and the courtyard, the wall to her left began to lose shape.

"Run!"

Marc's *Raijin* leapt for the open street as Alethea pivoted to face the bulging wall. A cloud of powdered mortar and stone washed over her *Thanatos*, blotting out the light. She figured she'd have a microsecond between the falling debris being too thick for missiles to pass and whatever was smashing through the wall smashing her. If she saw what she was shooting at, it would be too late.

Sunlight on metal high above—

She fired a narrow spread into the darkness directly ahead.

Shrapnel pinged off her canopy as all twenty birds exploded against something so close she could almost—

Her head snapped back as her BattleMech jerked forward, twisting to the left. Damage alarms hooted. Vibration rose through her command couch as the gyro below her suddenly altered rotation.

Instinctively Alethea hauled back on the yokes, fighting to stay upright. Her machine overbalanced and she staggered back against the far building.

Something swung upward through the billowing dust. She brought up her right arm—

There was no right arm. Her gyro was screaming because seven tons of missile launcher had disappeared.

The shape—

She threw herself left, staggering to keep her machine upright. Making the courtyard, she hauled her 'Mech around to face her attacker. The dust was thinning. The hulking shape of the one-hundred-ton *Berserker* in First Hussar two-tone green was clearly visible, pulling its axe out of the wall she'd been braced against.

Only twenty-five more tons than your Thanatos, she told herself. *But every one of those tons is* mean.

The huge machine turned toward her.

Alethea unleashed a full salvo of her remaining weapons. The paired large- and medium-pulse lasers on her left arm went true, further savaging the missile damage spread across the Hussar's torso, but the twin medium lasers flanking her cockpit wasted themselves against the pristine armor of the *Berserker*'s right shoulder.

A brace of large-pulse lasers answered. Her damage alarm squealed as armor peeled away from her 'Mech's right leg and side. The actuators still read green. She couldn't jump with the missing arm confusing her gyro, but she could outrun the bigger machine. *If* she could make the alley before it hit her in the back.

The *Berserker*'s left arm swung toward her.

She fired again before he could bring his PPC to bear. All four beams went true, carving deep into the holes blasted by her last flight of missiles. A spray of gray-green told her she'd taken out a heat sink, and the black, oily smoke of burning myomer curled out of the rents. But it wasn't much, and it surely wasn't enough.

Alethea shuffled left, the motion rocking her torso so she could fire only her arm weapons with accuracy. She fired. Again. Using only two lasers meant heat wasn't a problem. But it also meant she wasn't doing a hell of a lot of damage. A poor compromise between running for her life and trying to keep the *Berserker* pilot too wary of her weapons to aim properly, but it was the best she could do.

Suddenly the larger machine was haloed in blue lightning.

For a frozen second she thought its PPC had malfunctioned. Then she realized Marc had hit the assault 'Mech from behind. A fireball enveloped the *Berserker*'s head. Six hits from the *Raijin*'s short-range missile launcher.

The Hussar turned to face the new threat and Alethea reversed her course. Running now toward the enemy, she unleashed the combined lasers of her left arm, gouging away armor broken by Marc's missiles.

The *Berserker* ignored her. Standing square to Marc, he fired at the *Raijin*, content to let her minimal weapons do what damage they could while he dealt with the more deadly adversary.

Alethea realized that was sound tactics. She had no idea where the vital internal systems were on a *Berserker*, and with the amount of armor it carried it was going to take her a long time to find out.

However, there was one bit of damage she could do.

Bringing her 'Mech to a halt, she focused all four of her lasers on the back of the assault 'Mech's left knee. Alpha strike; alpha strike; alpha strike: she fired as fast as the capacitors would recharge.

By the time the *Berserker* pilot realized he was in trouble, it was too late.

The ruined left knee hinged sideways, hitting the right, and the BattleMech twisted as it went down. With the machine sprawled on its back, its torso lasers were pointed uselessly at the sky.

Alethea edged closer, scanning the building that had birthed the Hussar even as she moved to examine the fallen machine.

With the assault 'Mech down, she could see Marc's *Raijin* was a ruin. Armor had been scoured away from its entire torso; one turret was missing. As she watched, the birdlike machine staggered sideways a half step. A sure tell the pilot was injured.

The muzzle of the PPC on the *Berserker*'s left arm rose. Not much, not a meter, not enough to be seen if Alethea hadn't been looking right at it when it lifted. But with that tiny change the weapon was focused on Marc's stricken 'Mech.

Alethea leveled her large laser at the Hussar cockpit and blasted it to vapor.

Zenith Jump Point
Hellos Minor
Regulan Fiefs

"What is our status, Captain Flynn?" Lester asked.

"All DropShips secure," the flag captain responded, her voice edged with anticipation. "All JumpShips charged and ready, General."

Lester nodded, smiling slightly at the truncated title.

Aboard any ship there was only one captain—a tradition even captains-general knew enough to respect.

His chair had been bolted to the deck above and behind the captain's. Standard position for an admiral. Or captain-general of the Regulan Fiefs. He did not like JumpShip travel, but when he had to travel, doing so in command of a fleet was by far the most satisfying way to do it.

The Halas horde had attacked Atreus as he'd imagined they would. Risking lives and ships on dangerous pirate points for the sake of shaving a few days or hours off their assault. And while bypassing the jump points may have saved them an engagement with Regulan pickets, it meant they did not hold the jump points—leaving them open for Regulan reinforcements.

Regulan reinforcements that had been in place weeks before their assault began.

Lester shook his head. Halas in her hubris had thought her token "Atreus campaign" had held him in check. The thin bulwark of forces she could spare from her invasion of Andurien had done nothing but tax her resources.

Lester had known she would try to take Atreus away from him: her rape of the Free Worlds League would not be complete without the capital planet. And he'd known she'd use every asset at her disposal to get it. He'd deliberately stationed the First Regulan Hussars permanently on Atreus, publicly making it their homeworld, to ensure that she would throw every regular, reservist and recruit she had into the battle.

But the First were not the only Hussars to have a new home. When the First had moved to Atreus, the Fifth Regulan Hussars had moved from their native Olfsvik to Hellos Minor. And, as the Halas horde had gathered on Tongatapu and Loyalty, they had boarded DropShips and moved into position. Ready.

Lester had waited three days after receiving word Halas had attacked Atreus. He wanted to give the rabble time to mire themselves on the surface before the Fifth Hussar Regiment arrived in-system.

Lester and his forces would appear at the zenith jump point, like the rightful owners they were, and descend on the planet in an armada of DropShips. He wanted Halas' dupes to realize how much trouble the witch had gotten them into before his forces landed. He expected most to flee. He expected a few to turn coats and pretend to welcome him. He did not expect those who chose to fight to last long.

"Whenever you are ready, Captain Flynn," Lester ordered. "Take us to Atreus."

"Aye-aye, sir," she acknowledged. "Mr. Satchel, if you please."

The bridge distorted, seeming to stretch away in impossible directions as the jump field folded the vessel into something or someplace. Lester had no idea how it worked. But he knew it did work. And in the time it took him to remember yet again why he hated the sensation of JumpShip travel, they were in the Atreus system.

Around him the bridge crew moved with quick confidence. Checking screens and comparing numbers and murmuring into headsets as they confirmed that the JumpShips and their attendant DropShips had indeed made it safely to their destination.

Lester grinned as he imagined the consternation of the Halas ship captains as the jump signatures registered. Consternation that would turn to alarm when they realized three *Star Lords* and fifteen DropShips filled with aerospace fighters and BattleMechs had just irrevocably changed the balance of power in Atreus system.

How long before the first offer to surrender?

"Sweet mother of God."

Flynn's awed voice cut across Lester's thoughts.

"What—"

He stopped, transfixed by the image on the forward viewscreen.

"What the hell is that?" he asked.

"A bit over one-point-five kilometers of Clan WarShip, General," Captain Flynn answered. "Transponder says it's Clan Sea Fox, but I don't understand the identifiers."

"What the hell is a Clan Sea Fox WarShip doing in the Atreus system?"

"According to our sensors, General, it's aiming all of its weapons at us."

Zenith Jump Point
Atreus System
Free Worlds League

"Do you think your mother will truly appreciate the symmetry?" Rikkard asked.

Julietta smiled, more at the joy of moving weightlessly than his question.

How I used to hate space travel. Now—to move without having to walk is a blessing. She caught a handhold and reversed herself. Choosing a fresh objective, she pushed off, free-floating across the—she supposed it was a dining room of some sort.

"Oh yes, she'll appreciate it," she said aloud. "Once she gets over being furious about it."

"It only worked because Lester used the established jump point," Rikkard pointed out.

"That's because Lester is a man of tradition," Julietta said. "Rigidity is a quality one must always admire in an opponent."

"You are quoting Petr Kalasa," Rikkard accused.

"Does the source make it less true?"

Rikkard shook his head. She could tell he was amused by her constant flying across the room, but she didn't care. Choosing a new destination, she launched again.

"And if he had chosen to use a pirate point, you were aboard with enough Spirit Cats to make him forever regret being so clever," she said. "That would have spoiled the symmetry with Mother's 'support' of your conquest of Marik, but it would have had the same net effect.

"The Free Worlds League has Atreus because the Clan Protectorate kept its word."

58

The sky of Atreus. Jessica stood transfixed on the balcony. Ignoring the city of dreams spread across its dozen hills, she gazed up at the blue spring sky. *How long has it been since I looked up into the sky of Atreus?*

She remembered standing on her tiptoes to rest her chin on the railing beneath her fingers.

Memories of her childhood came welling up, memories of her father. Not memories of the savvy politician and determined warrior fighting to right the wrongs he'd found, the wrongs he'd been duped into abetting. Rather she remembered the gentle giant who had told her stories and lifted her up on his shoulders beneath this fine blue sky and listened with honest attention when she had shared her bright dreams of their future together.

Jessica felt her throat tighten as the world before her rippled and flowed.

That's enough of that.

Pulling a lace kerchief from the sleeve of her military jacket, Jessica dabbed at her eyes.

"Are you all right, Mother?"

"Yes. No." Jessica tucked the lace back out of sight as Nikol joined her on the balcony. "Just remembering. The last time I stood on this spot I was too short to know you could look down over the balustrade. All I ever saw from my father's favorite place to think was sky."

Nikol smiled at the image.

"You look good," she said.

Jessica looked down at herself, spreading her arms a bit. Her jacket was the traditional military tunic of the captain-general, cream with gold trim and purple at the shoulders and cuffs. Not so very different from the uniform Thaddeus had worn when he served as warden of the Covenant Worlds. Where she balked at tradition was the trousers; she had been too long on Oriente to change her ways. Below her jacket a pleated skirt of cream picked out in purple and gold fell gracefully to her ankles. Her boots were suitably martial.

Nikol wore a similar uniform, with trousers, of course, and considerably less purple and gold.

"How go the debates, Minister-General?" Jessica asked.

Nikol shook her head.

"If I'd known when I made up this job that it would entail sitting over the Parliament when it was in session, I'd have let the freedom fighters on Gallatin shoot me," she said. "However, I have established the tradition of the minister-general getting up and walking away without explanation when bored to tears.

"There are no debates," she added, answering the question. "Just an endless succession of MPs getting up and telling all the other MPs how vital *their* world was to the reestablishment of the Free Worlds League."

"That's healthy," Jessica said. "It means they're sure enough of success and of peace to want good vid samples to play for their local media."

"Oh, I know it's healthy. I just said healthy does not equal entertaining."

"Should I put up this uniform for another day?"

Nikol laughed.

"They have a schedule, and Farrow and his people are making sure they stick to it," she said. "These are the people who put together a provisional government in—how many weeks?

"It will not be long before the first captain-general of a unified Free Worlds League in over half a century is installed."

"Time being subjective."

"True."

"Michael and Elis have been taking the opportunity presented by the delay to tour the children's hospital," Nikol added. "Your daughter's gown is specifically tailored to ensure everyone notices that their heir is apparent."

"Is there any word on—" Jessica hesitated, surprised she found saying the names of her children difficult.

"There is a Sea Fox DropShip at Atreus Field posting Clan Protectorate colors," Nikol said. "I think we can assume Julietta is aboard, though in typical Clan fashion they are saying not a word. Christopher is with Duke Fontaine's delegation. I've sent a message, but he hasn't responded."

Jessica nodded. That Fontaine Marik took the time to appear so soon after losing his homeworld to the Lyrans a second time spoke volumes about the man's dedication to the League. That her son had not immediately sought her out spoke volumes about . . .

She wasn't sure.

I have unified the Free Worlds League and torn my family to fragments in the process.

"Do we at least know where the warden-general is, should we need him?" she asked aloud.

"The boys, as they style themselves, are strolling about the east garden pretending they don't know paparazzi are recording their every move." Nikol shook her head again. "There has been more crystal shot of Dad and Thaddeus palling around together than all the rest of Parliament's inaugural session combined."

Jessica shared her smile, then sobered.

"There's going to be political fallout from that," she predicted. She wasn't sure what form it would take, but she couldn't shake the feeling it was inevitable. "We are getting too complacent in the flush of victory. A mistake now would cost us dearly."

"Always the optimist, my dear," said Philip.

"Father and Thaddeus are no longer in the east garden." Nikol updated her earlier report before turning to grin at her father.

"In fact, Philip and I were discussing this very thing just now," Thaddeus added. "Or if not this very thing, several not so very things which are closely related."

Jessica smiled slightly. She appreciated their jovial mood, but somehow her husbands comfortably enjoying each other's company was always vaguely unsettling.

"Actually, it stems from something you said back when you and Philip first proposed this arrangement," Thaddeus said more soberly. "You made the case that your father—the Halas line—stayed true to what the Free Worlds League stands for when House Marik lost its way.

"Our marriage . . ." He spread his hands. "I don't think one citizen in twenty believes your marriage to me exists for any other reason than to bring your claim to the captain-generalcy into compliance with tradition. We—all of us—expected a great public outcry at our wedding. The reality proved to be a fraction of what we anticipated."

Jessica looked from one man to the other.

"If you're suggesting that the people of the Free Worlds League are ready for a captain-general who is not connected with the Marik family, you're mistaken," she said. "Do not confuse their appreciation for what was done on their behalf with evidence nothing needed to be done."

"The people had no problem with you restructuring the government by fiat," Thaddeus pointed out. "The minister-general for domestic affairs, the warden-general to oversee the military. Positions created out of thin air before you are even installed as captain-general. The people are ready for change."

"You read too much significance into what is essentially housekeeping," Jessica countered. "What brought the people of the League together was tradition, a shared history spanning centuries. And the core of that history is belief in the power of the Marik name—the power of the *first* Great House—to hold us together. Every step we have taken on this journey—every step—was necessary."

Julietta's canes clacked on the marble. That's why she didn't like the canes. They clacked. And they forced her to keep walking. There were days—days like today—when her legs weren't interested in listening to her brain's commands and she missed the steady push-step-rest rhythm of her walker.

But the walker's behind me and there is no going back.

No one made way for her. Or rather, no one made any more way for her than they would for any middle-aged woman on crutch-canes accompanied by a brace of Clan warriors and a two-hundred-kilogram elemental.

She wore a simple dress and no jewelry, and was making her way steadily toward the public observation gallery. None of her companions wore sign of rank or status other than their Clan affiliation. A few passersby looked sharp to be sure they were not Wolf patches, but most flowed past the slow-moving group without a glance. If anyone recognized her as something more than an ordinary woman in the company of Clanners, they gave no sign.

Each of her party had an observation gallery ticket, purchased by some Sea Fox apprentice, displayed prominently on a neck lanyard. Their verigraph invitations to the royal dais remained aboard ship; hers and Petr's and Rikkard's. She'd been a little surprised to receive those. Her mother hadn't acknowledged her since she'd declared the formation of the Clan Protectorate.

However, she supposed the invitations were of a piece with the notification, couched in truly beautiful diplomatic language, that the Clan Protectorate was entitled to seven seats in the League Parliament, one for each member world. Her mother believed too strongly in the Free Worlds League to deny the existence of a member state—even one of which she disapproved.

Julietta realized the sidewalk ran beside the portico to the Parliament building, waist-high to street traffic. Though the steps were still a block ahead, the entrance to the gallery was only a dozen meters to their right. All she had to do to avoid a few hundred painful steps was get over a marble railing that rose higher than her head and onto the raised portico.

Easily done.

"Penelope, I'd like to reach that door over there, the one with the guards checking tickets."

Without a word her bodyguard put an arm around Julietta's waist and lifted her clear of the pavement. There was a moment's wild swing through space as Penelope levered herself over the railing and then she was set down gently on the portico.

Julietta grinned up at Penelope as Rikkard and Petr swung easily over the balustrade. The vicarious experience of the elemental's tremendous strength always made her a bit giddy.

The guards at the door had not seen Julietta and her party scale the railing, and those spectators who had voiced no objection when the four made their way directly to the entrance. In fact the guards, focused on tickets suspended from neck lanyards, did not notice them at all until one obviously realized Penelope's prodigious chest was above his eye level.

"Um. Ah," he said brightly, taking in the full scope of the three-meter-tall elemental before noticing her companions. "Ma'am, I know it's open seating, but I'm going to ask that you sit in the back row so you don't block anyone's view.

"You," he said to Julietta, "can sit down front because of your—"

He stopped midword, dramatically noticing her green eyes and strawberry-blond hair shot with gray. His gaze traveled down to the canes cuffed to her forearms and then back up to her neck.

Realizing what was happening, Julietta stepped to the side, leading the young man and her companions clear of the doorway so the other guard, who was oblivious to the byplay, could continue to confirm tickets and direct people to the galleries. When she judged they could not be casually overheard, she raised her chin slightly to give him a clear view of her scars.

"Lady Julietta." The guard looked to Rikkard and then to Petr, taking in the scar tissue that covered half the Sea Fox leader's skull. "Khan Peter Kelso?"

"OvKhan Petr Kalasa," Petr corrected, not ungently.

"Star Colonel Rikkard Nova Cat," Rikkard supplied before the young man could hazard a guess.

"And the young lady you were admiring is Penelope Nova Cat," Julietta said, knowing the elemental would remain silent.

"Gentlemen, ladies," the guard acknowledged.

Julietta found herself marveling at the earnest schoolboy manners.

"Lady Julietta, you shouldn't be here," the guard said. Earnestly, of course. "I don't know what happened to your invitations, but I do know there's a place set aside for you in the noble's gallery."

Julietta read his name badge. "Mr. Pedersen, do you have specific instructions on what to do if the Clan Protectorate delegation appears at this door?"

"No, ma'am."

"Then let me assure you we received our invitations and we are choosing to watch the installation of the captain-general from the people's gallery," she said. "What I would like you to do for me is to follow the exact letter of your instructions regarding this. Do nothing. Tell no one. Let us keep our privacy."

The guard bobbed his head once.

"Yes, ma'am. You can sit anywhere you want. But, Miss Penelope? You're really going to have to sit in the back." The young man hesitated, visibly gathering his nerve. "Otherwise every guy in the place is going to be watching you."

"Another conquest of the Inner Sphere," Julietta murmured to the flabbergasted elemental as the blushing guard returned to his post. Not acknowledging Petr's laugh, she focused on putting one cane in front of the other, leading her Clanners among their fellow people of the Free Worlds League.

"Sir Frederick!"

Frederick paused midstep in guiding his consort toward their chairs and turned at the sound of his name. He found himself facing an imposing blond man with a piercing eye and features that had been honed by war. A MechWarrior, he thought in the half second before realization dawned.

"My God. Christopher?"

"Yes, sir."

"You look—well, good doesn't cover half of it. You've grown."

"Yes, sir." Christopher nodded, accepting the assessment. "Elis told me how you saved her life on Lesnovo."

"All I did was get knocked down and sat on," Frederick protested. "Your father did the real work."

"Perhaps. I just wanted to thank you."

On the verge of waving the words away, Frederick stopped. Meeting the young man's gaze, he dipped his chin. "You're welcome, son."

Remembering himself, Frederick looked to the woman on his arm. "My dear, let me introduce Christopher Marik, son of our new captain-general. Christopher, this is my fiancée, Lady Genevieve Bey-Hughes."

"Christopher Halas-Hughes, Sir Frederick," Christopher corrected. "And cousin Gen will remember me as the little boy in knee pants who used to follow her around when she visited Elis on Oriente."

"*Bey*-Hughes?" growled a voice before Gen could answer. A man half a head shorter than Christopher with a flowing mane of silver hair and matching beard appeared at the young man's shoulder. "Of the Albert Falls Beys?"

"Yes, milord," Gen answered. "On my father's side. Do you know them?"

"Know of them, don't know them. Good family." Turning his attention to Frederick, the man thrust his hand forward.

"Fontaine Marik," he announced. "Well met, cousin."

"The pleasure is mine."

Frederick hesitated, weighing whether to offer sympathy for Fontaine's recent military setbacks. He decided against it; Michael Cendar intended to broach a proposal addressing that very issue during his visit to Atreus.

"This is not a place I ever expected to be," he said instead.

"Nor I," admitted Fontaine. "I suspect the League—the entire Inner Sphere—is full of surprised people this day."

Regulus City
Chebbin, Regulus
Regulan Fiefs

"Is there nothing we can do?"

Emlia's drooping posture wounded Lester to his heart. But the answer to her question was that there was nothing he could say or do to relieve her grief. Or remove its cause.

"If I had a nuclear bomb I would use it," he said.

"Technically—"

"Gustav! A nuclear bomb in place under the house of Parliament on Atreus," Lester clarified.

"Don't know why I didn't think to plant one when we owned the place," he added. "God knows we sank enough else into that stinking planet."

Salazar opened his mouth, then wisely realized a response was not required and shut it again.

"What is our strategic situation?" Lester asked his security director. Not that he couldn't recite the data as effectively as Salazar; he just felt the need to have the worst confirmed.

"Our corridor to the Duchy of Andurien remains secure," Salazar reported. "A half dozen unaligned worlds remain sympathetic to proper rule and hostile to the Halas hegemony. Unfortunately, after its disastrously mismanaged war against Oriente, Andurien is not the capable ally it once was. In fact, in light of certain domestic alliances which have come to light, Andurien may be considered at best closely allied with the Magistracy of Canopus. At worst it may be regarded as a dependent state."

"What the hell was Humphreys thinking?"

"He was thinking the same thing you always think, dear," Emlia rallied to answer. "He was thinking that was the best he could do for his people."

Lester was grateful she did not add that allying with the Regulan Fiefs had not served Andurien well.

Lester stood in the open frame of the French doors staring out over the rooftops of the lower city to the expanse of the Brahma River. The water, dotted by hundreds of pleasure craft, glittered like a tapestry of silver threads beneath the white-hot sun.

How dare such a black day be so beautiful?

Snorting at his own foolishness, Lester turned away from the window. He saw Emlia was still wilted, despondent over the ascendancy of the Halas whore, and could think of nothing to say to her.

He had no idea what was the local time for Atreus City. The installation of the captain-general could still be hours away or it could have ended before he arose this morning.

Lester could have been there, of course, with Emlia. All the noble families of the Fiefs had received invitations. Just as weeks earlier—still reeling from the defeat at Atreus—they'd been notified that the Regulan Fiefs were allotted a mere twenty-eight seats in her mockery of a Parliament. One planet, one vote? Egalitarian nonsense that ignored the basic precepts of any intelligently run nation. Not that Lester believed for one moment that the Parliament would exist for any other reason than to give the illusion of legitimacy to the Halas harlot's despotism.

The third of July would always be a day of mourning throughout the Regulan Fiefs.

What had they now? What resources to fight the creature strangling the Free Worlds League?

The image of the star map formed in his mind. Enemies and stooges of Halas pressed close on three sides. Oriente, poised to strike at any moment; the Rim Commonality, equally willing but less ready; Tamarind-Abbey and the wounded remnants of the Marik-Stewart Commonwealth, like the distant orphans of The Republic, too preoccupied with their own troubles to threaten; and the unreadable enigma of the Clan Protectorate. Cut off from the rest of the Inner Sphere by the horseshoe of the ersatz Free Worlds League, Regulus had only one ally of doubtful ability to rimward, and they were closely entangled with a traditional adversary. An adversary whom necessity might well forge into a friend.

But we are not without assets.

"Salazar, how go preparations on Operation Firebreak?"

"Further along than expected, Your Grace. We're conducting final evaluations of the communications protocols now."

"Operation Bridge?"

"Phase one complete. We've begun phase two. And"—he anticipated Lester's next question—"Operation Mockingbird is in place awaiting activation."

Lester nodded, grateful for any good news on this nadir day.

"And what about our direct access to the *lady* Halas?" he asked. "What's the latest on Operation Vole?"

Atreus City, Atreus
Free Worlds League

Jessica stood alone on the balcony of her father's study, looking up into the evening sky.

Nikol and Thaddeus had left her to take their positions among the ministers of Parliament, to cast their votes with the rest. Philip had slipped away to the vantage point in the gallery that had been reserved for him.

The wind stirred, little more than a breeze. A strand of hair that had come loose from her severe braid blew across her face. She pulled it back absently, tucking it behind her ear.

Thaddeus had called the Free Worlds League a chimera. He'd been speaking of the military force gathered to liberate Atreus, but by extension his words applied to the entire League. Daughter of the whirlwind, a creature cobbled together out of mismatched parts. She could see why he had felt that way, could see what he saw when he looked at the assembled worlds, but he was wrong.

The parts of the Free Worlds League did not match each other, did not conform to a common model like the planets Thaddeus had organized into his "communities." But that was because each world—each citizen—was unique. They were not supposed to match. What they were supposed to do, all of them: the stubborn, bitter Regulan Fiefs; the worlds under the heels of the Lyrans and the Wolves; the scattered, chaotic worlds abandoned by The Republic; even those worlds closed up inside the mysterious Fortress . . .

What every unique and special world of the Free Worlds League was supposed to do—what every one did—was fit together into a perfect whole. A whole greater than the sum of its parts.

She had done what she had to do to rebuild that shattered whole. She had given orders that had cost ten thousand innocent people their lives; that she had never intended so many to die did not absolve her of responsibility. She had sent as many soldiers to fight and die on a dozen worlds. She had sacrificed her family.

Janos.

Everything she had and was—her honor, her compassion, her integrity—she had given all for the greater good. Because she had stood firm when others fell; because she had acted when others faltered; because she had been willing when others were afraid; because of *her* the Free Worlds League—

"Captain-General?"

Jessica whirled, startled, and found a round little man she had never seen before standing in the doorway to her father's office. He wore a formal jacket of a cut she did not recognize and the tab at his collar identified his home-world as—*Ariel?* She refused to squint.

"Captain-General," the man repeated, this time accompanying his words with a bow. "It is time."

Back straight, eyes bright with purpose, Jessica Marik stepped forward to meet her destiny.

FREE WORLDS LEAGUE

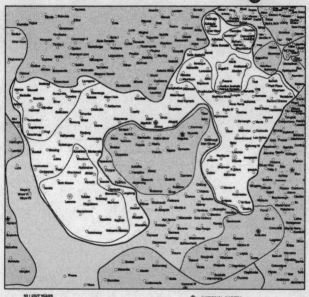

30 LIGHT YEARS

120 LIGHT YEARS OR 26,8 PARSECS

⊛ NATIONAL CAPITAL
◉ MAJOR PROVINCE CAPITAL
○ MINOR PROVINCE CAPITAL

COREWARD

ANTI-SPINWARD   SPINWARD

RIMWARD

THE INNER SPHERE

█ FREE WORLDS LEAGUE

6
5
4
3
1
2

1) Oriente Protectorate
2) Rim Commonality
3) Duchy of Tamarind-Abbey
4) Clan Protectorate
5) Covenant Worlds
6) Protectorate Coalition

© 3139 COMSTAR
CARTOGRAPHiC CORPS

About the Author

Kevin Killiany is delighted to be in his second quarter century as husband to Valerie. Though he is looking forward to the empty nest, he's also very glad their children—Alethea, Anson, and Daya—still seem happy to be around. Since the 1960s, Kevin has worked as an actor, a drill rig operator, a photographer, a warehouse grunt, a community college instructor, a drywall hanger, a teacher of exceptional children, a community services case manager, a high-risk intervention counselor, and a paperboy. He is currently a writer, with stories published in a variety of universes, including Star Trek, Doctor Who, Classic BattleTech, and, of course, MechWarrior. He is also an associate pastor of the Soul Saving Station in Wilmington, North Carolina.

MECHWARRIOR: DARK AGE

A Battletech® Series

AVAILABLE WHEREVER BOOKS ARE SOLD OR AT
PENGUIN.COM

The ShadowRun Series

THE ULTIMATE IN
SCIENCE FICTION AND FANTASY!

From magical tales of distant worlds to stories of
technological advances beyond the grasp of man, Penguin has
everything you need to stretch your imagination to its limits.

penguin.com

ACE
Get the latest information on favorites like
William Gibson, T.A. Barron, Brian Jacques,
Ursula K. LeGuin, Sharon Shinn, and Charlaine Harris,
as well as updates on the best new authors.

ROC
Escape with Harry Turtledove, Anne Bishop,
S.M. Stirling, Simon R. Green, Chris Bunch, Jim Butcher,
E.E. Knight, and many others—plus news on the
latest and hottest in science fiction and fantasy.

DAW
Mercedes Lackey, Kristen Britain, Tanya Huff,
Tad Williams, C.J. Cherryh, and many more—
DAW has something to satisfy the cravings of any
science fiction and fantasy lover.
Also visit dawbooks.com.

*Get the best of science fiction and fantasy
at your fingertips!*